HELSTRUM

CHRONICLES OF THE DAWNBLADE BOOK 8
ANDREW CLAYDON

ANDREW
CLAYDON

Helstrum

By Andrew Claydon

Published by Andrew Claydon

Copyright © 2025, Andrew Claydon

Edited by Danielle Fine

Cover Design by MiblArt

Written in UK English

Print ISBN: 978-1-0685190-4-8

Ebook ISBN: 978-1-0685190-5-5

Manufactured by:
Produced and bound by IngramSpark Australia: Ingram Content Group
AU Pty Ltd, Melbourne, Victoria. US: Lightning Source LLC, La Vergne,
Tennessee / Allentown, Pennsylvania / Jackson, Tennessee, United
States. UK: Lightning Source UK Ltd, Milton Keynes, United Kingdom.
Europe: Lightning Source UK Ltd, with facilities in Germany, France, and
Spain.The authorized representative in the European Economic Area is
Lightning Source France, 1 Av. Johannes Gutenberg, 78310 Maurepas,
France. compliance@lightningsource.fr

Published by:
Dawnblade Publishing
61 Bridge Street
Kington
United Kingdom
HR5 3DJ
andrew@andrewclaydonauthor.com
This book was manufactured using paper and ink products in accordance
with commercial standards.

Just because you're chosen, doesn't mean you want to be...

Crazed necromancers, vicious fauns, murderous demons and all manner of mayhem.
And it all leads back to one man, and one inevitable conclusion.
Tobias Helstrum needs to die.
Struggling with the idea of going from hero to assassin, Nicolas and his companions set off to hunt down and eliminate the man bringing misery to their world.
But it won't be a simple task, by any means.
Helstrum didn't get where he is today by being easy to kill. He has an army of minions, a few deadly tricks up his sleeve and more than a passing interest in seeing Nicolas dead.
But the soul of Etherius is up for grabs, and all Nicolas has to do to save it is murder a man he was already accused of trying to assassinate.

Dedicated to Lisa Heiser. Simply because Nicolas is an assassin in this tale, and I know how much you love the word '*ass*.'
And to everyone who loves a good adventure.

'Aren't words marvellous things? A few well chosen ones can make a person experience a virtual plethora of emotions. 'I love you', *for example. Or perhaps* 'You look like a mound of troll dung that has grown arms and legs and learned to speak'. *I heard the latter uttered with venom in the* Banshee's Wail *during my visit, and then I had a front row seat to the most entertaining bout of drunken fisticuffs afterwards. Words can be very powerful when used correctly, and equally so when they are used incorrectly with complete and utter conviction. Anyway, I digress. The menu in the* Banshee's Wail *is quite basic. I was unable to sample the stew properly due to my table being flipped over. However...'*
Etherius, A Traveller's Guide – Dieter Von Ostric

Allegard's Gallery
of Wonders

The Fort

Ivilar

Helstrum Manor

CHAPTER 1

Another good morning greeted Nicolas. Dreamily, he stared up at the ceiling. His eyes traced what on the face of it appeared to be bland stone. But he'd been doing this for many mornings, and now, he instantly picked out the discolourations and indents that made images his imagination had imposed on them. It was almost like picking out the constellations in the sky. There was the lion, the cyclops, and that shadowed part that looked exactly—and unnervingly—like a dick. He tended not to look at that one for too long.

Nicolas had been awake for a while now. It was becoming a routine, to just lie in bed, staring at the ceiling and revelling in the quiet life. With winter engulfing Etherius, he and his companions had been almost trapped in the city of Golthorak. There'd been no crazed enemies, no plots, no near-death experiences. Just...living. And it was damned intoxicating.

Especially considering who I'm sharing it with.

Closing his eyes, he bit his lips in the anticipation of turning over. Would he ever get tired of seeing Shift lying next to him?

I hope not.

Every night, he wondered if they'd go and find their own bed. And every night they'd chosen to share his.

Yippee.

Wanting to make the most of the moment, to milk it for all it was worth, he closed his eyes. When the anticipation reached its peak, he turned over and opened them.

'Morning, gorgeous,' said the most unexpected voice.

'Aaaarrrgggghhhhh.'

In a blind panic, Nicolas frantically tried to scrabble out of bed, getting his hands caught in the sheet in his chaotic attempt to escape. The rotund, very hairy, and extremely naked man watched him with a bemused stare. Shaking his hand free violently caused the sheet to pull, revealing more of the man than he wanted to see. Nicolas toppled backwards, his leg now somehow entwined with the damnable bedsheet. Bringing his arm up at the last moment, he managed to cushion his chin before it had an unpleasant meeting with the stone floor.

With a desperate pant, he got on all fours. At some point in his journey from bed to floor, the sheet had wrapped around his torso too. It was like a bloody snake. Fighting to get loose, he crawled across the floor, reaching for the *Dawn Blade*. His hands stopped just short of it as his brain finally caught up with what was happening, laughter cutting through the panicked fog that had caused him to make such a pig's ear of getting out of bed.

Oh for f...

'Shift,' he shouted, turning and sitting up. The sheet wound even more tightly around his leg, almost cutting off the circulation. '*Again*? Seriously? For Deities' sake. What's the matter with you?'

The hairy man slapped the bed several times in a fit of hysterics, causing an unpleasant belly jiggle, then wiped a tear from his eye.

Growling in annoyance, Nicolas fought himself free of the bedsheet—or it just finally deigned to release him. Either way, he balled it up in annoyance and threw it at Shift, which only served to increase their hilarity.

'That's the *fourth* time.' His rage, and his attempt to scold them, was probably undermined by the fact that he was completely naked and looking like an utter fool, but he was pissed off and wanted to make sure they knew it. 'When are you going to stop doing that?'

'When...it...stops...being...funny...' Shift gasped between laughs. '...your...face...' Breathing heavily a few times, they recovered themselves and put a podgy finger on their chin. 'So probably never.' They narrowed their eyes. 'Besides, I could practically sense your excitement before you turned over to look at me. You even closed your eyes to make it a *moment*. It made it much too tempting.'

'You're an ass.'

The big fellow's multiple chins pulled taut as they turned their head and angled downwards. 'Yup. Quite a hairy one too.'

'I could've killed you.'

They raised a sceptical eyebrow. 'You looked like you had your hands full with the bedsheet.'

'I thought you said after the sheep that...' Nicolas pinched the bridge of his nose. 'Look, can you change back please?'

Shift looked taken aback. 'Nick...do you have a problem with the male form?'

Nicolas sighed. 'No. The Deities made people in many shapes and sizes, and I'm sure they're all equally glorious...but I don't really want to talk to you while you look like a fat naked man. I'm picky like that sometimes.'

Shift sniggered and gave him a half smile. 'I'll see what I can do.'

Their form began to change. The belly retracted, as did all the hair, thankfully. Limbs became more slender. Shift propped their head on one hand as they lay on their side, other hand on their hip as they pouted their lip playfully and gave him faux doe eyes. 'Is this better?' they asked with fake contrition. 'Am I forgiven?'

Nicolas glared at Shift. 'Actually, I don't think...' Shift flicked their eyes downwards, and his gaze followed. 'You...you...' Suddenly, it was really difficult for Nicolas to keep his train of thought. 'You can't just change back to yourself...sprawled naked on the bed...and expect me to just stop being upset with you.'

Shift put their hand on their heart, staring at him in mock horror. 'Mr Carnegie, I was not expecting you to stop being angry with me.' They wrinkled their nose playfully. 'I was expecting you to let me make it up to you.'

And now I'm no longer mad. Dammit.

Closing his eyes, he shook his head and played back the last couple of minutes in his mind. He realised how stupid, and funny, he must've looked flailing around and trying to defeat a bedsheet, which had turned out to be a more difficult opponent than a minotaur. Despite himself, he let out a chuckle.

'You're forgiven,' he said grudgingly, trying not to smile as Shift stupidly fluttered their eyelashes at him again. 'But it's still not nice. And you have to stop doing it.'

Shift shrugged. 'I keep forgetting why.' They patted the bed next to them. 'Maybe you should come over here and explain it to me?'

He took a step forward and stopped. 'You aren't going to suddenly change into a chicken or anything.'

'Certainly not a chicken. We've already dealt with a talking chicken, and I like to be original.' Shift smirked then noted his unimpressed glare. 'No, I swear. The surprise is the best bit. That's why I always get you just when you wake.' Thinking for a moment, they tilted their head slightly. 'Besides, I'd never change whilst we were...you know. I do have a line.'

There's a revelation.

Tentatively, he walked over and sat beside them.

'You're lucky I like waking up next to you,' he grumbled, with one last final gasp of his annoyance.

With surprising grace, Shift was suddenly sat atop him. 'You are definitely a lucky bastard.' They smirked, before kissing him.

About half an hour later, Nicolas was staring dreamily at the ceiling again. Every so often, he let out a satisfied sigh.

'How many of those are you going to do?' Shift asked.

'Just let me enjoy the moment and...' Nicolas's eyes widened slightly as his stomach suddenly gurgled. Shift's joined in.

'I think the moment's over,' they said, patting him on the chest. 'Breakfast calls.'

So it does.

The shapeshifter kissed him on the cheek and got up to dress. Nicolas tried to make out that he wasn't watching them, but as Shift was pulling up their breeches, they half turned and winked at him, before jiggling their extremely cute behind into them completely.

Slapping the bed to motivate himself, Nicolas got up. As he rose, he stretched his arms out wide, which felt damned nice. Making to move, he stopped as he caught a glimpse of himself in the mirror. The artificial light in the room, generated by the faux sun that hung over Golthorak, was creating shadows on his body, defining the muscles that had developed since he'd begun training properly. Turning to the side, he moved his arm into poses, his muscles changing with each move, revealing different ones.

Wow. I'm starting to look pretty—

'Having fun there?'

Putting his hands by his sides too quickly, he gave Shift a hasty smile. 'I wasn't—'

'Yes, you were,' the shapeshifter interrupted, shaking their head. 'And it's fine. You've a lot to admire.' Their gaze lowered, and their mouth twitched slightly. 'I'm actually not sure you getting dressed is such a—' Both their stomachs grumbled in unison again. '...maybe we revisit this conversation after we've eaten.'

'I look forward to it,' he said with a wink, making a big show of flexing his left bicep.

They laughed as Nicolas got dressed. Things here had become nice, comfortable. So much so that everyone was ignoring the obvious: it wouldn't last.

Winter is nearly over.

CHAPTER 2

B y the time the pair got downstairs, their dwelling was empty. The
orcs of Golthorak had been very generous to their unexpected
guests, gifting them a large house in the centre of the underground city
they dwelt in. Built from the same grey stone the orcs mined to make
the rest of the city, it ought to look drab, but it was filled with ornately
carved wooden furniture, and drapes and tapestries broke up the grey
of the stone. It appeared some orcs had a real knack for interior design.

*I assume you develop one quickly when you're forced to hide in an under-
ground city. At least it's made a nice home for us.*

Nicolas almost missed a step as he realised that he'd used the word
home. It was the first time he'd referred to their dwelling as such, either
mentally or out loud. He'd not had one of those since his had been
burned to the ground and the people of Hablock taken. Guilt suddenly
racked him. His people were suffering who knew where or what, and
here he was cosily waiting out the winter.

I didn't have a choice.

The group had barely survived their journey to the hidden orc city.
Winter, in theory, should've been quiet, but they'd had to contend with
crazed monsters, armed morons with horned helmets, and more than a
few orcs—the more feral of Garaz's people.

'I think I might hide this,' Shift said, inspecting a small pouch left on the
dining table. Inside it was Silva's whetstone.

Despite them being in a place of safety, Silva was still nearly obsessive
about keeping her blade ready. And the warrior wasn't generally very
interested in what people around her were trying to do when she did.
Several evenings when Nicolas had planned to sit and read, his attempts
had been thwarted by the incessant noise of Silva engaged in her sword
care routine. Shift's idea was bloody tempting, save for one thing.

'Better not,' he said, going against his own desire. 'We don't want
to replace the constant *'schwing, schwing'* with Silva stomping around
interrogating everyone about her missing kit.'

With a sigh, Shift frowned at the pouch. 'Good point,' they relented. 'Annoying, but good.'

'Besides, if you're going to steal anything, take Garaz's bloody incense burner,' Nicolas grumbled. He wasn't averse to a bit of incense, but there were times when he'd had to go for a walk because the orc was meditating surrounded by a thick cloud of some funky herb that was making his eyes water.

Maybe it's his way of trying to drive us away, or keep us at a distance?

Even though a couple of months had passed since Garaz's treachery, which had brought them here, things with the orc were still tense. But only because Garaz was making it that way. He was always slightly aloof. Stand-offish. It was like the orc was refusing to renew their bond to punish himself.

And it's getting a bit old. Even I've gotten over the fact that he locked me in a cupboard.

And Shift had made sure Garaz had paid several penances for inconveniencing and lying to them. Some of them had been pretty funny. But really, no one had talked openly about any of it since they'd arrived.

They were all dancing around the orc because he felt so guilty. Sooner or later, though, a frank conversation would be needed. Preferably before they left. Garaz could be quite set in his ways, but Nicolas intended to be equally immovable about the orc not acting like he was part of their family again.

They walked to the door then came to a halt together. Beside it, against the wall, was leant a sword. Silva's sword. The warrior had worn it everywhere she'd gone since they'd been here. Even though they'd faced no danger since the Visitor had attacked this place. Still, Silva always liked to be on guard. For the most part, it was fine, but when they'd been invited to the homes of some of their new friends for dinner it had been a little odd.

And yet, here it is.

It was a sign that Silva was finally becoming settled. A minor miracle, by all accounts. It was also a very clear symbol of what they were about to give up. That wasn't lost on Shift either, who gave his hand a quick, sympathetic squeeze.

Typical. Only I could just start calling it a home when we're about to leave.

Emerging from the house, Nicolas took a deep breath of the morning air. Though Golthorak was an underground city—or at least an underground version of the ruined city above—numerous wind tunnels had been created to ensure that plenty of fresh air circulated throughout the large, connected caverns. As always, it was tinged with the smell of earth from its passage down here. At first, Nicolas had found it jarring, a stark reminder that he was underground. But now he was used to it. It was almost nice.

As was the city as a whole. The orcs had done an amazing job transforming vast, empty caverns into a community. Fleeing underground had been their only choice when their mighty civilisation was toppled by a disease that caused the peaceful and well-reasoned people he'd been living with for the past months to become the type of orc he knew from the many, many stories—all of which featured violence and carnage.

Way above them, attached to the roof of the cavern, was the vast globe that bathed the place in light during the day. You would believe it to be the sun unless you looked directly upwards at it. A mistake that had once caused brightly coloured spots on Nicolas's eyes for hours afterwards. Another mistake he'd made was asking Garaz how it worked. What had followed was a long, one-sided conversation, the only part of which he could remember was the word *alchemical*.

And I'm still not sure what it means.

Maybe he should try learning some science? Or at least something that wasn't fighting. He'd taken a lot of blows to the head in his short time as an adventurer and been knocked unconscious a few more. It might be a good idea to put his brain to use a bit more, even if just to reassure himself it wasn't damaged. It was a muscle that needed working like any of the others in his body.

The same thought I've had at least three times in the past few weeks...and yet I've done nothing about it.

'Good morning.'

'Hello, Gera.' Shift waved to the elderly orc currently in their garden.

Gera lived in the house next to them and had a green thumb, literally and figuratively. She'd insisted on tending their gardens during their stay and did so with the care of an artist creating a great work. Nicolas often marvelled at her precision. Gardening, like science, was lost on him. Though he could appreciate a nice garden.

Currently, she was on her knees pruning some flowers, blue shawl draped over her. Beside her sat a small blanket on which she'd carefully placed the off cuts.

'Ready for breakfast?' Gera asked, casting a sly glance at them. There was a mischievous tone in her voice.

'Yes,' Nicolas answered warily.

'We've worked up a bit of an appetite.'

Nicolas always cringed at Shift's frankness with the old orc. The pair had formed a bond when they'd discovered that the only thing Gera liked more than gardening were dirty jokes. Nicolas had sat with them once as they exchanged crude stories. He hadn't stayed long.

Shift turned and looked back at the window to their room. 'Were you listening, you dirty old mare?'

Gera let out a laugh. 'I do not need to get my excitement vicariously through you two. I guessed by the look on Silva and Garazs' faces when they left the house without you earlier. I am sure I heard young Garaz cursing you for being so *bloody loud*.' She did a perfect imitation of Garaz's voice.

Brilliant.

'Chin up,' Shift said, punching him on the arm. 'We all have our annoying habits. Silva and her damned sword sharpening. Garaz and his incense. And your absolute inability to be quiet in bed.'

If this is how the day is going...I may as well go back to bed right now.

CHAPTER 3

W hen they'd moved into Golthorak, Nicolas was worried he'd find the place claustrophobic. But the orcs had designed the city to be wide and open, with large streets and gaps between the stone houses. It gave the illusion of a sprawling place, when really only a thousand or so orcs lived here—not only a testament to their ingenuity, but to their spirit and their desire to remain a civilised race. Everything was made as if it were a work of art, a stark contrast to the ruins above. The once proud and scholarly people had been laid low by the curse they called *The Regression*. Yet it hadn't broken them. Those who remained...sane was probably the best term for it...had stayed true to who they were for generations. They'd kept their civilisation alive, albeit well hidden. Nicolas found it sad that nobody outside the wasteland knew about any of this, but the orcs that travelled beyond their borders were less interested in discussing history than they were chopping up any poor soul they happened across.

Making their way to the grand courtyard, where people often took communal meals, the pair passed several orcs along the way. Each time they were greeted with a hearty *good morning*. That had taken some getting used to on both sides. The orcs here were used to living in isolation from the rest of their world, and especially their own kin. Having newcomers must've been jarring for them. Likewise for Nicolas and his companions. Other than Garaz, the other orcs they'd met had all been quite invested in killing them.

And now they're my friends and neighbours.

The niggling voice in the back of his head reminded him that he would have to leave this, and them, behind soon. He didn't care for it. And he certainly wasn't comfortable with the reason they were leaving. But, as it often was in his life nowadays, he didn't have a choice.

He stopped himself dwelling on that quite quickly. He just wanted to enjoy the day.

As he walked down the path with Shift at his side, the city around them bustled with activity. There was the noise of friendly conversation, chores being completed, and even the humming of jaunty tunes.

'Nicolas and Shift,' a large orc greeted them. 'Well met.'

Grag was the head of the warriors who protected this place. He wore a simple toga, at odds with his muscular frame, and his thick black hair was tied in a tight top knot. Nicolas had learnt pretty quickly that even the fighters in this city didn't dress like warriors—possibly, it was too reminiscent of their barbaric brethren on the surface. He would never have expected someone so intimidating to be so genial.

'Grag.' He beamed, waving to the orc. 'Good morning.'

As their paths crossed, everyone slowed to a halt. Grag offered his hand, which Nicolas shook. 'Training today?' the orc asked in his deep bass voice.

Every day.

'Of course,' he replied. 'Still keen on putting me through my paces again sometime soon?'

The orc half smiled. 'I think I may have a trick or two to impart. I will admit, though, you are a deceptively tough fighter...for a human.'

'I wouldn't let Silva hear that,' Shift teased.

The orc's face dropped. 'That woman.' Nicolas wasn't sure if Grag was rubbing his ribcage knowingly, or if it was an unconscious memory of the last time the big orc had trained with Silva. 'Someone ought to teach her the difference between *training* and a *full and bloody battle.*'

I can sympathise with that.

'I'd heard she was a bit too much for you,' Shift said leadingly, drawing Grag's attention to his hand.

The orc gave an awkward smile as he lowered his hand. 'She is too much for anyone.' Grag said with a knowing nod. 'But then, this one is becoming quite the handful too.'

Trying not to blush with pride, Nicolas raised his fists in response to Grag doing the same. The pair playfully boxed the air around each other. He could feel Shift rolling their eyes without needing to see it.

It had been good for him to train with the orcs. He'd learned so much from Auron and Silva, and any other teacher he'd come across on his travels, such as Ramirez and Ban, but it was great to have stronger sparring partners. It helped him learn to utilise his speed and knowledge of where to strike to nullify their advantage. Besides, they were still deep in orc territory. There was no chance at all they would get back to the Nine Kingdoms of Man without at least one fight with a group of orcish marauders.

Grag stood up straight again, chuckling heartily as he slapped Nicolas on the shoulder. 'I took the nightwatch last night, and now my bed summons me. I will see you later.'

'What you'll see is a blur of motion then me standing above you in victory.' Nicolas chuckled.

'We shall see, human. We shall see.' Grag grinned as he continued on his way, wagging his finger.

'I could turn into him if you want?' Shift asked. 'I mean, that little display...the sexual tension...'

'Shut up.'

Shift's mouth broke into a broad grin, but they said nothing more.

More orcs greeted them—fellow members of their community—as they progressed down the main thoroughfare. Soon the buildings opened onto a large park, bordered by all kinds of wonderful florae. In its centre was a set of circular pillars with a domed roof on top. Just before it stood a group of orcs engaged in their daily meditation ritual. When Garaz meditated, he sat down. These orcs moved. Each movement was slow and focused, carefully timed with the pattern of their breathing. There was an almost perceptible aura of serenity around them. Which was why they did it: to fortify their minds and spirits lest The Regression take them, to banish any potentially violent or angry thoughts that might spur the curse on. In a rare moment when Garaz had talked about it, he'd voiced his belief that all the fighting they'd done in recent times had caused the curse to take him.

I should learn to meditate. Maybe there'll be a time when I don't have to focus on combat training and can work on some of that inner peace instead? That'd be nice.

And maybe that day would come sooner than he'd thought. Once their task – one he was not really comfortable with – was complete, this might actually all be over. What would that mean? Would he simply return to his normal life? Questions and possibilities entered his mind like a tidal wave, until he copied his hosts' example, breathing and quieting it. If he was mentally off chasing *what ifs*, he wouldn't be focused on his task.

'My hands are itchy.'

'Hmm, what?' he asked Shift, realising he'd been daydreaming instead of listening.

'My hands,' the shapeshifter repeated. 'They're itchy.'

Nicolas shrugged slightly. 'So...scratch them?'

Shift side-eyed him with a *tut*. 'Not literally. Do you know how long it's been since I've stolen something? Too long. My hands are getting itchy.'

'You haven't stolen anything since you've been here?'

'No.'

'…really?'

A fist hit him in the arm. 'No, you cheeky bastard. These people took us in, made us part of their community, so it seemed rude. And they've been through enough.'

'Since when were you worried about being ru—' Shift's glare made him change the direction of his sentence. 'I'm sure you'll make up for it when we leave.'

'That makes me itchy too.' There was a hint of disappointment in Shift's tone. 'I know we've got to go. And soon. But none of us have really talked about it.'

'Because we don't want to,' he admitted. 'I think we're all just enjoying being here for now. But the conversation is coming.'

Shift thought this over for a moment. 'Hopefully not for a few weeks yet.'

That'd be nice.

His nose caught the slight tinge of cooked food in the air, and his stomach reared up like an angry bear.

'Maybe when we have breakfast, you can steal some food from Silva's plate?'

The shapeshifter frowned thoughtfully. 'Get some extra food. Steal something. *And* piss Silva off.' Smiling, they kissed him on the cheek. 'I take it back, you're a genius.'

Chapter 4

'About bloody time,' Auron huffed as they entered the large food court.

A wide community space, it had a mosaic on the tiled floor of a multicoloured phoenix, its wings wide. Probably a metaphor for those who lived here. It was filled with benches and tables. Sometimes, the orcs ate alone, but mainly they gathered for meals. It reinforced the sense of community. Though, occasionally, Nicolas got the impression it was so people could keep an eye on each other, watching out for signs of The Regression.

Now he was here, the delicious aromas overpowered his nose.

Pork, if I'm not mistaken. Bacon, hopefully. Is that warm bread too...

Shut up, stomach. 'Calm down, we're here,' Shift said indignantly to the spirit, who'd been waiting by the entrance like an impatient tutor.

'I'm talking to *him*,' Auron retorted, pointing at Nicolas. 'He has training to do, and he's already late for breakfast.'

'I'll train as soon as I've eaten... Once my food's gone down,' Nicolas added hastily.

'Hurry up then,' the spirit replied, falling into step with them. 'We're over there.'

He didn't really need Auron to direct him to his other companions. In a sea of orcs in white togas, Silva stuck out. As did Garaz with his red cloak.

And Dieter's there too.

The famous travel author had joined them on their journey when they'd pursued Garaz to this place. He was an odd, and inquisitive, man. Very inquisitive. When they found Golthorak, he'd begun to quench his thirst for knowledge with all the enthusiasm of a drunkard who'd been accidentally locked in a tavern cellar. Though their hosts had, at first, been guarded with information, they'd quickly seen the benefit of having their culture recorded. Nicolas had passed the open door to Dieter's room once and marvelled at the piles of papers he'd already assembled.

'Good morning.' The writer smiled, putting down his drink. He'd spent so much time in the orc's library that he actually smelled like old books. 'Are we still okay to discuss the number of undead creatures you've encountered on your travels at some point today?'

That's quite a list.

'After training,' Auron said in a warning tone.

'Of course,' he replied, ignoring the spirit. 'We can sit down this evening and talk about all the animated dead things that have tried to kill me recently.'

A nice fun chat to look forward to.

'Fantastic.' And apparently that was that, as the writer set about his food once more.

'There's actually a handful you haven't faced yet,' Auron said with a knowing nod.

Nicolas's eyes widened slowly. There were more? He'd met enough already. Plenty. He didn't need or want to collect the whole decaying set.

'Good morning.' Garaz nodded, after an amused smirk at Dieter. 'I trust you are both well and have had a relaxing morning?'

Silva snorted into her drink.

'Actually, no, Garaz,' he answered. 'Shift did it again. Can you tell them?'

The orc grimaced in distaste as he eyed Nicolas and Shift. '...did *what*?' Then his orange eyebrows rose in understanding. 'Oh. That explains the scream from your room. What did they change into this time?'

'A hairy, fat naked man.'

Auron laughed out loud. Too loud.

'Can you tell them to cut it out before I have a heart attack? They'll listen to you.'

'Will I?' Shift muttered. 'I mean, he can tell me you're a cry-baby. I'll listen to that.'

'I am not your f—' Quickly, Garaz cut himself off. 'Would it make a difference?'

Nicolas tried not to fill in the blank, but he couldn't help it. That word was just another reminder that it was nearly time to go. It also brought on the guilt of his extended break from his quest to save his people.

'It'd make me feel better,' he replied.

'I already did that.' Shift chuckled.

'Enough,' Silva snapped, glaring at Shift. 'I'm eating.'

'And beyond that,' Garaz continued. 'Would it stop them?'

Nicolas opened his mouth, but he didn't want to admit to the answer. The orc shrugged at him as if to say, *'Well, there you go, then.'*

I suppose it—

Hang on a minute.

'You heard a scream from my room, and you *didn't* come running?' he cried.

The orc ruffled his nose. 'I had no wish to accidentally see what you two get up to.'

'I'm still eating,' Silva grumbled.

'But there are assassins after us,' he continued with an exasperated sigh. 'You didn't think that maybe—'

'In a hidden city?' Auron asked.

The spirit held up his hands in apology as the others looked at him. He wasn't quite right. The Visitor had tracked them here – well, to the ruined city on the surface, actually. That meant there was a chance the enemy knew where they were. Another unspoken thing that hung over the group.

'Well...' Garaz coughed awkwardly. 'There were...other noises afterward, so I assumed you were well.'

'Either that or you'd somehow seduced whoever'd come to kill you,' Silva said sourly. 'Neither me nor Garaz felt the need to hang around until we heard the *yippee*.'

'Ha bloody ha,' Nicolas said dryly, sitting down, taking a plate, and filling it. He'd hoped that everyone would forget that, but it seemed the word was destined to dog him as much as the nickname he didn't care for. 'How did I end up travelling with such funny people?'

That is not a fun tale.

'Don't worry, kid. I regularly pop my head into your room to check you're okay.' Auron grinned, putting his ethereal hand through the table from beneath and wiggling his fingers to hammer home his point.

'You'd better not,' Shift warned, pointing their fork at the spirit. 'I do not want you hovering over us in the night.'

'Excuse me.' Behind Nicolas stood a group of five orc children. Each of them shuffled awkwardly and expectantly as they looked at Shift. 'Do you think you could do the *thing*? Please.'

Shift rubbed their chin thoughtfully. '*Again?*' they said with a long exhalation. 'I don't know about that. I've barely had breakfast, and besides...*rrrrraaaaaggggggrrrrhhhh*.' Jumping up wide-eyed, Shift transformed their hands into claws and their teeth into fangs.

The kids squealed with fright and delight, scattering in all directions.

'Cute little green buggers,' they remarked as they reverted to their preferred form.

'You're really good with them.'

Shift cast a wary glance at him. 'Don't get any ideas about me bearing you many children, Nicolas Percival Carnegie. Thou shalt be disappointed.'

Something about that stung a little, and he wasn't sure why. 'Would I want a load of little yous' running around?' he asked glibly. 'It's bad enough having one of you make fun of me.' He pulled away as they ruffled his hair.

'I'm sorry you feel bullied.' Shift grinned.

'I'll put up with it for now...until I find someone better.'

'You two.' Auron sighed theatrically. It had to be for show; the spirit didn't breathe. 'I'm lucky I can't feel nauseated.'

'Some of us still can,' Silva said as she and Garaz exchanged a look.

Instead of responding, Nicolas reached over, grabbed some bread from Silva's plate, and bit into it. He instantly regretted it. The warrior looked poised to kill him. What she didn't notice was that as her attention was focused on Nicolas, Shift removed several other items from her plate.

Hopefully that soothes their itch.

And it'd also help their grumbling stomach. If he'd learnt anything about Shift, it's that they weren't always fun to be around when they were hungry.

Looking at his companions for a moment, Nicolas realised that he actually felt lucky for the first time in a good long while. And he was going to savour every moment of it.

'Chew faster,' Auron said as he crouched beside Nicolas. 'You're late for training.'

Or maybe not?

CHAPTER 5

K eeping his eyes ahead of him, knowing that if he looked down, he'd lose his balance and end up going in that exact direction, he walked along the thin beam. Arms outstretched to keep himself upright, he controlled his breathing, focused on his goal.

Shit.

His peripheral vision gave him a second's warning. Thank the Deities his reflexes were getting better. He stepped back, the swinging bag of flour missing his nose by a good inch. For a moment, he wobbled dangerously. Bending his legs slightly, he reset his centre of gravity until he became stable again.

'What in the *Underworld*?' he shouted to people he couldn't look at. Turning his head would mean falling.

'Doing the same course day after day breeds complacency.' Auron's scholarly tone gave him a perfect mental image of how the spirit was standing, arms folded with a haughty look on his face. 'We've been adding new things to ensure you're ready for what comes next.'

'You could've warned me...'

'Which would defeat the point of the exercise.' From the position of Silva's voice, she was below him to his left somewhere. He assumed that was where the release for the bag was. *Bags*. There was no way there would be only one.

Grunting, he continued along the beam. When Auron and Silva had first declared that they were going to build a training course for him, he'd thought it was a great idea. Now...he had the vague notion that they were trying to kill him.

With a little hop, he dodged another bag of flour, before coming to a halt to allow another to fly by, wafting a breeze across his face. He'd been sweating before he reached the beam. Now it was pouring from him.

Timing it perfectly, he slipped between the swinging bags and made it to the end stairway.

Oh fu—

Said stairway was now a steep slope that he was rolling down. Quickly, he took control of the roll, ducking into it so that when he reached the bottom of the slope he came into a standing position.

'Keep going, kid,' Auron bellowed.

Ahead was another slope. This one he hated with a passion, because he had to run up it. After bouncing on his toes several times, staring down the inanimate piece of slanted wood, he charged. Within two steps, his legs began to burn. Swinging his arms furiously, he pushed himself harder. There was barely any grip on the smooth wood. Gritting his teeth, he forced himself up it. Near the top, the muscles in his legs trembled, possibly about to give out. He ignored it. Giving it any time would break his concentration, and he'd be going back down, fast. Finally, his foot touched the top of the walkway.

Yes.

As his other foot began to hit the ground, he noticed the loop of rope he was stepping into. Too late. He was committed. The rope snapped around his ankle like a vicious snake and hauled him into the air. As he cried out, the world became a swaying blur. But he did notice various other loops of rope waiting on the walkway he should've been traversing now. For a few moments, he swung in the air, his breakfast threatening to return in a very unpleasant manner. There was a sharp jerk as the rope went slack, and he was lowered to the floor. As soon as his back touched the platform he'd been so unceremoniously snared from, he fought to free his ankle.

'You two are crazy,' he grumbled as he pulled his foot loose. 'How was I supposed to dodge that?'

'You are not going to improve if we do not keep pushing you,' Silva told him, offering her hand.

Taking it, with no comeback because he knew they were right, he allowed the warrior to help him to his feet. Letting out a deep breath, he dusted himself off.

'You're getting better, kid.' Auron nodded, looking at the course. 'I thought the flour bags would get you.'

'I had a little more faith,' Silva remarked. 'I thought you would end up flat on your face with the sudden slope.'

'So your *little more faith* extended for exactly a couple of metres. Thanks, guys.' He held his thumb up to the pair.

'Kid, with what's to come, you need to be ready for anything.' Nicolas and Silva gave each other an awkward glance, which the spirit noticed. 'I know we've avoided talking about it all this time. But rest-time is nearly over,' he said sternly. 'Soon, we'll be back on the road. And when we are...well, I want you to be prepared to best anything you come across...'

Nicolas straightened up at the tinge of emotion in Auron's voice. The spirit was concerned for him. He always knew that he and the spirit had the mentor-mentee relationship, but Auron was genuinely worried about him.

As he opened his mouth to reply, the spirit held up a hand to silence him. 'I figure we have at least another couple of weeks before we need to talk about what happens next. Make the most of it.'

He gave Auron an appreciative smile. Silva looked almost relieved, too.

'Good morning, all.'

Nicolas spun round at the sudden voice.

'I apologise for startling you,' Salrag, the leader of the community, said, putting his hand on his heart.

'It's easily done,' he replied with an awkward grin.

'Well, it shouldn't be,' Auron huffed. 'We're going to be working on that, kid, believe me.'

Great. Actually, it probably is great.

'Are you well?' Silva asked the old orc.

Her question prompted him to take a closer look. Studying his wizened face, he saw something in his gentle yellow eyes. Sadness.

'One of our people must take the Long Walk.'

The mood dampened instantly. A cloud settled above them. When the people of Golthorak showed signs that they were suffering from The Regression, they had to take the Long Walk. Leaving the city, they would journey into the wasteland, so they were no longer a danger to friends and family.

'I'm sorry,' Nicolas said. 'Who is it?'

'Grimog,' Salrag answered with a pained smile. Nicolas knew the orc vaguely. He was a bookish type, kept to himself but was always polite. That was a damn shame. 'Will you be there?'

'You want *us* to attend?'

He'd witnessed the Long Walk twice in the last month, but only from a distance. It was something the orcs took very seriously, so it seemed impolite to make themselves a part of it. But to be invited was a sign of their acceptance into the community

'Yes.' Salrag nodded. 'I believe Grimog was quite friendly with Lady Silva. He would appreciate it.'

Silva's eyes narrowed as she realised everyone was watching her. 'What?'

'I just never took you for the bookish type,' Nicolas replied diplomatically.

'You can read?' Auron asked, scrunching up his nose.

'He had many old tomes on the art of warfare and various combat styles,' the warrior retorted huffily. 'He would lend them to me, and we would discuss our thoughts once I had finished.'

'Wait,' Auron said, looking at everyone else as if a rainbow-coloured goat had just run across the table. 'You were in a *book club*?'

The warrior's face visibly reddened, though Nicolas wasn't sure if it was from embarrassment or rage.

'It was *not* a book club!' Rage, then.

Odd thing to be sensitive about.

'Well, as you killed me, I think I get to call it what I like.' Auron grinned broadly. 'Any issue with that?'

Silva clearly had all the issues in the world with it but kept quiet. It was hard to argue with someone when they threw the fact that you'd murdered them in your face. Though even Nicolas had to admit it was starting to get more than a little overused lately.

Maybe I should talk to him about it?

'So I take it you will attend?' Salrag might've been used to them all talking to Auron, who none of the other orcs could either see or hear, but he was clearly still a little perturbed by it every now and then. Understandably so.

'Of course,' he answered for the others.

CHAPTER 6

Within the hour, the entire community of Golthorak was assembled at the bottom of the stairway that led out of their city, standing in respectful silence. Everyone always attended, to say goodbye to one of their own. Nicolas hadn't noticed when he first entered the city, but the giant stone wall on one side of the stairway that led out of Golthorak had been smoothed and names were carved into it. One for each orc who had to leave over the centuries. One for each member of the community lost. It was too many names. Nicolas was no orc, but looking at it made his heart ache.

At the bottom step stood Grimog, his eyes downcast as he awaited the inevitable. His toga had been replaced by a simple shirt and breeches. Soon enough, that would be covered in scavenged armour, warpaint, trophies, tears and cuts from battle...

And probably blood.

Beside Grimog stood Salrag, talking quietly to the orc. It was hard to tell if Grimog was even taking in what was being said. He might've been too busy contemplating his fate, and what he was losing. Having lost his own home, Nicolas could feel the orc's pain. Yet this orc was determined to take one last vestige of his old life with him. He clung to a small worn red book—most likely a favourite—as if it were a crying child. The terrible thing was, when he finally turned, he would probably use it for toilet paper.

And he would turn. They always did. In all these centuries, the orcs had found no cure for their affliction. They just had to hope it passed them by. But once it began to take hold, that was it. Grimog had smashed up his own library in a fit of rage. Some said it was over the death of a character in the novel he was reading. Or due to a paper cut. Either way, he was on the road to losing himself. The only orc ever to be afflicted by it and not lose their mind was Garaz, but that was only due to the magic charm he now wore everywhere.

Nicolas found himself putting a hand on Garaz's shoulder. The large orc turned to him with a sad smile and patted his hand. Another thing he knew too well was survivor's guilt. Being the one running around free whilst his people—the people of Hablock—were suffering who knew what.

Taking Grimog by the shoulders, Salrag gave the other orc a burdened smile before turning to the crowd.

'Citizens of Golthorak,' the city leader declared, before pausing and lowering his head sadly. 'Today, we gather to say farewell to an honoured brother as he prepares to take his Long Walk into the wasteland that was once our home. The terrible curse that has dogged us for nearly a thousand years claims another good soul today.' The orc's mouth became a thin line. 'Even though The Regression claims him, he will always be one of us, one of our community. We will remember the person he was.' Salrag spread his arms out wide. 'Grimog Garlac, lover of books, writer of stories. Loving son and brother.'

'*Grimog Garlac, lover of books, writer of stories. Loving son and brother,*' the whole crowd repeated as one. Three times they repeated it, getting louder with each repetition.

Nicolas watched as each member of Grimog's family stepped forward and embraced the slender orc. For the most part, he just accepted it. But when his mother hugged him, he held her tightly for a moment.

'His leaving creates a hole amongst us that will never be filled,' Salrag continued. 'All we can do is hope, as we do with all our wayward kin, that your Long Walk one day puts you on the path back to us. Until that day, your name will be added to the Wall of the Lost, so in a way you may live on with us forever.'

Gog, the stone mason, waited quietly to the side with his tools. As soon as the ceremony was complete, he would get to work adding Grimog's name to the wall. But it was never just the name they added. There was always the description of who he was, the same one the assembled crowd had all repeated. That way it wasn't just a name carved in stone. It was a way for that person to be remembered and honoured for who they had been before they became lost.

Stroking his beard, Salrag turned to Grimog. 'Is there anything you wish to say?'

Even from here, it was clear that Grimog's face was streaked with tears. Coughing a few times to clear his throat, he spoke with a weak voice. Yet somehow, it carried across the entire crowd. 'I never knew most of you as well as I should've. You weren't books.' There was a smattering of chuckles. 'But you coming out for me today means everything.' For a moment, he stared at the book in his hand then looked up urgently. 'Silva? Where is Silva?'

Frowning, the warrior weaved past the couple of orcs in front of them and approached. As she did, Grimog held out the red book. 'Please, take this. It is a favourite of mine.' His gaze flicked lovingly to the book. 'I thought if I ever managed to translate it, it would give me the key to the universe. At least, it made me feel smart trying to translate it. Maybe one day you'll be able to learn what I could not?'

Silva took a slight step back. 'I...cannot take your last worldly possession from you...'

The orc pressed the book into her chest. 'If you don't, I'll just end up eating it.'

Slowly, and obviously reluctantly, the warrior took the book. She offered Grimog a bow before returning to the others.

'Keep it safe,' Auron said quietly to the warrior as she rejoined them.

'I intend to,' she replied after a brief pause.

Grimog turned to Salrag, standing up a little straighter. 'I am ready.'

It was probably a lie, but Nicolas doubted the orc would get any more ready.

'Then let us go,' the leader of the orc nation replied.

As the assembled crowd bowed their heads, Grimog walked up the stairs with Salrag at his side. An elderly orc shaman with a long, feathered stick followed them. He would conduct the final part of the ceremony. Once outside the city gates, the shaman would cast a spell to wipe Golthorak from the Walker's memory. It seemed so harsh, but Nicolas understood. If the other orcs found out about this place, they could return and tear it apart. That was one of the reasons the city had been built underground—to keep the remnants of the orc civilisation safe.

He'd asked Garaz once how his brother Shagraz had remembered him then instantly regretted the question when he'd seen the pain in his companion's yellow eyes. Garaz didn't know. But he'd told Nicolas of a chance encounter the pair had had before he'd left the orc wasteland. Shagraz's war party had happened upon Garaz on his way to the Nine Kingdoms of Man, in a journey that would eventually see him end up in the Academy of Magic to try to learn the skills to cure his people's curse. Garaz thought their blood tie might've dulled the magic that'd wiped Shagraz's memory, causing his brother to recognise him. In his disgust at seeing his kin so civilised, Shagraz had attacked his brother, Garaz barely managing to escape with his life. He'd thought that the end of it...until Hablock.

The respectful silence was kept until the trio had passed from sight. But even then, no one really spoke as the crowd dispersed. The pain of the loss always wounded the community grievously.

Beside him, Garaz's face was set in a strained expression.

Nicolas touched his arm to get his attention. 'Are you okay?'

'No.' His companion smiled thinly. 'I have seen too many of these. And every time I have seen one since our return, I want to rip off this amulet and give it to someone more deserving.'

Reaching into his cloak, Garaz pulled out the amulet he now had to wear. On the surface it looked like a simple green jewel embedded in the symbol for the Deity of Healing, but it contained the power to heal curses. It had been worn by Beba Greer, or the demon that had possessed her, to ward off the damage the possession caused as the demonic power consumed her body and soul. It seemed this power was also enough to keep the curse that plagued the orcs at bay.

He looked at the jewel in disdain before returning it to his cloak. Garaz and Salrag had had numerous debates—which both insisted were *not* arguments, despite sounding very much like them—about Garaz wearing the jewel. Garaz had spent years walking Etherius, working on the assumption that there must be a cure out there somewhere. Now he was wearing one, but it could only be used by a single person. Salrag had insisted that Garaz, being the best healer in the tribe, keep it and continue his work. Their orcish companion had been less enthused about the idea.

After over a thousand years, will the cure still be out there, if it ever existed at all?

'You're deserving,' Nicolas said. He didn't need to say more than that, the feeling behind it was quite clear.

Garaz smiled. The argument could be made that he shouldn't trust the orc, who'd knocked him out and stuffed him in a cupboard once, but their bond was beyond petty things like that.

Well, maybe petty *is the wrong word.*

Still, it was hardly like Nicolas had never made a mistake.

'Watching that reminds me how little I want to leave,' Shift said, staring at the walkway sadly.

'We still have time.' Silva's attempt at reassurance sounded hollow as she stared at the book in her hand. Then she shook herself off. 'Shall we return to training?'

'Not just yet,' Nicolas replied, looking away. 'I have something to do first.'

The warrior frowned for a second, before she nodded with understanding. 'It is that time of the week again.'

'It is.'

'Very well,' Silva said. 'Go do what you must. We can continue when you return.'

CHAPTER 7

After emerging into the light, there was the usual moment of blinking as his eyes adjusted to the sun again. As well-lit as the underground city was, sunlight just had a different quality to it. Raising his hand, he shielded his eyes for a moment and took a few lungful's of fresh air. When he'd first started living below, he'd been worried about the air running out. At first, he hadn't wanted to ask how everyone was breathing, because he knew it was a silly question. The city had been around for hundreds of years, and no one had died of suffocation. It had taken him days to try to figure out the way to ask how the city got its air and make it sound like scientific curiosity. He'd rehearsed it in his head numerous times to cultivate an appropriately casual tone, and the second he'd finally asked Garaz, Auron had turned around and gone, *'Panicking about running out of air, kid?'*

In the archway of the building that housed the secret entrance to the underground city, Nicolas stretched. When they'd first arrived, Nicolas had assumed it was a temple, but actually it had been a school. It, and the sites of the other secret entrances, had been put into what the orcs judged to be innocuous buildings that wouldn't attract looters or scavengers. Though if Dieter had come here with an expedition, the nearest school would've been high on his list of places to visit to learn about orc culture.

Lucky no explorers ever make it this far.

'It just tastes different, doesn't it?' One of the two orcs watching the gate chuckled. 'Fresh air.'

'It certainly does.' Nicolas kept his gaze outwards, so as not to give away the guard's hidden position, though he'd checked the street carefully before emerging. Although no one had come here in many years, it could happen.

I'm proof of that.

'It's the only reason I volunteer for this duty,' the orc told him, before adding. 'Stay safe.'

'See you soon,' he replied, walking down the steps and out into what had once been the proud city of Golthorak.

Now it was a ruin. Looking at it made him shudder. Not one building was whole. Rubble lined the street, sheeted with hundreds of years of dust. Nature had done its part to reclaim this place. The walls of the once-impressive buildings were covered in thick vines, plants and grass had burst through the paved walkways in numerous places. It was deathly quiet, as if the whole city was a giant gravestone for a now-dead race.

This could've been Yarringsburg, if the vampires had succeeded.

The sun cast its light over the ruined buildings, creating shadowed recesses that only served to add to the unnerving aura of the place.

The air was warmer than last week. Winter really was on its last legs.

It is *nearly time then.*

There was a bead of sweat on his brow. He'd worn too many furs. Quickly, he shrugged one off and placed it beside some rubble, ruffling it up in several variations until he was satisfied that it looked like part of the scenery. Even *he* wasn't daft enough to leave some neatly folded clothing in a supposedly dead city.

Walking down the streets, dodging debris and climbing over rubble, he finally allowed himself to ponder what would come next. It was easier when he was away from the place that had been his home since they'd arrived.

In his mind, he played back the final moments of Avin Hipmuck, the Visitor. A poor man whose life had been torn apart by a terrible accident that had left him a human-dragon hybrid, who was then used and corrupted for the goals of evil men. The idea that he'd been so close to getting Avin to stand down before that creature had taken his will and used him as a puppet stuck in his gut like a spear.

If I'd just done more. If I'd known what that creature was...

Then not only would Avin still be alive, but so would Tallith. The sergeant of the Babylon City Watch had sacrificed himself to save Nicolas, a man he looked up to. Right now, he didn't feel worthy of being looked up to by anyone. That battle was a failure. No one had needed to die, yet two people had.

But something had come of it. With his dying breath, Avin had written a name in the dirt, revealing the identity of the thrice-damned Maestro.

Tobias Helstrum.

A man already known to them as a spreader of hate and discord. Now it all became clear. He was causing chaos across Etherius to spread his xenophobic agenda. Nicolas had pondered Helstrum's potential endgame, where all this was leading, several times. He'd come up with nothing. But the plan didn't matter. In the end, all that mattered was what they were going to do next. None of them had really spoken of it since the decision had been made, but it had been made. As soon as winter passed, they would find Tobias Helstrum, make him reveal the location of the people of Hablock, then kill him.

He would've been lying if he said the idea didn't weigh heavily on him. Fighting enemies when attacked was one thing. But hunting down a man to end his life...

Am I a hero or an assassin?

He shuddered slightly. Really, he wanted neither of those names. He was just a man who'd had some extraordinarily bad luck, and yet somehow, he kept going. And the crazy path he'd had to follow ended up with him walking through a dead city wearing armour with the title of *Dawnblade*. With that title came responsibility. One that would see him and his companions moving on soon.

As much as he would've liked to stay here—not *here* here, but underground *here*—in reality, there was no choice. Helstrum needed killing. The place below, like so many in Etherius, was peaceful. If they didn't do this, it might end up like the one he was walking through now. Not to mention that Helstrum might know where they were. Had the Visitor reported their whereabouts before attacking them? It seemed not. Otherwise, he was sure he would've had a visit from the Maestro's demonic servant Koth before now. The creature didn't seem the type to be bothered by a bit of cold.

And yet he never came. So we go to him, soon enough. Hopefully, by the time I get there, I can figure out a way to kill him...for what he did to my parents.

Picturing them both, lest he forget their faces forever, he slipped between some of the old buildings. Following the alleyway, he came to the hidden courtyard. Nicolas imagined it had once held a garden similar to the styles of those below, but now it was just a patch of mud with numerous thick brambles growing between the weeds that peppered it.

After following the circumference of the dirt, Nicolas finally stopped and sat down, leaning against the nearby wall. Before him were a pair of simple, flat stones, unassuming to the casual eye but meaning a lot to him. Each one marked a grave.

Tallith, and Avin.

Avin had killed Tallith. It was hard to forgive that, even though he knew Avin had been a sick man corrupted by the Maestro. Even before that fight, he'd hurt countless others. Cursing those he visited who turned him away because of his appearance.

I would've done the same had a half-dragon creature knocked on my door. I could barely stand the travelling preachers we got occasionally.

The group had destroyed the cursed mask Avin had used before killing him. Despite everything he'd done, Nicolas couldn't help but hope that he was at peace now.

Where does the Maestro get all these magic weapons? Is there a shop for evil overlords? If there is he'll be their most valued customer.

Wherever it was, it'd be nice to find the place and burn it to the ground. And maybe piss on the ashes afterwards.

Sighing, he stared at the graves. Every week, he came to visit them. Burying them properly had seemed the right thing to do, and so did coming to pay his respects regularly. They'd get no visits from family or friends. Looking at the graves, anger welled in him at Tallith's unnecessary death and Avin's tragic one. He needed that anger to fuel him to do what they needed to do next.

In his mind, he pictured Tobias Helstrum. He was a scarred, old man. Several times, Nicolas pictured himself killing Helstrum, using the *Dawn Blade* to remove his evil from the world once and for all. Each time, it made him uncomfortable. It always did. He could never picture Helstrum defending himself. He had no doubt they would have to fight their way through scores of minions to get to the man, but simply ending his life without him being able to put up a fight...it seemed more like murder.

But he needs killing.

Staring at the graves, he thought of everyone else who'd died because of the evil man.

'I'm sorry you both died,' he whispered sadly. 'But it won't be for nothing. There's been enough wasted life already. It's just a shame that...'

Nicolas looked up. A glint of light had caught his eye, somewhere in the building across from him. He could've dismissed it as imagination, but he trusted his hero instincts. Narrowing his eyes, he scanned the roof of the building.

There.

He saw...

Is that a stick?

There was a boom like thunder.

CHAPTER 8

H e flinched at the sudden noise, and a lance of burning pain cut across his temple. There was an odd crunching noise behind him, and small chunks of loose stone showered his back. Before he could make sense of any of it, blood began to pour across his right eye. Furiously, Nicolas wiped it away. As he did, he caught sight of the man on the rooftop, finally revealed again after being briefly engulfed in smoke. He seemed to be doing something to his stick.

The world swam in and out of focus as he tore a strip of cloth from his shirt and furiously rubbed the blood from his eye and quickly wrapped it around his head wound. He hissed in pain as he pulled it tight. He had no idea how bad the wound was, but he was still in danger, so this wasn't the time to find out. However bad it was, it was enough to leave him disorientated.

Oh crap.

In between the blurring of his vision, he caught sight of the stick being pointed at him again. It was so long that the wielder had to use both hands, securing it against his shoulder. Quickly, Nicolas rolled aside. As he did there was another boom. A chunk of the wall he had been sat in front of blew outwards, sending rubble everywhere. For a moment, he stared aghast at the hole in the stone.

That could've been my head...might be my head.

As the man began to jiggle his stick again, or whatever he was doing with it, Nicolas threw himself over a small wall. Whatever magic this was, it appeared to need a moment to recharge before being used again. He had no idea what he could do with that information right now, but it was something.

How do I fight a wizard on a roof with a long stick?

It sounded like the start of a terrible joke. But it wasn't.

Shimmying up the wall he was crouched behind, he carefully peered out. Ducking down as soon as he saw the flash of light from the stick, he narrowly avoided losing an eye as another part of the wall turned to dust.

What do sticks have against me? First the choosing stick, now this.

Except the sticks themselves weren't the problem. It was those who wielded them.

He knew he wouldn't have long until the wizard's stick was recharged. And at the moment, there was nowhere obvious to go. The small wall he'd chosen to hide behind had no convenient door to allow his escape or window to jump through. He'd have to move. To his right and left were rows of pillars, with an open space between each—which seemed a lot wider now that he was under attack.

But I can't stay here.

Crawling to the edge of the wall, his head throbbing, Nicolas readied himself. Taking a runner's starting stance, he pushed his weight into his legs, ready to go. Mentally, he counted...

3...2...1...

Dashing from cover, he charged towards a pillar. He was almost there when the stick thundered once more. His leg jinked suddenly, as if something had grabbed and yanked it hard. Fire burnt his calf as he spun with force and fell to the ground, crying out in pain. Gasping, he quickly pulled himself behind cover. Gritting his teeth, he checked on his leg, which screamed at him in agony. There was a hole in his calf. There was a hole...in his leg. And worse, there was something inside it. He could feel it. A solid object just under the skin.

Between the dizziness due to his head, and now his injured leg, it was hard to concentrate. He was becoming woozy. Passing out now would be deadly, so he shook himself sharply. Ripping off more of his shirt, he quickly dressed the bleeding wound. He grunted in pain as he pulled his improvised bandage tight.

I hope Garaz can get whatever that thing is out again.

If only the orc was here to throw some fireballs at this stick-carrying asshole. Because right now, reduced to one leg, he was no use against a wizard with a fire-stick, or whatever it was.

How do I get out of this then?

Crawling home would be a long and painful job. Fighting would be just as difficult, especially as he was nowhere near his assailant and had no clue how to close the distance. Calling for help would announce where he was...

But he already knows where I am.

'Heeeeeeeelp,' he cried at the top of his voice. It wasn't the most heroic move, but he understood his current limitations well enough. Bugger his pride all the way to the Underworld.

The answer was silence. In fact, too much silence. No calls of rescuers, and no more booms. Once the silence and the not-knowing, became too much, Nicolas tentatively poked his head out of cover. No holes were put in it.

Good. I have enough holes as it is.

Except it wasn't good. A brief glance at the rooftop told him the wizard was no longer there. Poking his head out again, he tried to look around, to see where the attacker had gone.

Bugger.

The slight shuffle behind him told him he had company. And in all the chaos of the last couple of minutes, he hadn't even drawn his sword. Turning, he went for the blade.

'I wouldn't.'

His hand stopped short of the hilt as he caught sight of the stick, pointed directly at his head. Now that it was closer to him, he could see it had an opening in it. There were also bits of metal attached to it, and something that looked like the trigger he'd seen before on crossbows. At one end of the stick, looking at him down what Nicolas guessed was some kind of sight, was a face covered in a leering demonic mask—the kind frequently worn by any asshole who served the Maestro. In an instant, he saw the man's conviction in his eyes. The choice to kill him had been made, and there was nothing he could do about it.

I'm going to be killed by a stick... That's just embarrassing.

'You called for help, kid?' Auron skidded to a halt as he appeared through a wall and took in the scene.

'Yes, please. Kindly do something nasty to this guy,' he said, with a gesture towards his attacker.

'What?' The masked man turned his head, trying to see who Nicolas was talking to. Which lined him up nicely with Auron's finger.

'Finger poke of doom.'

The man screamed as the spiritual appendage jabbed him right in the pupil. Auron's attack worked like a charm, except for one issue. As the man roared in pain, his trigger finger flexed. This close to Nicolas the noise was deafening, making his ears numb until a high-pitched ringing began. There was a hole in the wall not four inches from his head, but better there than between his eyes. Opening and closing his mouth, Nicolas tried to get his hearing back. His ears were having none of it.

The idiot deafened me.

Even his eyes were stinging, due to the sudden flash and smoke they'd been subjected to. But he couldn't wait for the dancing light to clear. He felt the stick hit his foot as his attacker dropped it. Through the smoke, he could make out the hazy form of the man stepping backwards, clutching his eye.

Drawing the knife from his boot, Nicolas winced in anticipation of what came next. The pain was nearly unbearable as he leapt to his feet and threw himself at the man. In fact, his leg nearly betrayed him completely. But he didn't have to go far. When he crashed into his attacker, the pair fell to the ground. Landing atop the assassin, Nicolas was racked with pain as his injured leg connected with the man's knee. For another moment, he thought he was going to pass out. Somehow, he managed to stay conscious.

His attacker's eye widened behind the mask as he saw the knife in Nicolas's hand. The warrior got his arm up just in time, blocking the blade before it skewered his throat. A battle of strength began, the warrior using his forearm to try and hold back the knife that Nicolas very much wanted to stab him with. Nicolas had the dominant position, but also loss of blood to contend with. He was getting weaker, and he knew it.

Pressing his entire bodyweight behind the blade, Nicolas drove it an inch closer to his attacker's head. The man grunted with the effort of trying to hold him off, using his free hand to reinforce his blocking arm. Both their limbs shook as the struggle continued. Then the warrior played his final gambit.

Breaking his reinforced hold, the warrior grabbed Nicolas's damaged leg. There was no word for the pain as his body spasmed, and he fell away, rolling around on the floor, clutching his leg with his free hand. The fact that he still held the knife was a miracle. The warrior moved with him, grabbing his throat with one hand, as he picked up his fire-stick with the other, holding it by the narrower end, most likely to use it as a club.

A year ago, Nicolas would've had no idea what to do, but this wasn't Nicolas a year ago. With a quick slash, he cut the wrist of the hand gripping his arm, enjoying the brief elation as the pressure on his neck subsided. He then turned the knife point forward and drove it straight into his attacker's throat, ensuring to twist it before removing it, just as Silva had taught him.

With a sickly cry, the warrior grabbed his throat and fell back to the floor. By the time Nicolas crawled back against the wall and managed to bring his ragged breathing back under control, his attacker was already dead. With a sigh of relief as he watched the killer's spirit leave his body and vanish completely.

Good riddance, you stick-wielding asshole. Have fun in the Underworld.

Then he did actually pass out.

CHAPTER 9

T hrobbing brought him around, but he didn't want to open his eyes straightaway. Even behind his eyelids, the world was swimming. It took him a moment or two to remember what had happened.

There's...a man with a stick...that put a hole in my leg...

Well, he appeared to be alive. And lying on a bed. Which was a good thing. In his experience, being captured by a villain did not involve them putting you on a bed. Especially not one as comfortable as this one. He would've expected a hard cell floor with some decorative straw. Possibly being chained to a wall or manacled as an optional extra. But no. He was in a bed. And he was alive.

Thank the Deities.

The ache in his leg was a vast improvement over his last encounter with it. But there was something else. Stinging. Garaz must've used his healing magic. Meaning it was an emergency and he'd been pretty close to death. There was a time when all the orc's healing magic had done was actually heal him, but since his brief visit to the Underworld, it had burned him too. A seer had told him he now had a foot in both worlds, so healing magic would help the living part of him but also burn him as it did the undead. Since then, he'd stuck to healing potions, which were slower acting and thus safer. There was still a question mark over what other side effects his trip to the *other side* might've caused, but so far it was just that and being able to see the souls of the dead more frequently.

Focus on the fact that you're alive.

And surrounded by familiar people.

'Before I open my eyes, how bad is the scar?' Internally, he winced as he waited for the answer.

'Not bad...by your standards.'

Brilliant.

Considering his *standards* were whip marks all over his back, the harpy talon scars in his shoulders and the various other cut and stab marks that adorned him, he wasn't any the wiser about what to expect.

When he opened his eyes, he wasn't interested in finding pictures in the stone roof this time. Tilting his head up, he saw his companions standing around him. None of them looked overly concerned, so he was either all right or they'd gotten really good at acting.

Looking down, he could see his bare leg. The flesh around where the hole had been was fiery pink, like it had been burnt a while ago.

'Your condition was serious, and it was imperative that I get that wound closed, so I had to use my healing magic,' Garaz informed him. 'But I used little amounts frequently. I think the fact that there are no internal organs in your leg helped. I hope the scars will fade.'

Little amounts frequently? *How long was I out for?*

'If not, I'm the only one who sees your legs, and I don't mind,' Shift added.

Nicolas didn't feel like celebrating, especially when the shapeshifter's gaze flicked to his temple.

'What?' he asked shrilly. Then he remembered the blood in his eyes. 'Mirror,' he said, reaching out and gesturing urgently with his hand.

Silva handed him a mirror. As he took it, he noticed that her sword was on her belt once more. A wise precaution.

Not giving himself time to be nervous and hesitant, he put the mirror up to his face.

Dammit.

In truth, the scar wasn't terrible. It ran across his forehead, drawing a line parallel to his right eyebrow. An angry red line, criss-crossed by the stitches that had sewn it shut.

'I was reluctant to use more magic on you than I needed to,' Garaz offered.

'I appreciate that.' *I don't want my brain melted.* 'Any side effects I should be worried about?'

'There are herbs on the side for the headaches you will be getting.' The orc pointed to the bedside table. 'And I suggest a crutch for a few days until your leg heals properly. But beyond that, you should be fine.'

'Except I'm becoming more scar than skin,' he joked. Sort of. The thought unnerved him, and he found himself needing reassurance. 'Auron,' he said quickly, 'you must've had a few scars in your time, right?'

'No.' The spirit stepped back as everyone turned and looked at him. 'What? I don't. I was just that good.'

Oh Deities, he's right. I'm not good. I'm just going to continue getting scarred until I'm some kind of deformed...

Shift flicked their hand through the spirit's head in a mock slap.

'Okay, okay.' The spirit sighed. 'So, this one time, I was chasing this wizard whose gimmick was controlling animals.' *I've faced one of those before.* 'Except instead of going for the obvious ones, bears, wolves and such, he had a weird perversion for taking cute animals and making them feral.'

'*Cute* animals?' Silva frowned.

'You know, squirrels, kittens…that sort of thing.' Auron shook his head. 'He had some sort of vague idea about setting up a nature reserve to shield animals from destructive people, or some such.' The spirit held his hands in the air. 'Now, I'm all for saving animals, but his idea was that if no one was alive within a certain radius then no one could hurt the animals. *That* was an issue. So, I go after him. I'm staying in this tavern overnight, and I'm getting undressed. What I didn't know was that he'd sent a rabbit…a bloody rabbit of all things, to try to kill me.' Auron scowled for a moment. 'I bend over to drop my breeches, annnnnd…'

'Wait a minute,' Shift said, holding their hands up. 'Do you mean to tell us that you have a rabbit bite scar…on your ass?'

'It took out quite a chunk,' the spirit grumbled.

Suddenly, I feel better. It's no harpy talons, but it is *hilarious.*

'Thank you for sharing.' He was sure Auron didn't appreciate the snigger afterwards.

'You're welcome,' the spirit replied dryly.

'So, how long was I out for?' he asked the others.

'Not long.' Shift smiled warmly. 'You're getting better at this.'

'Only because I've been rendered unconscious so many times.' He chuckled, though it was almost a sigh. 'It's not a skill I'm pleased to have developed.'

Nicolas Percival Carnegie. Twenty-one years old. Born in Hablock. Son of…

Going over the facts of his life in his mind reassured him that constantly being knocked out wasn't causing any permanent damage. Though would he even know if he'd forgotten anything or gotten any of the facts wrong?

'You're okay, kid,' Auron said, obviously noticing his worry.

'Of course he is.' Shift smirked. 'He's whined already.'

The spirit grinned. 'Thank the Deities. He'll be all right.'

'But I nearly wasn't,' he huffed. 'So being nice to me for a few minutes wouldn't hurt you guys.'

'…*He whined.*' Silva allowed herself a small smirk as he glared at her. 'And I still might not be for long. I think it's safe to assume that Tobias Helstrum knows where we are.'

That sobered the mood of the room quickly.

CHAPTER 10

With Garaz and Silva's help, he sat up. His calf was stiff and sore, but it could've been worse.

And at least it's still attached to my leg.

'So...' He caught sight of something odd on the bedside table, beside the orc's herbs. 'What's that?'

Leaning over, Garaz picked up the small bowl, holding it out for him to see. Sat inside was a small metal ball, partially covered in blood. It rolled around noisily as the orc tilted the bowl to let him see. It took Nicolas a second to realise what it was.

'Wait...*that* was in my leg?' he cried.

'I think you were lucky,' the orc told him. 'I believe that the weapon that fired this did not hit you directly, but the projectile it launched ricocheted and caught you in the leg. If it had gone deeper...'

'You may have lost your leg,' Silva clarified helpfully.

'Weapon...projectile...'

Silva reached behind her and grabbed the fire-stick from where it was resting against the wall. Here, in front of him, it looked almost innocuous. Save for the way Silva held it as if it were a long and very rotten sausage.

Garaz gestured for the warrior to pass him the weapon, and Nicolas flinched as she threw it across the bed, directly over him. The orc turned the weapon, probing it with a gentleness at odds with his large hands. Nicolas flinched again as the holed end pointed at him for a second.

Flinched? I nearly shat my pants.

'Is it some sort of wand?' Auron asked as Nicolas eyed it nervously.

'No. It is actually mechanical in nature.' Nicolas wasn't too keen in the childlike enthusiasm Garaz had for something that had put a hole in him. 'If I had a basis for comparison, it is like a crossbow, in that you squeeze the trigger to make it fire.'

Above said trigger was some kind of small metal lever. Garaz pulled it back with a couple of clicks. Pointed the weapon at the roof and squeezed the trigger. Nicolas came a little closer to shitting his pants as the weapon clicked.

'Garaz, what in the Underworld?' he cried. 'That thing's dangerous and you just go pressing the trigger willy-nilly?'

The orc frowned at him. '*Willy-nilly?*' he repeated. 'You need not worry, Nicolas. It is safe.'

'Are you sure about that?' Shift asked. 'I mean, I'm not as jumpy as my lover there, but maybe you shouldn't be so comfortable with a weapon you've only just discovered.'

'Ah,' the orc said, looking down its length. 'This is where it gets interesting...' *I think we need to leave him and that weapon alone in the room for a bit.* '...the weapon operates on some sort of combustion principle. The man you killed had black powder on him. It appears to create a small explosion when struck, which propels the ball out of the end of the weapon—'

'And into my leg,' Nicolas interrupted harshly.

Garaz's face dropped as he realised how excited he'd been getting. Quickly, he leant the weapon against the wall. 'Quite.'

'It's certainly noisy to launch something so small,' Nicolas remarked, eyeing the metal ball in disgust. 'Every time it fired, it was like a clap of thunder.'

'That's what made me come running,' Auron said. 'I was taking a stroll and heard the bangs, I sped up considerably when I heard you calling for help. If the thing was silent, I might not have known what was going on.'

The room shrank for a moment as Nicolas realised how close he'd been to death. The weapon had been pointed right at him. If Auron hadn't come along, he'd be sat propped against that wall right now, the sunlight shining through a hole in his head. He internally shuddered at the thought of the masked face looking down the weapon at him.

'Helstrum knows where we are,' he said quietly. 'And winter has passed enough that he can get to us.'

The room went quiet for a moment, as the implications set in for everyone.

'I can't believe he sent one guy to kill me,' Nicolas remarked, dwelling on the man again.

Shift snorted with laughter. 'Oh Deities, listen to you.' They chuckled. '*They only sent one man, to kill* me? *Outrageous.*'

'Well...it's a little insulting,' he said sourly. 'Even if the guy did have a fire-stick.'

'Fire-stick?' Silva frowned.

Nicolas shrugged. 'You come up with a better name for it.'

'No, no, no,' Shift said, raising their hands. 'We've gone off on a tangent here. We need to go back to Nick's upset that they would only send *one man* to try to kill the legendary hero.'

'I did not say it like that,' he protested.

'It was inferred,' Shift said, wrinkling their nose in disagreement.

'Why don't you infer my—'

'Hey,' Auron shouted. He looked at each of them in turn as the room silenced. 'You're all going off on tangents. We need to get back to the real issue. Helstrum just tried to kill us, well you. *And* he has some kind of new weapon.'

'Helstrum's made the first move,' Silva said with bravado. 'Now it is our turn. It's...' the warrior hesitated for a moment. 'Time to go.'

Again, the room went quiet.

'So, we are doing this then?' Nicolas asked. 'Hunting him down and killing him?'

Auron gave him a sympathetic look. 'He's the Maestro, kid. He needs killing.'

Nicolas looked away. He knew that. It was just the idea of seeking someone out to end their life. It didn't sit right.

Auron opened his mouth to speak.

'We're going,' Nicolas said firmly. 'I'm just uncomfortable with it.'

'Being an assassin?' He winced at Shift's use of the *A* word. 'I'm just teasing. Don't take it personally.'

'I'm not.'

'Uh-huh,' Shift said with raised eyebrows. 'Besides, it's not the first time you've tried to assassinate him.'

'That wasn't me,' he protested with an exasperated sigh.

The last, and only, time Nicolas had been near Tobias Helstrum was in a town called Narus, where Helstrum had been holding a rally so he could vomit hatred on some poor folk who didn't know better than to listen to it. At that rally, someone had tried to kill him. Nicolas had foiled the attempt, but due to a misunderstanding, he'd been believed to be the killer. As far as he knew, he was still a wanted man in the kingdom of Nalbina because of it.

'Yes, random mysterious archer,' Auron mocked. 'We know. Hopefully you do a better job of killing him on your second attempt.'

Funny. Very, very funny.

'As much as we have found a modicum of peace here, we all knew this was inevitable,' Silva interjected

'Of course, it's just...a shame.' Shift sighed. 'I almost feel at home here.'

'If we don't go and do this, soon enough nowhere in Etherius will be peaceful.'

Shift side-eyed him. 'Getting Auron's flair for the dramatic?'

He sighed. 'Don't pretend you can't sense it. After all we've seen happening. It's all building to something, you can almost feel it in the air. Like Etherius is holding its breath.'

'Yes, I do agree, *Auron the Second*.' The jest came with no smile. 'But still, it's nice here.'

Nicolas felt the same. He'd grown oddly attached to this very strange place, and the comfort it had offered them these past months. 'Maybe we'll come back one day.'

'We're about to take a run at one of the most influential—if disgusting—men in Etherius.' Shift smiled wanly. 'I think maybe there won't be much coming back from that.'

The thought had occurred to him too. Tobias Helstrum was the Maestro, but he was also a powerful man in his own right. Killing him without evidence of his identity would lead to them being arrested and likely executed for the crime. At best, they could expect a lifetime of being hunted by the authorities.

Still, he needs killing.

'Before we do, your leg needs to heal,' Garaz warned. 'The damage could have been worse, but it will still take some few days for you to be able to walk properly. You may all travel then.'

The implication of the orc's choice of phrase wasn't lost on anyone, but no one argued with him...*yet*.

'It's settled then,' Auron said with a thin smile. 'A few days to recover then it's adventure time.'

More like assassin time.

CHAPTER 11

Assassin time was delayed by Nicolas's need to heal. Strangely, it turned out the slightly burnt scar tissue from the healing magic bothered him more than the wound it'd healed, pulling tight with every step he took. The pronounced limp that came with his injury had eased off after the first few days.

But the fate of Etherius wasn't about to hang around, patiently waiting for him to get better. And neither was Silva.

'Lie down,' the warrior told him as he hobbled down the stairs, two days after the attack.

'Hmm, pardon?' he asked, having been concentrating so hard on not falling down the stairs that he hadn't listened properly.

'Lie down.'

Now Nicolas was confused for a different reason. The warrior appeared to be indicating to the floor.

'On...the floor.?'

The warrior frowned at him in confusion. 'Yes. Where am I pointing?'

'You...want me to lie on the floor.'

'Are you well?' Silva asked, narrowing her eyes. 'I know it's early, but you appear to be confused.'

The conversation was starting to get awkward, so Nicolas decided it'd be better to just comply. Slowly, he limped over to Silva. At least she was pointing to a part of the floor that had a rug on it. Carefully, he lowered himself until he was lying with Silva standing over him. Things were getting more awkward by the second.

His head was abruptly lifted and a pillow shoved under it then Silva knelt by his leg and straightened it. Before he could ask what she intended to do—not that he was sure he wanted the answer—the warrior began to massage his leg.

It's actually...nice.

Silva did look as if she were chopping a slab of meat rather than administering a massage, but it was relieving the stiffness in his leg.

Then he made the mistake of flicking his eyes to the side. Silva wasn't known for wearing a lot of armour and *was* known for her muscular physique. When a woman with such a physique is rubbing a man's leg...well...there's usually a very natural response. Nicolas stared at the ceiling, wide-eyed, doing everything in his power to interrupt that response.

Trolls. Giant, hairy, angry trolls. Alric Tavish. Pirates. Big, sweaty, angry pirates. Auron's stories. Auron's scarred ass.

He let out an *eep* as Silva suddenly raised his leg and positioned herself to his side, so she was leaning over him and her...chest-plate...was directly in his line of sight. Keeping his leg at a ninety-degree angle, she took hold of his knee and pressed his foot towards his head.

Oh, please Deities, no...

It was getting very hot in here. Very hot.

'How does that feel?' the warrior asked, matter-of-factly.

Nicolas could only answer with a coughing nod.

'What in every undead soul in the Underworld is going on here?' Shift asked as they stared aghast at the scene from the bottom of the stairs.

'I am assisting Nicolas with the tightness in his leg,' Silva replied with a frown.

Shift put their hands on their hips and nodded several times. 'And helping make his breeches tighter?'

The warrior frowned again then stood up. 'Your dirty mind is unbecoming. I am trying to help him walk properly again.'

The shapeshifter walked over to them and stood directly over Nicolas. 'Looking a little warm there, Nick,' they remarked with wide eyes. They then leant down with a smile and flicked him between the legs, hard.

Coughing again, Nicolas curled into a ball on his side, hands on his groin. 'I wasn't doing anything,' he protested with a wheeze.

'I didn't hurt my finger doing that, so you're forgiven.' Shift smiled then winked at him evily. 'But it's always good to be warned. Just in case.'

Noted.

Tutting at Shift, Silva helped Nicolas to his feet. Surprisingly, his leg did feel better. Though he wasn't sure if this was due to Silva's ministrations, or he was just distracted by the pain of getting flicked in the balls.

The door of the house opened, and Garaz walked in, followed by Auron. A few steps into the room, the orc stopped, tilting his head at Nicolas curiously.

'Do you need my assistance?'

'No,' he said, waving the orc away. 'I'm good.'

He could tell from the smirk on the spirit's face that Auron had guessed, at least broadly, what had happened.

'How is the leg?' he asked.

'Getting better,' Nicolas said as he sat down at the small table they ate at. 'I can probably travel now. By the time we've actually found him, it should be healed up nicely.'

'Any ideas about that?' Shift asked, sitting across from him.

Auron shrugged. 'We find a population centre and ask,' the spirit replied. 'Tobias Helstrum likes to make a big show of himself. I'm sure he won't be that hard to find. It just depends what end of Etherius he's at.'

'I have begun to gather supplies for our journey,' Silva informed the group. 'The orcs have no horses here, so we will be on foot until we can buy some.'

My leg best improve quickly then.

'At least it'll give me plenty of time to think about the best way to kill him,' Nicolas remarked sourly, staring at the fruit bowl.

'You cannot have a sense of honour when it comes to killing an enemy,' Silva said.

'Yes,' Auron remarked with a snarky tone. 'You do whatever it takes to kill them. Maybe you wait for them to take a shit and shoot them with a crossbow.'

The unsubtle jab wasn't lost on the warrior, who winced very slightly.

'Maybe we could just hire someone to do it?' Nicolas asked, picking up an apple and looking at his dark outline reflected in it.

'You know that's worse than just killing him ourselves, right?' Shift asked.

'Yes.' He didn't know how exactly, but it was. 'I didn't mean it anyway. This is our job. I'd hardly entrust the fate of Etherius to Alexi and Emelina. Or any of their colleagues.'

'We will be fine,' Auron said. 'We've got the new *Dawnblade*, Silva bloody Destrone, a shapeshifting thief, an orc who throws fireballs, and the most handsome spirit to grace the afterlife. Killing him won't be a problem.'

A cough got everyone's attention. 'On that note,' Garaz began slowly. 'I should tell you that I will not be coming with you.'

Here we go.

'What?' Auron scoffed. 'What do you mean, you *aren't coming with us?*'

Nicolas had been defensive enough times in his life to know what it meant when Garaz straightened up the way he did. It was like some form of mystical energy shield appeared around the orc.

'I believe my meaning was clear.' Their companion ensured he was looking away from all of them when he spoke. 'This quest is yours. I have my work here.'

'By which you mean *I'm going to use a piss-poor excuse to get out of going with my friends because I'm still racked with guilt about lying to them and trying to kill them.*'

Clearly, that hit a nerve, because now Garaz was happy to make eye contact. Spinning around, he stared at Shift furiously. 'You are not funny,' he growled, before storming back out of the house. The door slammed hard enough to shake the items on the nearby cabinet.

'I wasn't trying to be,' Shift remarked dryly.

CHAPTER 12

Nicolas rose from the floor awkwardly. He couldn't let Garaz leave in such a manner. And out of the four of them, he was going to be the most empathetic when he caught up to the orc, and therefore the most likely to calm him down. Shift would take the piss until he really lost his cool. Auron would tell him a story, which his companion didn't need right now. And Silva...would probably just scowl intently at him until he relented. None of that would be productive.

Standing, he tested his leg for a moment. Despite nearly causing an awkward situation, and a fight with Shift, Silva had actually helped. His leg was still stiff, but not as bad as it had been only an hour before.

Perhaps I should ask her to do it aga...actually, I don't think it's worth incurring Shift's wrath.

'That's healing nicely,' Auron remarked, pointing at his calf. 'Which is good, because you have an orc to chase down.' It seemed the spirit had come to the same conclusion as he had. 'And then we really need to start getting ready to go.'

'It'll be fine.' Nicolas wasn't sure if he was saying that to himself or Auron. But he was saying it.

'Of course it is, kid.' The spirit grinned. 'I've seen people attempt more with worse wounds.'

'Here cometh the tale,' Shift whispered quietly.

'So, this one time, there was a raider name Paiter. He picked the wrong fight and lost both his legs, but to give the stubborn bugger his due, he survived.' Auron appeared almost impressed. 'Even then, he didn't give up on his—rather stupid—dream to rob people on the road. He got two peg legs fitted and went about his business. One day, he happened to try to rob a carriage I was travelling in. Well, I wasn't about to have that.' The spirit shook his head. 'I felt kind of bad killing him. He could barely manoeuvre with those legs, but he refused point blank to let me take him alive. Sometimes, you have to kill someone when it seems distasteful to do so.'

'Is that the lesson?' Nicolas asked. 'Because I already said I'd kill Helstrum.'

Auron narrowed his eyes thoughtfully. 'That, and you can work to overcome any wound or disability if you try hard enough.'

'Until some passing hero cuts your head off on the side of some random road,' Shift smirked.

'That won't happen to you though, kid,' the spirit said quickly. 'You don't have any peg legs, just one stiff one. So, it could be worse. That's three lessons in one tale.' Auron was clearly pleased with himself about that.

Sometimes I wonder if there's actually any wisdom in his stories, or if he just likes telling them...

Luckily, it wasn't hard to figure out where Garaz had gone. If he wasn't in the house, or the food court, he could be found in his workshop just a few streets down. The orc had a habit of locking himself away in there for long hours at a time. The others knew not to disturb him when he did.

Until now.

After leaving the house and shutting the door much more carefully than his companion, Nicolas walked down the street. This was the first time since the attack that he'd walked a distance without some kind of support. But his leg needed to be worked. He couldn't rely on his crutch forever. And, thankfully, it seemed to be okay. It was sore, of course. But it could've been a lot worse. If the ball had actually struck him, instead of bouncing off something beforehand, he could've lost the leg completely. Then he'd be halfway to Paiter's situation. With that in mind, a little soreness didn't seem much of a bother at all.

There was no sign of Garaz on the street, so he'd been quick once he left. Walking slowly, to give the orc a little extra time to calm down, Nicolas made his way to the workshop. The place itself was an unassuming stone building with a flat roof. Stopping at the door, Nicolas hesitated with his knuckle raised just before he knocked. He was sure the response would be very Sarus-like, and he didn't feel like being told to bugger off. He wouldn't anyway. So, turning the handle quietly, he let himself in.

His companion was hunched over a bench. And clearly still aggravated, judging by the way he snatched things around him and slapped them back down on the table again. Beyond that, the workshop was neat to the point of regimented. Each thing was in its proper place, and the things that weren't would be returned there after use. Everything was clean and well-kept. There were devices and magical implements whose uses he had no interest in trying to discern, and numerous books that would make him cross-eyed if he tried to read them all. None of that was the purpose of his visit.

Garaz half-turned as he approached. He was sure the orc was going to say something to the effect of *'I have made my decision and that is that.'*

'What are you working on?' he asked as he craned his neck to look over Garaz's shoulder.

'I do not appreciate you sneaking up on me,' the orc replied gruffly after a second.

'Sneaking up on you?' Nicolas laughed. 'Haven't you heard my legend? I can blend with the very shadows themselves, appearing at will to smite evil. If I wanted to sneak up on you, you'd have screamed like...me when I wake up next to Shift pretending to be a fat old man.'

Garaz's lips made several odd movements. The orc was wrong-footed again. 'I am not coming,' he persisted.

'Trying to find the secrets of various powders?' Nicolas asked instead, nodding to the two dishes in front of Garaz.

One contained the red substance they'd come to know as *Boost.* A potent narcotic for wizards that temporarily boosted their power, whilst leaving them open to potentially exploding. The other, he guessed, was the black powder taken from his attacker, the thing that powered his fire-stick.

'Indeed,' Garaz said, turning his attention back to his work. 'These powders are very similar. They are both combustible. Watch.' The orc took a pinch of the black powder and put it on a separate dish. With a click of his fingers, he created a small flame. In an instant, there was a flash, a *whumph*, and a puff of smoke.

Nicolas coughed, waving his hand in front of his face to bat away the sudden cloud. 'Deities,' he cursed. 'Be careful with the rest of it.'

'I will be.' Garaz smiled. 'The red powder, this *Boost*, is equally volatile. We know this because it blew Oleg Hobranth into many small pieces.' There was a hint of satisfaction in the orc's voice at recounting the death of his nemesis. 'But I cannot fathom what triggers it. Maybe it is physiological?'

Whatever it was, the loony trader, Snaggle-toothed Joe, had managed to use it to transport them across a vast distance. And he hadn't exploded even a little.

Which is surprising, considering how much of the stuff he inhaled.

'Just be careful testing it,' Nicolas cautioned. 'And I know it's addictive, so...'

Garaz looked at him and raised an eyebrow, causing Nicolas to shrug awkwardly. It needed to be said. Or at least implied.

Nicolas's gaze moved down to the amulet around the orc's neck. 'How about that?' he asked. 'Any luck yet?'

Garaz sighed, cupping the amulet. 'It is hard to have breakthroughs when the item that you intend to study must remain around your neck, lest you turn into a rampaging maniac and smash your workspace to pieces.' The orc let the amulet go and the chain swayed slightly.

'I was wondering about that,' Nicolas asked, staring hypnotically at the amulet. 'It worked when it was around your neck, but why did you turn fully after I broke the chain? You still had it on your person.' The question brought back an uncomfortable memory of Garaz shooting him through the air with a fireball.

'That, at least, I have a decent theory about,' the orc said, turning back to the table and leafing through the pages strewn across it in a very unscientific fashion. 'I believe the amulet needs a measure of skin contact to access its healing magic. It seems powerful enough to fight off *The Regression* but not remove it completely. If I take it off for more than a few minutes, I begin to get...irked.'

I have no wish to see Garaz 'irked' again. Ever.

'At least it matches your skin.' It was a poor attempt to be reassuring, and he knew it, but he had to try. Not that it mattered. Garaz's mind had drifted off again, back to the scrawled notes in front of him. For such a particular fellow, his handwriting was not even vaguely legible.

Back to the purpose of my visit.

'So, you're coming then.'

The big orc sighed before looking at him incredulously. 'Are you serious?' He stared at Nicolas for a moment, before deciding that he was indeed serious. 'I do not deserve a place with you, after what I did. Why would you even want me?'

'Personally, I'm just hoping to return the favour and stuff you in a cupboard at some point.' He grinned.

Garaz chuckled. 'I see Shift is continuing to rub off on you.'

'You know we want you with us, right?'

'If it is healing you are looking for, my magic should not be used on you. I can make up enough potions for—'

'Hey,' Nicolas interrupted sharply. 'We want *you*. You're one of us. Yes, things went a bit bad, but I think we're all adult enough to let it go. Except maybe Shift...and Auron.' He made sure he looked the orc right in the eye. 'We have the chance to really make the world better. I know you want to be part of that. Or you can shut yourself away from the world, feeling sorry for yourself and staring at that amulet in the hope *something* may happen.' He smiled a little. 'Plus, I do get punched in the face a lot.'

After a long pause, the orc laughed aloud. 'You do keep me busy.' Garaz's face became solemn again. 'But I betrayed you all. I cannot be trusted. If the amulet were to fall off or somehow be lost...'

'Then we will beat the sense back into you.' Nicolas shrugged. 'We've done it before.'

'All jesting aside—'

'All jesting aside,' he interrupted quickly. 'You're *family*. And when people in a family make mistakes, they get forgiven. None of us hold you in ill will. You had your reasons, and they were damned good ones. I wish you'd talked to us before running off, but it is what it is. The idea of going out there without you, and your wisdom... Well, I might as well go out and leave one of my arms behind.'

'I—'

'Look,' Nicolas interrupted abruptly, 'I came here because I can give you a nice, well-reasoned argument why you should be with us. Now, if I fail...one of the others will come and try. Ask yourself, do you really want Silva in here glaring at you until you relent? Or Auron telling you stories to try to spur you on? Or, even worse...' Nicolas allowed himself a dramatic pause. '...Shift wandering around...touching stuff.' Garaz's eyes widened in shock at the very thought of Shift being unleashed on his workspace. 'And they'd all do it because they care. Please. Garaz. It won't be right without you by our side.'

Garaz's gaze dropped to the floor as he thought. The conflict was clear, even without being able to look into his yellow eyes. 'Well, as your healer I could not let you walk around missing an arm.' The orc smiled finally then offered Nicolas his hand. 'I have said this many times, but I am truly sorry. Still, it will be my honour to travel with you once more.'

Nicolas took the hand and shook it. 'But you walk in front of me at all times. I don't trust you behind me again,' he said with a wink.

'Noted.' Garaz smiled.

CHAPTER 13

'*A dventure time*,' Auron bellowed with wide open arms as they strolled down the street towards the exit to Golthorak. His voice echoed from house to house and his aura shone brightly. Suddenly, the spirit turned, wagging a finger at Nicolas with enthusiasm. 'If you're going to be the new me, you need a catchphrase.'

'He has one,' Shift informed the spirit. '*My name isn't Nick Carnage.*'

'Funny,' Nicolas said, shaking his head.?'

Auron rolled his pupilless eyes. 'Spoilsports. Where's your sense of adventure? Of theatrics? Of passion?'

Auron was the only one who appeared happy. Nicolas and the others were trudging along quietly. They were all going to miss this place. Privately, he suspected that the spirit's bluster was because he was going to miss it, too, and he was trying to take their minds off it.

I wish something would take my mind off the long walk.

That was another thing Auron had to be happy about. He didn't have to walk. Having an undead horse that appeared whenever you summoned it was very handy, provided you yourself were undead. Yesterday, Silva had suggested they steal mounts from the nearest orc camp. It had seemed a good idea until Garaz reminded everyone that the orcs rode barely domesticated giant wolf creatures to battle. That had taken the lustre off the idea quickly.

Still, he could've used a horse. They'd only spent a couple more days preparing, and Nicolas recovering, before they left, and his leg was still stiff and starting to hurt even though they'd only made it down a few streets so far.

*Speaking of...*The streets were quiet today. Dead, actually. They'd chosen to leave early, so maybe people were still asleep?

At least the lack of people meant they were making good time. There were no well-wishes or lengthy goodbyes. Just...

As the group rounded the corner to the staircase that would take them out of Golthorak, they all came to a stop. Ahead of them was the entire population of the city. The orcs looked back at them, waiting patiently.

'Huh.' There was emotion in Shift's seemingly simple response. Most likely the same emotion he was feeling himself right now.

Glances were exchanged before they continued on their way. As they reached the crowd of orcs, it parted for them. Smiling, familiar faces wished them well on their journey. Nicolas shook the hands of several he'd become close to, especially Grag and Gera.

As the final few orcs allowed them to pass, they revealed Salrag and Dieter, standing by the stairs waiting for them.

And no shaman.

'There will be no wiping of your minds,' the orc leader said with a half-smile. 'We hope you return one day. You can hardly do that if you cannot remember where we are.'

He smiled awkwardly, embarrassed his mind had been read. 'Thank you. It means a lot,' he said, as he and Salrag clasped each other's shoulders. 'And thank you for making us part of your community.'

'And you always will be.' The leader nodded to the stone mason, who was waiting dutifully for them to leave. Nicolas could guess why. He then went about fighting to keep the tear welling in his eye from dropping out.

Today it's us taking our Long Walk.

After patting Salrag on the arms, he turned his attention to Dieter. 'You're staying then?' he asked the writer, when he noticed the lack of pack and supplies.'

'Yes, indeed, my dear boy.' The explorer beamed. 'I have only just started scratching the surface when it comes to putting together a historical picture of how the orcs of old lived.' Dieter leaned in and whispered conspiratorially, 'Do you know, they apparently were the first to invent a constitution as we understand it.'

'I thought the elves would've had that first?' Nicolas knew little about the race, who'd left Etherius nearly a thousand years ago, but Dieter liked to talk history and he hadn't been able to help but pick up a fact or two. One of which was apparently how civilised they were.

'Good question,' Dieter said, clicking his fingers with a smile. 'In fact, the elves were more casual in that respect. There was no official constitution, per se, just an understanding that all elves knew the correct way to behave and would act as such. The only recorded edict I've found is the very simple, '*elf shalt not kill elf.*' Beyond that, it just seemed to be a case of use your best judgement. Whereas the orcs set out a specific list of rules and guidelines for people to live by. It's quite fascinating'

Good job the elves are gone then. I don't trust many people's best judgement *nowadays.*

'Best judgement is good if you don't have any weird creatures on your shoulder controlling you,' Shift muttered with a shudder, referring to the odd tentacled creature that had sapped Avin's will when he'd been on the verge of realising who he'd once been.

'You know, mentioning that thing on his neck reminds me of a story I heard long ago.' Auron squinted thoughtfully, tapping his chin. 'What was it...what was it...oh yes, an old King of Hoflar, Ragin the Crazed, went mad many years ago.'

I'm assuming he was given that moniker after, rather than before, it happened.

'They said he ran around screaming that he had something on his back. Then one day he just threw himself out of a tower window.' The spirit clapped his hands together to mimic someone splatting on the ground far below.

'Hang on,' Shift said in surprise. 'You listened to another person's story? Were you gagged or something? Trying to bed them?'

'My wisdom is never appreciated,' Auron huffed.

'...and I cannot wait to start probing the city above a bit more. I think it will give me a real insight into how the orc culture has evolved.' Nicolas hadn't realised Dieter had still been talking all this time.

Nicolas often likened the writer to a child with a net chasing butterflies, constantly on the move, full of wonder and curiosity. But it was good he wasn't coming. The explorer had joined them for the opportunity to learn first-hand of the group's exploits, explore the fabled *Orc Wastelands*, and not die doing so. In that, they'd all nearly failed a few times. And what they'd be doing now would be a lot more difficult and a lot more dangerous. Besides, he was happy here.

But who will chronicle my epic deeds without him?

Nicolas frowned. That thought sounded more like one of Auron's than his. But when he checked, the spirit was stood off to the side. He hadn't been cheekily possessed. Though he wasn't likely to miss that. The one and only time it *had* happened had been a terrible experience. Like someone shoving icicles down his throat and up his ass simultaneously.

But the fact that he wasn't possessed made the errant thought worse. That meant Auron was rubbing off on him. He didn't want anyone chronicling his deeds, and he especially didn't want an official account of him sneaking around to kill someone recorded for all of time.

'It's been a pleasure,' he said, holding out his hand to Dieter. 'I hope we meet again.'

'That's more than likely.' The explorer chuckled as they shook hands. 'I have a habit of getting around.'

Now it was Nicolas's turn to chuckle. 'As do I, it seems.'

Beside them, Salrag gripped Garaz firmly by the shoulders. The orcs then touched foreheads, closing their eyes. 'Good journey, my friend,' Salrag said with feeling.

'Be well,' Garaz replied.

Goodbyes were crap, save for the relieved ones when visiting a relative you didn't particularly care for. Here, though, they were crap. Nicolas and his companions assembled at the bottom of the grand stairway leading to the surface.

'Anyone else struggling to make their legs move?' Shift asked.

'Yes,' Silva answered flatly.

'We do need to go,' Nicolas said. 'Everyone's watching us. Besides, Tobias Helstrum isn't going to kill himself.'

'It would be handy if he did.' Garaz chuckled.

Handy, but unlikely. There was only one way that Tobias Helstrum was going to be taken care of. Forcing his legs to obey, Nicolas placed a foot on the first step. *Would* it be possible to just hire Alexi and Emelina to do it? No. It was too important to entrust to anyone else. Slowly, he walked up the stairs. Three sets of feet followed him. He assumed Auron was behind them.

A strange sound made him turn. The orcs were patting their chests rhythmically. It was a farewell for them. He cast a longing glance over the city, wondering if he'd ever see it again.

I hope so.

'Do you think a cold shiver just ran up Helstrum's spine, wherever he is?' Shift asked as they continued.

'It should,' Silva remarked. 'Because his days are coming to an end.'

'Another dark lord to add to the pile of legitimate threats and sad pretenders who've tried to take over Etherius over the years, only to die before their schemes bore fruit,' Auron scoffed.

His companions made it sound like this task was going to be an easy one, but Nicolas had an inkling that it could turn out to be very difficult indeed.

CHAPTER 14

E merging into the ruined city that had once been the seat of orc culture, Nicolas and his companions kept to the shadows. Moving slowly, they approached the hidden sentries.

'There is no sign of activity,' one orc told them. 'Nor from any of the others.'

Due to the attempt on Nicolas's life, watchers had been stationed throughout the city. He'd never known Helstrum's minions to travel alone, no matter what type of weapon they carried. Yet there'd been no sign of anyone else since. And Silva had tracked the man back to the gates of the dead city.

Beyond the city might be a different matter entirely, but they wouldn't know until they left. Still, erring on the side of caution, the group checked the adjoining roofs. They appeared empty.

Slipping out onto the streets, Nicolas and his companions stayed in single file on one side of the street, unless they had to move around debris – or at some points climb over it, which Nicolas's injured leg was none too fond of. Proceeding quietly through the ruined city, back towards the remnants of the mighty gate that would've once protected it from the outside world, Nicolas found himself mentally rebuilding the ruined homes and businesses they passed. If his imagination was even vaguely right, this place would've been majestic in its heyday.

'What do you think caused it?' he said in a whisper.

'Hmm?' Garaz replied, broken from whatever deep thought he'd been immersed in. The orc wasn't one for shallow thoughts. That was Auron's area of expertise.

'*The Regression*,' he continued. 'You have no idea at all what caused it?'

Garaz looked around at the city, as if finally noticing it. Nicolas couldn't blame him for blocking it out. 'History says it was preceded by a mighty storm, the likes of which has never been seen since. Emerald clouds lit the sky and forks of green lightning lashed the ground.' The orc's mouth curled in a snarl.

'What is it?'

'A suspicion,' Garaz growled. 'One I have had for many years, that has gained more credence since I began to wear this amulet.'

'That it was a spell?' Silva guessed.

'Yes. But the power and malice to do that to an entire species is unfathomable.' Yet the orc appeared to be fathoming it. His hand was clenched tightly around his staff.

But why would someone do something so terrible?

An accident, maybe?

'There is another theory, one I like even less.'

'Go on,' Shift said when the orc was reluctant to continue.

'At the time when the storm struck, Etherius was in the midst of an age of unbridled peace. We had built a civilisation based on reason and learning, and the elves ruled over a mighty empire, keeping order in the world. Humanity was a new race, just beginning to appear in numbers on the Western fringes. It has been suggested by some that nature needed to restore some sort of balance between order and chaos, and our race drew the short straw.' Garaz shook his head in annoyance. 'We do not take those who follow that train of thought seriously. It does not hold up to any sort of logic, especially when my people nearly exterminated the elves.'

'I can see why you aren't fond of that,' Shift scoffed. 'That's some absolute troll shit.'

'I'm more inclined towards the spell,' Auron chimed in. 'Wizards can be sadistic little bastards when they want to be.' The spirit rode nonchalantly on his spectral steed, Mare, looking ahead with a deadpan expression. No one bothered to try to speak; they all knew what was coming. Suddenly, Auron spun in his saddle. 'So, this one time, an entire town was suffering a rabid case of the pox. All the men were infected and going insane with the pus and the itching...but no one could explain where it'd come from, as it was a religious community and very *'thou shalt keep it in thy britches before thou art wed.'*

'You really think that'd stop anyone?' Shift said with a raised eyebrow.

'Wouldn't stop me.' The spirit shrugged. 'But I happened to be passing, stayed in the local inn overnight, and *bam*, next day, I have the pox. There was itching, and oozing and—'

'Get to the point,' Nicolas said quickly, worried his breakfast might reappear.

'Well, that was too much of a coincidence for me, especially as I'd been tired that night and *did* keep it in my breeches. And as it felt like I had a colony of fleas down there, I thought it worth investigating.' The spirit shifted uncomfortably in his saddle, as if haunted by the ghost of the itching. 'Turned out the local wizard, Ramas the Wise—*Ramas the Spiteful Asshole,* more like—had a marriage proposal turned down. So, he decided to make sure no one else could *have* the woman he loved...or any woman, for that matter. *If I shalt not lie with a woman, nor shalt any of you lucky bastards either.*'

'How did you catch him out?' Garaz asked, lips slightly curled in distaste.

'Simple,' Auron said grimly. 'I went to the local town meeting, and he was the only man there not scratching his groin.'

'Some of your stories are disgusting,' Nicolas said, wrinkling his nose.

'Important, though,' the spirit replied, wagging his finger knowingly.

'And what was the moral of this story, o' mighty teller of tales,' Shift asked with faux reverence.

Auron looked at Shift, pursing his lips for a moment. 'Always keep your eyes open for something out of place.'

Shift opened their mouth, but after a second, they closed it again. 'That is actually a decent lesson, I suppose,' they admitted grudgingly after a few moments.

'I know.' Auron grinned with his normal level of modesty.

'I'll keep that in mind,' he said, nervously scanning the roofs of the buildings around him. 'It'd have been nice to hear that one *before* I was attacked, though.'

'I don't know about you, kid, but I'd be massively insulted if they sent just one guy to kill me.'

'If that's how they insult me, I'm quite happy to continue being insulted.' Nicolas chuckled. 'One at a time is plenty.'

'Still, only one? Does he not know what a big deal you are?' Shift asked, mirth creasing the corners of their mouth. 'Especially after you've already tried to kill him once.'

'That *wasn't* me!' Nicolas caught his rising voice and glanced around nervously before dropping it to a harsh whisper. 'How many times do I have to repeat that?'

'Shame you just didn't let him die,' Silva said. 'It would have saved many people a lot of bother.'

That's a good point. Still, if I ever meet that damned archer again...

But he doubted he would. It was a big, wide, terrifying world, and all he had to go on was a glimpse of a bushy beard. Walk into the average tavern and you can probably see five guys with a beard, at least two of whom would be hunters or adventurers and carry bows.

'Do you think Golthorak will be... He won't send more people here, will he?' Nicolas asked, suddenly worried about Salrag and the others.

'I don't think so,' Auron mused. 'It will take him time to realise his assassin has failed. Once he does I doubt he'll think we'd just sit here and wait for the next one. He'll know we'll be on the move. Sending more people here would be a waste of time.'

Good. The last thing Nicolas wanted was more people coming to the city looking for him. Though he knew the orcs would keep careful watch for a long time to come.

'So now begins the real hunt.' Garaz sighed as he stepped over some rubble. 'He does not know where we are, and we do not know where he is.'

'It does not matter what corner of Etherius he hides in, we will find him,' Silva said with a determination that made Nicolas feel almost sorry for Helstrum.

'That's the spirit.' Auron grinned before unsheathing his sword and gesturing forwards. 'Onward, friends. We have a man to kill.'

'A man whose weakness is overconfidence.' He could tell from Shift's tone that a joke at his expense was coming. 'Because who in their right mind sends one man to kill the new *Dawnblade*?'

Nicolas had seen Helstrum in person. He already knew the man was not in his right mind at all.

CHAPTER 15

N icolas's mouth kept opening and closing, but no words were coming out. Keeping his eyes on the scene ahead, he turned slightly to his companions. When he risked a glance at them, they were all equally confused and shocked. Nice not to be the only one with a slack jaw for a change.

'He sent a lot more than one guy,' Auron said after a long whistle.

The group had been warned of trouble before they reached the overlook they now stood on. By the smell. Nicolas hated that he knew the smell of decay by now, but it was definitely that, in large quantities. Yet it hadn't prepared him for this.

'Damn,' Shift remarked, shaking their head as they stared wide-eyed ahead of them.

What should've been a long stretch of uninteresting wasteland was instead a horrific scene of carnage and death. Bodies lay strewn across it, pecked at or gnawed on by the numerous scavenging creatures that slunk between them.

No. Do not focus on any of that.

'Helstrum sent a whole army after us,' Silva remarked slowly. 'That makes more sense.'

Even from here, they could make out the unmistakable masks of the enemy. The blood stains decorating the ground were faded, suggesting this battle had taken place a while ago. Nicolas knew exactly when it'd happened. Not long before a killer shot him in the leg.

'A lot of good it did,' Shift scoffed with raised eyebrows.

Nicolas wasn't good at guessing numbers at a glance, but there had to be at least two hundred of Helstrum's men lying dead on the hard, cracked ground. On either side of them was a similar number of dead orcs.

'It looks like they formed ranks with those fire-sticks, which took a toll on the orcs,' Auron noted, pointing to the trail of bodies leading to the main scene of death and destruction. 'But once the orcs got amongst them, it went very badly for Helstrum's men.'

'My people are not so easily deterred when there is the promise of a good fight.' Garaz sighed. 'The ones who live above ground, anyway.'

'But the orcs didn't get them all,' Nicolas said, paling. 'One survived. One man survived this slaughter, and instead of running home, he continued. He kept walking until he found the city. Then he tracked me down and tried to kill me.'

The sheer will displayed by Helstrum's followers was unnerving, as was the parallel. They intended to continue until this was done, just as the masked killer had.

'It is unsurprising that a man with such rhetoric as Helstrum attracts fanatics.' Garaz sniffed. 'Which makes our quest all the more daunting.'

Quest. He makes it sound like we're popping into a dungeon to find treasure, not tracking a man down to end his life.

Again, the idea of hiring someone to do it popped into his head. With an annoyed frown, he chased it away. He hadn't palmed off his job to deliver a message; he wasn't palming this off either. It was just nice to dream occasionally.

'We'd best go and see if there's any intelligence we can gather from the dead,' Silva declared, already beginning to walk towards the scene of carnage.

'Great,' Nicolas muttered as he followed.

As the group approached the battle scene and details manifested themselves, everything became worse. An orc lay on his back, eyes rolled upwards toward the hole in the centre of his forehead. A human warrior had become several pieces of a human warrior. The flies were already about their work, the incessant droning of their massed wings making it hard to think. Some of the scavenging creatures were pretty fat by now. Other than Auron, everyone had to wrap cloth around their faces to try to mute the terrible stench.

'So, they all just killed each other then?' Shift said from behind the rag they were using to cover their nose. 'Deities, this place stinks. You know what...' Their brow furrowed in concentration, and as they removed their rag, their nose disappeared and they began to breathe through their mouth. 'That's a little better.' They sighed, before cocking an eyebrow at Nicolas. 'How do I look?'

'Different,' was all he could manage. Their lack of nose was bloody odd.

'Judging by that look on your face, that's the polite answer.' Shift shook their head. 'You know what, it's worth it to save myself from that terrible stench.'

'Isn't it uncomfortable?' Silva asked as she dug through the pockets of the dead human who looked to be the leader of the army. The cape and gold mask were dead giveaways. The warrior took out a piece of parchment, read it, then discarded it.

Shift shrugged. 'A little. It's more effort to change a single part of my form than my whole form. It's like being pulled in two different directions and requires more concentration. But still, better than gagging on death stench.'

Yeah, I think not having a nose right now might be nice.

'There are no survivors, as far as I can tell,' Garaz said, as he examined a few of the bodies.

Nor were there likely to be. Many of the bodies were already decaying. Anyone too wounded to leave likely never would. Luckily, there wasn't a necromancer around. This would make a handy instant army.

'Here.' It seemed Silva had found something worth reading. The warrior unfurled a letter. '*General Karass. I write to you today on a matter of grave importance. Though I knew misguided souls amongst our own people would try to push back against our crusade to secure a future for our race, I never realised the lengths some of these fools would go to. There are those humans—if they deserve the title anymore—who have taken up arms against us. The most prolific of these is a vile young man named Nicolas Percival Carnegie. He sometimes goes by the moniker Nick Carnage...*'

'I bloody well do not,' Nicolas protested.

'*...or the Dawnblade.*' Silva continued to read. '*This insidious young man has gathered a cadre of followers to enact his ambition to thwart our noble efforts. He even goes as far as to consort with orcs and shapeshifting creatures. We know the location of this young reprobate. As you are a man of utter conviction as to the righteousness of our cause, I charge you with eliminating this disturbing threat once winter eases enough to allow you and your men passage. I enclose a map to the location of this scum, that you may wipe them from Etherius. As you can see, it is in the orc wasteland. I understand the severity of the task and the difficulties in executing it. But I will supply you and your men with the finest weapons to aid this effort. For be warned, though he looks meek, this rebellious cur is a dangerous foe. Just recently, he attempted to kill me in the most cowardly way imaginable, to silence the voice of righteousness that cries into the dark of this world. And may I ask one more favour of you? The shapeshifter that travels with them. It needs to be captured and brought back alive. This is important to our cause, though the reason must remain secret for now. I wholeheartedly trust you with this endeavour and wish you all speed in killing such a despicable race traitor. Yours sincerely, Tobias Helstrum.*'

'*It?*' Shift repeated the word with disgust. 'Bloody charming.'

'You just got *it*,' Nicolas said, shaking his head. 'I got *vile young man, insidious man, rebellious cur* and *despicable race traitor*.'

'I don't believe Tobias Helstrum likes you very much, kid.' Auron smirked.

'The feeling's mutual.' He glanced back at the letter. 'But why do they suddenly want Shift so badly?'

During their encounters with the Visitor, they'd learned that the Maestro wanted to capture Shift. They had yet to learn why.

'Who cares?' Silva said, tearing the letter in two. 'They can't have Shift. And any who try shall die in the attempt.'

'If I wasn't with Nicolas already, such talk would make me go weak at the knees,' Shift said, faux biting their lip. 'But I would like to know what these assholes want with me.'

'Well, once we've beaten the location of my people out of Helstrum, we'll give him a few extra kicks to tell us,' Nicolas said with a firm nod.

'Deal,' the shapeshifter said, pointing at him and winking.

Picking his way across the battleground, Nicolas avoided pools of dried blood, spilled innards that had been seasoned by the weather, and various weapons and supplies from the troop sent to kill him. 'Do you think there's anything here we can use?' he asked thoughtfully.

'If you're willing to clean the gore off it,' Shift replied, taking some coin from a dead man's pouch and pocketing it.

'I think we might have some competition for the looting rights,' Auron said with a tone that instantly caused the phrase *uh-oh* to pass through Nicolas's mind.

CHAPTER 16

With a heavy sigh, Nicolas looked at the spirit then turned in the direction Auron was looking. Sure enough, a group of orcs mounted on giant furred beasts were watching them from beside a scattering of dead trees. They could've been survivors of the battle, coming back around to loot the dead. Or another clan who'd happened by. Either way, these weren't the toga-wearing, civilised, orcs he'd spent time living with. So, battle was imminent.

Nicolas was suddenly very aware that neither he, nor his companions, were mounted.

Maybe they'll be sporting and dismount to fight us?

Nope, that was about as unlikely as a giant's foot suddenly appearing and treading on them all.

'What do we do?' he asked, slowly drawing his sword and backing towards his companions.

'Kill them all, or die,' Silva said, readying herself.

'Not exactly the thorough and tactical strategy I was hoping for,' he grumbled.

'Let them come to you,' Auron said. 'You'll only wear yourselves out by running. Maybe one or two of those creatures will get distracted by the all-you-can-eat intestine buffet on the floor here.'

'Maybe some of these are still loaded?' Shift said, picking up one of the fire-sticks.

After jabbing his sword into the ground, Nicolas tried to check the ones lying around him. But he wasn't sure how to do it. Looking down the barrel yielded no results, nor did poking them. Finally, he shook one. Though he only did that to try to get the dismembered hand off it. When he did, there seemed to be a slight rattle, which he assumed was a good thing.

And it was definitely good timing, as the leader of the orc party raised his weapon in the air and roared ferally. This verbose and well-thought-out invite to his kin to join him in the slaughter of some innocent passers-by was met with multiple hoots of delight as the orcs charged.

Shit.

Thinking back, Nicolas tried to remember how the killer had held the fire-stick. After a few variations, he tucked the stock into his shoulder and looked down the metal sight, just as the man had. Beside him, Silva and Shift were doing the same. Garaz had a fireball ready to fling.

'Wait for it,' Auron counselled.

The war party had yet to reach the edge of the bodies from the previous battle, which probably marked the range of these new weapons.

'Wait for it.'

Orc raiders bounced up and down on their mounts, waving their weapons in the air with snarling glee.

'Now.'

His tongue poking out slightly, Nicolas lined the sight up with one of the oncoming orcs, making sure to pick a big one so he was less likely to miss. Breathing out, he squeezed the trigger. There was a click, and the weapon fired. With a flash, the barrel unleashed smoke with a mighty roar. The stock of the weapon drove back into his shoulder with sudden and jarring force. The violent strike threw him backwards, and he dropped the weapon as he flapped his arms in an attempt to do who knew what. But he was already overbalanced, and he toppled, directly into a dead body's open gut wound. He heaved as something wet and fleshy slimed the back of his neck before he began scrabbling to get up.

And I've bitten my tongue.

Getting to his feet, he furiously brushed his hair to get whatever he could feel in it out and to encourage the flies now buzzing around his head to piss off. Quickly, he lunged for his sword, pausing when he saw that the big orc he'd aimed for was still riding towards him. Two more of the small band lay dead on the floor, and another one was being dragged in the wake of his shrieking mount, whose fur was aflame.

Their bloodlust fully awakened now—as if it hadn't been already—the war party spurred their beasts to go faster. Judging by the snarling grin he was getting, the big one realised Nicolas had tried to shoot him and was intent on making him pay for it.

Lifting his sword, he flexed his now-aching shoulder. It would have to be ignored. Just like his leg. Then he noticed something odd. The big orc, as well as several others, were carrying fire-sticks. Appearing unable to discern how to load and fire them, the orcs had defaulted to using them as fancy clubs.

Is it better to be shot by one or beaten to death by one?

That's a stupid choice. I'd rather live.

'Split them up just before they reach us,' Auron told Garaz. 'Take the thunder out of their charge.'

'Very well,' the orc said, brandishing his staff and gathering his magic. The whooping and hollering feral faces grew closer.

'Now?' Silva asked as the pack came closer.

'Nearly,' Garaz muttered, energy building around him.

Nicolas could see the drool on the wolf creatures' fangs, in anticipation of the meal to come. 'Now.'

'A few more seconds,' the orc growled, sweat beading on his forehead.

Nicolas could pick out the rust on the leader's battle axe. *'Now. Now. Now. Now. Now.'*

With a grunt of effort, Garaz swung his staff down. It struck the ground, and a wall of flame shot from it, bisecting the attacking marauders and forcing them to split into two groups, suddenly breaking formation to get away from the fire.

At least we won't get mown down now.

As the smoke cleared, Nicolas laughed. The big orc was sat atop his mount, which had stopped to munch on the guts of a dead soldier. Growling with rage, the orc yanked on his beast's reins, trying to get it to move, but it was intent on its meal.

Lunging forwards, Nicolas made the orc pay for his lack of attention to the battle, sliding the *Dawn Blade* between the seams where two pieces of patched-together armour met. The orc squealed in shock and pain then again as Nicolas withdrew his sword—whose reflective blade was now stained with blood—before it fell to the ground dead.

Several of the orcs had also been thrown by their beasts when the sudden blast of flame appeared, and one wolf creature was dead, the smell of burning fur overpowering the stink of death. Already the riders were getting to their feet, snarling furiously.

'Nicolas,' Silva shouted. 'You take the ones on foot, and we'll handle the mounted ones.'

Here we go.

Nicolas parried a rusty cleaver meant to cut him in two, before drawing his sword across the torso of its wielder. A club swung at him, but he ducked it, driving the tip of the *Dawn Blade* into his attacker's gut. Grabbed by a third orc and hauled from the ground, he stabbed the warrior directly in the throat before his axe could be brought to bear. Hitting the ground as he was dropped, Nicolas rolled to prevent the blade coming towards him from reaching its target, pushing up quickly when the roll was complete and cutting his attacker across the stomach twice.

Beside him, he caught a glance of Shift, ducking and weaving the attacks of a giant mounted orc, stabbing with their knives wherever a target presented itself. The wolf snapped at them, and Shift allowed themselves to fall back to the ground, driving the knives into either side of the creature's neck. As the wolf fell dead, it landed on its rider's leg, trapping the orc so Shift could finish him quickly.

Silva had removed an orc's leg, but surprisingly, the warrior still had some fight left in him, hopping forwards and swinging his weapon wildly. It wasn't a long fight.

An orc ran past him, aflame, so Garaz was giving a good account of himself too. He caught a glimpse of the orc using his staff as a club to crack the skull of a rider as he passed.

Fortunately, with so many dead bodies around them, there were plenty of knives to throw, so Auron was having a merry old time. His aim was immaculate.

I need to practise with throwing knives more.

After deflecting another blade, and dispatching the orc holding it, Nicolas's vision tunnelled as he saw the bow being drawn back, its lethal projectile being pointed at him. The archer's mouth curled in killer satisfaction then widened in disbelief as an axe embedded in its head. The arrow hit the floor a second before its owner.

'You're getting good at that,' Nicolas shouted.

'If I can only do one thing, I'd best do it well,' Auron called back, hands on his knees and aura visibly weaker. Throwing something that large must've taken it out of him.

Shame these aren't demons then he could actually fight...

Why am I wishing for demons?

A hand grabbed the back of his neck, and he cursed his lack of awareness. But as fortune would have it, his neck was still caked in blood from the dead soldier he'd fallen on, so he slipped out of the grip easily, turning and gutting his attacker.

A thick green shoulder struck Nicolas in the side and sent him sprawling to the floor. Over him loomed a large orc with a scarred face and skulls hanging from chains on his rusty spiked armour. A totem on his back denoted him the leader of the tribe, something Nicolas had learned listening to the Golthorak orcs educating Dieter. What were they called? *Bosses?*

Boss fight then.

From his lying position, Nicolas pushed his torso off the ground, slicing the *Dawn Blade* across both the orc's shins. The beast roared as it stumbled backwards yet somehow remained standing. Nicolas threw himself forwards, driving his sword deep into his attacker's gut...where it stayed. The orc stepped back, and the hilt of the *Dawn Blade* was prised from his grip, the sword stuck deep in the orc boss's stomach with no apparent effect save enraging the beast.

Taking advantage of his moment of confusion, the orc lashed out at speed, grabbing him by the throat and hauling him in close. 'Got yer sword, humie,' he growled, his voice filled with smugness and bloodlust, his breath just nasty.

'It's not my only weapon,' Nicolas managed between choking noises. In a fluid motion, he raised his foot, slid the knife from his boot, and put it right in the orc's eye. The Boss dropped him as it reared back, clutching its ruined eye. Using a foot to brace himself, Nicolas yanked his sword from the orc's stomach and slashed its throat. Finally, the orc fell to the ground, giant clawed hand attempting to stop the blood pouring from its neck. Nicolas finished it quickly, stabbing it straight in the heart. With a choked cry, the orc boss finally died, the last of his warriors already awaiting him in the afterlife thanks to his companions.

He tried not to notice the souls of the orcs vanish as he stretched. Taking one last look to ensure all the enemies were dead and staying that way, he found some cloth to clean his sword on and returned it to its sheath. Not so long ago, he'd have been doubled over trying to catch his breath. But not now.

'You know that leaving your sword in an enemy's gut also counts as dropping it, right, kid?' Auron sighed as he approached.

Nicolas didn't dignify that with a response, retrieving his knife from the orc boss's eye without looking directly at it. As he pulled it out, he saw Garaz staring and scowling into the distance. 'Are you okay?'

Garaz turned and furrowed his brow before realising the implication of his question. 'I am well, thank you. The amulet still does its work against my violent nature. Despite...*this*.'

That wasn't all Nicolas had meant by the question. He was also concerned about the toll killing his own people might take on the orc, mentally. Then the sobering thought hit him that he'd killed more than a few of his own kind himself...and there was at least one more to go.

CHAPTER 17

N eeding a breather but not wanting to take one somewhere the air was so foul, the group trekked across to the dead trees the orc war party had watched them from. There were a couple of rocks that made serviceable, but not comfortable, chairs. Resting his legs, Nicolas looked out over the pile of the dead, which they'd just added to.

'Nothing like fighting some orcs to get your blood pumping,' Auron declared jovially, hands on hips.

'And you know what exactly about pumping blood?' Shift asked as they inspected one of their knives, before returning it to the custom sheath they'd had made for it.

'Ha bloody ha,' the spirit replied. 'You know I meant metaphorically, smartass.'

Whilst they talked, Garaz got to his knees, closing his eyes and bowing slightly. His lips moved as he brought his hands to a prayer position. Nicolas assumed he was wishing the souls of his errant kin a safe passage to whatever afterlife orcs believed in. They deserved it. It wasn't their fault they'd been made into animals. Not only were their lives lost, but all the potential they'd had, if the curse had never touched them.

'At least it is good practise for what's to come,' Silva remarked, keeping her eyes peeled for more war parties.

Practise? Nicolas looked around at the carnage they'd just walked away from. If this was the warm up, what in the Underworld was to come?

'Still, kid, you handled yourself well.' Auron nodded. 'I know you don't like the end result, all the bodies and whatnot, but you stood your ground. I've seen knights with piss trickling down their armour at the sight of an orc war-pack charging them.'

That's something, I suppose.

For a moment, his gaze flicked down, just to check he *hadn't* pissed himself and somehow not noticed. Nope. His breeches were nice and dry.

Maybe he was just so used to orcs now after living amongst them that even the feral ones weren't such a big deal? Either way, the idea that he'd done better than a seasoned knight was actually quite the confidence boost.

'I suggest we do not dally here for long,' Garaz said, rising. 'I doubt this will be the only group coming here. You heard those weapons fire. They will have been heard for miles around. And anything that sounds like a battle is sure to attract more of my feral brethren.'

That was an excellent motivator to get up and get going.

Fortunately, those were the only orcs they saw close-up over the next few days of travel. It could've been a shorter journey, but the group took big diversions whenever they sighted settlements on the horizon, or orc patrols. Their path wasn't even close to a straight line. In fact, if Nicolas had cared to try to trace it on a map he'd likely have gone cross-eyed.

But soon the harsh ground of the wasteland gave way to defiant tufts of greenery. The air was still cold, but not the-heart-of-winter cold. Their feet sloshing in slush from melted snow was a welcome sound, marking their return to civilisation. Mounds of snow still decorated parts of the ground, but winter no longer had a firm grip on the lands of humanity.

The group passed into the kingdom of Ivilar, the largest of the Nine Kingdoms of Man and considered chief amongst equals. It was the only one of the human kingdoms to keep its original elven name—a tribute to acknowledge the gift humanity was given by the elves and the trust placed in them to lead the new world, as its former rulers left for parts unknown. Garaz and Dieter had spent many a night in furious conjecture as to where the elves—those not butchered by the Great Orc Horde, anyway—had gone. Nothing came of it save boring the rest of the room.

'Oh no,' Shift said dryly as they pointed ahead of them in mock horror. 'How shalt we stalwart adventurers circumvent this mighty fortification? It seems our journey may be finished before it hath even begun.'

His companion's oh-so-subtle sarcasm was directed at the fortified fence that ran the length of the border, with spiked sticks planted in the ground before it. Apparently, a wall was too costly to build so it was decided to build *this* to act as a deterrent.

In all the years since this thing was built, I'd bet a pouch of gold that the sum total of those it has deterred is zero.

It certainly wouldn't dissuade the orcs it was trying to keep out. How many orcs had urinated on it over the years, whilst their brethren watched and laughed?

A lot more than zero.

'I'll manage because I can walk through it.' Auron chuckled. 'But you sorry lot may have to construct a siege tower.'

'I can practically step over it.' Silva sneered. 'I could certainly kick it down.'

Nicolas looked at a piece of the fence listing forwards. 'It looks like nature's already taking care of that.'

'I imagine my people only leave it standing at all because it amuses them,' Garaz remarked, shaking his head.

When they reached the fence, the group slid between the sharpened logs in front of it before clambering over. Nicolas drew the short straw for giving everyone a leg up. Shift made a meal of it, purposely taking their time as they revelled in his discomfort.

Silva was next. He hoisted her up, his gaze following her as she rose and grabbed the top of the fence, pulling herself up. As she did, he realised that he was looking, very accidentally, directly up her skirt. Quickly, he averted his eyes.

Thank the Deities she didn't notice.

Garaz was the toughest one, but Nicolas tried not to let it show. His breathing became heavy as he heaved, concerned his wrists might give out. But soon enough, and with great relief, the weight was taken from him and the orc pulled himself over the fence.

'Give me your hands,' Silva said as she appeared over the fence, reaching for him.

Taking the offered hands, he walked up the wall to Silva, only to find himself suddenly being dangled mid-air. 'Do not look up my skirt again,' the warrior snarled.

'I di— It was an accident,' he stammered. It felt like his soul was dropping right out of his body through his feet.

'I know,' the warrior replied. 'That is why I haven't just let you drop.'

'Sorry,' he said sheepishly as the warrior hoisted him over and he made the short drop to the other side.

'What was that?' Shift asked, looking at him askew.

'What?' He really hoped they hadn't noticed the thing with Silva. It was a complete accident but...

'Did you just sigh?' Shift asked him.

'What?'

'Just then.' His companion pointed behind them. 'When we crossed the border. You actually sighed in relief.'

'No.' Nicolas hoped his uncertainty didn't show. In all honesty, he wasn't sure.

'He did,' Silva interjected helpfully.

'I breathed out as I landed,' he protested. 'That's what you're supposed to do.'

'From an actual drop.' Auron smirked. 'Not...*that*.' The spirit pointed dismissively at the fence.

'You can't lecture me about falling from a height when you walked through the bloody thing.'

'So, the question is,' Shift asked thoughtfully, 'did you sigh in relief because we're away from the orcs now, or because you weren't sure you were going to survive that mighty drop?'

'First of all, I didn't bloody—'

'*Halt. Stay where you are.*'

CHAPTER 18

W here the group of soldiers had appeared from would forever be a mystery to him, but there they were, plain as day. Twelve men armed with halberds in a semi-circle surrounding them. The men all wore the polished silver plate and red crested helms of Ivilar, the sides of which were fashioned like wings. The fancy armour was just another marker of how prosperous the largest of the Nine Kingdoms of Man was. It also should've made them pretty noticeable when they approached. At least all his companions looked as surprised as he was.

Nicolas and the others huddled together at the epicentre of the pointing spear tips. He made sure to keep his hands up where they could be seen, and well away from his sword. The pose was a signal for Silva to do the same, as she was the most likely to start any trouble. And they definitely didn't want that.

'Identify yourselves and state your business,' demanded the thickly bearded captain, who'd secured his red cape behind him to allow easy access to his sword should he need it.

Knowing he was the most personable one of the group, Nicolas allowed himself a slight step forward, making no sudden movements. 'We mean no—'

'Did you come from the wasteland?' the captain shouted.

You should let me answer the first question before asking more, but okay.

Nicolas looked back at the fence. It was a stupid question. The soldiers must've seen them climbing over it. 'Yes.'

'Orc spies then, is it?'

'Whoa, whoa, whoa. No orc spies here, friend,' Nicolas stammered quickly.

'I am not your *friend*,' the captain snapped back sternly. 'I am a captain of the Border Guard of Ivilar. You will address me as *sir*, understood?'

This is not going well. 'Yes...sir.'

'So then,' the captain continued. 'If you are not orc spies, do you care to explain *that*?'

Nicolas bit his lip to prevent him from saying anything rash, knowing without looking that the captain was gesturing to Garaz. But he had a very pleasant mental image of smacking the officious prick right in the nose for the inflection he'd used on the word *'that.'*

'I can assure you, sir, that he is no spy either,' he replied patiently. 'I know this looks bad, but—'

'Do you know who would say something exactly like that?' Inwardly, Nicolas sighed. He could see where this sentence was going. 'An orc spy.'

'Do you see humans travelling with orcs often?' Shift's smile matched their sarcastic tone.

'What I've never seen before are humans coming out of the wasteland.' The captain's glare suggested he held sarcasm in little regard.

Best not let Shift talk too much then.

'Because humans don't survive out there. Unless the orcs allow it. And why might that be?' There was a perfectly patronizing pause. 'Because they are orc spies.'

'We aren't spies,' he said firmly.

The captain looked him up and down with complete distrust. 'Then, pray tell, why are you coming from the orc territories, with an orc in tow?'

'We've been living with...' Nicolas caught himself before he said something that was sure to be taken as incriminating.

'With the orcs,' the captain finished for him. 'And that is how they turned you to spies, to be let loose upon your own kind.'

'Have you ever known orcs to use spies?' Silva asked incredulously.

'No,' the captain admitted. 'But mayhap the spies are normally better than you are at not getting caught.'

'You know this is going nowhere, right, kid?'

Auron was wrong. It was going somewhere; it was headed directly toward them being locked up, and he wasn't sure he had time for that. He had to take control of this.

'I think we've got off on the wrong foot here,' he said calmly.

'Any feet spies plant on our land are the wrong feet,' the captain declared.

'I bet that sounded better in his head,' Shift said exactly loudly enough for the captain to hear.

The man scowled. 'Spies or not, you will surrender your weapons and be taken to the nearest fort for interrogation.'

The situation was getting worse by the second. The captain had clearly already made his mind up. The only thing Nicolas could think of to get out of it was a daft, and potentially brilliant, idea.

I really don't want to say what I'm about to say.

Closing his eyes, he prepared himself. 'Look, I don't know if you know who you're talking to here.'

The captain's eyebrows leapt up his forehead incredulously. 'I *beg* your pardon?'

'And I will give it to you.' Nicolas nodded. 'Because I am Nicolas Percival Carnegie, the new *Dawnblade*. Apprentice of the original *Dawnblade*, the legendary Auron of Tellmark. I am the slayer of Avus Arex, saviour of Sarus, peacekeeper of Merida, lawman of Babylon. I'm not saying that to brag. I just want to be sure you know exactly who you're dealing with here and to prove beyond a shadow of a doubt that we aren't spies.' He winced as he realised what he needed to add. 'Some around these parts know me as *Nick Carnage*.'

The feeling of eyes on the back of his head churned up some awkwardness in his gut. Turning slightly, he looked at his shocked companions.

'Have you been rehearsing that?' Shift asked, mouth agape.

He hadn't, but it sounded too smooth for his denials to be believed. Auron was beaming at him in pride whilst both Silva and Garaz were shaking their heads slowly. Wishing to try to pretend the awkwardness in his gut wasn't there, he turned back to the captain and looked at him expectantly.

The man's eyes narrowed, revealing some crow's feet that normally remained hidden. 'Never bloody heard of you,' the soldier scoffed. 'Auron of Tellmark, I know. But you can't just carve a rising sun on your armour, go around calling yourself the *Dawnblade,* and expect people to swallow it.'

What?... I... What? 'You've never heard of me?'

'Stings, doesn't it, kid?'

Nicolas glared at Auron. This really wasn't the time to be reminded of his own past mistakes, which apparently the spirit was still irked over.

Of all the random folk I've met who know me, and the one bloody time I need someone to know who I am and... Bugger it.

'No, I haven't,' the captain replied dryly. 'And in all honesty, you trying to pass yourself off as the squire of a deceased hero is in extremely poor taste...spy. As I said, you and your questionable companions are going to come with us, and we can discern whether you are really spies in a less informal setting.'

Considering you just called me 'spy' I don't fancy my chances.

'You will of course note that I did not use the word *please*. That is because this isn't a request, and failure to comply will be met with deadly force.'

Nicolas held up his finger. 'One moment, please.' Gesturing to his companions, he had them huddle in close to him as the captain glared at him. 'What do we do?'

'Fight them.' Silva shrugged.

'I do not think assaulting the border guards will help our protests that we are not orc spies,' Garaz said.

The warrior's brow furrowed thoughtfully. 'Oh, so you'd prefer to be locked up then?'

'Do not be facetious.'

'I am being practical.'

'We aren't fighting border guards,' Nicolas told Silva. 'If we do, we'll be hunted down and arrested, which won't help us get to Helstrum. We need another way out of this.'

'Just let them arrest you,' Auron suggested.

Shift looked both shocked *and* offended. 'That goes completely against my nature as a thief.'

'It's simple.' The spirit shook his head as if they should all just understand what he meant. 'You let them lock you up, and I break you out at night.'

Shift pursed their lips thoughtfully. 'Okay, that is more my style.'

'And we'll still be hunted down,' Nicolas said, shaking his head. 'We don't have time for this. Every hour we're delayed in reaching Helstrum is an hour he can spend doing whatever evil crap he does. We may actually need to subdue—'

A soft thump on the grass made them all look down. In the centre of the group was a strange glass globe with a dancing light inside it. It reminded Nicolas of the globes they'd used in Yarringsburg to unleash a gas cloud to confuse the vampires guarding the castle. His eyes widened as the light got brighter, and he heard a whistling sound.

'Oh no...'

There was a flash as bright as the sun, and then darkness.

CHAPTER 19

Instead of rocking him further to sleep, whatever was rocking him served to bring him around slowly. The darkness behind his eyes swelled and contracted repeatedly, as blobs of light danced around. He knew the headache that would welcome him when he opened his eyes would be a mighty one.

Is it a sign of brain damage? How many times can I get knocked out before something up there breaks?

He needed to check. Which meant going through his usual mantra. Nicolas knew it was a silly one. Because if his brain was broken, then the facts he was about to recite would be wrong and he wouldn't know it anyway.

My name is Nicolas Percival Carnegie. My mother's name is...was...Elsbeth Vivian Carnegie and my father's name was Ronald Albert Carnegie. I'm twenty-one, originally from the village of Hablock, and I hate the way my life has gone with a passion...except meeting Shift. Shift is amazing. Yes, that all seems in order. Now to find out what that clammy thing is sticking to my cheek.

There was a sudden jolt. Someone nearby groaned. The voice was familiar. Silva maybe? It finally dawned on Nicolas that they were in a wagon. The rhythmic creaking, the rocking. Definitely a wagon. And since he could remember clearly what had happened before he'd been rendered unconscious, it meant he was once again riding in the back of a prison wagon. Huffing, he finally opened his eyes. It took a few blinks for reality to become clear. And when it did, it was confusing.

Why is everything green?

Not entirely green. There was orange...straw? His nose twitched at the odd odour. Luckily, his brain wasn't damaged, so he managed to quickly figure out what he was looking at. Nicolas retched as he got as much distance away from Garaz's armpit as he could, as fast as he could. It wasn't an easy task. For some reason, his cheek was stuck to the orc's skin. The pulling motion as they parted made him gag again—and caused the orc to stir.

I bet his head feels as bad as mine.

In Nicolas's, there were currently several minotaurs dancing to a jaunty tune. Reaching up, he grabbed one of the bars on the window of the wagon and hauled himself to his feet. His legs did not want to take his weight.

'Hey, kid,' Auron said with sympathy as he rode alongside the wagon on Mare. 'You've been arrested. And they were none too careful about how they threw you in there.'

Glancing back, he saw the others in a heap on the wagon floor. But they were all moving. Shift was clearly cursing under their breath. Nicolas almost jumped with fright as Silva's eyes shot open like some sort of vampire who'd just awoken with a mighty thirst.

Leaning against the window of the wagon, Nicolas took a moment to get a few breaths of air that weren't infested by the smell of sweaty orc pits. Alongside the wagon marched the soldiers, three on each side. The captain rode ahead of them. Nicolas glared at the fluttering cape and imagined how bloody pleased with himself the captain must be.

'*Owwwww.*' Shift groaned as they sat up, tentatively opening a single eye. 'This is all Garaz's fault, you know.'

'And you have come to this conclusion how?' If it wasn't for him speaking, the orc would've appeared sound asleep. Though the lack of snoring that sounded like an oncoming avalanche was a dead giveaway too.

'Simple. We wouldn't be accused of being orc spies if we didn't have an orc with us.'

'I humbly apologise for joining the quest you vehemently invited me on,' the orc scoffed sourly.

Shift managed a pained smile. 'Accepted.'

'By the Deities, you all talk constantly,' Silva grumbled. She pulled one of her arms out from under Shift's butt, but it hung limply at her side. Silva looked at it in annoyance, as if willing it to move by sheer force of glare. It did not comply. With a sneer, she brought her other palm up and put her hand to her head.

Nicolas had to agree with Silva: the amount of talking taking place was excessive whilst they all tried to recover from whatever that globe thing had done. Yet there were things that did actually need to be discussed.

'So, what's the plan then?'

'Well,' Auron began thoughtfully, arms behind his head. 'When we reach wherever we're going, they're going to put you in cells. Most likely split you up into different ones. At nightfall, we break out, which will be facilitated by either me or Shift. We create a distraction and slip away in the confusion. Classic and simple.'

'I think we just need to wait for a magistrate to talk to and straighten this out,' Nicolas told the others. 'If not, we could be wanted. It won't help our task if we have to dodge every patrol we come across between here and...him.'

'If you're happy to wait two weeks, fine, kid.' Auron shrugged as Nicolas held his head and groaned. 'They'll have to summon him. He'll have to travel to wherever they're taking you. There will be an interrogation. That'll need to be thorough. They don't want to mess around with potential spies. Then he has—'

'Fine, I get it. The first plan it is then.' Nicolas huffed. 'What about any guards we come across?'

Auron shrugged. 'Silva roughs them up.'

'Gladly.' The warrior snorted.

'And leaves them alive,' Nicolas added hastily.

Silva was clearly unimpressed he felt that'd needed saying.

'Sounds like a solid plan.' Nicolas frowned. There'd been a time when being thrown in a cell would've caused him all sorts of worry, concern, and pants-wetting terror. Not anymore. Getting imprisoned and getting out was becoming par for the course. Right now, this was merely an inconvenience.

Though given the choice, I'd rather not be locked up at all.

'Guards won't be a problem,' Shift said casually. 'If we can find some armour, I'll just change into one. If anyone asks where I'm taking you, I'll say, *'I be takin' these miscreants to the cap'n for interrogation.'*

'Nice guard voice.' Nicolas grinned.

'Quiet in there.' The command was accompanied by banging on the side of the wagon.

The group fell silent—not because of the guard's command but because suddenly the clopping of hooves on a dirt road switched to the clopping of hooves on stone. The shadow of a stone arch passed overhead. Through the window, Nicolas watched as they passed into a courtyard. Soldiers who were milling around or doing drills stopped to watch them curiously.

There are a lot of guards.

Pressing his face to the small opening, he could just about make out the nearby fortress.

There was a sudden jolt as the wagon came to a halt.

'We're here,' Auron declared.

'I think we all figured that out.' Silva sighed.

'Don't get snotty with me because you all got caught again,' the spirit huffed.

'I will cheer up immensely when Garaz removes his elbow from my cleavage.'

The orc's eyes opened wide, and Nicolas could've sworn Garaz's green skin reddened slightly, though it might've been the residual spots of light in his eyes. Either way, the elbow was retracted at speed.

The door of the wagon swung open, revealing two lines of pointing halberds marking a path for them.

'Right, you lot, *out*,' the captain demanded. 'Any funny business or lip and it'll be our steel you get a taste of this time.'

With the perfect motivation, Nicolas scrabbled to his feet and promptly jumped out of the wagon. The others weren't far behind. The wagon creaked with every shift in weight as one of his companions jumped from it.

Ahead of them, a gate was being pulled shut. It was situated in a solid wall that ran around the circumference of the fort they were in. The fort itself didn't look huge, but it was well-tended and well-garrisoned. Men were training with swords against each other and against straw dummies while others marched in formation or patrolled the battlements, now that the show of them being brought in was over.

'What have we here then, Captain?' an officious man in fancy armour asked as he approached. What hair he had left was white and faded, revealing the liver spots on his head. He walked as if he had all the time in the world, hands clasped behind his back. 'Quite the strange collection of fellows, I'd say.'

The captain snapped off a quick salute. 'Found these orc spies crossing the border, milord.'

The old man studied them lazily. 'I see, I see,' he replied with barely any enthusiasm. 'Fortunate you had the prison wagon with you then.'

'Standard protocol with border patrol, milord.' By the slight exasperation in the captain's tone, it was clear this wasn't the first time they'd had this conversation. 'We mean to interrogate them to confirm their allegiances and—'

The officer gave a dismissive wave of his hand as he turned away. 'Yes, yes, Captain. Whatever you think's best.' Already he was heading back towards the fort.

'Very good, milord,' the captain said with another salute.

'Cream of the military, that one.' Auron snorted. 'Considering this fort borders orc territory, you'd think they'd put someone in charge who had a bit of passion for keeping their kingdom safe. There's a lot to be said for meritocracy, you know.'

'Time to get you lot locked up until we can determine whether you are friend or foe,' the captain declared, pointing beyond the wagon. 'Get moving.'

'This guy.' Auron chuckled, dismounting Mare. 'I'll have you out before first light.'

CHAPTER 20

The plan wasn't ideal—getting arrested crossing the border hadn't been ideal—but it was simple. Wait until it was dark, then break out of their cells. Unfortunately, the plan was completely embuggered by the fact that they weren't put in jail cells, but instead placed in separate cages hanging from a gallows in the very centre of the fortress's courtyard, where the entire garrison could watch them. Even now, when night had fallen, a ring of torches lit the gallows up, so guards on the wall could keep half an eye on them and ensure they didn't get up to mischief.

I don't want to get up to mischief. I want to get out of here.

Fidgeting slightly, he tried to find a way to sit where the bars of the cage weren't cutting into either his legs, his ass, or both at once. Currently, he was allowing his legs to dangle from the cage. He sighed again. He'd been doing that a lot in the past few hours.

'Dammit,' Auron grumbled as he watched spear-men patrolling the battlements. 'This is going to be more complicated than I thought.

'That's understating it,' Shift confirmed, flicking the bars of their cage. 'I could change and slip between the bars and then free the rest of you. But the way they've been watching us by the time I've freed the first of you the alarm will be raised, even if I could use the magic key.'

Usually, Shift hated the idea of using the gift from T'goth, a Deity they'd once met in the form of a crazy old man. But now they didn't have it, they actually needed it. The key, along with the rest of their personal effects, was in a locked box at the bottom of the ramp that led up to the gallows. So tantalisingly close, yet so far.

Why would you leave the belongings of orc spies so close to them? Shouldn't they be rooting through them for clues or something?

'They had best hope we do not escape these cages,' Silva growled. 'Lest some of these *funny men* require a long stay at the local healer's temple.'

Earlier in the day, Nicolas had made the apparent mistake of asking a guard for some water. The one he'd asked fancied himself a court jester. With an obliging nod, the man had taken a ladle of water from a nearby barrel and walked towards Nicolas, only to *accidentally* trip and spill it just as Nicolas reached for it. This had gotten a laugh from the other guards. So the man, finding his audience, continued to do this routine for another ten minutes. As the novelty began to wear off for those watching, the jester decided to up his game by spilling the water over Silva. Even now, Nicolas shuddered at the glare the man had received. He'd found himself edging back into his cage when the warrior had unleashed it. Suffice to say that the jester decided to end his performance there.

'I do not believe that will help our case,' Garaz said with a sympathetic smile. It was the first time the orc had spoken in a while. He'd been in quiet meditation for most of the day. The guards had taken his amulet when they'd confiscated their personal effects.

'I don't think much will help our case,' Shift said. 'They've made up their mind.'

'This misunderstanding can still be settled without violence. Once the magistrate arrives.'

'Hmm.'

Nicolas frowned at Auron. 'What?'

'I don't want to be a doomsayer,' the spirit began. 'But have any of you seen a messenger leave the fortress?'

Shared glances suggested not.

A suppressed growl escaped Garaz's lips. 'That is...irksome,' the orc said, struggling to control his voice.

'Are you okay?' Shift asked, eyeing him nervously.

The orc looked at Shift for a moment then his mouth became a thin line. 'At the moment. But this is the longest I have been without the amulet. I can sense...*it* coming.'

'Can you get it?' Nicolas asked Auron urgently.

The spirit looked at the locked box. 'Sorry, kid. I can do a lot, but I can't pick locks.'

Dammit.

He didn't want to lose Garaz. And he was also very aware of how having his companion suddenly become a crazed monster would look when they were trying to reinforce the notion that they were good folk.

The clomping of boots on wood got his attention. A guard was stomping up the ramp towards them.

'That's enough talking out of you lot,' a helmed guard snapped as he approached. 'Stay silent or we'll have one of you lashed as an example.'

Nicolas didn't need daylight to see the whitening of Silva's knuckles as she gripped the bars.

'Sorry,' he said softly.

A stick jabbed him painfully in the rib. 'I said *quiet.*' The guard's chiselled jaw curled into a snarl before the stick slipped out of his hand and he knelt to pick it up. Which was quite a way down for the tall fellow. Something about the way he bent down to pick it up was oddly awkward looking, but Nicolas couldn't put his finger on why.

Rubbing his tender side in annoyance, Nicolas frowned at the guard. He wasn't picking up the stick at all; he was unlocking his cage.

'You don't have much time,' the guard whispered hurriedly. 'It was no coincidence that you were found at the border. The captain was on the look out for you, specifically, and has been for some days now. That is why he had the wagon with him already. I believe he hoped you'd resist so he could justify killing you all, but you didn't, so he had to bring you back lest the true men of his party protested. Now you're here they will come for you. They will throw your gear around and make it look like you attempted to escape when the guards discovered you and cut you down.'

Shit. Shit. Shit. Shit. Shit.

'Shit,' Auron said at his side.

'Umm...how do we know you aren't part of this?' Nicolas asked. 'You seem to be setting us up for exactly that.'

Standing, the guard, who had a deep voice and an almost noble bearing—plus an impressive jaw line—tucked his stick under his arm. 'Because you have friends, Nicolas Percival Carnegie. More than you know. Governor Morrow says hello.'

'Governor—'

The guard snarled, kicking the cage hard. It juddered and began to swing slightly under the force of the blow. A couple of the men on the battlements looked down to see what the disturbance was.

'You keep those defiant eyes off me, worm,' he snapped, waving his stick. 'Or I'll rob the executioner of one more head on the block.' Spitting at Nicolas's feet, the guard turned and stormed off.

'You all heard that, right?' Nicolas asked, dumbfounded.

'Yes,' Garaz confirmed. 'It seems we are in more danger than we knew.'

'And we have support,' Silva added. 'If he is to be believed.'

'I'll take it,' Nicolas said. 'My gut says we can trust him.'

'Your *hero instincts*,' Auron corrected.

'Whatever. Shame they didn't warn me about the captain.'

Wait. So the captain lied when he said he didn't recognise me?

On some level, that was oddly satisfying, but a little beside the point. Right now, they had more pressing concerns.

'Okay,' he said, shaking the thought off. 'We're almost free, but we're also in danger. What do we do?'

'You'll have to let us out of these cages,' Silva told him. 'And you'll need to do it fast.'

'I can't do that,' Nicolas scoffed. 'I'm not Shift. I can't pick locks.'

'He should've let *me* out,' his companion confirmed, before tutting and rolling their eyes. 'Actually, never mind. I can get myself out. It'll be the Silva and Garaz who need help. Nick and I will have to take a cage each.' The shapeshifter turned their attention to Nicolas. 'I can teach you the basics of lock-picking. These are very simple locks, so even a twitchy amateur should manage. But like I said, the guards will raise the alarm the instant we make out move. We'll be surrounded before we're all free, then they have an actual excuse to kill us.'

'That is a good point,' Garaz agreed. 'There are too many guards on the wall for us to do this unnoticed.'

'Not for long,' Auron said, watching a couple of the armoured men patrolling the battlements. 'Whoever is coming for you is going to want as few actual witnesses as possible. Those guards will get relieved so the only ones left are the ones intent on killing us...you.'

'How can you know that?' Nicolas asked.

The spirit tilted his head in a look that clearly imparted *'c'mon kid. I know my stuff.'*

'That'll be our window to act,' Auron continued. 'When it comes we'll need to be ready for it. We surprise them, overpower them, and get out of here like Sha'then himself is chasing us.'

The others exchanged worried glances, but soon nodded in agreement. It wasn't a great plan, but it was infinitely better than sitting in cages waiting to be butchered.

Making no sudden movements, Nicolas slipped the unlocked padlock from the cage door, holding it to ensure it didn't just fall open and drop him to the ground. Tentatively, Nicolas tested the bottom of the cage. It moved a little, with a slight creak that sounded in his mind like a banshee's howl.

'Right then,' he said quietly. 'If I'm going to try to pick another lock what am I using to do it?"

Shift, keeping one eye on the guards, slipped a hand towards their boot. Reaching inside it, they produced a couple of pieces of metal. 'I've got one for both of us,' they said. Shift threw one to him and Nicolas was surprised when he actually caught it. 'As you get out, I'll change quickly and slip through the bars. I'll unlock Silva. You unlock Garaz.'

'I'll see about creating a distraction to try and buy a little time,' Auron said quickly.

'Once we're all out, I'll get that chest open. We get our gear and run.' Shift closed their eyes and sighed. 'I don't think I'm going to have time to get redressed either. Dammit. I don't want to escape a fortress naked again.'

'*Again?*' Nicolas asked.

'Focus,' Silva hissed at him.

'Once free I will create a fire to keep the guards busy whilst we make our escape,' Garaz added. 'Nothing too big. That straw wagon over there should do.'

'And the men who come to kill us?' Nicolas asked. 'They aren't just going to stand by and let us prance out of here.'

'They die,' Silva replied as if it was the most obvious thing in the world.

'They do not,' Auron corrected. 'You kill any of the soldiers here, corrupt or not, and you'll be hunted for the rest of your life.'

'Auron's right,' Nicolas agreed. 'But I don't think I have any qualms about roughing them up.'

All of the group agreed with that notion wholeheartedly.

Plan set, all they had to do now was wait for someone to show up and try to kill them.

CHAPTER 21

Another hour passed. Nicolas found that waiting for someone to come and kill you was quite tedious. For some reason he couldn't fathom, he just wanted them to get on with it. Eventually, another soldier exited the fort and began to walk the length of the battlements, stopping to exchange brief words with each guard he passed. As he did, said guards would leave their post and head back towards the fort.

Here we go.

'You ready?' Shift asked him.

'No,' he answered honestly.

'Well you'd better get ready fast, kid. This is happening.' When Auron felt the need to talk in hushed tones, it was time to worry.

All eyes turned to the fortress's door as it opened. Figures appeared, checking the battlements before striding across the courtyard, where their companion who'd dismissed the guards joined them. It was the captain and four of his men. But they were walking away from Nicolas and the others. This was getting curiouser by the minute.

The group assembled around the fortress's gate. At the captain's behest, two of the guards opened it a little. The crack allowed some moonlight to enter the shadowed archway, enough that he saw a figure slip into the courtyard. Nicolas couldn't make out any details, but he watched as the figure talked to the captain then handed him a pouch.

That'd be some coin to kill us, I'm guessing.

The group approached the gallows. At the bottom of it, they came to a halt. The newcomer had a beaked leather mask across the top part of his face, covering his nose, eyes and forehead. Around it sat his shoulder length black, wavy hair, most of which was tied back in a loose ponytail. He wore the tunic of a fighter, or an assassin maybe. Tilting his head slightly, he studied Nicolas as much as Nicolas studied him.

'That's them,' he said finally.

'You are sure?' the captain asked, half turning to the man.

The man nodded once. 'Definitely. They're troublesome, so I suggest you make it quick.'

Oh, taking the time to check they're killing the right people. How delightfully thorough.

'Hmm,' the captain began thoughtfully. 'We stab them in the cages and dress the scene after. The old idiot won't know the difference or even bother to check.'

'As long as it doesn't come back to us,' the masked man told the captain, before adding, 'You have Mr Hesltrum's thanks for your help in this matter.'

'He is welcome,' the captain said, patting the new pouch on his belt.

The captain nodded to his four men then towards Nicolas and the others.

Taking a deep breath, Nicolas dropped from the cage and sprinted towards Garaz's. Instantly there was a cry of surprise and the sound of drawing swords behind him. Fumbling slightly, he put the lock-pick Shift had given him into the lock. One twist and the delicate piece of metal snapped in his hand. It was accompanied by a heavy sigh from Garaz.

Simple lock my ass.

Staring at the broken piece of metal, Nicolas sighed himself and discarded it.

I wish our friend had left us a handy sword when he unlocked my cage. Can't have everything, I suppose.

All he could do now was buy Shift as much time as possible to release the others.

Readying himself, Nicolas sprinted towards the edge of the ramp and launched himself into the air. The four soldiers, confused by his sudden action, slowed to a halt.

'Yeeeeeee-haaaaaaaa.'

As much as Nicolas hated to admit it, his outburst wasn't intended to further confuse the soldiers. He was just caught up in the moment. Even if it did potentially end up waking the rest of the fort.

He crashed into the four men. The two he hit directly stumbled backwards into their companions, who lost their footing completely and fell back down the ramp, ending up at the feet of their shocked captain and the masked man.

Using his momentum, Nicolas grabbed the head of the nearest guard and introduced it to the edge of the gallows platform. Kicking the back of his knee to drop him to one leg, Nicolas smacked his head against the wood a second time, before stepping back and booting him in the side of his helmet. He began to tumble down the ramp, impeding the progress of the captain, who was now storming up it.

'You little bastard.'

Stepping to the side, Nicolas dodged the sword swing from the second guard. The blade caught in the wood for a second, a second Nicolas used to kick him right in the balls. With a wheezing groan, the man let go of his stuck blade to put both hands on his damaged genitals. Nicolas drove the man's forehead into the hilt of his own sword, before sending him sprawling with a punch to the jaw.

'Have at you.'

Even Nicolas knew you shouldn't really announce it when you were attacking someone from behind. Stepping around and into the captain's attack, he blocked the oncoming sword, driving his elbow into the captain's elbow joint. Quickly, he circled his arm under the captain's and then over his attacker's shoulder, causing a surprised curse as the man doubled over, his arm locked into place. Nicolas punched him in the face five times—venting a little bit of his frustration—before kneeing him in the side of the head and finally releasing his shoulder so his body could crash to the wooden floor. Picking up the captain's sword, Nicolas raised it, then stopped, Auron's words echoing in his head. For a moment it was bloody tempting to kill a man set on killing him, but instead he took a big swing and threw the blade out of reach, so at least it couldn't be used against him.

By now the two at the bottom of the ramp had gotten their wits about them and were charging him. One disappeared into the air as Garaz came from nowhere, tackling him with his shoulder. The other was intercepted by Silva. Nicolas winced at the violence she unleashed on him. She was an expert in venting her frustration through her fists, where Nicolas was merely a novice.

For a second, he stared at the masked man, until urgent voices within the fortress got his attention. When he looked back, the man had vanished. Lights appeared in windows as people, guards specifically, began to wake. He looked at the carnage around him.

Bugger. Me and my big mouth.

When they come out here and see all this, they definitely aren't going to ask questions first.

Shift appeared beside him, half dressed. Reaching down, they grinned in triumph as they snatched the purse off the captain's belt.

'What?' they asked, seeing Nicolas looking. 'He was paid to kill us, and he failed. He doesn't deserve the coin.'

'It's not that, you're, um...'

Shift looked down at themselves. 'Breasts are out? I had noticed. Best I could do on short notice.' Their top was bunched under their arm.

Breeches had been the priority. Nicolas could respect that. Though Shift used the moment of a lull to quickly slip their shirt on again.

'Here.' Nicolas turned at Silva's voice and barely got his hand up in time to catch the *Dawn Blade*. Quickly, he ran over and grabbed his pack from the chest whilst the others collected their belongings.

The door of the fortress opened, and several half-dressed guards stepped out. There was a moment of surprise, a moment of confusion, and then...

'To arms. The prisoners are escaping. To arms.'

Subtlety out the window completely, Garaz threw a fireball towards the gate, exploding it into flaming shards and causing a flash so bright Nicolas had to shield his eyes. The orc then ignited the straw cart, as was the plan. It went up with a *whoosh*, causing the soldiers to stumble back, shielding their eyes from the flash.

'Go,' Auron shouted urgently.

Jumping over the unconscious bodies, Nicolas sprinted across the courtyard towards the open gate. Ahead, several men ran onto the battlements. Archers. Nicolas zigzagged as arrows plinked into the ground around him. That was the only way to do it. Running in a straight line when someone was trying to shoot you with an arrow would be suicidal.

Bolting through the gate, the group made for the treeline. Several arrows followed, but fortunately they hit nothing save the trunk of a poor tree that was minding its own business.

Leaves rustled angrily around them as they tore through the foliage. They couldn't rest yet, or for a while. Pursuers would be on their heels in no time. The battle cries behind them were very enthusiastic for people who'd only just woken up. It spurred them on even faster.

CHAPTER 22

C oming to a halt, he looked around, aware something was amiss. Trying to focus on the feeling, he finally realised that it was a trembling in the road beneath his feet. Frowning, he looked down. Some of the smaller stones were vibrating. A distant rumbling was growing louder.

What is...?

Nicolas's eyes widened as he answered his own question. Panic gripped him.

'Get off the road,' he cried.

But when he turned, his companions were no longer there. Frantically, he scanned the bushes for the others.

'Hey, fool,' Shift shouted from a bush on the other side of the road, urgently waving him over. 'Get off the road.'

As the rumbling reached its crescendo, Nicolas threw himself into the bushes. Trying to ignore the scratches of sharp branches, he got onto his belly and manoeuvred so he could see the road.

At his eye level, numerous pounding hooves passed by, throwing up a cloud of dust. It tickled his nose, threatening to make him sneeze. Quickly, he grabbed his nose and held it shut. He doubted anyone would hear a sneeze over the din the horses were making, but better safe than sorry.

Even when the roar had receded into nothing, the group stayed where they were, fearful of walking into a rear guard or stragglers. Now was the time for the utmost caution.

'Looks clear,' Auron declared from the middle of the road.

'Considering they're looking for us, they aren't exactly doing a good job of it,' Shift said as they rose, brushing the leaves from their tunic.

'Charging up and down roads does seem a strange method to hunt fugitives,' Garaz replied.

'Tactically inept.' Silva sniffed, staring with disgust in the direction of the knights.

As stupid as their tactics of just charging up and down roads were, the kingdom could mobilise impressive force at speed. This was the fifth patrol they'd seen, and it was barely lunchtime. Nicolas supposed it was a necessity when they lived this close to orcs. On the one hand, it was good that the kingdom took its security so seriously, but on the other hand, it was a royal pain in the backside when they had places to be.

Wait? Did Garaz say fugitives? A sobering thought struck him. *By the Deities, we're being hunted by the authorities. Again.*

Of course they were. They'd escaped after being accused of being spies and given several of the kingdom's soldiery—albeit corrupt soldiery—a thorough kicking on their way out the door. At least they hadn't killed any of them, though Nicolas doubted the one Silva had beaten would be up and about for a good long while. Either way, they were wanted people on the run from troops of knights. Assuming, of course, those men on horseback were the actual authorities and not a group of dressed-up killers.

Why has this gotten so complicated all of a sudden? We literally just want to kill one man.

That thought was a strange one. No wonder people were hunting them. They were technically assassins.

'The hunters are now the hunted,' Auron said sagely, echoing Nicolas's thoughts.

'Any suggestions?' Nicolas asked. 'Preferably not in story form?' With an army out hunting them, someone was bound to get lucky sooner or later.

'So, this one time,' the spirit said with narrowed eyes, drawing out the pause as long as possible, 'there was a mouthy little jackass named *Nick Carnage* who didn't appreciate good wisdom when it was imparted.'

Oh, I'm the jackass, am I?

'His question still stands,' Garaz said, diplomatic as usual. 'What shall we do?'

Auron pursed his lips. 'We need somewhere to lie low for a few days, until they get bored of not finding us. After that, we'll know which ones are the killers, because they'll be the ones still looking.'

'And where exactly do we *lie low*?' Silva asked. 'Nowhere obvious comes to mind. I doubt the locals will want to give a group of potential orc spies a safe haven.'

'That's because you lot have no friends.' Auron grinned. 'Whereas, in life, I was quite the sociable chap and never short of people willing to do me a favour or owing me one.'

'Any of them happen to be local?' Nicolas asked. He already knew the answer, but sometimes it was best to just let Auron have his moment.

'Of course,' the spirit replied, with a nod and a wink.

'Good.' Garaz stared in the direction the knights had gone and sighed. 'Is this how it felt when you were wanted in Nalbina for attempted assassination? I do not care for it.'

'When I was *wrongly accused* of being an assassin,' Nicolas corrected. 'And yes. Not nice, is it?'

'Pfft,' Shift scoffed. 'I've been wanted plenty of times. I just make sure they're looking for the wrong face.'

'Maybe we do not continue this conversation on the road?' Silva suggested with a huff, before turning to Auron. 'How close is your friend?'

'Nearby,' the spirit answered vaguely.

Deciding the road was getting a little too exposed, the group travelled through the forest itself. It made the going slower, but caution was preferable to speed right now. Still, travelling parallel to the track, they stopped several times and hid as patrols passed, riding like their horses were on fire. Nicolas was beginning to believe it was the same patrol going in circles.

Moving carefully, the group remained quiet and vigilant. That was why when Silva motioned for them to halt, they all stopped and got to the floor. Even Auron. Probably a reflex left over from when he was alive.

Ahead of them, Silva nodded to a large tree. Auron jogged forward. Craning around the tree, the spirit held up four fingers.

Listening, Nicolas picked up the neigh of a horse and then voices.

'By the Deities, all this riding around plays havoc with my bladder,' one bellowed.

Nicolas suddenly realised why the men had stopped.

'Well, Lord Farnsworth wants those prisoners back,' another voice added. 'First time I've seen him animated about anything other than having a nice sit down.'

'Not as animated as Captain Jax, mind.' Another laughed. 'I've never seen him so pissed. Did you see his face, black and blue.'

'Serves the wanker right,' the first scoffed. 'Never liked him. I don't know how he made captain. They'll promote anyone nowadays.'

'Because the man licks ass with the passion of a succubus shagging the soul outta someone,' a fourth chimed in. 'I'm sure he greased a few palms with coin along the way.'

'*Gasp.*' One of the men laughed. 'You cast aspersions on the honour of a captain of the Ivilar border guard?'

'Damned right I do. The man's a twat.' There was a dramatic pause. 'But I'll never do it in earshot of him, that's for damned sure.'

The other men laughed.

'So what about these fugitives then? Think they're spies?'

'Nah,' the first man replied. 'You ever heard of orcs using humans instead of chopping them up? Plus, that orc was bloody well spoken. Don't see that often.'

'I heard of an orc healer who travelled around Yarringsburg that was like that,' one of the men mused. 'Apparently quite a nice fellow, by all accounts.'

Nicolas glanced at Garaz, who nodded in agreement at the praise.

'Who bloody knows or cares?' one of the men said. 'Ours isn't to reason why, ours is just to stab whoever they bloody well tell us to.'

'That what we're doing then, stabbing them?' another asked.

'Old Jax was quite adamant about killing them on sight. I think we should bring them back alive, just to piss him off.'

'If we ever find the buggers. All this riding...'

'Ahhhhh.' The first man sighed in loud satisfaction. 'Done. That's a bloody relief.'

'We're all relieved.' One of the men chuckled. 'That was the longest piss ever.'

'Just mount up, you mouthy sods. There's fugitives to hunt.'

Soon enough, Nicolas caught a glimpse of the men as they rode towards the road. None of them bothered to look back or check the forest around them. Though Nicolas had already guessed these weren't the cream of the Ivilar military. They waited a while before Auron gave the signal that the coast was clear.

'So, they want to kill us on sight then?' Shift remarked as they rose. 'So much for summoning a magistrate to straighten this out.'

'I should've snapped that captain's neck,' Silva growled, clutching her hands.

'That would've made it worse,' Nicolas told the warrior. 'At the moment, they're just looking for potential spies crossing the border. The whole kingdom will be up in arms if we go around breaking officer's necks.' Silva rolled her eyes. 'Though it's nice to dream,' he added quickly.

'We need to get where we are going quickly,' Garaz said, looking in the direction the soldiers had gone. 'We are too exposed out here.'

'Agreed,' Nicolas said firmly.

All chatter ceased as the group continued on their way.

CHAPTER 23

As it turned out, Auron's definition of *nearby* wasn't quite as nearby as Nicolas would've liked. When you're on the run, the best place to lie low is within a couple of metres of you. Auron's mysterious friend was several miles away. But after the close call with the urinating soldiers, fortune seemed to favour the group. Though they still moved with all due caution, just to be on the safe side.

Auron, who'd been scouting ahead for any potential surprises, appeared through a tree, nearly making Nicolas start.

'We're here,' the spirit said excitedly, before disappearing back through the bark.

There was a time he'd make an effort to walk around it.

His companion was clearly becoming more comfortable with his...was condition the right word?

Circumventing the tree, Nicolas and the others followed, moving carefully. The foliage around them began to clear, revealing an open area just off the main track, which was occupied by a longhouse, of sorts. It was clearly no drinking hall. Numerous brightly coloured wooden signs peppered its front and sides. Each had a picture of some random item with writing underneath. Beside the building was a collection of hitching posts, with many horses attached. There were even a handful of wagons, waiting for their owners to return.

'This doesn't look like a place to lie low,' Nicolas whispered urgently.

'There are a lot of people here,' Silva said warily.

Nicolas appreciated the support for his concerns.

'They'll be busy,' Auron said in much too breezy a manner for Nicolas's liking. 'Just walk in naturally, and don't draw attention to yourselves. No one will notice.'

Nicolas and Garaz shared a look. An orc walking into whatever this place was bound to raise at least one eyebrow. His companion wrapped his cloak around himself as tightly as he could. Somehow, this made him more conspicuous. They just had to hope Auron was right and that no one paid too much attention to them.

'Do you lot not trust me?' Auron's scowl matched the defensiveness in his tone.

'Of course we do,' Shift replied quickly. 'But you don't get hung if we get caught.'

'No one's getting hung,' the spirit scoffed with an eyeroll. 'You heard the pissing soldier. They're going to kill you on sight.'

'Thanks for that,' Nicolas muttered.

'Which they won't,' Auron continued loudly. 'Because my old pal will see you right.'

Nicolas couldn't deny Auron's experience and wisdom. If he trusted this guy, so should they. So he didn't feel the need to argue.

Besides, I'll get a story if I do.

Shaking himself to try to remove any signs of tension or nervousness from his body, Nicolas followed the others towards the building. Halfway there, Shift caught his eye and nodded at him purposefully. He realised quickly that he was *trying* to walk casually, instead of actually walking casually. With an awkward cough, he adjusted his stride and gave Shift a sheepish grin.

As they approached the long house, Nicolas realised what the pictures around the building were. They were products. Beneath each was its name and a price. A bright red sign above the door read *Allegard's Gallery of Wonders.*

'This is a store of some kind?' Garaz asked from beneath the hood of his cloak.

Auron went almost slack jawed. 'You've never heard of the *Gallery of Wonders?'*

The red hood shook. The spirit looked at each of them in turn, searching their expressions. Well, Shift and Silva's. The spirit knew Nicolas wasn't very worldly. 'The rest of you?' From the incredulous look on Auron's face, he would not be at all impressed if the answer was *no.*

Shift shook their head and Silva shrugged.

'Deities, people,' the spirit gasped in disbelief. 'Allegard's isn't just a store, it's *the* store. He sells *everything* you can make coin from, and what he doesn't have in stock, he can get. Provided it's legal, of course,' he added quickly.

'I'd never assume you'd associate with criminal elements.' Shift grinned.

'When I was alive, anyway.' Auron half smiled. 'My standards have slipped somewhat since my death. Hence me now aiding wanted fugitives.'

Nicolas had to admit he was curious. There was something enticing about the doorway and what lay beyond. But he got the impression that was the point. The bright signs, the open doors. It was all to entice people inside. And it was working. Speeding up slightly, he was the first one through them.

'*Welcome to Allegard's Gallery of Wonders. The* where *for all your* wares.'

Instinctively, he jumped back across the threshold. The feminine voice came from everywhere and nowhere. And there was no actual person visible.

'Take your hand off your sword, kid.' Auron tutted. 'It's just one of Allegard's little magical touches. A welcoming voice when you enter. He reckons it *'enhances the shopping experience.'* Nicolas was hesitant to let go of his blade. 'And he *really* doesn't take kindly to people brandishing weapons in his store. He has...*measures* in place for that.'

Nicolas quickly took his hand off the hilt of his sword, holding it up palm open, just in case.

'Very smooth.' Shift chuckled, walking past him. The voice again greeted them as they entered. In fact, it repeated the welcome for each of them in turn, save the obvious one.

Passing the voice again, Nicolas stood in the store's entrance and looked around in wonder. The place looked much bigger on the inside, and it was crammed with stuff. There were displays of fine robes, some mounted on posed wooden people so that one might see what they looked like on, racks of weapons of all varieties, cooking implements, and curiosities he couldn't immediately identify.

I see why he calls this a gallery of wonders.

It was hard to know what to focus on first as his head turned this way and that. In the end, he decided to go for the four-sided counter that dominated the centre of the room.

At the counter, serving a customer buying a fine silk gown, was a large man whose generally irritable expression suggested that he shouldn't work in customer service. Much of his hair had migrated to his chin, leaving only a few tufts at the side and some lingering strands on top. His head was peppered with grey. At first glance, he appeared fat, but there was something about the way he moved that gave Nicolas the impression that more than a little of it was muscle.

Allegard, I presume.

Finishing his transaction with the barest of smiles, Allegard leant on the counter and drummed on it with his big sausage fingers as he glared in the direction of the door, exactly where Nicolas was standing. He found himself suppressing a gulp.

'He doesn't look very friendly,' Nicolas whispered to Auron.

'Hmm,' the spirit was too busy looking at a suit of armour by the door to pay attention. Finally, he realised what Nicolas had said. 'He's fine. He's a darling once you get to know him.'

Though he undoubtedly looked strange talking to thin air, he couldn't help but turn and address the spirit directly. 'A *darling*? Are you serious?'

'Always, kid.' The spirit grinned. 'Now, let's go and have a chat. I'll do the talking, you just repeat what I say.'

Auron started forwards then stopped when he realised Nicolas wasn't following him. 'C'mon, kid,' the spirit urged. 'Before half the Ivilar military pile through that door.'

Fine.

CHAPTER 24

Once again trying not to let his nerves or awkwardness show, Nicolas walked down the aisle towards the counter whilst the others—except Garaz, who stayed close to the door—followed. Yet his nerves kept prodding him for attention, demanding to know why Allegard was staring at him with such a piercing and impatient glare. Did the trader already know who they were? Was he ready to sell them out? Was he one of the random people who knew about Nicolas? Judging by the expression, Nicolas might've killed a relative of his in battle or something. He didn't get the feeling—

Wait. He isn't looking at me.

What Nicolas's paranoia had failed to take into account was the three young mages stood between him and the counter. At least, he assumed they were mages. If not, they were going to a fancy dress party of some kind, because the star covered robes screamed that they were magic users. The trio stood beside a rack of wands, crafted in various sizes and styles. One held a long wand with a curved handle reverently in his outstretched palms. It didn't appear to be made of wood, but Nicolas couldn't have told you what it was actually made from even if he'd held it.

'...the great mage, Ander the Shaper, knew the importance of a good quality wand,' the one who held the wand declared knowingly.

'I get what you're saying,' the second one exclaimed with an exasperated tone, raising his hand. 'But the point you're spectacularly missing is that wizards don't *need* wands. They are a focusing tool at best, and a show-piece at worse.'

'But as a tool, that is a very lovely one,' the third cut in with his slightly nasal voice.

'Oh, there's no denying that,' the first agreed with a raised finger. 'But you must understand that all the greats had wands.'

'Magus the Elemental didn't,' the second one replied abruptly.

The first mage rolled his eyes. 'Oh, here we go.' He sighed. 'Can we not have *one* conversation where you don't bring up *Magus the bloody Elemental*.'

'He was an innovator and one of the most powerful wizards in history,' number two snapped. 'And he didn't need a wand.'

'He carried a staff,' mage three scoffed. 'It's the same thing, but longer.'

'It was a *walking cane*, you absolute simpleton.' He clutched his hands in frustration. 'By Magus's beard, you two are—'

'*Oi*.' Allegard's voice rumbled through the store like an erupting volcano.

Everyone in the Gallery came to an abrupt halt, including Nicolas and his companions. Suddenly, Nicolas really wanted to put some distance between himself and the now very awkward mages.

'For two whole hours you three have been stood there mooning over those wands,' Allegard snarled, palms flat on the counter as he leant over. 'Waffling about *Magus this* and *Greybeard that* whilst you pick them up and waft the bloody things around one by one like you're conducting a Deities' damned orchestra. Are you three planning on actually *buying* anything today, or are you just waiting for me to turn my back so you can stick those wands up your bum-holes to prove which of your sad little asses is more enchanted? Hmm?'

Nicolas found himself edging away from the mages, who'd become considerably paler in the last minute. Every other customer in the store was either engrossed in the show or trying to make it look like their interest lay in the items they were looking at, whilst secretly watching so they didn't miss anything.

'Well...' the first mage stammered. 'You see...well...we were...it's like this...really...'

Allegard narrowed his eyes. 'Are you buying anything today?' His voice had a faux sweetness.

'We...are a bit short on coin until next week,' the second one admitted with an awkward cough.

'Ah, in that case, I will see you next week.' Allegard smiled evilly. 'Until then. *Out!*' The roar echoed around the store as the shopkeeper pointed towards the door, just in case they weren't already aware of its location.

Strange for a man so clearly irritable to choose to open a shop. Is this how the oracle got so cranky? Too long dealing with people?

Sheepishly, the mage holding the wand placed it into its holder on the shelf.

Allegard stood upright, folding his arms and growling.

Quickly, the mage took it back off the shelf and wiped it thoroughly with his robe, before replacing it again. Then, keeping their eyes on the shopkeeper, the trio backed towards the door. Nicolas had to sidestep so they didn't bump into him. Just as they reached the threshold, the mages turned and exited the building with all due haste. As they passed the door, the feminine voice called out three times, *'Thank you for shopping with us today. Please come again.'*

I'm not sure Allegard shares that sentiment.

Nicolas didn't catch the whole of what Allegard muttered in response, but the first word was *better* and the third word was *not*.

'You sure we should be talking to him?' Shift muttered. 'He has a temperament that makes Silva seem calm and collected.' Shift bucked slightly, and it took Nicolas a second to realise that the warrior had punched them on the arm.

'He's fine,' Auron soothed. 'You just need to know how to talk to him.'

With only the evidence of this experience to go on, Nicolas would have to put Auron's assurances down to *if you say so*. But they really had nowhere else to go. Though, were he looking at the positive side, after that outburst, everyone else in the store was keeping to themselves, so no one was paying attention to the proverbial orc in the room.

Approaching the counter, Nicolas opened his mouth to introduce himself when Allegard held up a hand.

'Shut up a second,' he said gruffly as he looked past Nicolas.

Um…okay then.

Nicolas closed his mouth. As he did, he heard a familiar sound.

'Welcome to Allegard's Gallery of Wonders. The Where *for all your* Wares.'

Suddenly, he realised that Allegard's frowning eyes were looking towards the door, and specifically the two men who'd just walked in and were doing a very bad job of making it look like they were casually browsing. Each wore light leather armour, with the occasional metal plate attached, and had unkempt hair. It didn't take long for Nicolas to realise that they were heading towards a demure young lady who was examining a long, curved dagger. She let out a disbelieving breath as she looked at the price tag attached to the hilt, not even realising that the two men were closing on her.

I need to interve—

'Oi.' Allegard's shout, and his proximity to it, made Nicolas's ears ring. Both men stopped dead where they stood, hands hovering above the daggers they'd meant to draw and presumably plunge into the young woman. 'You bloody bounty hunters,' the shopkeeper snarled. 'I don't want none of that guild feuding bullshit in my shop. This is neutral territory, and it's staying that way. And if I have to mop blood off the damn floor, I'll be doing it with that tangled mess atop your damned heads. If you don't want to find out where the mop handle is going, I suggest you leave. Now.' The shopkeeper's voice could do a threatening rumble with the best of them.

Backing away from the men, the young woman opened her shawl to reveal a sheathed blade under each armpit. She rested her hands on the hilts but didn't draw them. The bounty hunters, on the other hand, drew their knives. One pointed his towards Allegard. Though what he intended to do with such a short blade at this distance was anyone's guess.

'Do it, brother,' the man said. 'Slit the assassin bitch. I'll watch the fat man.'

His companion advanced. Still, the woman didn't draw her knives.

Allegard shook his head with a huff and caught Nicolas's eye. 'Stupid bastards,' he moaned. Slowly and deliberately, the storekeeper put two thick fingers to his lips and let out a short, sharp whistle. 'Pixie, Dust...' A malicious grin creased his face. 'Playtime.'

A door at the back of the shop crashed open. Nicolas took a step back from the counter as he heard frantic padding. Then two giant shapes jumped on the counter, causing Nicolas to take a few more steps back, his hand scrabbling for the hilt of the *Dawn Blade* but missing it every time.

'What in the Underworld are those bloody things?' he gasped, finally giving up and letting his hand flop to the side.

They were dogs, but they were also not dogs. He didn't have time to fully get his head around what the things were before Allegard pointed towards the paling bounty hunters and said, 'Those wankers.'

With a roar, the creatures leapt from the counter. Nicolas's head moved as he followed the sound of their paws slapping on the ground. But he couldn't see them. What he could see was the bounty hunters suddenly vanishing from sight. Pulled to the ground with a shrill cry. And then the screaming started.

'Silly sods.' Auron chuckled, shaking his head.

Nicolas tracked the screaming until the bounty hunters came into view again, being dragged kicking and thrashing out of the store by the jaws firmly secured to their nether regions. Each was yanked from the establishment by their testicles, before disappearing around the corner.

'*Thank you for shopping with us today. Please come again,*' the magic voice chimed twice, barely audible over the screaming.

'Troll-brained assholes.' Allegard chuckled before his face dropped again. 'The High King needs to hurry up and get the Guilds talking around a table. They all know it was a bloody shit-stirring faun behind it all. This feuding crap is bad for business.' Huffing, he slapped his palms on the counter again. 'Right. What can I do for you then?'

CHAPTER 25

Nicolas had no idea what Allegard could do for him. He'd completely forgotten why he'd come in here in the first place. The storekeeper pursed his lips in annoyance. Nicolas guessed he wasn't blessed with an overabundance of patience. Finally, he opened his mouth to speak.

'Shut up a minute,' Allegard interrupted, raising his palm, before turning. 'You can put your hands down now, love. You're all right, as long as you don't start any shit. And make a purchase.'

Slowly lowering her raised hands, the woman covered her knives again, picked up the blade she'd previously decided was too pricey, and ran over to the counter to pay for it. With a nervous smile, she put the coins on the counter.

'A fine choice.' Allegard smiled genially. 'A solid blade. That'll do some good killing for you. And because of the trouble, I'll throw in some resharpening, should you ever need it.'

With a nervous noise that could've been a *yes, thanks,* a chuckle, or neither, the woman promptly left the store.

'Right then,' Allegard huffed to Nicolas, gesturing with his hand. 'Out with it. I haven't got all day.'

Steeling himself to talk to this generally angry-looking fellow, Nicolas found the words from his open mouth halted by Allegard's raised palm. Again.

'Shut up a minute,' the storekeeper growled, pointing at Nicolas's chest plate. Specifically, the symbol on it. 'What, pray tell, is *that*?'

Nicolas opened his mouth and waited to be interrupted. When it didn't happen, he began to talk. 'Well, I am Nicolas Percival Carnegie. I'm the new *Dawnblade.*'

Allegard's eyebrows rose slowly and he began to nod. 'Ooooh, I see how it is.' There was a forced sweetness to his voice that was worrying. 'You carve a rising sun on yer armour and go around calling yourself whatever you fancy. Is that how it works? Get some nice clothes and go around pinching the identities of your betters.'

Betters?

'I...uh...I have the sword.'

He jumped as Allegard slapped his palms on the counter once more. 'Are you threatening me?' he growled. 'Because if you are...' The rest of the sentence hung in the air as the storekeeper purposely brought two fingers to his lips and gave a little blow.

Nicolas turned his head slightly as he heard padding. Behind him, the two dogs were approaching. Except they weren't dogs. Each was thickly muscled with patchy tufts of fur. Beneath the fur was thick red skin. Sharp fins adorned their backs, and their eyes were hollow and black. Each growled softly as it approached him. Thankfully, his companions were close, ready to back him up should they attack. Except Auron, who looked frustratingly at ease. Shift gave him a look to suggest that he should be doing a much better job of talking to Allegard.

It's not like I'm not trying. He keeps bloody interrupting me.

Right now, he wasn't sure what combination of words was going to stop the shopkeeper siccing these beasts on him. But he had to find them.

'I think we've—'

Nicolas started as Allegard roared with laughter. A meaty hand reached across the counter and slapped him on the shoulder. 'Your face,' the storekeeper boomed. 'Your damned face. I wish someone was here to paint a portrait of that. I'd hang it behind the counter and every time one of my customers pissed me off, I'd look at it and laugh my ass off.'

Behind Nicolas, more than one of his companions had a raised eyebrow.

Allegard let out a deep breath to calm himself and wiped a single tear from his eye. 'You don't need to go soiling that fancy armour. I know who you are.'

'Ah, brilliant.' Nicolas thanked several Deities personally that his testicles were going to remain out of a dog's mouth, at least for now. 'You do know me then.'

'Not personally,' the storekeeper said, shrugging his broad shoulders. 'But I heard the tales. Pasty, skinny kid going round doing good. Taking up the *Dawnblade* mantle. People say *Nick Carnage*, but I knew that was wrong. Nobody has a daft-soundin' name like that. You know what gossips are like.'

Maybe he isn't so bad after all.

Allegard clapped his hands together. 'Now. I hear that undead bastard Auron is with ya. Is that right?'

Having no idea what was going on, Nicolas simply nodded.

'Ha.' The storekeeper looked to his creatures. 'Go say hello then, ya buggers.'

I am so bloody confused.

The creatures took the stance of regular dogs, charging Auron with their tongues hanging out. As one, they jumped at the spirit, knocking him to the ground and licking at him as Auron play fought with them.

'I missed you boys, too,' he said between laughs, trying to fight the tongues away from his face.

'I do not understand,' Garaz said, frowning intently as he approached.

'I think that is the general feeling,' Silva replied.

'There he is...' Allegard chuckled as his dog creatures bounced on what, to him, would be thin air. 'Got anything to say to your old pal then?'

'Kid, tell him, *so this one time...*' Auron said as he fought his way to his feet. He stopped halfway as both creatures dropped to the floor and presented their bellies. With an indulging smile, he began to rub them.

'He says, *so this one time,*' Nicolas repeated dutifully.

Allegard's face dropped. 'Of course he bloody does. Only good thing about him being dead. I don't have to hear his damned stories anymore.'

'Yet he has so many,' Shift cut in.

Allegard blew a raspberry. 'Doesn't he just. And he'll damned well tell you them.'

'Won't he just,' Silva said, closing her eyes.

'It's the hand gestures as well.' The shopkeeper mimed a series of dramatic hand movements whilst turning his nose up.

'He does like to tell a story with flair,' Garaz agreed.

Scowling, Auron walked to the counter and stared appraisingly at an expensive looking vase sat neatly on it.

'*Finger poke of doom.*'

Allegard's mouth dropped open as the vase smashed to pieces on the floor. Growling, he pointed a finger at the air around where it'd been. 'I know that was you, you asshole. Do you know how much that was worth?'

Auron had already moved and was highly amused at the storekeeper telling off thin air. 'I know that if you ungrateful goblin turds keep this up, none of you will have the benefit of my wisdom.'

Muttering curses under his breath, Allegard turned back to Nicolas. 'Despite what just happened,' he began, casting a glare where he thought Auron stood, 'any friend of Auron's is a friend of mine. So what can I do fer ya? Some muscle-building tonic? A magic comb that styles hair? Maybe a potion of fortitude?'

'All right,' he cut in quickly, before his pride took more of a kicking than it already had. 'Actually, we need somewhere to lie low.'

For the first time, the storekeeper really looked at his companions. 'Ah, you're the ones who roughed up the border guards and fled then.'

'It really wasn't like that...' He wanted to explain it, but that'd end up being a potentially very long tale.

Allegard pursed his lips as something behind them caught his eye. 'Do me a favour,' he said casually. 'Split up and look like you're browsing around the shop.'

It was an odd request, to be sure, but there was a slight tone in his voice suggesting urgency. No sooner had they split up than...

'*Welcome to Allegard's Gallery of Wonders. The* where *for all your* wares.'

Peering over the shelf as casually as he could, ensuring that he still appeared to be engrossed in the book in his hand, he watched three soldiers stride up the main aisle, their armour clicking and clacking as they advanced.

'Mr Allegard,' the leader said in an overly officious voice, 'we are hunting fugitives. Orc spies.'

'Orc spies, you say,' the storekeeper huffed, stroking his beard. 'Bloody typical in these troubled times.'

'Just trust Allegard.' Auron must've picked up on Nicolas's worry, or he was wearing it openly. Quickly, he brought his expression into line.

'Indeed,' the soldier said. 'There are four of them. Two women, an orc, and a boy.'

Nicolas's eyes shot over to Shift. Thankfully, they were just mouthing curse words at being referred to as a woman, rather than shouting them openly. Garaz had managed to vanish somehow, whilst Silva hung around near the door, just in case. Beyond his companion, out the door of the shop, he could see more soldiers on horseback. This had the potential to get messy.

'They assaulted a group of our men and fled,' the soldier continued.

Allegard made a *pfft* noise. 'If they are on the run then they're keeping their heads down. Only an absolute fool would go into the premier store in Ivilar when they are wanted by you. The king of fools in fact. The high emperor of fooldom.'

Okay, no need to hammer it home.

The soldier was obviously in no mood for chit-chat. 'Have you seen anyone unusual around.'

'No,' Allegard answered flatly. 'There are plenty of unusual characters around these days, but no one like you describe.'

Internal sigh of relief.

'And if you...' the soldier began leadingly.

'I will be a good citizen and report them at once.' The storekeeper smiled.

'Excellent.' Without as much as a *thank you* or *ta-ta* the soldier turned on his heel and marched with his comrade out of the shop. Just before he left the store, he stopped and turned back toward the counter. 'There were two men running down the road with bloody...ahem...testicular areas.'

'Shoplifters,' Allegard said causally. 'They're lucky they've got anything left down there.'

The soldier seemed to have no idea how to respond to that. 'Very well then. Good day.' And he left.

'Thank you for shopping with us. Please come again.'

Sigh of relief number two.

'Good book?' Shift asked as they sidled up to him.

Finally able to take his eye off the soldiers, who were already riding away, Nicolas turned the tome he held over in his hand. On the cover was some scared-looking fool surrounded by tentacles, all laid in gold filigree. The blue leather against the gold made it hard to read the title of the book.

Someone should've brought that up with the author when he printed it.

Squinting, he finally managed to make out the writing on the cover

'The Odd Sea,' he read aloud. Quickly, he put the book back on the shelf. 'Not my thing. That one nautical adventure I had was enough for me. I don't need to go reading about them too.'

'Ramirez would be crushed to hear you say that.'

For a second, a fond smile crossed his lips. He would like to see the old sea dog again, just on land this time. Proper land. Not an island.

We have met some interesting people on our travels.

Perhaps there was a side to this adventuring lark he'd never considered before. Though it wasn't really worth the constant near death experiences.

Checking that no one was paying undue attention to them, the group returned to the counter.

'Don't worry, I won't turn you in,' Allegard said with a chuckle. 'The local soldiery have begun to expect a military discount for their part in protecting the kingdom, and by extension, my shop. I disagree. My opinion is that a mooching bastard is a mooching bastard, whether they wear armour or not, so up theirs. Besides, I owe Auron big, and Allegard always repays his debts.'

Turning, the shopkeeper summoned a young boy to mind the counter in his stead, before leading them to the back of the store, the dogs following.

'Quite the character, this fellow,' Garaz whispered.

'You have no idea,' Auron said, rolling his pupilless eyes.

CHAPTER 26

Entering the corridors behind the shop, Allegard led them to what appeared to be an innocuous back room, storing several barrels of who knew what. Moving one of the barrels aside revealed a small trapdoor in the floor. Bending down with a grunt, the storekeeper pulled it open. A set of wooden stairs led into darkness.

'For customers who try to leave without paying.' Allegard smiled at Nicolas's questioning look. 'Let them rot down here for a few weeks and see if they've learnt their lesson.' After a moment of intense eye contact, Allegard let out a laugh. 'Calm down, young man. You're so nervous. I jest.'

Nicolas really didn't care for the storekeeper constantly keeping him on the back foot. Something nudged his hand, and he looked down. One of the dog creatures was putting its head into Nicolas's hand. Tentatively, he scratched it. When he got to the ear, the beast nuzzled in harder with a pleased growl.

That'll be the spot then.

'I'm sorry,' Nicolas asked. 'But what are these?'

'Demon hounds.' Allegard's answer only served to raise more questions. 'Ask the storyteller. I wouldn't want to deprive him.' He gestured vaguely around the room, unsure where Auron stood.

The spirit pursed his lips, clearly trying to work out whether to be flattered or offended. 'So, this one time, old Allegard here was a bodyguard for a very bad man. In all fairness, he was no sweetheart himself. Had a bit of a bad life that led to him doing some very nasty things.' Auron's gaze flicked to Silva. The comparison was not lost on the warrior. 'Said bad man got all hot and bothered when he met this demon-worshipping cult. Thought he could summon a demon and order it around. So, they did this big summoning ritual to bring it forth and bind it—'

'You can bind demons?' Garaz asked.

'Not that I know of,' the spirit answered quickly. 'But it didn't stop him trying. And lo, things went to shit fast. Demonic energy everywhere, and a very annoyed demon tearing apart anyone stupid enough to still be in reaching distance. By the time I got there, Allegard was the only one left alive. So, I did what I do best and sent the demon back where it came from..' Auron smiled at the dogs. 'But it left us these. And they took some bloody taming, I'll tell you. It's nice they can still see me. Must be the demon in them.'

'But you let Allegard live?' Nicolas asked.

'*Well*...I saw in his eyes that he was seriously rethinking his current life, so I decided to help him out.'

'He didn't just let me live,' the storekeeper said solemnly. 'He helped me raise the money to build this place. Really put me back on my feet. Deities know what he saw in me to make him do that. But I'm forever thankful that he did.'

'How many other people have you spared in the past?' Shift said with a mock frown. 'You never tell us those stories.'

The spirit shrugged. 'Because they're boring. Who wants to hear about me *sparing* people?'

That was hardly boring. That story had a demon in it. And...

'Why did you call them *Pixie* and *Dust*?' Nicolas asked, raising a finger.

'Because I'm a funny guy.' Allegard smiled. 'Now. In you go.'

At least Nicolas knew now why he should trust Allegard. Shame Auron hadn't felt the need to volunteer that information before they'd gotten here. For someone who talked about his life in often unpleasant detail, he could be annoyingly vague when he fancied.

Descending the stairs, Nicolas found an entire living area beneath the shop. There were separate rooms surrounded by wood-panelled walls. The irony that he was underground again was not lost on Nicolas. Still, for somewhere so odd, it had an almost homely quality to it. The others seemed equally impressed.

'Deities damn it, I need to lose weight,' Allegard grumbled as he squeezed through the opening. Garaz had managed to sidestep into it, but he didn't have the belly the storekeeper had. Finally, he popped through and joined them. 'There are only two beds, but you're hiding from the authorities. So if you complain, I'll turn you whiny little shits in.' Allegard boomed with laughter. 'I'll get the boy to bring some food down. Is there anything else you need?'

'What do you know of Tobias Helstrum?' Silva asked.

Allegard's face dropped faster than the temperature when winter came. 'I know my sales of weapons go up every time he releases a new pamphlet.

'So he's good for business then?'

'War and hate are never good for business,' the shopkeeper fired back. 'Not in the long run. Odious little man has got everyone on edge, and there is enough of that around without him vomiting his nonsense to any fool who will listen. The Nine Kingdoms of Man has its problems, but people seem to forget that it's *always* had problems. That stuff isn't new. Kicking the shit out of a family of kascats doesn't make the economy better. Driving out some hardworking Serian folk doesn't suddenly make the crop yield larger. You mark my words,' Allegard solemnly looked back towards the surface, 'we're heading for some really bad times, and that's what men like him want. They thrive on it.'

'I don't suppose you have a location for him?' Shift ventured.

The storekeeper narrowed his eyes in thought. 'I have several,' Allegard huffed. 'Now winter has broken, he's back on the road, touring towns and villages so he can fill people's ears with dung. I think I have some leaflets upstairs. One of those robed morons brought a load in for me to hand out just yesterday. I used them to line Pixie and Dust's cage. If I can find one that hasn't been crapped or pissed on, I'll send it down with the food.'

Please find an unsoiled one. Please find an unsoiled one.

'How long do you think we should stay here?' he asked Allegard.

'At least a couple of days,' the storekeeper said thoughtfully. 'Enough for the local patrols to think you've moved on. But I'll keep my eyes and ears open.' Narrowing his eyes with a smile, Allegard pointed at the group. 'And no spying whilst you're here.'

'We will try to contain our need for espionage,' Garaz replied dryly.

'That's the spirit.'

The orc seemed genuinely shocked when Allegard slapped him on the back with a laugh.

With that, the shopkeeper left them to settle into their new home. Nicolas put his pack on the floor...and that was pretty much all he could do.

'This is cosy,' Auron remarked, looking around.

'At least you can go outside,' Nicolas lamented. 'And there are only two beds.'

'That's okay,' Shift said with a slight tilt of their head and a naughty gleam in their eye. 'We're used to shar—'

'No,' Silva said firmly, appearing from the bedroom after looking it over. 'The beds are nearly next to each other. You two are not sharing.'

'But we wouldn't,' Nicolas protested. 'Not with you guys sleeping so close...'

'I'm not giving you the chance,' the warrior replied. 'Shift will share with me, Nicolas with Garaz.'

Shift narrowed their eyes. 'But you don't look like a good cuddler.'

'I am not,' Silva answered firmly.

Nicolas looked at Garaz. *That* snoring...right by his head. The orc gave him a sympathetic smile.

That's me not sleeping for a few days.

Then, of course, there was the size of the bed versus the size of the orc. He eyed the wooden floor. Putting some furs on it and sleeping there might be a better option.

CHAPTER 27

S creaming made his eyes flash open. In a second of drowsiness, he almost rolled to the wrong side, bumping into Garaz. Correcting himself quickly, he reached for his sword, which was wedged in the very small gap between the two beds. It was half drawn by the time he noticed Silva pressing herself to the far wall, looking terrified as she panted heavily.

Oh.

Slowly, he sheathed his blade. When he looked at Silva's bed, he started and almost drew it again. There was a giant snake in it. The creature flicked its tongue out playfully, half covered by the sheets. Part of Nicolas wanted to laugh, but he'd been on the receiving end of this often enough to understand the warrior's pain.

Nicolas turned and frowned at the thunderous snore in his ear. How was Garaz sleeping through this?

Beside him, the snake changed form to a familiar humanoid one. Shift propped themselves up on their elbow as they looked at Silva. The change had raised the bedsheets slightly, and Nicolas became very distracted by Shift's exposed ass pointing in his direction. For a moment a dreamy smile crossed Nicolas's face.

At the wall, fearful eyes turned to furious ones.

'Something amiss, darling?' Shift asked with poorly faked innocence.

'Youuuuuuuu.' Silva stalked around the bed, picking up their pillow and brandishing it like a war hammer.

Silva lunged at Shift, sitting astride them and unleashing a mighty barrage with the pillow. Shift laughed at their own nonsense as they held their arms up to defend themselves from the onslaught. Nicolas's dreamy smile returned. This time it took a little more shaking off.

I suppose I should break this up. She doesn't look like she's going to stop. And I imagine it takes a good while to beat someone to death with a pillow.

'Silva, if you could just—'

'Stay out of it.'

He was stunned into silence as the pillow struck him across the jaw. Incredulously, he rubbed it for a moment as Silva's attention returned to Shift. It took him a moment to decide it'd actually happened. But when he did...

Cheeky cow.

Before he knew what he was doing, he'd launched his own pillow. Silva froze mid-swing as the pillow Nicolas threw hit her in the side of the head. The warrior's head turned slowly toward him, eyes wide.

Oh shit.

'What did you just do?' Silva asked threateningly. The fact that she wasn't looking at him directly somehow made it worse.

Deciding to take responsibility for his actions, he gave himself a little shake and pushed out his chest. 'I think you know exactly what I—'

From the force behind the blow, it seemed Silva had thrown her pillow with the purpose of taking his head off his shoulders. Scooping up the pillow indignantly, Nicolas brandished it and charged at Silva.

'Well, this is all very kinky,' Auron remarked from the doorway with a bemused expression.

He managed to get two blows in before Silva clocked him with a pillow-based uppercut. Turning and stumbling backwards, he caught his legs on the side of his bed and fell back onto it.

A bleary yellow eye opened and regarded him with displeasure. 'Please explain why you are draped over me,' Garaz grunted, licking his lips and wincing slightly at the taste of his own morning breath.

'The children were having a pillow fight, and it got out of hand,' Auron said from the corner of the room.

'I was awoken by a giant snake,' Silva growled as Shift pulled the sheet tactically over themselves.

'Calm down,' Auron replied, smirking. 'I doubt it's the first time.'

The spirit blinked twice as the pillow passed through him and hit the wall. 'That was uncalled for,' he said in a haughty tone.

'I do not know why I have tethered myself to such frustrating people,' Silva huffed.

'Because no one else would have you,' the spirit ventured.

'Because you love us.' Shift grinned.

'Because we're the penance you have to go through for your redemption?' Nicolas suggested.

'Because, like me, you never wish to have a good night's sleep again,' Garaz muttered angrily.

'Please,' Nicolas scoffed. 'Your snoring tells me you slept fine. Unlike the one with it in his ear.'

A loaded silence followed. No one was sure if this was camaraderie anymore or the beginnings of a full-blown argument. As grateful as they were to Allegard, they'd been in this pokey basement together for three days now, and it was starting to wear thin. They'd lived together for months in Golthorak, but not in such close proximity. Each day it seemed like the place was a little smaller.

The worst bit is Auron having a captive audience.

The stories were relentless, to the point Nicolas was starting to suspect that the spirit was making half this stuff up. Surely no one could've had such an eventful life? Actually, his life had been pretty damned eventful since leaving Hablock. Either way, Auron seemed bent on keeping them entertained, whether they wanted it or not.

The door on the stairs creaked open, and Nicolas's hand was on his sword within a second. He released his grip on the hilt as soon as he heard a familiar padding on the stairs. Pixie and Dust ran to them, jumping on the bed with excitement. Pixie enthusiastically nuzzled into Shift's side as Dust bounded up to Nicolas, pinning him to the bed and licking his cheek with enthusiasm. When they weren't biting people's testicles off, these creatures were big softies.

How can something so horrific also look so damned cute?

'Wakey, wakey,' Allegard boomed as he walked down the stairs. 'Your lowly servant is here with a meal for his guests who don't pay rent.'

This was the same joke he made every morning. Granted, they'd only been here for three days, but it was starting to feel a lot longer. Finally wrestling the demon hound off him—which was quite difficult, because Dust decided it was a game—he got up and walked into the main room of their hideout.

'Look at you all, wide awake and fresh-faced for a new day.' Allegard chuckled as he put down a tray. 'You can tell Auron I didn't bother plating him up a portion. Decent food is wasted on the dead.'

'And you tell him he should be thankful. It means more food for fat bastards like his good self,' the spirit retorted instantly.

Nicolas repeated Auron's words, and Allegard belly-laughed. 'Even in death he still has his quick wit.' Stepping back, the storekeeper gestured to the tray. 'Now, my fine fugitives, eat up. I bring glad tidings with your breakfast.'

Nicolas was already sat at the table and bringing a piece of bread to his open mouth when he stopped. 'Glad tidings?'

Leaning heavily against the wall, Allegard watched the others enter—save Shift, who was still putting some clothes on. 'They appear to have called off the search.'

That is *good news.*

It had been relentless. Allegard had been questioned six times in the last three days, turning them away each time, keeping true to his promise to keep them safe. Their pursuers had showm no sign of giving up...only to suddenly stop.

'Those are glad tidings indeed,' Garaz said thoughtfully. 'What has changed?'

'Your lot,' the storekeeper replied, pointing to Garaz. 'A raiding party crossed the border. Big one. Seems they're a bit riled up about a human army stomping into their lands. Took it as a challenge.' The storekeeper rolled his eyes. 'Somehow, they made it past the imposing border fortifications, and they've been roughing up some local villages. All available troops are being gathered to go and send them to wherever orcs end up after they die.'

Shit.

Should they go and help?

Granted, turning up to aid the people bent on arresting them would likely be a disaster. And he couldn't ignore the fact that this was their chance to go and get Helstrum, the bigger threat.

Still...it doesn't sit right.

'Greater good, kid,' Auron said, reading his expression. 'Let the army handle the orcs. We handle Helstrum.'

'How long do you think before we can leave?' There was still anger in Silva's tone. Unsurprising, given her rude awakening.

Allegard shrugged. 'I'd give it a few hours to make sure no stragglers come by, but other than that, you should be good to go.' Allegard pulled something from his belt and handed it to Garaz. 'And it appears luck doubly favours you today.'

The orc unfurled the parchment. 'There is a Custodians of Humanity rally today. Tobias Helstrum will be speaking to his followers. And it is nearby.'

Wow. That is fortunate.

Silva looked over the orc's shoulder. 'I know this place. It's beside an abandoned fortress.'

Sounds like a delightful place to go commit murder.

Nicolas chided himself. It wasn't murder...really. They were just killing him...assassinating him. Closing his eyes, Nicolas ate his bread. Wrestling with the terminology and moral ambiguity wasn't getting any easier. But he had to admit, this was a golden opportunity. They couldn't waste it.

'Garaz will have to stay,' Auron said from nowhere.

The orc gave him a quizzical look.

'We can hardly turn up to one of his rallies with an orc in tow,' the spirit explained. 'And with orcs raiding hereabouts, I don't think the locals will think twice about lynching you on sight. Unless you have some sort of shape-changing ability you have neglected to mention...'

The orc sighed. Auron wasn't wrong. There was only so many times pulling his hood over his head was going to work. 'I do not care for the idea of you doing this without me,' Garaz said thoughtfully, 'but I cannot deny your logic.'

'I don't care for doing it without you either,' Nicolas said hesitantly. Having to leave behind one of the most powerful of their team, and their healer, wasn't something he relished. 'But if it helps our chances of success...'

'We could always appear at the gate with Garaz in chains and use it to ingratiate ourselves with the Custodians.' After being subject to their withering glares, Silva said no more on that matter.

'It appears all your efforts to convince me to come with you have led to me being left in a basement.' The orc didn't seem upset. He knew the logic of the situation as much as the others, and Nicolas very much doubted Garaz fancied being surrounded by hundreds of Helstrum's followers.

Shift entered the room and put their hands on his shoulders. 'Don't worry, we have a shapeshifter, a ghost, and two mighty warriors. We can do this,' they whispered, before kissing him on the cheek.

Two *mighty warriors? Who's the oth— Oh.*

He reddened. He wasn't mighty, yet, but he appreciated the compliment.

'You know this room is small enough that I heard you call me a *ghost*, even though you whispered it,' Auron remarked tartly. 'I'll remind you *again*. Ghosts float around haunting things. I am a spirit. A useful undead entity and companion. Do you see any chains here? Do you hear any rattling of said chains?'

'I hear a bit of prattling.' Shift smirked.

Auron scowled at the shapeshifter.

I can't wait to be out of this room.

'We will need disguises for the road,' Silva said. Thankfully, someone was thinking of logistical matters. 'We can hardly appear as we are. I am sure the enemy will be on the lookout for us.'

Allegard waved his hand dismissively. 'Don't worry about that,' he scoffed. 'I am the *where* for all your *wares*, remember? Old Allegard will kit you out so your own mothers won't even recognise you.'

CHAPTER 28

Irritably, he scratched his neck again. Fidgeting his shoulders, Nicolas tried to move the heavy hessian material he wore to a better position—though he had yet to find any that didn't cause him to itch somewhere. Allegard had insisted that the simple outfits he'd fashioned for them weren't old sacks he'd cut up, but that was troll-shit. The store-keeper hadn't even attempted to hide his smirk.

And all the clothes he stocks that he could actually have lent us. The tight bugger.

It wasn't even much of a disguise. A cut-up sack. He'd voiced his concerns to his tailor.

'Nonsense,' Allegard had bellowed, looking him up and down. 'You look like the salt of the Deities-damned earth. Proper peasant folk.'

Now, walking down the road with Shift, Silva, and Auron, he had to admit that they did look like *proper peasant folk*. Well, Nicolas and Silva did.

Shift had balked openly at the idea of wearing the sack, especially one that stank of potatoes. So to travel inconspicuously, they'd turned themselves into a dog. The side benefit of that was that he hadn't been teased in a while. It did mean, however, that he had more to carry as he was responsible for their spare attire, which was slung in a bag over his back.

'Can you stop walking like that?' Silva asked from inside her own potato-sack disguise, her neck red where she'd been scratching it.

Nicolas frowned. 'Like what?'

'You're limping,' the warrior hissed back. 'And I know your leg is fine, so you're doing it on purpose.'

'Oh,' he said quietly, glancing down at his leg. It had healed nicely, though there was still stiffness in the morning and after long walks. 'I thought it'd make us look more...I don't know, peasant-like. People would ignore us because they don't want to hear about how I hurt my leg. I don't know.'

'The way you're doing it will draw more attention to us,' Silva replied. 'You are making it extremely noticeable.'

'Sorry,' he said sheepishly. 'I didn't realise.'

Shaking his leg, which had ironically started to ache from the forced limp, he began to walk normally. Suddenly, he felt Auron's gaze on him.

'You came up with a story to go with your limp, didn't you?' the spirit asked coyly.

'No.'

Auron let out a single chuckle. 'Yes, you did.'

So what? Taking an arrow to the knee escaping raiders would earn me more sympathetic.

Not that he was about to admit that to a certain spirit.

'*Woof.*' Shift's bark made Nicolas glance down at the shapeshifter. For a moment he shuddered, remembering his brief time as a dog courtesy of The Visitor.

I'll take it the bark is agreeing with Auron. Nicolas frowned. *This is the second adventure in a row where one of us ends up a dog. I hope it isn't a pattern.*

'You won't break into any acting companies with that level of theatrics,' Auron added.

'Is your leg well, friend? I saw you limping just now.'

Nicolas turned and made a big show of shaking the limping leg out. 'Yes, I am well, thank you. Just an old injury. Plays up every now and then. Especially on long journeys like this one.'

I hope my theatrics are better than Auron claims.

'Ah,' the man at the crossing ahead of them said with a nod. 'I can sympathise with that myself.' He gave a burdened smile. The man was middle aged and wore the white robe of a pilgrim, his possessions in a bag around his shoulder. Judging by the slight twang in his accent and his stoic bearing, Nicolas guessed he was from the kingdom of Hoflar. There was a sadness in his eyes, the sort that was embedded and would probably never leave. It most likely had something to do with the ghost of the woman by his side, who Nicolas was trying not to notice. Auron and the female ghost nodded a greeting to each other.

'I don't suppose you're on your way to the Helstrum rally?' Silva said, eyeing the man's robes.

'That I am,' the man answered. 'Yourselves?'

'Aye.' Auron gave Nicolas a double take. It must've been his attempt at a southern accent. ''ave heard a lot of people say his message is powerful. Thought we'd make t' journey and see for ourselves.'

Beside him, Shift let out a derisive snort.

The man nodded solemnly. 'In times like these, it's comforting to find a man who has answers.' *Even terrible ones.* 'I'm an Initiate member of the Custodians. Only joined a couple of months ago. Never had the chance to see Helstrum, but after the incident, all he said made a lot of sense. Now I get to see him in the flesh and see if he's the man they say.'

'*Initiate?*' Auron repeated. 'I didn't know they had levels of membership. So he's a scumbag *and* he's pretentious.'

'The *incident?*' Silva prompted.

'Tell them then,' the female ghost said with a huff. 'Tell them why you're wandering around in a fancy cloak instead of raising the young 'uns like you should. Just...' Her white eyes widened as she caught Nicolas looking at her.

Quickly, he averted his gaze.

With a sigh, the man strolled to the nearest tree and sat down. He was a big man, with thickly muscled arms, and lowering his impressive bulk took time and effort. Nicolas and Silva joined him. Apparently, they were doing this in a proper '*story time*' format. Shift sniffed random things. Nicolas knew Silva well enough to tell that she found this interruption annoying. But being rude to someone going to the same place as them might end up spectacularly biting them on the ass, so she played along.

'It was a couple of months back now,' the traveller began. 'I was a miner. Worked on the crew of a small silver mine. Nothing fancy, just enough to keep our collective in food and furs. Then we dug too deep. Cracked open into a new tunnel, but it wasn't ours. Full of damned rat-men. Filthy creatures swarmed the mine. We fled, of course. A couple of us didn't make it, but we managed to blockade the entrance before they spilled out towards the village.' He shook his head sadly. 'I breathed a sigh of relief, praising the Deities we were safe. How stupid I was.' Suddenly, his eyes looked lost. 'I look up, and there are my children... The look on their faces... I just knew. It...it turns out my wife had entered the mine to bring me the lunch I'd forgotten that day.' With each word, the man's voice became more choked.

Nicolas moved closer and put a reassuring hand on his shoulder. Silva was unlikely to do it. Judging by the near flinch, no one had touched the man in a while.

'I charged at the entrance, started throwing rocks aside, but the others, they held me back. They were right to do it. After I'd calmed, I petitioned the local militia and Hall of Guardians to come and clear the mine so I could find her body. But apparently it was happening all over and,' his hands closed into fists, 'bigger mines took priority.'

'And instead of looking after your children, like a man, you decide to run around Etherius following the banner of any malcontent who pours honey in your big daft ear.'

Nicolas had to agree with the ghostly woman. If something like that had happened to him, he'd be sure to keep those most precious to him close. He also got an inkling about what unfinished business was keeping her tethered to Etherius.

'I knew I couldn't let it go,' the man continued. 'I couldn't let other people suffer as I have. Couldn't just wait for my children to be taken. So I joined the Custodians. Apparently, they're raising an army, and if Helstrum's the man they say he is, I'll be first in the queue.'

Nicolas shared uneasy glances with his companions, even the one who was currently a dog.

'I'm hoping he has answers for me too.' *Not exactly a lie. I want to know where my people are.* 'I've been attacked by fauns more than once. And my whole village was abducted.' *I'll just leave out the bit where Helstrum ordered it.*

The traveller's jaw set in a scowl. 'Little bastards,' he spat. 'Nowhere is safe anymore.'

'Which is why you ought to be minding *our children*,' the ghostly woman snapped in his ear.

'It only helps if he can hear you,' Auron told the woman.

'It helps me.' She sighed. 'Shouting at this stubborn ass of a man is all I have left.'

The traveller held out his hand to Nicolas. 'Piotr,' he said with a strained smile.

'Tallith,' Nicolas replied, shaking the hand as he said the first name that came to mind. Grief stabbed him in the gut.

'Well met.' Piotr's smile was a little warmer now. Reaching down, he began to smooth Shift, who was not opposed to it. 'Listen, these roads aren't exactly safe. The army has been charging around hunting fugitives. Mayhap we can travel together, seeing as we are all going to the rally?'

'Of course.' That was the exact opposite of something he'd guess Silva would suggest, but the warrior had said it. 'I'm Sasha.'

Maybe she thinks we'll look more legitimate travelling with another pilgrim?

It sounded dangerous to him, but at the same time, they could hardly ditch the man when he was going the same way. Hopefully, the rally wasn't far, because he wasn't sure he could remember to use the false name he'd given Piotr for long. But they were fixed on that course now, so he'd just have to try his darndest.

'A pleasure,' Piotr said, inclining his head. 'And what is this one's name?' he asked, scratching Shift under the chin.

'Ruffles.'

Silva's eyes widened slightly, but she caught herself. Auron didn't need to, so he openly stared at Nicolas in disbelief. Shift was also clearly displeased with their new name.

'An odd name for a dog, to be sure.' Piotr chuckled. 'But who am I to judge?'

'The villager we bought her from had already named her, so we were stuck with it,' he said quickly.

Quietly, he was pleased to think on his feet so well.

CHAPTER 29

For twenty minutes, the group shared some food and made general small talk. Then Piotr rose, stretching his arms wide before shouldering his pack again. 'The road awaits,' the traveller added as he turned in the direction they were going.

'The road to stupidity,' the woman huffed. 'The children are back the other way.'

Nicolas and Silva stood and grabbed their own belongings. Together, they followed Piotr down the track.

'Have you all travelled a long way?' their new companion asked.

'Yarringsburg.' *And it's certainly been a long journey since then.*

'Oh, I thought I heard a southern twang in your accent when we first met.'

Silva sighed slightly.

The pilgrim spoke again, his brow furrowed. 'You're coming from a strange direction to have set out from Yarringsburg.'

Oh shit.

'We had to visit Allegard's Gallery of Wonders first,' he answered quickly. 'I've heard so much about it.'

This thinking on my feet is getting bloody hard.

The pilgrim wrinkled his nose. 'Oh, I've heard that Allegard is a very...temperamental soul.'

'Accounts were underexaggerated,' Silva interjected.

'And his prices are overexaggerated.' Nicolas chuckled.

Piotr chuckled. 'Well, I hope you bought your beloved something nice anyway.'

It took Nicolas a second to understand what he meant. 'Oh, of course.' He smiled, taking Silva's arm. *Deities, her bicep is impressive when it's tensed.* 'Well, I planned to, but...'

'Say no more, friend.' The pilgrim smiled. 'I can tell you aren't affluent folk. That's good. It's important people like us support Helstrum as much as all those lords and ladies.'

He must be referring to the sacks.

'We don't have much, but we have each other.' Leaning in, he kissed Silva on the cheek.

The warrior turned and offered him a warm smile, though her eyes fully imparted how annoyed she was with him. A dog quietly growled to his left.

'And that's all you really need,' Piotr remarked. 'You're lucky to have a woman like that.'

'I know.' He nodded. 'Since we crossed paths on a bridge, we've been inseparable. When you're destined to be together, you just know it.' Fully immersed in the character and story he was creating for himself, he slapped Silva on the ass.

Oh, no.

'What can I say?,' Silva smiled. 'He isn't my usual type, but he just has a sweetness I find adorable.' She wrapped her arm around Nicolas and pulled him close, feigning nuzzling his cheek whilst she whispered in his ear, 'You *ever* slap me on the ass again, I'll kill you.'

Nicolas kept a smile on his face, hoping his eyes didn't betray his fear.

'Sweet men in this age are hard to come by.' Piotr smiled. 'Like a troll with table manners.'

Something bumped into his leg. Nervously, knowing what to expect, he glanced down. Ruffles had a surprisingly expressive face. Checking that Piotr wasn't watching, he mouthed, *Sorry.* If they were going to travel together, Nicolas knew he'd be watching Piotr nearly obsessively for some tell that he'd seen through their story. The man was nice, but Nicolas wasn't exactly an expert at disguise and deception.

'So how come you're following this lot about?' the ghost of the traveller's wife asked Auron.

'The kid there was the one who found my body,' the spirit replied. 'I've been hanging around him ever since.'

'That must've been a shock for him.'

Auron chuckled. 'You have no idea. He passed out twice. Then I had to watch him try to get my body up on a funeral pyre. It was painful.'

'Yeah, him and muscle don't appear to be well acquainted.'

Hey.

'Name's Vanya, by the way,' the ghost added.

'Auron of Tellmark.'

'Oh,' Vanya's eyes widened slightly. 'I didn't realise I was travelling in such fine company. I know he found your body, but why's a fancy hero following around pil— Ah, they aren't really pilgrims, are they?'

'No.' Auron chuckled. 'We're on our way to kill Helstrum.'

Why are you telling her that? Nicolas wanted to shout at Auron to shut up, but Piotr might have questions if he started screaming at thin air.

'Good,' the ghost huffed. 'Hateful little man preying on the grief of others. If I had my choice, I'd give him a frying pan around the head. People like that don't make things better, only worse. But Piotr's got a mind that the best way to protect the children is to leave them with my grandparents and go sign up to some ridiculous cult.'

I need to do something about that.

'We're pretty sure he's behind all the bad stuff that's been happening anyway,' the spirit continued.

'Makes sense.' Vanya nodded. 'What better way to get dumb sacks of rock like my husband to listen to you than by stirring up trouble? Make sure you give him one for me. And if one of your companions could try to talk some sense into my thick bastard of a husband, I'd appreciate it.' That last sentence was directed at Nicolas, and he knew it.

Though discouraging Piotr might give the game away, what he was doing just didn't sit right with Nicolas.

'Tell me about your children,' he asked their travelling companion.

After a moment of hesitancy, Piotr smiled. 'Rolf and Anya. My little dumplings. Great children, full of energy. Rolf has the makings of a good miner someday.'

'Who did you say you left them with, when you left?'

'My wife's grandparents. They protested, but they never liked me anyway. Not good enough for their granddaughter.' Pitor shook his head. 'Deities', if I heard that once I heard it a thousand times.'

'That never mattered to me.' Vanya sniffed.

'I suppose I get where they're coming from.'

Piotr came to an abrupt halt and turned to Nicolas with a questioning look.

'What I mean is,' he continued quickly, 'I'd find it a little strange if someone left their children after such a tragedy.'

The traveller looked down the road in the direction they were headed then back at him. Nicolas got the impression Piotr could get defensive at any moment. 'I am making this journey to protect them,' he said firmly.

'Oh,' Nicolas replied. 'I just thought...'

'What?' Piotr asked with narrowed eyes.

Silva's eyes fiercely questioned what he thought he was doing.

Nicolas shrugged. 'I just thought the best way to protect them would be to be with them, that's all.'

Piotr's face darkened. 'If I can help purge the filth from Etherius, then I'm helping to protect—'

'I was really upset when my parents were taken from me,' he cut in quickly. 'Devastated. It felt like my whole world fell into a big dark hole. Those two people who raised me, were with me every day, suddenly gone.'

'They lost Vanya. They haven't lost me,' Piotr snapped.

Theatrically, he looked around Piotr. 'They aren't here, and you aren't there,' he said softly. 'Their mother is dead, and their father marches off to war. How long did you give them before you left? Did they have time to properly grieve with you?'

'No, they didn't,' Vanya growled.

Piotr's face gave the answer away.

'For all they know, you could already be dead on some battlefield,' Nicolas pressed. 'Or on some backwoods road. If it were me, I'd be worried sick. All I want is for my parents to be back and to have some semblance of family again. I'm always stronger when I'm with my family.' Now he meant Shift, Auron, and the others, as much as his parents. 'I just...I get why you thought leaving was the right thing. But maybe you're actually hurting them even more?'

Piotr's mouth opened and closed a few times. 'I... I... You... *Shit*.' Realisation dawned on his face as if it'd punched him wearing metal knuckles. 'But I couldn't protect Vanya. She... I couldn't save her...'

'And you're saving them, being here?'

The traveller's head turned in all directions. 'But she is gone.'

'That she is,' Nicolas said with sympathy, before pointing down the trail they followed. 'Going that way won't bring her back. Go the other way and be with your children. Grieve with them. Protect them by being in their lives and bringing them up right.'

Piotr's eyes became unfocused. He stumbled backwards a couple of steps. 'I need to go home,' he said hoarsely when he finally looked up. 'I think I have been a fool. Will...will they forgive me?'

'They'll be too happy to see you return to hold any grudge,' Nicolas said with a sympathetic smile.

Piotr rubbed his eyes then dropped his pack and embraced Nicolas. When he broke it, he held Nicolas by the shoulders. 'I think my grief clouded my eyes so much that I couldn't see what was important. Thank you, Tallith.'

Who? Oh, yes.

Nicolas put his hands over Piotr's. 'Go be with your children.'

The traveller marched back down the road with purpose. As he did, Vanya followed, taking a second to bid Nicolas an emotional thank you before she left.

124

'Once he gets home, his soul will be at peace. Hers too,' Auron said with a smile. 'That was a good thing you did, kid.'

'It would've been much easier to infiltrate the rally with a member of the Custodians in tow,' Silva noted.

He didn't take his eyes off Piotr walking away. 'It was the right thing to do.'

As Piotr disappeared into the distance, there was a warmth in him. Somehow, he knew, no matter what, that Piotr would make it home.

At least Helstrum will have one less minion. It's a shame I can't convince the rest of them to bugger off home too.

CHAPTER 30

I t took another half a day's walk before the location of the rally was in sight. And it appeared the abandoned fortress was, in fact, very occupied. A stone blot on an otherwise open landscape, the fortress was tall and formidable. Its outer wall housed a large courtyard with numerous buildings, and a shanty town of tents had been erected before it. Several lines of people converged from various trails to fill the road leading towards it. It was hard to make out details at this distance, but there were numerous white robes amongst the travellers. He couldn't help but make the comparison to a line of ants marching towards food.

Except there's nothing nourishing here, just some ideas likely to give you the worst shits of your life.

Yet the people weren't headed to the fortress *exactly*. Beside its right-hand outer wall, a large field had been fenced off, and a stage erected. It seemed Tobias Helstrum was taking no chances with his security. There were watchtowers at regular intervals along the fence—which he assumed were manned by archers—and what looked to be a small army patrolled the grounds and the crowd.

Nicolas's eyes wandered from the towers back to the line of people making their way to the gate. It was a herd of Piotrs—misguided souls who'd seen Helstrum's message as some kind of revelation of hope. He knew he couldn't talk them down one by one.

When we do eventually finish this, his message will fade too.

Except it didn't seem like it'd be as simple as that. The organisation and manpower on display here was impressive and scary in equal measure. With Helstrum dead, would his men just throw down their stupid masks and wander off home? What seemed more probable was someone else stepping up to take his place.

We'll kill that guy when we come to him. But best focus on one assassination at a time.

'Just keep calm and act like you want to be there,' Auron counselled. 'You'll have no problem blending in. There are all sorts in that procession.'

'Leaving Garaz behind was a wise move.' Nicolas wasn't sure whether Silva was just stating a fact, trying to comfort him, or trying to comfort herself. Maybe all three. Either way, he would've rather had the orc on hand in case the men in those watchtowers got itchy bow string fingers.

Approaching the road, he fought the urge to try and fake a limp again. It wasn't going to do anything extra to help him blend into the crowd. All he had to do was walk in silent reverence like the rest. They were treating this as if it were some kind of religious experience. And if Nicolas knew anything, it was that Tobias Helstrum was pretty far from being a Deity.

As the gate came into clear view, he saw gangs of guards around it, watching attentively as people passed through. Each had a sword on one side of their belt and a heavy club on the other. All of them wore the masks he associated with the Maestro's men.

He isn't even trying to hide it anymore.

Anger welled up in him at the sheer arrogance. Here they were, sneaking around, wanted men, and Tobias Helstrum was just strutting wherever he fancied, wafting his evilness in people's faces. If Helstrum had been in front of him in that exact moment, he would've had no trouble killing the man. How could such evil stand there, plain as day, pretending to help people? It was disgusting. He had half a mind to start shouting at the crowd until they came to their senses. But that would only get him a meeting with those clubs...or the swords.

The vigilance of the men by the gate was matched by those in the watchtowers. Nicolas started as he realised that the men weren't armed with bows as he'd assumed, but with fire-sticks. There was a sudden phantom pain in his leg as he focused on one of the weapons.

Someone grabbed his collar and yanked him out of the crowd, and Nicolas fought his instinct to defend himself and make the owner of the grabbing hand pay for it. Instead, he went with the force of the pull, feigning a stagger. No one else batted an eyelid as they continued onwards.

'Nice sack,' the guard said in a very uncomplimentary manner. He didn't need to see the sneer behind the mask; he could sense it. 'Let's see who we 'ave 'ere then.'

Discreetly, he gestured for Silva to stay put, knowing the warrior would be ready to defend him should the need arise. Fortunately, they hadn't brought any armour or weapons with them. Well, that wasn't strictly true. He had his boot knife. And he was sure Silva was somehow armed to the teeth. Strip the woman down to her skeleton and she'd still be able to produce a hidden battleaxe from behind a rib. Still, the sack disguises would've been pointless if they fell off to reveal fully armoured torsos. The idea was to get in first then improvise.

I doubt there's any shortage of weapons to grab here.

Pulling open his hessian cloak roughly, the guard patted him down. Nicolas kept his gaze low and humble. Though having the man feel him all over and just allowing it to happen was a weird sensation.

Then, a hand grabbed him roughly by the chin and pulled his head up. 'Don't I know you?' Behind the mask, the guard's eyes narrowed as he tried to put a name to his face.

'No, sir,' he answered quickly, keeping his voice weak sounding.

Slowly, the masked head shook. 'No. I'm sure I know you. I just can't think wh...at in the Underworld?'

The guard began to hop on the spot, shaking his leg furiously to try to get at least some of the piss off it. Finally dropping his foot, he clenched his fists and glared at the dog that had ruined his boot.

'You dirty little shit,' he growled angrily as he drew his club, but the dog was already making its escape. Whilst his comrades weren't openly laughing, their masks were shaking slightly.

Nicolas took the opportunity to slip back into the crowd. Thankfully, he'd been forgotten in the chaos.

Thanks, Shift.

The closer they got to the gate, the more the crowd was funnelled, until it had closed in on Nicolas. On the one hand, it was good because he could hide in it. But on the other, it was getting difficult to breathe. Guards ensured everyone stayed on the path with judicious prods from their batons. Though it wasn't much of a problem. Everyone wanted to be here. Even Nicolas, after a fashion.

After passing through the arch, the crowd began to break apart. As those pressing against him moved away, Nicolas practically felt like he'd been born again. Frowning, he looked at Auron, who'd been walking beside him all this time.

'How did you walk through those people and not possess any of them?' he whispered from the side of his mouth.

The spirit shrugged. 'I assume it's an intention thing. I have to want to possess them? Who knows.'

Silva took his hand and led him away from the main gate. They were surrounded. There were people everywhere. Many were sat on the grass or walking around trying to find their spot. A few had even thought to bring picnic baskets and chairs, as if they were attending some bard's poetry reading. Guards moved amongst the crowds, keeping order. The sight of so many of those masks made Nicolas shudder.

A little grunt of pain escaped him as Silva squeezed his hand, but he kept his face neutral despite the vice-like grip on his hand, suggesting that she was still a little annoyed with him.

I swear by each individual Deity that I will never smack her on the ass again. Just please don't let her cripple my hand.

Though really he was happy to be holding Silva's hand. With people everywhere, the large open space seemed more confined than the basement they'd lived in for the past few days, and it would be very easy for them to become separated.

Voices rose above the murmuring of the throng. At regular intervals, crimson-robed preachers manned smaller podiums to 'warm-up' the crowd for the main event. Their necks were taut and veins protruded on their temples as they rabidly spouted their nonsense, shaking their fists in the air as if they were surrounded by annoying flies. Elsewhere, people were dancing to music played by fellows in their makeshift groups—at least that was what he guessed they were doing. Cloaked men and women gyrated with closed eyes and blissful expressions. The most disturbing thing was the number of children present. One woman, thoroughly engrossed in a preacher's jabbering, was actually feeding a baby at the breast.

'This is all very culty, isn't it?'

Nicolas nearly cried out. Shift stood beside him, wearing a white robe.

'Weren't you a dog just now?' he whispered.

'Yes, and now I'm not.' They shrugged. 'Do I need to school you on the concept of *shapeshifting*?'

'No,' he hissed. 'But you're...clothed.'

Shift looked down at their robes. 'Oh. Well, some of the gyrating ladies over there decided that clothes restricted their movement too much, so I just ensured their garb was used by someone who'd appreciate it. Me.'

Nicolas looked in the direction Shift indicated then very quickly looked away again.

'It's all very disturbing,' Auron noted, shaking his head in disgust no matter which way he looked. 'It'll only get worse in a minute. It was definitely wise not to bring Garaz. He'd be wrapped in his cloak so tightly to keep this filth out that he'd die of suffocation.'

'Medallion?'

A bright young man stood behind him holding a tray with what looked suspiciously like trinkets on it. There were a few medallions with the symbol of the Custodians of Humanity and a few crudely carved statues of Tobias Helstrum.

'No, thank you,' he said politely.

'Okay, sir.' The young man went to leave but stopped abruptly. 'Death to the inhuman menace.' He smiled as if he'd said, *'Have the loveliest day.'*

'Ah, yeah. Okay.'

He was about to remark how insane this place was when the nature of the crowd changed. Suddenly, the preachers were silent, and the rather improper dancing ceased abruptly. All eyes now looked towards the stage as the crowd swayed.

A gong sounded once, twice, three times.

'Tobias, Tobias, Tobias.'

'I cannot stand chanting,' Silva snarled, wrinkling her nose.

The chanting became a cheer that grew in pitch and fervour until it was practically deafening as a figure appeared on the stage. It was difficult to see, but those at the front were reaching forwards. Several people even attempted to climb the stage. The guards were very liberal with the use of their clubs.

Here he comes.

CHAPTER 31

'That's Tobias Helstrum?' Shift scoffed. 'I was expecting some-thing...more.'

He tried to control his scowl as Tobias Helstrum hobbled into view. At first impression, he looked unassuming. An older man, short and stocky. He was dressed simply, which Nicolas was sure was purposeful. Wearing a plain black robe and a wide brimmed hat to cover his orange hair. From this distance, Nicolas couldn't make out the burn scars that covered one half of the man's face.

Tobias was escorted onto the stage, and towards the podium set up for him, by four heavily armoured warriors. Five other figures followed in his wake. Nicolas cast a glance at them then did a double take.

'There's our new friend.' Shift glared.

One of the five following Helstrum was the leather-masked man from the border fort. Hands clasped behind his back, he took in the crowd.

'Gasp,' Auron said in mock horror, having managed to find a spot where someone wasn't stood in him. 'Helstrum sent that man to kill us? I am shocked to my core by this surprising revelation.' The spirit chuckled at his own nonsense.

It was actually strangely comforting, seeing the man up there.

At least we know it was Helstrum, and we haven't somehow made other enemies on our travels.

Nicolas rolled his eyes at the idea that the satisfaction in his life now came from knowing exactly who was trying to kill him.

The other four walking with the man were a curious bunch. One was a hugely muscular man with hair and beard like the mane of a lion, long and bouncing as he walked. Other than leather straps criss-tcrossing his chest and some fur pants, he wore nothing. Probably because he'd struggle to find clothing that would fit over his massively muscled torso. There were bulging bits where Nicolas hadn't even realised bits could bulge. His arms were so thick it was doubtful he could scratch his back if he wanted to. Yet his legs were significantly thinner. So much so that

Nicolas wondered how they carried his top-heavy weight. Oh, and he looked as mean as a hungry dragon.

To the left of the man in the mask was a gentleman who was clearly a wizard. Long black robes draped over his thin frame. His cheeks were so gaunt that his cheekbones stuck out like a pair of spear tips. His eyes were so sunken it gave the impression the man had no pupils.

Practically a walking skeleton.

If Nicolas had to bet some coin, he'd put it on this man being some kind of necromancer.

And he wasn't the only magic user. Another wore a long blue robe. His black hair was slicked back, and his pointed moustache was clearly the product of strict cultivation. There was a haughty look to him normally found on a lord of some note. For a moment, Nicolas couldn't work out what was off about the man. Then he realised. It was the way he moved. He didn't appear to walk; instead, he glided across the floor, his legs concealed by the robe.

At the end of the group was a tall, muscular woman with ebony skin and a long, braided ponytail that extended nearly to the floor. She carried a formidable mace and had the expression of someone quite keen on breaking things. In the *'I'll wear some armour, but only grudgingly'* stakes, she could've given Silva a run for her money.

'Ooh,' Auron said with sudden excitement. 'It seems old Helstrum invested in some specialist bodyguards after your last attempt on his life.'

'That *wasn't* me,' Nicolas hissed. 'It was the bearded archer.'

'Who vanished, leaving you holding a bow.' Shift nodded in a disbelieving way.

'Oh, you can both—'

'She is magnificent.'

Nicolas turned and frowned at Silva in harmony with Auron and Shift. The warrior didn't notice. She was too busy staring wide-eyed at the stage.

'Is she?' Shift asked, eyeing the warrior strangely.

Silva continued to stare at the woman in awe. 'That is a true warrior,' she whispered. 'Strong and proud. A specimen of the art of war.'

'Mayhap you two can go for dinner together later,' Auron remarked with distaste. 'Though romantic relationships with the enemy are frowned upon.'

'There is no romance here.' Silva's voice had a dreamy quality to it. She'd obviously completely missed the spirit's sarcasm. 'We will fight. She and I shall do battle with one another. And it will be legendary.'

'Not now you won't,' Nicolas chided. 'So calm down and save it for later.'

Silva shook herself and finally looked at the others. 'One day, I shall,' she said with certainty. 'And when that time comes, she is *mine*. Understood?' There was a firmness in her voice that brooked no disagreement.

Nicolas and Shift exchanged a glance.

'I'm quite comfortable with you taking them all if...' His gaze lingered on the leather masked man for a moment, his jaw setting in a scowl. 'Actually, if it comes to it, the masked guy is mine.'

As Helstrum reached the podium, the armoured guards continued onwards, stepping off the stage and forming a human wall in front of their master, keeping their thick shields in front of them and brandishing their long spears to attention. Behind Tobias, his five bodyguards spread out. Nicolas eyed them warily.

There was clearly a reason Tobias had chosen them. And that reason meant this quest was about to get a lot more difficult.

Five of us. Five of them.

Oh crap. Garaz isn't here. That's five against four them.

He guessed each one had been chosen to fight a specific one of them, even the member of their party who wasn't with them. A couple were obvious, a couple less so. Either way, Silva was right. At some point, they would have to go through them. He doubted there'd be a handy route around them. That just wasn't how these things worked.

Sighing, he studied the leather-masked man. He was clearly the foremost of the group. From here, the man looked thin and unassuming, but Nicolas could tell he was a warrior. It was the way he carried himself.

And here I am. Weaponless in a sack.

His sword hand twitched slightly, wanting to seek the comfort of the *Dawn Blade*, which wasn't there to comfort him. Sweat beaded on his temple. He was in the midst of Helstrum's camp, surrounded by enemies. And enemies specially hired to kill him.

What about the crowd?

Would these dancing zealots turn on him if Helstrum commanded it? Would they descend on him as a horde, tearing at him with tooth and nail?

I can't fight them. I can't fight them all.

The world began to blur. He remembered the guard Shift had pissed on. That man had nearly recognised him. What if he was, even now, drying his leg off and it suddenly occurred to him: 'Hey. That was that Nick Carnage guy.' Right this second, he could be gathering his comrades. Nicolas was afraid to turn around, lest he see a group of soldiers searching the crowd, working their way towards him.

And I'm stood here in a sack. I stand out. They'll find me.

Should he just do what he'd come here to do, before they were discovered? Nicolas pictured himself moving through the crowd, moving toward Tobias with the knowledge he was about to die, but hopeful he could kill Helstrum before he did. Where would he get a weapon? Slip it from a guard's belt? There were plenty of those around, hence the problem.

Can I do it? Can I make it to Helstrum before they get me?

His heart began to pound, and he struggled to breathe. It was as if he could feel hands reaching for him from behind, ready to grab him and drag him away. Trying to look casual, he glanced over his shoulder. There was nothing. As soon as he looked forwards again, the feeling returned with interest. His legs started to weaken.

They're going to find us. Any minute...

'Shhh.' Shift took his hand. 'It's okay. We are fine. They can't know. Calm.'

Somehow, their words worked. It was as if they were sharing their calm with him. Slowly, his heart and breathing became regular again.

That's why I I—

A sudden hush descended on the crowd, drawing his attention. Tobias Helstrum was about to speak.

CHAPTER 32

H aving hobbled to the podium playing the perfect humble and weak old man, Tobias Helstrum held out his cane. The masked man stepped forward and took it, before returning to a respectful distance. Pursing his lips, Tobias cast his gaze over the crowd as if in awe that so many people would come out to listen to little old him, the unassuming fellow. And the crowd loved it. It began to shuffle forward, hoping to get closer to the man they took to be some kind of saviour. Nicolas went with them, keeping up appearances lest they were noticed.

Leaning forward, he rested his hands on the podium. In an instant, his entire persona changed. This was no longer some crippled old man but a demi-god, ready to perform miracles. His presence projected across the entire crowd. Presumably, most of the people here got all tingly when it happened, but when the presence reached him, he felt only disgust. The crowd murmured reverently. With a single raised hand, he silenced all of them. Nicolas had to grudgingly admit that it was an impressive display of power.

Ever the expert orator, Tobias allowed the silence to hang just long enough to raise anticipation. 'My people.' His gravelly voice carried across the field like it was nothing—most likely some spell to enhance his natural speaking voice. 'It does my heart good to see so many of you here today, that so many humans are open to receiving the message. That so many minds are open to the truth.' Again, a pause as he scanned the crowd, nodding thoughtfully, like he was thinking about what to say next, as if he hadn't fully prepared for this. 'And what is our message? What are those three words that humanity should stand together and say in this cold, dark world? *'I love you?' 'Let's be friends?'*' For a moment, Helstrum let his head hang low before slowly raising it again, his face as fierce as any monster in the world. 'No, my people. The message is clear. Here, today, we need to come together and utter the three words we should've said years ago. Except we do not simply utter them. Instead, we shout them into the darkness descending on us. And those three words are, *'We've had enough.'*

A wave of cheering broke out, interspersed with random whoops of agreement. Within moments, the cacophony of noise settled into a united cheer: 'We have had enough!'

Helstrum nodded along with them, allowing the chanting to die down of its own accord.

'But what have we had enough of?' Tobias asked his followers. 'I can answer for myself. And I believe my answer is the same each and every one of you would give.' Stepping back, Tobias put his hand on his heart. 'I, Tobias Helstrum, have had enough of being a victim. I have had enough of giving in to fear. I have had enough of looking the other way whilst our people are torn asunder by those who wish us ill.' The hand went from his heart to his scarred face. 'These are not scars. These are a lesson. Trust and acceptance come at a price. How many kingdoms have learnt that lesson over the past few years? How many kingdoms of man have suffered because they trusted those they who were allowed to live alongside them? How many of you bear your own scars, even if they are not visible to the eye?'

There were cries of agreement from the crowd.

'I do not like this,' Shift whispered as they regarded the rapt audience around them.

'Hoflar's mines are attacked by rat men. Tannath suffers a rot on their beloved sacred forests. Secos's seat of learning is burned to the ground by a kascat dignitary after a failed coup. Sarus's economy is wrecked by a dwarven gangster. Merida is besieged by mer-folk.'

That one, at least, is an outright lie.

'And who is doing anything to stop this?' Helstrum cried incredulously. 'Do you see the Guild of Heroes stepping forward to banish this evil? No, you don't. And why is that? Why are our heroes no longer protecting us?' He clutched the podium again. 'Because they are a shadow of their former selves. Once-great heroes are no more than drunken mercenaries, living on the reflected glory of their ancestors.'

'Drunken bastards,' someone in the crowd yelled.

'They never came,' another shouted.

'Asshole,' Auron snapped, glaring around at the jeers of agreement.

Tobias nodded along. 'And what of our kingdom's armies? Where are they? Where are the local militias when creatures like the Visitor stalk the land, terrorising innocent families and unleashing vicious curses upon them?'

Nicolas's fists clenched in rage.

If I ever enjoy killing anyone, it'll be this guy.

'It's not sufficient anymore that just *I* have had enough of these things, or *you* have had enough. Or *you*,' Tobias bellowed, pointing to individuals in the crowd. 'We cannot be individuals anymore. We must stand as one and say that *we* have had enough.' Tobias's voice rose in tone and fervour with each word. '*We* have had enough of sitting by whilst chaotic elements rampage through our kingdoms. *We* have had enough of standing idle whilst our land is sold off to agenda-driven interlopers. *We* have had enough of being besieged in our own homes.' A fist slammed on the podium. '*We* have had *enough* of bending over backwards in the name of *friendship*, only to find a knife in our backs when we do. *We* have had *enough* of turning the other cheek. *We have had enough* of barbarity, victimisation, and integration. *We have had enough* of not standing up and saying *stop. We...have...had...enough!*'

As both Helstrum's fists slammed on the podium in outrage, the crowd became frenzied, their shouted grievances overlapping into a furious roar. Everyone began trying their darndest to punch the sky, throwing their fists into the air wildly. Hesitantly, Nicolas and his companions joined in. Groups of guards stalked through the crowd, and not joining in would make them stand out. Auron stood by with his arms crossed, scowling in disgust, just as Nicolas wanted to.

Tobias Helstrum sagged over the podium, as if unleashing such truth—his version of the truth anyway—had physically drained him. Slowly, he rose again, his raised hand hushing the crowd instantly.

'But *how* do we get this chaos to stop?' Tobias asked quietly. 'Do we petition our kings and queens? Do we wait for our *champions* to sober up and finally remember that they are supposed to stand up for us? No, we can do neither.' Theatrical pause. 'And why not? Because we have given them chance after chance to step up and defend us, and they have *failed*, time after time. We shouldn't need to *summon* people to protect us. They should already be here doing it.'

Apparently, Nicolas and his companions weren't the only ones here not enthused by Tobias's message. Getting up on one of the preacher's stands, a man gestured towards the stage, shouting to all those who could hear him, trying to talk some sense into the crowd.

'You can't listen to this nonsense,' he shouted passionately. 'This man is stirring up hatred and making you all drink it like ale. Can't you see—'

Four guards dragged him to the floor, and he disappeared into a flurry of swinging clubs.

'Without those we should count on to protect us, what do we do? Do we just give up?' Tobias asked, unperturbed by the interruption. 'I, for one, won't do that. And why is that? It's because I know humanity is strong. Right now, we are divided and weakened by the constraints we have imposed on ourselves. But when we come together, nothing can stop us. Was it not humanity fighting together that turned the tide of war when the great orc horde descended on the elves over a thousand years ago?'

Nicolas had to admit that the first humans had been brave indeed to take up arms and face the horde happily driving the elven race to extinction. He couldn't imagine facing down a horde of anything. Yet they had, and somehow, they'd won, being bequeathed the elves' kingdom in gratitude before they left Etherius. Nicolas didn't like the fact that Helstrum had a point and was twisting it for his own sick agenda.

'We can be strong again, my friends,' Helstrum continued with passion. 'We can stand as one. One people. No more division or politicking. Just humanity, fighting as one to survive in a hostile world. That is why I am beseeching all right-minded lords and ladies of Etherius to stand with me, that we may call our leaders to account. I am demanding a King's Moot, a meeting of our rulers not called in many a year. We will call those who govern us together and demand a resolution for the chaos plaguing our lands. We will demand that they banish this evil from our lands and drive it back across our borders and beyond.'

The term *and beyond* had some very interesting connotations. Because he doubted Helstrum's wrath would stop at the creation of some kind of buffer zone. No. Nicolas could see it clearly. Tobias would settle for nothing less than total annihilation.

Of everyone who isn't human.

Nicolas's qualms about assassinating Helstrum were waning with every word the man spoke.

'And when we finally rouse our rulers to action, what can they do?' Tobias asked thoughtfully. 'Each kingdom has an army, true enough, but even they may not be enough to vanquish these monsters. That is why we need to stand together. Right-minded men and women need to join the fight, not just on the battlefield, but in the towns and villages, ensuring that we are ever watchful for the enemy that stalks amongst us.' He punctuated the end of each sentence by hammering his fist on the table. 'We have spent so many years drawing borders between us that we have forgotten our common lineage. We have forgotten that we are a single people. We have forgotten that together we are strong. Well, I implore you to remember. I implore you to stand together. I implore you to prepare to face the oncoming storm with bravery and dedication. Just as we always have. Because we are *humans*. And once we remember that and pull together, there is no force in this world that can tear us back down.'

A rhythmic beating began, the crowd slapping closed fists against their chests.

'It is time to stand up and say *we have had enough*. We have been pushed too far. It is time to banish the evil from Etherius. We didn't make it *us or them*, but by God, we will answer their challenge and strike them down. And we will continue to do so until every single human is free from fear, free from threat, and free from tyranny.'

God? Doesn't he mean the Deities?

Tobias Helstrum cast his hands high into the air and lifted his head to the sky. '*Humanity!*' The cry echoed around the arena like a giant's fart, taken up and carried by the crowd.

Remembering what had happened to the man who'd spoken out, Nicolas realised they'd best try to fit in with the crowd. 'Fauns suck,' he shouted, waving his fist in the air. Even that made him feel awkward and uncomfortable, so he didn't say anything else.

'By the Deities,' Shift gasped, staring at Helstrum. 'He's insane.'

'What an odious fellow,' Auron shouted over the din. 'I'm glad we're here to kill him.'

'Same here,' Nicolas agreed.

'Either he dies, or countless others will,' Silva added.

Once again, Helstrum doubled over the podium as if uttering his almighty revelations to the masses had drained his very soul. Assuming he had one.

'You have all come here today to hear the truth of the world,' Helstrum began with conviction. 'Now you know it, I pray you can help defend our world, our way of life, from the circling vultures.' He looked around thoughtfully. 'But doing so is no easy task. Vigilance is something we can all do. It is our common responsibility. But for those who wish more, who wish to make the defence of our people their purpose, you have a chance to take the first steps today.' With a sweeping gesture, he indicated rows of tables with scribes seated behind them on the far side of the arena. 'Join us. Stand with us. Fight with us and win with us.' His voice dropped to a low growl, yet still it carried to every corner of the crowd. 'Because we have had *enough*.'

By the Deities, he's building a damned army.

Nicolas watched in horror as people began moving purposefully towards the tables, queues forming in an instant. As they did, Tobias Helstrum was escorted from the stage. People reached out, as if hoping to touch him.

'This is madness,' Silva muttered. 'He cannot just build an army unopposed.'

'And yet he is trying to,' Shift said. 'We need to finish this. Quickly.'

His companion was right. This army would not be for defence, though he was sure those fools signing up would believe that was the case. How long until they finally realised the truth?

'I bet he's staying in that fortress tonight,' Auron mused, pointing at the building that towered over all of them.

'And that he's surrounded by a small army,' Shift added. 'Getting to him won't be easy.'

Nicolas looked towards the tables, and a potentially suicidal idea came to mind. 'Then perhaps we should join the army.'

CHAPTER 33

U nsure whether this idea was absolute genius or absolute insanity, Nicolas and the others took the next step, which meant joining another queue. This one didn't move anywhere near as fast as the queue to enter the arena, due to the scribes taking fastidious details of the new recruits. There was a palpable air of excitement from the people around him that sickened and horrified Nicolas in equal measure. These people were signing up for the army of a very evil man. He wanted to shake and slap each person in turn until they came to their senses. But really, there was only one thing he could do.

Stop all of this before the army is put to use.

The desks gradually grew closer, until Shift was stood in front of it.

'Name?' the scribe asked in a way that gave the impression he was very disinterested in the answer.

'Saraya Sturn,' the shapeshifter replied with a smile the clerk didn't deserve.

'Place of birth...?'

The voices trailed off as he suddenly realised he needed a fake name. He couldn't use the crappy one that dogged him everywhere, because it was likely well known amongst his enemies. Bad enough that any of them could recognise him at any given moment. And he didn't feel comfortable using Tallith's name again. So what then?

John? No, I don't look like a John. Tobias? Shit, I definitely can't use that. Patricia? Oh, for Deities sake Nicolas, that's a girl's name. C'mon, man. Think. Thinkthinkthink...

'Wake up, kid,' Auron shouted at him, snapping him to attention.

He was now at the front of the queue, and the scribe was staring at him with a raised eyebrow. How long had he been considering names for?

And I still don't have one.

'Name.'

His mind went blank. The scribe had his quill hovering over the parchment, but when no quick reply came, he cocked his eyebrow again.

'Name.'

'Billy, Billy Bobknobs,' he blurted. *Of all the names I could've picked.*

'That's your name?' the scribe asked, wrinkling his nose.

'Yes.' He chuckled nervously. 'People tell me it sounds made up all the time. It's a family joke.' Nicolas shook himself. 'Sorry. I'm just so happy to be joining up and fighting for what's right that my brain is all over the place.'

'Indeed,' the scribe said warily. After a glance at his sack outfit, the scribe seemed content that Nicolas was some sort of village idiot. 'Place of birth?' And yet they were still signing him up.

Somehow, he managed to catch his tongue in his mouth before he accidentally said *Babylon.* He doubted the name of that integrated city would be well received here.

'Yarringsburg,' he said finally.

'Oh,' the scribe said after a pause.

'Those filthy vampires descended on my home,' he cried. 'I was a tradesman, and my shop, my livelihood, gets torn down, and I'm reduced to living in an alley wearing sacks.' Nicolas yanked on his clothing for effect before slamming his fist on the table. 'I knew I had to find a way to stop such atrocities happening to other good people. That's why I was drawn to Mr Helstrum's message and—'

The scribe rubbed the bridge of his nose wearily. 'Please just stick to answering the questions. I have a lot of people to get through.'

Nicolas looked back behind him at the long line. 'Of course, yes, sorry.'

'And cut down on the amateur dramatics,' Auron scolded. 'You're drawing too much attention.'

The spirit wasn't wrong. A few people nearby, including guards, were looking at him.

With a sigh, the scribe continued. 'Any physical ailments?'

'Well, I—'

'A simple yes or no, please,' the scribe interrupted tartly.

I think I need to make this as quick as possible. 'No.'

'Thank the Deities,' the scribe muttered, quill scratching on the parchment.

Now that he was in the rhythm, he managed to get through the rest of the questions quickly.

'Why are you here?'

That one caught him by surprise, and his mind stalled again. 'I've already answered that...' he said nervously.

'No, you haven't.' Suddenly, the scribe fixed him with an intense gaze. 'You don't travel all this way and take up arms just because a vampire burned down your shop and you have to wear...sack clothes. Why are you really here?'

Shit. Damn me and my crap theatrics.

This was obviously a make-or-break question. His answer would either allow him entry or see him beaten all the way home, if he was allowed out of here alive that is. His peripheral vision picked up on guards' grips tightening on their clubs, muscles tensing, ready for use.

'I was whipped once,' he said, channelling the old anger of that wound and using it. 'I was on a ship. Hoping to make a new life for myself. A faun attacked me and my friends, captured us. He had me tied to a post and lashed. And he did it for nothing other than his own entertainment. Can you believe that? Someone doing that to another being, for fun? For amusement? It's disgusting.' His hands were clenching into fists. 'Do you want to see the scars the filthy bastard left?' Quickly, he began to raise his shirt and turn.

'No, no,' the scribe said, raising a hand. 'That's quite all right.'

'I will see,' one of the guards said, stepping forwards. Obviously, he was less inclined to believe him than the scribe. The masked man circled him and lifted the back of his shirt. He caught his breath in surprise. Lowering the shirt again, the guard returned to his post, nodding to the clerk.

'It's all in order,' the guard said after an awkward cough.

Nothing about the state of my back is 'in order,' *asshole. Though I never knew the scars would come in handy.*

A tear gathered at the corner of his eye. He had no idea that the emotion over the whipping was still so raw.

And yet it seems like an age ago.

Maybe it would always be like that? Like the scars, it was destined to never fade completely, instead, just resting in his subconscious, waiting to be woken and called forward as a reminder. How much else was hidden in there, waiting for its moment to strike?

Quickly, Nicolas tucked his shirt back in. It gave him a pang of relief to know the scars were covered up again. He didn't mind being topless around Shift but leaving himself exposed to anyone else made him nauseated.

The scribe handed him a slip of paper and indicated he should follow Shift. Part of Nicolas wanted to say thank you as he walked away, but for what? And did anyone in this organization deserve thanks for anything?

'Billy bloody Bobknobs?' Shift said as he caught up to them. 'All the names you can pick, and you choose *that* one.'

'I know, I know,' he whispered. 'Just another example of how strangely my mind works. What about you, where'd *Saraya* come from?'

143

'In the past, it paid to use a lot of aliases.' Shift shrugged. 'That's one I always seem to gravitate back to, though I change the last name. I shouldn't really reuse a name, but I'm oddly fond of it, so there you go.'

'Heroes don't use aliases,' Auron added beside them. 'How do you get the glory if you go around using made-up names?'

'Okay,' Nicolas replied. 'Next time, I'll slap my hand down on the table and declare *'I am Nick Carnage, defeater of evil and destroyer of my enemies.'* Then you can enjoy the show as I fight my way through the thousand or so men who descend on me.'

'There's no need to be facetious, kid,' Auron replied flatly.

'Ha.' Shift chuckled. 'You used the name.'

I wh— Oh shit, I did use that bloody name. What's the matter with me today?

Once Silva joined them, they were funnelled to another desk, where they were given some simple white garments in a pack. After shouldering the packs, the new trainees were split into vague columns and marched around the circumference of the fortress, until they came to the shanty town of tents in front of the main gate. Except it wasn't a shanty town; it was a training ground. There were several large wooden buildings, which he guessed were storehouses, and longer tents on the far side where the recruits would sleep when they weren't being prepared for war. It was all disturbingly efficient.

They passed small open areas where men in masks barked at groups of trainees who wore the same simple white shirts and breeches that were in their packs. Shouting voices demanded that they run or climb or spar. Pairs of men wrestled each other whilst others took their swords to training dummies shaped like minotaurs. There was the din of training all around. And something else. Nicolas jumped at the sound of thunder, knowing instantly what it was. The group was marched past a row of men reloading the fire-sticks they'd just used to shoot at straw dummies that were set well away from them. Nicolas was nearly sick in his mouth at the images of fairies and centaurs crudely painted on the targets, which were already filled with holes. With practised precision, the men poured the black powder into the hole at the end of the weapon, before adding the projectile then ramming it in place with a metal stick that slipped out from under the barrel. They then took aim, fired and repeated the process. This time, Nicolas counted. One shot then about a half minute to reload. That could make a difference in a fight. Just seeing the weapons made his leg ache.

'Someone is building quite the army,' Auron remarked as he watched a group of men jabbing spears into straw dummies in the shape of kascats.

'Can he do this?' Nicolas asked in a hushed tone. 'Can you just *build an army*? Surely the king would raise an eyebrow at someone raising their own fighting force right in the middle of his kingdom.'

'Helstrum isn't being subtle about it at all,' Silva remarked as she looked around. 'So, he must have ample support to bring enough pressure to bear on High King Martius to allow this. Or he has agents ensuring everyone looks the other way.'

Martius was the king of Ivilar, the first and largest of the Kingdoms of Man. *High King* was more of an honorary title, a sort of *first amongst equals* thing. He was famed for being wise and just, so the other kings often took his counsel. Nothing about this seemed wise *or* just so certain people in power must be ensuring that word of this didn't reach the wrong ears. The sheer level of planning behind all of this was astounding.

'That is disturbing,' Silva said, watching the instructors teach their charges with slightly narrowed eyes. They were clearly men who knew their stuff.

'Everything here's disturbing,' he replied. They were right in the belly of the beast.

I hope it doesn't swallow me before I can cut its head off.

'Line up,' bellowed a masked man.

The new recruits assembled themselves in rough ranks on a patch of dirt in front of the large man, whose head moved slowly from left to right as he scrutinised his new charges. His mask was fancier than the others, with a pair of horns protruding from the forehead. It must be a symbol of rank.

Walking the line, the man looked every recruit up and down, fingers flexing around the baton he carried behind his back. Nicolas felt practically naked when it was his turn. Part of him wanted to introduce himself, to break the awkward tension, but he knew that even making eye contact with the man would be a mistake.

'I have never, in all my years, seen such a slovenly bunch of goatherders,' the instructor shouted as he returned to his position, gripping his baton as if he were about to snap it. 'Well, there are no goats to herd here, or shag, if that's your inclination. You are here to be made into warriors. You are here to fight for your homes and earn this...' From behind his back, the man produced one of the masks the enemy soldiers wore. 'Once you are trained here, this will be your new face. This is the face of the Custodians of Humanity. Our enemy wants to scare us into submission, but with these masks, we turn terror back upon him and all his kind. The enemy will learn to fear this face because it brings with it their obliteration. By wearing this mask, you will be sending a message to the non-human enemy that you are prepared to do whatever is necessary to protect humanity.'

I want to be sick. There really is only so much of this crap I can stomach.

'Yes,' one of the recruits, a young man with sandy hair cried with enthusiasm, brandishing his hands with glee. 'Let's take it to that inhuman scum.'

The instructor strode forwards and smacked the man on the leg with his baton. The strike was so loud that Nicolas winced. The man crumpled to the side with a cry.

'Stand up straight,' the instructor barked. 'I am here to teach you discipline as well as how to fight. Fighting is what an army does. Discipline is how it goes about doing it. We are not some crazed horde like our enemies. We defeat them by being better than them. And we do that by *being quiet until you are told otherwise!*'

Though his leg obviously pained him, the man stood up straight, at rigid attention.

'If he even tried to hit me with that baton, it'd be stuck right up his ass by now.' Auron tutted.

Which would do nothing to keep our disguises intact.

The instructor returned to his position in front of the assembled group. 'Right now, you are nothing. You are lumps of clay. I will mould that clay. I will shape it. Through hard training, I will turn you lumps of clay into mighty warriors of humanity. I...'

Nicolas couldn't concentrate on the instructor's words. He was trying too hard not to laugh at Auron, who stood beside the instructor, copying his mannerisms in an overly exaggerated, comical way.

Does he want us to get caught?

He really wanted to shout at the spirit to stop, but the instructor might think it was directed at him and introduce him to the baton. So, he stood at attention and tried to stay that way.

Today is going to be a long day.

CHAPTER 34

A s they rounded the corner of the fortress's outer wall, several of the recruits failed to make the turn, stumbling and falling to the grass in panting heaps. There they were yelled at and belittled by enraged instructors who demanded they *get up and show the strength humans were born with.'* They'd already lost a few since the start of the run, and judging by the pained looks on some of the other faces, there would be more before the end. Even now, a couple of men were clutching their ribs, grimacing with each step. One had some thick red veins on his temples. Nicolas was genuinely worried that he'd have a heart attack.

Shit. I should look like this too.

Catching himself, he began to stumble slightly and let out a few heavy breaths to feign exhaustion. This was one of the most difficult parts of their ruse: pretending to be crap. If he or either of the others showed any kind of skill, questions would be asked. Easier to appear on the level of the rest of the recruits, for now.

'Move it, you stumbling bastards,' the head instructor bellowed from where he stood, which marked the finish line of their lap around the wall. 'You're a disgrace. Utter filth.'

Apparently, being trained to serve in an army required you to be called *filth* a lot. Nicolas wasn't sure why. Surely you got better results from praising people, instead of insulting them?

Spurring himself on, Nicolas made sure not to run in a straight line, as none of the others did. As difficult as he was finding it, he could tell from the tension in Silva's face that she was struggling with it more than he was. Shift appeared to be revelling in the chance to act. Auron was just living his best after-life, standing by the instructor doing a hand gesture that expressed his belief that the instructor had a habit of interfering with himself regularly.

Nicolas slowed when he began to lead the group. Allowing himself to drop back, he was the third to cross the finish line. Doubling over, he got onto all fours on the grass and did some lip-service panting as exhausted bodies fell all around him. Truthfully, this had been less exhausting than the lecture on the weakness of inhuman species the group had been forced to endure before they set off.

They certainly want to make sure their people are indoctrinated as well as knackered.

Longingly, he cast his gaze to the fortress gate. So far there had been no chance to go inside. He'd hoped that the new recruits would be paraded in front of Helstrum, or something like that. But no. Only regular soldiers could enter the fortress grounds. For the new recruits, it was forbidden.

Slowly, the stragglers flopped across the finish line, urged on by screaming instructors with batons. But they had no chance to rest. A bellowing voice commanded them to line up. Even the most tired of the group managed to force themselves to stand.

'I suppose you could call that an effort,' the instructor snapped as he walked the line, tapping his baton on his hand. 'Even if it was a bloody disappointing one. But do not fear. This is just day one. We have tomorrow, then the day after, and the one after that.' The instructor stopped, tucking his baton behind his back. 'I have every day I need to turn you peasant lumps into an effective fighting force, whether you serve with the army or not.'

A shudder went down Nicolas's spine as he felt the burst of rage from Silva. Risking a glance, he noticed the pink armbands both the warrior and Shift wore. Apparently, fighting in the army was for the men. But they would train the women too, to send them home so they could protect the young and infirm whilst rooting out inhuman treachery.

They're good enough to fight, as long as they don't go too far from the home to do it.

Nicolas wasn't surprised by the attitude. Neither were Silva and Shift. They were just annoyed. Though he was quietly impressed neither of them had made a scene about it. That showed how seriously they all took their mission.

'Disperse,' the instructor barked. 'Eat and sleep. Hopefully, in the morning you goatherders will wake up with more fortitude.'

Nicolas didn't need the instructor's mask to be removed to know he was giving his charges a look of disgust as they all moved away from the training ground, most to find food.

The feeling's mutual.

Whatever you could say about Helstrum—so many bad things—he didn't skimp on training his men. Nicolas had seen enough evidence of that while running around the camp. This would be an effective army, if it was ever unleashed. Though it might take a while. The instructors had tempered themselves, not throwing the recruits into a full day right away.

Just about...

Already, the sun was lowering in the sky.

Following the herd, Nicolas and his companions slowed until they were lagging behind. Finally, the group slipped between the pair of tents Auron gestured towards.

'This way, folks,' the spirit said jovially as he led them on a winding trail through the camp.

'This is unproductive,' Silva remarked, keeping her eyes sharp for people watching them. 'We won't get closer to finding him if we stay here until the rest of those people are up to scratch.'

Which will take a damned long time.

'We just need to find Helstrum and get the job done then all of this will...' Shift frowned.

'It'd be really nice if all of this just withered and vanished when he dies, but I doubt it,' Nicolas said solemnly.

'You'd be surprised. Without an arguably charismatic fellow to rally them, all these fools will more than likely just wander home,' Auron explained.

'As easy as that?'

'Not at all.' The spirit chuckled. 'I imagine there will be splinter groups, and warbands, but they won't last long. I've seen it more than once, kid. I'd stop and tell you a story about it, but now's really not the time.'

Whilst they'd 'enjoyed' their lecture and run, the spirit had been scouting the camp and the fortress for them.

'So Helstrum's still here?' Shift asked.

'Yes,' the spirit confirmed. There was an urgency in his tone. 'Though I heard he intends to leave soon. So we need to get to him now.'

That worried Nicolas. Rushing was not the same as having a plan. If they were entering Helstrum's fortress, where his army and bodyguards were, a plan would be a really good idea.

But we aren't going to have one, are we? This is going to be an improvising adventure. I hate those.

Though most of his adventures were improvising ones, truth be told.

Between the tents, he caught a glimpse of the fortress gate. It was heavily guarded.

'So how do we get in?'

'This'll be a start,' Auron said, pointing at the storage shed he'd led them to.

'Ah.' Nicolas nodded knowingly. 'There's arms and armour in there we can put on to slip past the guards at the gate.'

That's actually a good idea.

Auron screwed his face up. 'Kid, do you really think they'd just leave that out here for anyone to grab?' *Dammit.* 'No. This is where we'll store the bodies of the guards you lot are going to knock out and strip.'

'Oh. That'll work too.' Nicolas shrugged.

'Give me a second.' Shift crouched and worked the lock as the others kept lookout, with Nicolas very aware that they were in the open. No one seemed to be paying them any attention, but that could change in a second.

'Hurry up,' Nicolas hissed after a few seconds became an eternity.

Shift shot him a glare. 'Stop interrupting, and I will.'

'Can you not just use your magic key?'

His companion eyed him incredulously. 'You don't tell an artist what brush to use when they're painting.'

'Artists don't get killed when they're found loitering around canvases,' he shot back.

The next thing Nicolas knew, he was fumbling the padlock which Shift had thrown at him. It took several attempts before he got a firm grip on it, much to the shapeshifter's amusement. With the door opened, the pair slipped inside. Seconds later, Silva joined them.

'Right then,' Nicolas whispered. 'We just need some guards now.'

Silva ripped the neckline of her shirt slightly, to expose a little more cleavage. 'Leave that to me,' she said, before slipping outside.

CHAPTER 35

Auron stood up straight, his head appearing back through the wall it had been popped through.

'She's coming.' The spirit nodded.

Flexing his fingers, Nicolas took up a position behind the door. Shift slipped behind a shelf filled with neatly folded training clothes. The room became silent. Dark, save for the glow of Auron's aura and the muted light coming through the murky window at the back of the shed. In that silence, Nicolas heard voices.

Slowly, the door opened, and two figures slipped inside. Silva led the guard by the chin of his mask. She was pouting slightly and definitely pushing her chest out as the man, smaller and slighter than her dutifully followed.

'I just...I don't know,' she said in a faux demure voice. 'There's something about being in a military camp that just...enflames certain passions.'

'Oh, I know what you mean.' Nicolas could almost picture the guard's leering grin. 'And believe me, love, I know how to deal with an enflamed passion.'

I've heard enough.

Stepping forwards, he wrapped his arm around the guard's neck in one fluid motion. Grabbing his elbow, he locked in the hold and kicked out the back of one of the man's knees, before dragging him backwards. The man let out strained gasps as he clawed at Nicolas's arm. Five seconds later, he was unconscious.

With an impressed nod, Silva pulled him by the legs into a dark corner of the room. Efficiently, she and Shift stripped the guard. Not long after, Shift was a masked and armoured enemy soldier. Silva ensured the guard was tightly bound with a shirt stuffed in his mouth, lest he wake and scream for help.

'I'll go and get another one,' Silva said, before exiting the shed.

'How do I look?' Shift asked.

'It doesn't enflame my passions at all,' Nicolas replied with a grimace.

The masked head cocked to the side. 'I'm not feeling particularly enflamed in this get-up either,' they admitted.

'That was nice and smooth, kid,' Auron remarked with a proud nod. 'Now, back to your position.'

As Nicolas readied himself, the spirit poked his head through the wall again. It came back almost instantly. 'That was quick,' the spirit remarked. 'These men must not see women that often.'

The scene played itself out again. Silva led the guard in, he said something indicating he was horny, and Nicolas knocked him out. This time, it was Nicolas's turn to play dress-up. Well, switch one disguise for another really. He was half dressed when he realised that the guard was pretty much exactly his size. Silva was picking her targets well.

Bouncing his shoulders up and down a few times, and fidgeting, he got the leather armour to a position where it finally sat right. It wasn't a great fit, and it wasn't *his* armour. But beggars couldn't be choosers when infiltrating an enemy fortress. Picking up the mask, he stared into its empty eye holes in disgust. He couldn't bring himself to put it on just yet. Instead, he laid it on the ground beside him.

'One more then.' Silva sighed, adjusting her top again.

Within minutes, the warrior returned. The door opened, and Silva led the guard in. This one was bigger, Silva's size. He'd have to be quick. As the man crossed the threshold, Nicolas's nose twitched. He could smell piss.

Whatever.

Once the door was shut, Nicolas took a step forwards.

'Ow.'

'You tit,' Auron chided as Nicoles stepped on the pointed nose of the mask he'd left lying by his feet. The thing was bloody sharp.

Instantly, the guard turned around and stared at him. 'Hey,' he snarled, looking him up and down. 'I recognise you. What are you doing wearing that? You only signed up today and...' The guard gasped and took a step backwards, pointing at Nicolas. 'Hang on. I do bloody recognise you. You're Nick Carnage. You're— *Urk.*'

The man went for his sword, and Silva snapped his neck. His limp body tried to crash to the ground, but Nicolas and Silva caught it and lowered it gently.

'That nearly went badly,' Shift remarked, leaning over to inspect the body. 'We should probably just kill the other two as well.'

'I... It doesn't seem right,' Nicolas said sheepishly. 'They're already unconscious and bound. It's...gratuitous.'

Shift rolled their eyes and said nothing.

'You still have a lot to learn,' Silva grumbled, stripping the guard. 'Like how to not give us away when...oh.'

The warrior had picked up the unconscious guard's boot and sniffed it. Her nose wrinkled in disgust. For a moment, the warrior pointedly looked at Nicolas's feet, clearly considering forcing him to swap one of his boots for her piss stained one. Thank the Deities' he had smaller feet than her, making a trade impossible. A few minutes later, leaving it until last, Silva closed her eyes and tentatively lowered her foot into the boot. She was still scowling about it when she put her mask on.

'You sure this will work?' he said, stretching out his arms and looking over his new gear.

'We've done this before,' Shift said with an impatient sigh.

'And as I recall, we got caught.' Which had nearly led to their deaths at the hands of a dwarf gangster.

Shift gestured for him to put his mask on. 'And we learn from our mistakes.'

'But—'

'Stop worrying, kid,' Auron interjected. 'The guards at the gate have been watching soldiers pass all day. They're used to it. With that comes a certain complacency. They won't expect you to be anything but exactly what you look like.'

Stop worrying? What's he going to try to do next? Stop the moon from rising?

Eyeing the metal mask in his hand with a sigh, he finally put it on to his face. Instantly, he felt enclosed. Constricted. Wearing the armour and mask of the enemy was distasteful, but it was a necessity. Just like travelling all this way to kill a man. Necessity.

'How do they wear these things?' His voice was slightly echoey with the mask on.

'Fanatical fools have low standards,' was Auron's pearl of wisdom on the subject.

'Sometimes, I really wish I could shift my clothes as well as my appearance,' Shift grumbled. 'It'd make my life a lot easier.'

'And you'd be naked less of the time,' Nicolas noted.

'Unless you ask nicely.' He didn't need to see their face; he felt the grin.

'Enough,' Silva snapped.

Checking the guard's sword could be drawn when he needed it to be, he got ready for the next stage of their quest. The blade was basic, but it'd have to do.

It's good enough to stab Maestros with, anyway.

Leaving the shed, the trio got into formation and marched toward the gate leading to the fortress. Ahead of them, a troop of guards were milling around it. None of them looked very attentive. Beyond them and the open gate, he could see the courtyard of the fortress.

We can do this.

Walking like they belonged, Nicolas fought to control his worry as they approached the group. With each footstep, he waited for the challenge. The gate's archway loomed over them. Soon, they would be stopped and questioned. Then he was covered by the shadow of the arch. Either side of him were the thick wooden gates. The challenge would come now.

And then they were in the fortress.

Oh.

Nicolas wanted to look back, to see if the guards had even acknowledged their passing. But he couldn't. So they just kept walking. That was it. They were in.

And the guards think they're earning their pay, do they?

CHAPTER 36

It turned out that the courtyard surrounding the fortress was broken up into walled sections. Each connected to the others via archways with portcullises. Nicolas guessed it was a way to try and confound invaders. Should they fight their way through the main gate they'd find themselves having to do it all over again on two sides, giving the defenders a chance to wear them down until they couldn't continue the assault. The entrance to the fort wasn't visible, so he guessed it was on the other side of the building. It'd be a bit useless having the courtyard sectioned off like this if the way into the fort was right in front of anyone who got in.

All around them were armoured masked men, marching in formation, standing guard or milling around talking and eating.

'This is where we split up,' Auron said, looking around. 'I'll go into the fortress itself. Shift can check the buildings here, and you and Silva can check the courtyards to the left and right. We meet back here in twenty minutes with Helstrum's location then we go and kill him.'

There is no way, by all the Deities, that it'll be that easy.

No, he corrected himself. It can be that easy. It *has* to be, for Etherius's sake.

Not acknowledging the spirit, the group broke up, moving in different directions. Nicolas watched as Shift slipped into the nearest thatched building, whilst Auron passed through the wall into the fortress itself. He guessed Silva was going where she was supposed to.

Making sure he was walking casually, he passed through the next gateway. How long would it take him to find Tobias Helstrum? They needed to be quick. There wasn't much of the day left now.

Oh. There he is.

On the far side of the adjoining courtyard, the hatemonger was standing before a pair of wagons, with his bodyguards and a number of other troops. The man he was talking to caught Nicolas's attention. He was covered head to toe in black armour. The helmet had a single visor slit, and spiked plates going backwards like the scales of a dragon. On the armour's chest plate was a carving of something that looked like a heart. The man reminded him of Alric Tavish, the black knight who'd been one of Helstrum's chief lieutenants, before Nicolas killed him. Well, Gornak had been the one to implant his axe in the man's torso and finish him off, but Nicolas had definitely softened Tavish up first.

Auron will be thrilled to see another black knight. He loves them.

Whoever the man was, he was clearly important. That was obvious from the way Helstrum talked to him and the soldiers around looked upon him with reverence.

His gaze flicked to the carriages again. The horses were ready to go, the drivers simply awaiting their passengers. Helstrum was leaving.

We can't miss our chance.

But what could Nicolas do? Helstrum was practically surrounded. And he was alone. There was no time to go and gather the others. This was the best chance he'd get, and maybe his only one. In his mind, he weighed up all the lives the Maestro had taken already, and all those he would take. Especially when his army was unleashed. There was no choice. He had to do this. And there would be no coming back from it. Not with all those soldiers around him.

But it's the right thing to do.

The thing that hurt the most was that he'd not have the chance to question Helstrum about his people. All he could do was hope they found their way home once the Maestro's forces scattered, as Auron suggested they would.

Realising that standing idle might draw attention to himself, he began to walk. He needed to get closer to strike anyway. In his mind, he played it out. Approach Helstrum from the side, one quick slash of the sword, and it was done.

No. It can't be just a cut.

Nicolas needed to be sure he'd die. That meant beheading him or driving the sword into him somewhere it'd definitely prove fatal. It wouldn't be easy. But if it saved Etherius, he'd do it. Mentally, he said goodbye to Shift and the others.

But then the black knight bowed, and Helstrum boarded the carriages with three of his bodyguards. The door shut with a firm click as the rest of his escort entered the second conveyance and a troop of knights pulled up alongside the carriages.

Shit.

There was nothing he could do now. If he went for the carriage, there would be little to no chance of him getting within shouting distance of Helstrum, never mind killing distance. All he could do was watch, disappointment gripped him as the the drivers spurred their horses into action. Soon, the convoy was leaving through the gate. Nicolas found himself wishing he could throw fireballs.

Glancing back, he saw the leather-masked man who seemed to pop up everywhere he went mount his own horse, a particular looking black mare with a white mane, and ride off. Somehow, he got the impression that he was going somewhere else. That just left the black knight and his men.

Dammit. Shit. Bugger. Bollocks. Crap.

They'd missed their potentially best chance. Frantically, he racked his brain for what to do next. He had no idea where their enemy was heading. All he could do was hope that the others would find something.

Or I could.

The black knight was still there, talking to his men. If Nicolas could get close enough, he might be able to eavesdrop. Maybe that way he could learn Helstrum's destination?

Then at least all of this won't have been for naught.

Nicolas approached the black knight, but as he did, the man removed his helmet. Nicolas skidded to a halt. For a moment, eyes wide, breath held, he was unable to comprehend what he was seeing.

What? How? But. What? How? But...

His brain seemed to stop functioning for a moment, overcome by the sudden burning questions filling it. Slowly, his mind took him back to the well outside his house on one fateful night. Ahead of him, as clearly as if it were that night again, stood Koth, the Maestro's terrifying demonic *fixer*, who'd been sent to kill him. Who *had* killed him, after a fashion. And then killed his parents. Nicolas could practically feel the chill of the demon-host's presence as he readied himself to lay down his life to defend his family. He recalled every horrifying detail of what had happened next with crystal clarity. The arrow struck him in the chest, and he fell to the ground. His body actually juddered slightly as he recalled the impact.

But it isn't right.

Mentally, he rewound time again. Closing his eyes firmly, he played the whole scene out a second time. There was Koth, in front of him. Then *thunk*, the arrow hit him in the chest, killing him.

Again.

Koth, the stand-off, the arrow. It was fired so fast he didn't even see Koth move.

Again.

Thunk. Arrow in the chest. He fell backwards. Briefly, he saw Koth, the creature's hand reaching down towards him.

A terrible realisation set in. Something he hadn't even noticed until now. Something that connected to what he was seeing right here and now.

When he said it aloud, his voice came out as a hoarse whisper. 'Koth wasn't carrying a bow.'

Once the declaration was made, he knew it to be fact. Koth hadn't been carrying a bow, or any other weapon that night. Yet somehow, an arrow had hit him in the chest. And now he knew exactly where it had come from.

But it can't be...

For a moment, he attempted to rationalise what he was seeing, to find some reason he was wrong. But he couldn't argue against the truth, because that was what it was...the truth. And the evidence was standing across the courtyard from him, plain as the mask on his face.

Betrayer.

With understanding came the purest rage he'd ever felt. His whole body shook with anger, his fists clenching so tightly he was sure he'd break the skin of his palm with his nails. Suddenly, the mask was stifling him, cutting off his air flow. He couldn't breathe. Fiercely, he tore it from his face and tossed it aside, along with his helmet.

Red mist descended over his eyes as a single idea filled his mind.

Revenge.

The thought grew and grew until the pressure in his head was immense. The wrath boiled over inside him until he screamed the name of his enemy for all Etherius to hear.

'Potttttttttter!'

CHAPTER 37

T he cry echoed to every corner of the courtyard. Confused, Garus Potter swung around. Nicolas's *friend* from Hablock, the man who'd shot him in the chest with an arrow, was here, dressed in black armour and cavorting with his enemy. His beard was neater, but he was unmistakable. And he was about to die.

Potter's frown of confusion became a broad grin as he realised who'd shouted his name. 'Nicky boy,' he shouted jovially. 'You're here.'

Around the black knight, his men gathered. Nicolas paid them no heed as his mouth curled in disgust at the greeting. Seething, he pictured himself ripping the traitorous bastard's head clean off, once he'd taken the time to ensure that every limb Potter had was at the wrong angle.

You know what...I'm actually going to do it.

With a growl, he began to stride across the courtyard. Potter's face dropped quickly as he realised the force bearing down on him, if not the havoc that force intended to wreak when he arrived.

And I am wrath incarnate, you filthy bastard.

He wanted to yell out every obscenity in his brain, but the trembling anger kept his lips sealed shut. All he had now was a single puprose...

Revenge.

Finally, the traitorous bottom-feeding scum decided he should probably do something to prevent the horrible fate that was about to befall him. Taking a couple of steps back, Potter gestured to his men.

'Stop him,' the black knight snapped. 'But make sure you take him alive.'

I'm not the one who needs to worry about living.

With a cry, the men surged forward, drawing their clubs from their belts as they ran at Nicolas.

Come on then.

Shaking fists clenched, paying no heed to the fact he actually had a sword on his hip, Nicolas continued onwards. All he could see through right now was Potter's neck. His fingers flexed in anticipation of closing around it and squeezing. An insistent voice nagged at the back of his mind. *'You can't kill him. He knows where your people are.'* It was drowned out by the fierce roar of the anger that had consumed him. His focus only shifted at the very last second, just as the first of Potter's men reached him.

Number one got nothing fancy. Nicolas barely broke his stride as he booted the oncoming attacker right in the face, sending him sprawling backwards to the ground with a heavy thud. The second swung his club in a wide arc. Nicolas drove forwards, ramming his shoulder into the man's chest before flipping him over his back. He barely registered the sound of the soldier crashing to the ground as he carried on towards his intended target.

Another charged him. Nicolas caught the man's arm in a downward swing, before laying him out with a vicious uppercut. As the man fell away, a soldier grabbed Nicolas's collar. Before he could bring his club to bear, Nicolas gripped the hand holding him and twisted it. The guard shouted in surprise and pain as his body moved with the motion, doubling him over. Keeping him in that position, Nicolas kicked him in the chest four times, before booting him in the side of the head, his gaze locked on Potter the whole time.

Ducking down, a club sailed over his head. Driving his legs upward, Nicolas cracked the attacker across the jaw, barely even registering the pain as his knuckles struck the metal mask he wore. Shaking his head, the dazed man didn't have time to react before Nicolas began working his torso over with a flurry of furious blows. When he was done, the soldier swayed on the spot for a moment, blood trickling from beneath the leering face he wore. Nicolas pressed a single finger into the man's forehead and pushed, forcing his limp body to topple over and fall to the ground.

'Get some more troops in here.' The tinge of fear in Potter's voice was so damned satisfying.

Turning, he saw his former friend backing towards the nearest wall.

Fine. Bring a whole army, I don't care. Nothing is going to save you.

Stumbled movement in his peripheral vision caught his attention. Guard number one had risen and was making his way toward him. Not standing on ceremony, Nicolas turned and stomped towards the guard. Reaching him, he tore the man's mask off and smashed his nose with a thunderous headbutt.

Huffing in frustration, he saw the second guard stirring, slowly trying to push himself from the floor. Nicolas booted him in the side of the head to ensure he didn't succeed.

Now for Potter.

As he turned his attention to his back-stabbing former friend, he saw the sweat on his stupid bald head. It was even more pleasing than the tremble in his voice. Especially as Nicolas was about to take that head and smash it into every wall he could find.

You are right to fear me you filthy bastard.

Another guard, from somewhere unseen, tried to grab his shoulders from behind. Turning and circling his arm, Nicolas broke the man's grip before grabbing the back of his head and introducing his face to the ground. Another guard ran at him. He dodged the poor attack and turned his fingers into a spear tip, which he drove into the man's throat. Spinning, he kicked a third in the jaw, sending him flying through the air.

'*You*,' he hissed as he turned his attention back to Potter, pointing an accusing finger at his former friend.

He was so close now. In his mind, he pictured squeezing Potter's throat until his eyes popped out of his head. New questions were posed by that voice that was trying to put a dampener on his sweet revenge.

Was he complicit all along? Did he watch my parents die? Did he have a hand in it? Does he know where the people of Hablock are?

Even through the haze of his rage, he knew he'd never have the answers to those questions. Because Garus Potter would die this day.

His head swung to the side, his attention summoned by a battle cry. From the next gateway charged ten men, clubs at the ready.

Fine.

Uttering his own battle cry – which was very close to a bestial roar – he charged them, causing his attackers to slow in confusion. Putting his foot on a nearby hitching post, Nicolas launched himself into the air at a group of enemies for the second time in a week. His teeth clenched in rage as he fell towards the silly bastards trying to get between him and his vengeance. Then he crashed into them. The force was enough to knock all the men backwards, most of them falling heavily to the cobbled ground.

From there, his anger consumed him completely. There were no fancy techniques; it was a flurry of fists and elbows as he lost himself to his rage. Hands clawed at him as he tried to rise, only to be answered by furious punches that broke bone and tore skin. Anyone who grabbed him soon regretted it.

After flooring the guard who took hold of his collar with a one-two combination, Nicolas finally rose from the pile. Standing tall above the groaning men.

Time for Potter.

He took a single step then his motion was arrested by a pull on his ankle. He dropped his other boot onto the jaw of the man trying to hold him then, in a blur of motion, caught the club swinging at him and plucked it from the guard's hand. The soldier made an *urk* sound as his own club was introduced to his neck.

'*Potter!*' he cried again, spittle flying from his mouth.

Vengeance.

His vision tunnelled again as he ran at the black knight, hands already reaching out, ready to tear that stupid beard right off his face.

Now.

Nicolas grunted in pain as a guard tackled him from the side, lifting him into the air and carrying him away from his target. He drove his elbows down onto the man's back until he fell to the ground. With a cry, Nicolas swung his knee into the side of the man's neck. Before he could move, two men took hold of him roughly, throwing him into the nearby wall. His cheek smacked against the cold stone, jarring his vision for a moment. The soldiers tried to pin him to the wall, but Nicolas poured his rage into his arms, pushing himself away far enough to put his legs on the wall and shove off. All three men fell backwards, and Nicolas elbowed each in the stomach and tried to rise. But it was too late; the others were on him.

Nicolas flailed and kicked furiously as he was dragged back down to the ground. He continued to punch and kick—even bite once—but they were over him now, swarming him. And they had the high ground. Club blows rained down on him. Between their legs, he saw Potter, standing tall, thinking he was safe. The black-armoured bastard was even walking towards him. The cockiness in his strut caused another volcanic explosion of anger in Nicolas.

I will not be denied.

Bellowing a curse, he burst from the group, scattering men in all directions. Snarling like a hungry wolf, he threw himself at Potter.

His hands were inches from the cockroach's neck when his arms were intercepted and pulled in opposite directions until his muscles strained, threatening to tear under the pressure. Arms wrapped around his neck and torso. His legs were secured. Yet still he struggled, spitting more curses and obscenities. Somehow, he managed to move forward a couple of steps.

In front of him, Potter exhaled theatrically. Crouching, he picked up a club, examining it briefly before turning his attention back to Nicolas.

'When you've had a chance to calm down,' the bearded bastard began, 'you and I need to have a little chat, Nicky boy.'

'You can go f—'

The club struck him hard in the jaw, knocking him unconcious.

CHAPTER 38

'Your tongue's out again, Nicky boy,' Potter noted with a bemused stare.

Nicolas glanced at his friend. 'I know,' he said, strain in his voice. 'You keep telling me.'

'And you keep doing it.'

'Well, I...' He grunted with effort. 'I can't talk about this right now.'

Potter held up his hands in apology and gestured for him to continue.

That was going to be hard, as the entire bow was shaking. Actually, it wasn't the bow. It was his arms. Both the one holding the bow, and the one pulling the string back. They ached as if they were being pulled in two different directions by charging horses. Trying to line up his shot, Nicolas knew his tongue had slipped out of his mouth again with the concentration. But it was impossible to get the bow to stay still, never mind aim at something. In the end, the arrow was loosed less due to his intention to do so and more due to his inability to hold the string any longer.

Thunk.

Nodding with raised eyebrows, Potter strolled over to the tree and looked up. 'I don't know if you're aware, Nicky boy,' he regarded the shaking arrow sticking out of the lowest branch, 'but generally when hunting rabbits you should aim at the ground. Where the rabbits are.'

'Ha, bloody, ha.' Nicolas grimaced as he rubbed his sore arm tenderly.

Stroking his beard thoughtfully, Potter suddenly clicked his fingers. 'I know. You've discovered some never-before-seen type of climbing rabbit.'

'I already said ha, bloody, ha, once. I'm not going to keep doing it for every joke you make.'

'Best stop giving me material then.' Potter grinned.

Despite himself, Nicolas chuckled. Potter joined in quickly. Soon the forest echoed with their laughter.

When it finally subsided, his friend put his hands on his hips and looked around. 'Well, I think we've successfully scared away every rabbit in a ten-mile radius.' Potter smirked. 'Not that they had anything to fear from you.'

Staring at the bow, Nicolas twanged the string a couple of times. 'Sorry.'
A twig hit him in the chest.

'Don't apologise to me.' Potter laughed, crouching and picking up the three rabbits he'd killed. Rising, he presented them like a trophy with a broad grin. 'I'm not the one going hungry tonight. Maybe you're just too nice and don't like the idea of killing rabbits? Or maybe hunting's not your forte?'

'What is?' He smiled. 'Beyond being nervous of course...and missing the target.'

Potter narrowed his eyes and gave him a sly grin. 'Maybe you've got hidden depths.'

Nicolas stopped short of picking the quiver up from the forest floor. 'What do you mean?'

Potter clicked his tongue and sighed. 'You know exactly what I mean, Nicky boy.'

Oh, that.

Ever since he'd returned home from his unexpected trip to Yarringsburg, Potter had been dying to prise the events of his near-death experience—experiences—from him. He'd told a barefaced lie when he'd suggested his trip was uneventful. He wasn't massively comfortable lying to his friends and family, but he didn't want to relive what had happened. The problem was, it was hard to believe him when he'd been overdue by several days and looked like he'd fallen down a cliff on his return. Still, most people had respected his right to keep it to himself.

Save one.

And questions like this were embuggering his plan to forget all about it. It had only been a week, and twice now he'd jumped at tree trunks that looked suspiciously like that armoured lunatic Silva.

She is dead. She's dead and can't hurt me anymore.

Night-time and all the shadows it brought was the worst, but he quickly shook the thought off before images of bloody fangs popped into his head. Instead, he picked up the quiver and began to walk back towards home.

'I told you what happened,' he replied, as Potter fell into step beside him.

'You told me a lot of nothing,' Potter said as he scanned the forest floor for signs of rabbits. 'And expected me to believe it. Yet you act as skittish as the rabbits today.'

Instantly, his hackles rose. 'No, I don't.'

His friend turned to him and raised an eyebrow. 'Yes, you do. You eye every shadow warily and start at any surprising noise. Don't pretend you don't.'

Shadows are scary. They could contain vampires.

Vampires. Once a simple myth. A scary tale. Now he knew the things in tales could be real, and very deadly.

Save the stupid vampires who just pose and kill themselves.

'Suit yourself.' Potter sighed.

'What about you?' Nicolas asked, hoping to deflect from the long and traumatising tale he most certainly didn't want to tell. 'When's your big adventure?'

When Potter had been drinking, he would go off on long tangents about what would happen when he finally struck out and left Hablock. The way he told it, it all sounded very grand and glorious. He would make a mighty name for himself. But it had yet to materialise.

Maybe that's why he's so desperate to know what's out there, to be prepared? I should tell him.

Nicolas cursed that it was so difficult to talk about. He promised himself if Potter ever looked like he was actually leaving, he would tell his friend the whole story.

There was a flash of seriousness on Potter's face, which melted away almost as soon as it'd formed. 'Plans are in the making, Nicky boy.' His friend grinned.

'Oooh, he has plans,' Nicolas mocked.

'I do.' Potter smirked. 'At the moment, I'm trying to come up with a decent adventurer name. I think adventurers need a good name. It helps tales of their deeds carry on. Potter the Fierce maybe? Or Potter the Slayer?' He scrunched his face up thoughtfully. 'Though I like the idea of a grand title. Something with Sir in it, maybe? Lord.' His eyes widened in excitement. 'Ooh, I like that. Lord Slayer. Lord Evil's Bane.'

'Keep it simple and accurate,' Nicolas suggested. 'Potter the Bullshitter.'

His friend wagged an accusing finger at him. 'You'll see. Just gotta get me old mother better and then I'm off.'

Nicolas furrowed his brow. 'She's unwell again? Is it serious?'

Potter shrugged. The nonchalance in his expression was confusing.

'Have you taken her to the healer?' he pressed.

'Over and over,' he said tartly. 'Yet it keeps recurring.'

There was something in Potter's tone that made it clear he didn't want to talk about it. Nicolas could respect people wanting to keep something to themselves more than certain other bearded individuals.

Sucking his teeth, Potter eyed the foliage around them. 'I don't think there are any more rabbits about today, Nicky boy.'

Thank the Deities.

The idea of killing fluffy little creatures wasn't one he savoured.

Truth be told, he probably wouldn't have even done it. Killing just wasn't in his nature, and he was set on keeping it that way.

'Well, at least you got the lesson in archery I promised.' Potter smiled broadly. 'Keep at it, and maybe one day, you'll almost hit something, instead of completely missing it.'

Nicolas slapped his friend on the arm. 'Thanks for the vote of confidence.' His tone became more serious. 'I hope she's okay. Your mum, I mean.'

Potter finished pushing aside the branch that was in his way and waved his hand dismissively. 'That tough old trout always gets better. I'd rather have your mum.'

'Well, I'm not trading.' Nicolas smiled. 'Though you're still coming to dinner tonight, right?'

His friend stared at him incredulously. 'There's no monster in all the lands that could keep me from your mum's cooking. What's she making?'

'Pie, apparently.'

'I hope it isn't rabbit pie, or it'll just be an empty crust. You ain't having any of mine.'

'Funny man.' Nicolas nodded. 'Funny, funny man.'

'It's nice your parents take me in like they do,' Potter mused as he looked up at the forest canopy.

'Well, they aren't used to me having a friend.' He shrugged.

A half-smile creased the edge of Potter's lips. 'You went from no friends to the best friend of all.'

'Shame I'm not trying to hit your ego with this bow.' Nicolas scoffed. 'I couldn't miss.'

'You'll miss me...' Potter replied coyly. 'When I'm gone. As will all the maidens in the tavern.'

Nicolas let out a sharp laugh. 'Oh, I can see it now. They'll all be swooning in the village square, crying 'Potter, Potter, Potter.'

Potter...

Potter...

Potter...

CHAPTER 39

P *otter!*

The wave of rage shocked him into consciousness. With it, he surged forwards, seeing the source of his ire directly in front of him. Within an instant, his motion was arrested, the manacles on his wrists cutting into his skin. Somehow, he managed not to slip and fall. Growling, he tested the restraints angrily. The chains clattered as he pulled against them again and again. But neither budged from their fastening in the wall behind him. So instead, he lashed out a kick, which wasn't even close.

'Not calmed down yet then, Nicky boy?' Potter commented, shaking his head sadly.

'I'll be nice and calm once I hold your heart in my hand so I can feel its last beat, you traitorous son of a bitch,' he snarled.

Holding his gauntleted hand up, Potter stopped the big guard who was taking a step towards Nicolas, fist raised. Finally, Nicolas realised they weren't alone. In fact, the black-armoured bastard was taking no chances. Four men stood in a semi-circle around him, crossbows loaded and aimed. Two more stood by the door and another four around the edge of the room. Then there was a big guy. Even with the mask on, Nicolas could tell he was a mean one.

'That's quite graphic for you, friend.' The black knight smirked. 'You've changed. Or have you *grown up?*'

Licking his lips, Nicolas looked around the room. It was a classic jail. Beyond the window, it was the dead of night. He had no idea how long he'd been out. Finally, he began to register the pain where he'd been beaten. Mentally checking himself over, he found numerous bruises. But he couldn't tell if he had any worse damage. For now, it all seemed superficial. Or his rage was pumping so much adrenaline through his veins that he couldn't feel the worst of it.

'Send these men for a walk, unlock my chains, and I'll happily show you how much I've grown up,' he snarled.

'Look, I understand you're a bit aggrieved—' Potter began.

'*Aggrieved?*' he spat. 'A-bloody-ggrieved. Yes, I tend to be *aggrieved* when someone betrays me and shoots me in the chest with an arrow. How would anyone take it any other way? That isn't exactly something you turn the other cheek for even when you *don't* know the person.'

Potter looked at the floor and nodded a few times. 'Okay, I understand your anger. I do.'

Thank you so much for your understanding, asshole.

'But in all honesty, I wasn't expecting to ever have this conversation with you. I mean, the arrow should've done the job. But you just won't die, will you? Koth, Tavish, the demon-host in Babylon, Avin...you just refuse to let us kill you.'

'*Us?*' Nicolas sagged against the chains. The betrayal was even deeper than he'd realised. 'You know all that?'

Potter gave him a self-indulgent half-smile. 'Of course. I'm privy to a lot of tasty information. I am kind of a big deal around here, if I may say so.'

Nicolas raised his head and narrowed his eyes. 'Go on then.'

Potter frowned. 'What?'

'What stupid name did you give yourself?' he asked, shaking his head.

Potter gestured to the sigil carved on his armour. 'They call me *Lord Blackheart.*'

Nicolas burst out laughing. His former friend glowered before nodding to the big guard, who punched him in the stomach. He was too busy laughing to think about the pain of the blow. 'Lord Blackheart? *Lord Blackheart?*'

'It's how they know me.' Potter was trying to be smug, but there was an edge of defensiveness in his voice.

'No, it really isn't.' Nicolas laughed. 'No one ever looked at you and thought, *'Huh, that guy looks like a Lord Blackheart.'* You picked a ridiculous name and demanded people call you it, as if you can change who you are.'

'Oh,' Potter said in a menacing whisper. 'And who am I then?'

'A sad little asshole, desperate to prove himself a big man.'

The guard struck him again, this time with his fist across the cheek.

'Harder, please,' Nicolas spat at the guard. 'Knock me out so I don't have to listen to this idiot.'

'Now, Nicky boy—'

'Don't *Nicky boy* me,' he cried. 'They raided our town and took our people, and you *joined* them. They killed my parents. And you joined them. You bloody joined them.' He tilted his head. 'Or were you already one of them?'

Potter refused to look at him.

Good, I hope the guilt burns you inside and out.

'I was out hunting when they came,' his former friend explained. 'I returned home to see them taking my family. I watched as they were dragged out of our house, and I couldn't help but think...screw them.'

'That's your mother.' He laughed incredulously. 'A sick woman who—'

'Let me tell you something about my *sick mother,*' Potter snarled, now holding his gaze. 'She was sick when it suited her. All the time, all I heard was *'You're just a layabout, why don't you go and make something of yourself, do the family name some good.'* Yet the minute I attempted to it was, *'Oh, my son. I'm ill and can't possibly care for myself. I need you.'* Constantly belittling me for not making anything of myself like my dad, yet desperate that I didn't walk out like he did. Only thing useful about her was her womb. Good riddance.'

'Sorry, I wasn't listening to your self-pity,' Nicolas replied with a theatrical apologetic shrug. 'I was too busy picturing sticking a sword in your gut.'

The guard grabbed him by the hair and cracked him across the cheek again. This time when he spat, there was blood in it.

'I saw my chance, didn't I, Nicky boy?' Lord Blackheart continued. 'It was time to go and make that name for myself. No more excuses. Screw the little people who'd held me back.' His tone softened for a moment. 'I actually came to help you, you know.'

'Bloody funny way of going about it,' he retorted dryly. 'I didn't find the arrow in the chest particularly helpful.'

Potter glared but just continued his monologue. 'So, I get to your house, and I see you making some kind of stand against Koth. Then I get to thinking. The sheer power to be able to unleash such a creature and abduct an entire village...well, I saw an opportunity.'

'One that required me to die?'

'It wasn't *necessary,* but it was my way of introducing myself, of showing that I could do what needed doing, that I had that killer instinct they might be after.' The level of smug pride on display made Nicoles want to vomit. 'All in all, Koth was quite impressed with me and offered to become my sponsor. He got me a seat at the table and gave me some sweet jobs, ensuring my name got heard in all the right places. The rest is history.'

'You're welcome.' Nicolas tested the chains again.

'I *should* be thanking you.' Potter chuckled. 'You paved the way for all of this. You even got me a promotion when you killed Tavish. You did nearly ruin it when you threw that knife at me in Narus, mind. I almost actually hit Helstrum because of you. That would've buggered up my career prospects no end.'

It took Nicolas a moment for it to sink in. When he did, he let out a groan and rolled his eyes. 'It was fake. I bloody knew it.'

Potter shrugged. 'It was supposed to make the message look good. But it worked out well enough, and I got to be where I'm meant to be.'

'You get a chance to reinvent yourself, and *this* is what you choose?' Trying to gesture to someone's outfit with chained hands was quite difficult.

'I saw the potential in my new masters, just like they saw the potential in me.' Potter smirked. 'Here, we're going to change the world. What else would you have me do?'

'You could've helped me,' he cried.

'Against Koth?' Potter blew a raspberry. 'C'mon, Nicky boy.'

'So help me or kill me were your *only* choices?'

'In all fairness, I didn't expect to have to listen to you whine about it.'

'*Whine?*'

'Yes.' Potter scoffed, gesturing to him. 'You have all this amazing stuff happen to you, and all you do is *waaaaaahhhhhh*. It's kind of pathetic, let me tell you.' Stepping forward, Potter grabbed his collar roughly. 'You could've shared it. I gave you chances. You could've taken me with you, helped me realise my destiny. But nope. You wanted all the glory for yourself. So when I saw my opportunity, I took it.'

'I never wanted glory,' Nicolas cried. 'I just wanted a quiet life.'

With a harsh laugh, Potter let go of him. 'Please, Nicky boy. *Everyone* wants glory. Big glory, small glory. Whatever. They all want it, but don't want to do what they need to do to get it.'

Nicolas was dumbfounded. How could someone he'd counted as a friend justify this to himself. 'But our people...'

'We're building a better world, and I'm building a legacy. If I have to step on a few people to do it...' Potter shrugged again.

'*My parents*,' Nicolas snapped. 'Who took you in and treated you well. Did you help with them too? Or did you just watch and clap like a good little minion?'

'I'm no minion.' The sneer on Potter's face suggested that had hit a nerve. Then his faced softened. 'Your parents. I *am* sorry about them. But Koth wanted to do it. I...I left.'

'Well done, sparing yourself that sight.'

'I'm not proud of that, but it got me here.' Potter gestured around him with an almost dreamy quality. Which was weird, because they were in a cell. 'And so are you. I *was* hoping you'd join me. Nicky boy and Potter, back together. Imagine what we could do?'

'You *what?*'

'You and me, together.' Potter grinned. 'I use my clout to get you off the hook for all the crap you've caused, and you can be my right-hand guy. I know you know how to fight now—I have an infirmary full of men who'll speak to that—so you've got the skills, you're just using them for the wrong side.'

Nicolas shook his head in disbelief at what he was hearing. For a moment he wondered if he'd finally been struck in the head too many times. Had his brain been broken and he was making up absolute nonsense like this? No, this was real, horribly real. And Potter's argument wasn't even slightly compelling.

'I'm going to say this slowly and clearly, so you understand it,' Nicolas said. 'I am going to kill you. Not for revenge, or for Hablock, or even for my parents, but because you clearly need killing.'

Potter rolled his eyes. 'Nicky boy—'

'Asshole.'

'Nicky boy—'

'Prick.'

'*Nicky*—'

'Wanker.'

'When you come around again, I'll give you one last chance. Hopefully, you see sense.' This time, Potter was the one to punch him. His gauntleted knuckles cut the flesh of Nicolas's cheek.

Nicolas snapped his eyes back to his former friend. 'Are you going to knock me out soon?'

Potter punched him again.

'I don't like being tickled.'

With a grunt of frustration, Potter grabbed a club from one of the guards. That did the job.

CHAPTER 40

Every muscle in his body tensed as freezing water shocked him awake. Gasping, he desperately tried to catch his breath as his lungs pumped at furious speed.,. Coughing and spluttering, he tried to focus as all his senses screamed at him. The only thing he was sure of was that he was still chained to the wall.

Roughly, a hand grabbed a wad of his dripping wet hair and yanked his head upwards. His feet had to follow, and soon he was standing. His legs betrayed him, but the hand held him up, pain searing his scalp as he was kept upright despite the rest of his body being limp. One by one he planted his feet and managed to stand of his own accord.

Potter was watching him with a half-smile. 'Right then, Nicky boy.' His former friend grinned. 'Now you're awake again, let's try banging my head against this wall one last time.'

How am I the one in chains, and he's stood here large as life? I'm the Deities-damned good guy.

Once again, Nicolas was surrounded by crossbow-armed guards. It was still night, so he couldn't have been unconscious too long. But his arms were numb from taking his weight for however long he had been.

The last few shivers left his body as he glared defiantly at Potter. 'I'll happily bang your head against every wall in this place, you treacherous bastard.'

He doubled over, wheezing, as he was punched in the stomach. His head was lifted up just in time for the backhand blow to catch him across the cheek. For a moment, his body threatened to go limp again, but he managed to stay on his feet.

'Are you out of your mind?' Potter cried, throwing his hands into the air. 'Do you not understand what killing you will do for me? I'll be in the Maestro's favour until the end of time. And yet here I am, still intent on giving you one last chance to join us.'

'No.' It was one of the easiest answers he'd given in his life, even though he knew it'd be the answer to end it. Part of him wondered if he could try to fake it, to convince them to unshackle him. But he knew he'd try to kill Potter the minute he did.

'Fine,' Potter said instantly. 'If you're so intent on dying, I'm too important to waste my time trying to convince you otherwise.'

Bless you for gracing me with your presence at all.

There was a long pause, and no sword gutted him. No crossbow bolt shot him down. Instead, Lord Blackheart stared at him with folded arms.

'What do you want?' Nicolas asked after a moment of clarity.

Potter narrowed his eyes and sneered slightly. 'Where are your companions?' he asked slowly.

'Ha,' Nicolas's laugh echoed around the room. 'If you think I'm giving them up, you're stupider than you look. Which is pretty damned stupid, considering you walk around with a heart on your armour.'

The guard hit him several times. Potter came back into view once the man stepped back, his assault complete.

'You're a stubborn little bastard,' his former friend mused. 'I have no idea why fate chose to gift you that message, instead of me.'

'Fate? *Fate*?' Nicolas shook his head in exasperation. 'Fate had nothing to do with it. You were there. You saw that bloody choosing stick.'

'And I saw it choose you.' Potter's tone was ice cold. 'And since it has, you have fame. People know your name. People respect or fear it.'

'A lot of good it's doing me,' he said, gesturing to the chains with his head. 'But if it bothers you so much, have it. Have my fame and whatever else you were prattling on about. I hope you choke on it.' Nicolas thought for a moment. 'Actually, part of me hopes you enjoy it. Then one night, as you sleep, it'll hit you just what you had to do to get it. Betraying your best friend. Selling out your village. Participating in the murder of innocent people who loved you. And all the other dark shit you've done since then. And when you do, when it dawns on you how utterly despicable you are, I hope you throw yourself off the damn roof of a place just like this.'

The black knight chuckled dryly. 'What I'll do when I realise that, is open my eyes, turn over, and make love to the four beautiful women sharing my bed.'

Nicolas's fist clenched. It was a futile gesture, and he knew it. But he couldn't help himself. 'Do you know where they are? Our people?'

'Yup,' Potter replied as he drew his sword and studied himself in the blade. 'There's no point telling you, though. It wouldn't do you any good, Nicky boy. Because you're right. You aren't going to tell us where the orc, the traitor bitch, and that shapeshifter you're so fond of are, are you?' He didn't wait for an answer. 'So, I have no reason to keep you alive. Might as well finish you off then enjoy the sweet fruits of my labour.'

The certainty in Potter's eyes shocked him. Lord Blackheart would kill him and not lose an hour's sleep over it.

If only I had a chance to take him with me.

A sudden, bright light filled the window then vanished again just as quickly. All eyes turned to it.

'What was that?' Potter asked.

His answer came in the form of a horn sounding a deep note that resonated through the night air. It was an alarm, if Nicolas guessed right.

Potter looked around in confusion before stomping towards the window and peering out. 'What in the Underworld is going on out there?'

If only I could kick him in the ass and out that window.

In his mind, Nicolas measured the distance. He'd never reach. But it was still tempting to try.

There was a sound of urgent footsteps outside the cell. A guard burst through the door, panting heavily. 'Milord, we're under attack.'

'What?' Potter cried. 'Attack? By who?'

'Orcs, milord,' the soldier said, keeping his head bowed. 'They're attacking the outer camp and the training grounds. They'll be at the gate soon.'

'Dammit,' Potter growled. 'Seal the fortress. Musketeers and archers to the battlements. Prepare to drive them back.'

'What about the men stuck outside the walls?' the soldier asked.

'Let's hope they learned a lot in the last day, enough to give the orcs a good fight. If not, they died for a noble cause.'

Who is this man?

Potter glanced out of the window as another flash filled it. 'We need to get out there.' He pointed to the crossbowmen. 'You lot, with me.'

Even now, Nicolas could hear the sounds of battle in the distance. The orcs were certainly coming in hard.

Good. Hopefully one of them eats Potter.

Potter, with most of the men, filed out of the room, leaving just one man and the four by the door.

'What shall we do with him?' the guard who liked to punch Nicolas called after his master.

'Kill him, moron,' came the already distant reply.

The guard drew his sword and stalked towards him. 'Right then, you—'

The end of that sentence was lost forever as the guard's neck snapped with a wince-inducing crack. Before the others could react, the second guard who'd been stood by the door lunged forwards, stabbing another in the gut.

The fight was short and sweet. As the last guard fell, Silva and Shift took their masks off and discarded them.

'Much appreciated.' He smiled. 'I was hoping a couple of the guards were you guys. But when you weren't jumping in...'

'We couldn't risk it,' Silva said as she checked the corridor. 'Not with four crossbows pointed at you all at once. We needed to bide our time.'

'How's my face?' he asked as Shift approached.

The shapeshifter regarded him with narrowed eyes. 'A bit messed up. But I'd still kiss you.'

'Get these chains off me, and you have a big kiss coming your way.'

As Shift went to reach for the manacles, they stopped briefly. 'I assume you'd prefer me to use my magic key this time?'

'If you wouldn't mind.'

CHAPTER 41

Rubbing his arms—and his sore wrists—vigorously, Nicolas tried to get the feeling back in them. Fortunately, it didn't take long, probably egged on by a desire to find Potter and administer a healthy amount of retribution. Which was good. He had a building to fight his way out of.

Speaking of...

Standing over the dead guard who'd been so passionate about beating him, Nicolas crouched down and took his sword. As he rose, his eyes were focused on the dead man, whose head was at the wrong angle. Anger demanded that he kick the man. But he was dead; there was no point. Then he noticed the man's ghost in the room, caught in the brief moment before passing on to the Underworld. Locking eyes with the man's ghost, he kicked his body hard in the ribs.

'Tell Sha'then I said hello,' he growled at the apparition.

The soldier sneered, opening his mouth to speak, but then he and the others faded into nothing. He hoped all their eternal souls had spikes right up their asses.

Outside the jail, the corridor was quiet. It seemed like the majority of the soldiers were at the walls trying to repel the orc attack. Even through the thick stone walls, he could hear the din of battle. And the shooting of numerous fire-sticks.

Silva threw aside her mask and helmet. 'I tire of sneaking around,' she declared, circling her sword in her hand. 'I prefer a straight-up fight.'

'Oh, I am definitely in the mood for a fight,' Nicolas said, focused on the sword he was swinging so he could get used to the weight. It wasn't the *Dawn Blade*, but it'd bloody well do for now.

'I don't think we'll have a choice anyway,' Shift remarked. 'We can hardly say we're escorting these guys' most-hated enemy out of the building.'

Moving down the corridor single file, the group kept silent. But there was no sign of anyone. Finally, they came to a window.

'Silva, you know you said you wanted a straight-up fight?' Shift asked, peering out. 'I think there's plenty to go around.'

Nicolas joined his companion at the window. Beyond it, he could see the wall surrounding the fortress. Numerous men manned it, moving with haste as they fired their weapons then reloaded them as fast as they could. Every so often, one would fall, his body limply crashing to the ground below with an arrow sticking from it.

Beyond the wall, there was inhuman snarling and the clashing of metal. And the blasting of those new weapons.

Oh, and the death screams. How I pray for the day I don't hear death screams anymore.

The way his life was going, he'd more likely go deaf well before that was achieved.

'Where's Auron?' he asked as he looked around, awaiting a story about escaping a castle under attack.

'When we realised you were captured, he went to get Garaz.'

He looked at Shift askew. 'But that's a long walk.'

'He summoned his horse and rode,' Silva said, curling her mouth slightly. 'He was quite showy about it too.'

Auron? Gasp.

If only they all had undead horses they could summon from thin air. According to Auron, Mare, his ridiculously named horse, ran even faster post-life.

'What's the plan then?' he asked. 'I doubt we've got time to search the place for a handy secret passage?'

'That'd be nice,' Shift said dreamily. 'But no. This is a *make it up as we go along* type thing.'

Nicolas didn't feel it necessary to point out that it was exactly that type of planning that had gotten them into this mess in the first place.

'First things first. Get to the courtyard,' Silva told him. 'We will figure out our next move from there.'

Silva checked the corner and ensured that the way was clear. With her nod, the trio progressed carefully. Though it was likely any soldiers were occupied with the battle outside, it never paid to be complacent in an enemy stronghold.

'So, you and the prick in the black armour were once friends?' Shift kept levity in their voice, but the look in their eyes suggested they were worried for him.

'Once,' Nicolas said with a growl. 'I think it's fair to say that's right out the window.' His hand moved up to his chest unconsciously, rubbing the arrow scar.

'Well, at least your taste in company has improved,' they replied with a wink.

'It was slim pickings back in Hablock. I wasn't exactly a popular fellow.' Talking about his hometown stung, but he couldn't pretend it never existed. Just like he couldn't pretend he and Potter had never been friends.

Shift gave a theatrical gasp. 'You don't sa—'

'*Halt!*'

Silva swung around, giving Shift and Nicolas a well-earned filthy look, as neither of the pair had thought to keep an eye behind them. Three soldiers stood down the corridor from them. Two had fire-sticks which were levelled at them, and the third, a tall and broad man, stood back a little way from the others. In this narrow corridor, Nicolas didn't like the odds of them missing if they fired.

'Drop your weapons,' one of the soldiers commanded.

This was a tricky situation. If they did as they'd been asked, the men were likely to kill them anyway. But at the same time, they didn't want to do anything to bring on their fate.

Still, I think I'd rather go down fighting.

He was preparing himself for what might be his final charge...when the problem was solved for him. The third guard stepped forwards and, with a blur of his hands, cut the throats of the other two. The fire-sticks clattered to the ground as the men desperately attempted to stop the freely flowing blood. They failed and were dead soon enough. The soldier who was left standing removed his mask. Instantly, Nicolas recognised the strong jawline.

'*You*,' he cried, pointing. 'You were in the border fort. You're the one who helped us.'

The man gave a noble bow. 'And it looks like I am set to do so again.'

Silva stepped between them, sword at the ready. 'Once you explain who you are.'

Nicolas might've labelled her paranoid, but his *best friend* had turned out to be a low down, good for nothing, back-stabbing – well, front-ar-rowing, if that's a term – sneaky, despicable bastard. So who was he to judge?

The man indicated the sound of battle in the distance. 'Do we have time for that? Please, I am a friend. I will explain all once we are clear of this place.'

I love the optimism. Just two armies to get through first.

'I think we should trust him,' Shift offered. 'He has saved our lives twice. That should earn him some leeway.'

Silva pursed her lips thoughtfully. There was an undeniable logic in that. 'For now,' she relented finally.

'This way,' the man said, turning and running back down the corridor.

Nicolas and the others followed quickly. When he got close to their saviour, though, he seemed to bump into something directly in the walkway. He glanced around for a moment yet couldn't see anything. Must've been his imagination.

When he reached the window, the man turned to them. 'Out here.'

'Out where?' Nicolas cried.

'The window.'

Nicolas peered out of it. They were pretty high up. Jumping out of this window would certainly break some bones. Possibly prove fatal. Down below—way below—chaos still reigned on the battlements. Soldiers were desperately fighting back orcs who'd found a ladder somewhere and made it up to greet them with their blades. Ahead of them was the main gate they'd entered the fortress through.

It was really high up. 'Throw ourselves out the window?' he scoffed as he pulled himself back in. 'Why in the name of the all the Deities would you think that's a good idea?'

'There's a hay wagon directly below us,' their saviour said.

Nicolas leant out the window. *Oh yeah, there it is. That tiny dot.* 'Off you go then,' Nicolas said, presenting the window to their saviour.

'Trust me,' the man replied awkwardly, 'you want me to go last.'

His attention was caught by the sound of an angry cry and boots charging up the corridor.

They know we've escaped.

Still, he couldn't bring himself to just chuck his body out a window. His survival instinct put it's foot down and refused to let him do it.

'We need to go,' Shift urged.

'Look, if you think I'm—'

'Stop over-thinking it, Nick.'

'Yaaaaaahhhhhhhh.'

CHAPTER 42

As he was shoved from the window, he managed to turn mid-air and give Shift a stupefied look, until they disappeared from view and all he saw was the rapidly moving castle wall. His arms flailed as he screamed. He closed his eyes tightly and prayed.

Please don't miss. Please don't miss. Please don't miss.

With a thump, he hit the hay. Thankfully, it was thick, but the impact still drove the air from him as he rolled to the side and out of the slanting wagon. When his body finally came to rest on the stone floor, he glanced up at the window from which he'd come. Instantly, he became nauseated. Looking away before he was actually sick, he realised there was a pair of feet directly in front of him.

Following the legs up, he found himself staring at a shocked guard holding a fire-stick. The man was making an *'uuuuhhhhh'* sound from beneath his mask, suggesting his mouth was open as he tried to process what he'd just seen. When he had, he began to shoulder his weapon.

Driving himself up from the floor, Nicolas punched the soldier in the throat. Choking, the soldier dropped to the floor as there was another thump in the hay behind him. Nicolas kicked him to make sure he stayed down. Then he noticed something.

Potter.

There, atop the battlements, the black-armoured asshole was marching about, shouting orders like he was someone important and not just a village rabbit-hunter. Who'd have thought murdering your friend was a solid route to getting your dream job? Scowling, Nicolas picked up the fire-stick. Pressing it into his shoulder, he took aim. There was another bump in the hay behind him.

'Nick, wait...'

Shift's words were lost in the thunder of the weapon as he squeezed the trigger. With flame and smoke, it launched its metal projectile. Nicolas jerked backwards slightly, but this time he'd been ready for the weapon's mighty kick. Part of the battlements next to Potter shattered.

Slowly, Lord Blackheart turned around, first looking at the hole in his cape with wide eyes then looking at Nicolas, his mouth an exaggerated O.

Nicolas started at a massive crash behind him. When he turned, the hay wagon had been shattered. Amongst the debris was their saviour.

But how?

The man was a tall fellow, to be sure, yet he'd fallen like a giant stomping onto the wagon.

In that moment, Potter got over his surprise and came to life. '*Kill them. Kill them all,*' he screamed, pointing toward them. The paleness of his face from his near-death experience becoming the bright red of rage. '*Killllll themmmmm.*'

It was hard to really hear what Potter was saying over the sounds of battle, but he was exaggerating it enough that Nicolas could lip read. His soldiers nearby had a better time hearing him. Several who were manning the gate, which kept bulging as something bumped hard against it from beyond, left their post and formed a line, fire-sticks at the ready.

'Didn't we *just* do this?' Shift asked.

Again, he winced as fingers began to squeeze triggers...and then the gate exploded.

Shards of wood flew across the courtyard, impaling several men. Suddenly, Nicolas and his companions weren't a priority as orcs thundered into the courtyard, hacking and slashing at anyone who didn't have green skin. Within moments, the entire courtyard was in the grip of a violent battle.

Only one of the soldiers set to kill them decided to try to follow through on the order. He raised his weapon again and aimed...then screamed as he turned into a flailing ball of fire.

From the throng of fighting bodies, a familiar, red-cloaked figure emerged, knocking a soldier aside with his staff as he did.

'Garaz?' Nicolas cried in relief. 'This was you?'

The orc smiled then closed his eyes with a sigh. 'And him,' he said, gesturing to the castle wall.

Timing his cue perfectly, Auron rode through the wall on Mare as if jumping a wide chasm. The spirit then did a lap of the courtyard and settled before them, Mare rearing dramatically as he saluted them. 'Yes, I, Auron of Tellmark have come with reinforcements to save you from your plight.'

Give me strength.

'But how?' Shift said in wonder.

'Once Auron informed me of your situation, we rushed here. On the way, I became aware we were close to my tainted kin—which is hardly difficult, considering how rowdily they usually travel. Before they killed me for being *'not orc-like,'* I told them where they could find a really good fight.' Garaz gestured around him as if to say *and here we are.*

A masked head flew past them and struck the wall with a squelch that made Nicolas gag.

'I doubt this will do much to shake their hatred of non-humans,' Shift remarked, eyeing the head in disgust as it hit the floor.

'I doubt even a wizard powerful enough to summon the fiercest earthquakes could shake *that* foundation.' Garaz sniffed in annoyance.

Despite that foundation, these were just men. Yes, they had joined the army of a very evil man. But really, they were misguided people who'd might've been through some tragedy, one bad enough to allow them to buy Helstrum's bullshit. And now more than a few of them were dead. He doubted many on the outside of the wall had survived. Something about that made him sad, deep inside. The use and waste of life. But he couldn't dwell on it now. All he could do was see his companions to safety—or they him, more likely.

It quickly became apparent that Garaz's plan had a single hiccup, and a major one at that. Once the *reinforcements* were in the midst of battle, they weren't fussy about which pink-skinned folk they killed.

Or orcs.

Before Nicolas could shout a warning, Garaz ducked the orc swinging its oddly improvised blade at his head. Spinning as he ducked, Garaz turned and gave his attacker a fireball directly to the face. The pained squealing from the orc was almost as bad as the smell of cooked meat.

A large shape came at Nicolas out of the chaos. Swinging his sword, he blocked the blow from the orc, before cutting the creature diagonally across the torso. Thank the Deities they thought furs were effective armour.

'I believe my idea may have just put us in more danger,' Garaz admitted, suddenly alert.

'Be a shame to make this too easy,' their saviour said, ushering them back to the wall.

'Who is th—? Oh, it is you.' Garaz recognised the man, who nodded back politely.

But is he really an ally? Knowing my luck, he's a faun in disguise.

Nicolas eyed the broken wagon nervously.

He's certainly heavier than he looks.

Right now, they had bigger issues. Like how to get out of here. There was a literal war between them and the gate, the closest exit. Worse, the battle had closed in around them, in a large semi-circle that was going to keep them pinned to the wall. Fortunately, the Custodians and the orcs seem bent on annihilating each other, so their small group garnered little interest.

But little *is still* some.

Several orcs broke from the fray and charged them. Nicolas quickly raised his sword, intercepting the old cleaver the one attacking him carried and catching it on one of the many nicks in its blade. With a deft circle, he disarmed the orc and ran him through.

'What are these things they're using?' he asked as he parried another blow. The majority of the orcs carried the same type of weapon.

To be honest, in the midst of a battle was not the time to be making enquiries about arms and armaments. But Nicolas's mind just worked in a funny way sometimes.

Especially when I've been punched in the head repeatedly in a short space of time.

Garaz picked up the human trying to stab him by the face and hurled him into a pack of orcs. The man disappeared into them with the nausea-inducing sound of chewing and tearing flesh.

'They are called...' Garaz gave a brief sigh before finishing his thought. '*Choppas. The Regression* does terrible things to an orc's vocabulary.'

Why can't it also affect their ability to swing a sword...I mean choppa?

A large orc barrelled into their group, belly first, sending them all flying in opposite directions. Nicolas stumbled to the ground, sword slipping from his grasp to end up on the far side of the orc, who...

Shit.

...had Shift dangling in the air by their legs like a rabbit in a butcher's window. Shift swung their blade at the orc, only to have it slapped away before the enraged creature grabbed their arm and began to pull. Time slowed as he saw the pain on Shift's face. His sword was too far away.

'Nick,' Shift cried, pointing at the floor. 'Get to the *choppa*.'

To his side was a discarded orc weapon. Flinging himself toward it, Nicolas rolled as he landed, grabbing the weapon and launching it as he smoothly rose from the roll. With a thud, it embedded itself in the side of the orc's head. It's red, feral eyes rolled backwards as it let go of Shift and slowly toppled to the ground, dead.

'Enough of this,' Garaz roared as he rose.

He slammed his staff on the ground. Two lines of flame burst from it, pushing the fighting parties back—and burning some—as it created a corridor for them to use. Though the heat was oppressive, like being stood inside an oven, the group quickly charged down the walkway Garaz had created. Sweat poured from Nicolas's body as he made for the gate as fast as he could, knowing the flames protecting him wouldn't last forever.

Potter.

There he was, standing on the battlements, right in his line of sight. Not breaking stride, Nicolas grabbed a knife from a dead soldier's belt as he passed his body. With no time to aim properly, just a hope that it would sail true and find its target, he launched it. The blade spun through the air, to stick in the shoulder pauldron of Lord Blackheart's armour, rather than between his eyes as Nicolas had hoped. Potter staggered back in shock as he glared at Nicolas, who raised his thumb and index finger in a narrow gap. A reminder of how close he'd come.

His former friend yanked the knife out of his armour and threw it to the ground, raging and flailing his arms. Though he couldn't hear what he was ranting about over the battle, Nicolas guessed it was something to the effect of *'I'll get you Nicky boy. Just see if I don't. Lord Blackheart always gets his vengeance.'* Or some such bollocks.

Lord Blackheart *loves the sound of his own voice.*

With a smirk, Nicolas simply pointed to the three orcs bearing down on the black knight. Hopefully, these orcs had a taste for human flesh.

As the carnage continued, Nicolas and his companions fled the embattled fortress.

CHAPTER 43

W heezing and panting, he made it to the next rise with his companions. There, the group finally stopped to catch their breath. Nicolas had plenty of experience running, but this had been a frenzied flight, and he had to admit he was pretty badly beaten. So he put his hands on his knees and waited for the world to stop spinning. His sweat-drenched body tingled as the cool night air settled on it.

Rising, and stretching his aching body, he caught sight of Shift doing the same. 'You pushed me out the window,' he said irritably.

The shapeshifter shrugged. 'It got you down, didn't it?'

'That's not the—' He waved his hand in the air lazily. 'Never mind.' He was too tired to argue.

Turning, he dropped to the grass with a sigh. The fortress should've been hard to make out in the dark, but it was lit up by numerous fires. Several looked big enough to threaten to consume the place entirely.

Good.

They might've missed their shot at Tobis Helstrum, but at least he could take solace in the fact that his training ground was being burnt to cinders. Though he highly doubted this was the only one. Either way, it should at least set the Maestro's plan back considerably, giving them time to hunt him down and finish their job.

I also hope an orc is currently shitting out Potter's remains.

His hands tore at the grass beneath his fingers as his friend's betrayal hit him again. Then he frowned. Looking up, he searched the sky for a reason for the thunder he'd just heard. But it was clear, save the twinkling stars. Nicolas wondered if the stars were enjoying the show as some villains got punished.

'There,' Shift said, pointing towards the main road to the fortress.

Torches. Lots of them.

It wasn't thunder; it was cavalry. The soldiers of Ivilar had finally caught up to their prey. Ranks of armoured knights charged towards the fortress. It didn't take long for the orcs to notice, either. A number of them exited the gate to wait for the newcomers, only to be barrelled aside as the knights charged through them.

Hopefully, they arrest all Helstrum's men too. And if Potter isn't dead...well, that'll give me something to do after I've killed the Maestro, won't it?

'Getting betrayed is tough,' Shift said softly, putting their hand on his.

They're being sympathetic? Deities, I must look bad.

'You have experience?' he asked.

Shift gave a slight chuckle. 'Thieves Guild. It's happened once or twice. Soon learned to wise up and not trust people...until I met you lot,' they finished sourly.

He turned his hand so they could interlace their fingers. 'I'm sorry for your troubles,' he said, trying to fight back his smirk.

They gave an exaggerated sigh. 'It's okay.' A mischievous look crossed their face. 'I could tell you about it, if you like. You look like you're in the mood for a *'So, this one time....'*

'I am quite all right, thank you.'

A gasp of surprise from behind got their attention. Silva had her sword to their saviour's throat. 'It is time for that explanation,' she growled, matching his steps as he backed away.

She's right, but not like this.

Giving his own sigh, Nicolas got up and walked over to the soldier. Gently, he put his hand over Silva's and pushed her blade away. 'He can't tell us anything if you cut his throat. Besides, he did save us, twice. I think that earns him a couple of sentences without having a sword pointed at him. At least.'

Silva glared at Nicolas as if he'd just overstepped his bounds, which surprised him more than a little. 'As you are helping me grow as a person, he gets three sentences,' she said finally.

'Glad to see her journey of growth is paying off,' Auron remarked snarkily.

Silva sheathed her blade but gave their saviour a look that suggested it could quite easily come out again. The soldier backed away a couple of paces. 'Is she always like that?'

'Yes.' Shift grinned. 'But in all fairness, we do get betrayed a lot.'

That was certainly true. Which was probably why Garaz had a sly fireball simmering away in his hand right now.

He's one to talk.

'Ah, I understand,' the soldier said. 'I am aware of your tales. Unfortunately, circumstances have not allowed me to be forthcoming until now. I apologise for the subterfuge. It is necessary in my line of work.' Putting one hand on his heart, he bowed low. 'I am Jorish, Commander of the Eighth Centaur Battleherd, now attached to the League of Light.'

Nicolas went to open his mouth then stopped. He wasn't entirely sure if he was about to ask a stupid question, but now it was in his mind, he couldn't *not* ask it. Carefully, eyeing his companions for signs he was about to make an idiot of himself, he asked, 'Don't you need to be a centaur to be commander of a centaur battle-thingy?'

'I am a centaur,' Jorish answered simply.

Leaning to the side, he looked behind the soldier then at his companions. Was he the only one missing something? Again, he was hesitant to speak, but the confused looks from the others was enough to make him continue.

'No, you're not,' he said slowly.

'I can assure you I am.'

Oh, for Deities' sake. He's mad.

On very uncertain ground, he turned to Garaz. 'Centaurs are half-horse, right? I mean, that's what I've always heard. Am I right? I'm sure I'm right.'

The orc nodded, as perturbed as he was.

'I think what my bumbling love interest is trying to say,' Shift began, 'is if you're a centaur, *where's the rest of you?*'

'I've done some amazing things, but I've never misplaced half my body.' Auron chuckled.

As Jorish went to reach into his armour, Silva took a menacing step forward. Suddenly, his hands were in the air. Sensible move. 'I can explain if you allow me,' he said sheepishly.

This ought to be good.

When Silva didn't immediately stab him, Jorish reached into his armour and pulled out a small charm on a chain. 'This is a perception warper,' he explained, holding the medallion aloft. 'It ensures that people see only what they expect to see. Here, everyone expects to see a human, so that's what they see. Nobody expects to see a centaur, so nobody does.'

When did everyone start getting charms on chains? Where's mine?

'But you're still a centaur?' Nicolas asked warily.

'Yes.'

'Oh, come on,' Nicolas cried. 'You're wearing human clothes. And how would you stop your horse half from bumping into people?'

'I walk carefully.'

Suddenly, he remembered the castle corridor. He *had* bumped into something when he got too close to Jorish. 'I... You... I...' He raised his hands in surrender. 'You know what, I completely give up on understanding this world. I'm not even going to try anymore. Anything anyone tells me I'm just going to smile, nod, and accept it. Otherwise, all my hair will fall out by my next birthday.'

'You'll be saner for it,' Auron added sagely.

'Please,' Jorish said. 'Look at me with the expectation of seeing a centaur.'

It seemed ridiculous. Just look at someone and *expect* to see something which clearly wasn't there? But his new philosophy was to smile and nod, and Jorish was so darned certain of himself. Taking a deep breath, Nicolas closed his eyes.

Centaur, centaur, centaur.

He opened his eyes again. They widened instantly. 'Well, shit.'

Lo and behold, suddenly Jorish had half a horse sticking out of his rear. No wonder the wagon had been pulverised when he landed on it. Nicolas found himself blinking, a lot, as his mind attempted to wrap around what he was seeing.

'Fascinating,' Garaz said.

'Necessary.' Jorish shrugged.

'I sense a good story coming,' Auron said with glee.

CHAPTER 44

S haking his head in disbelief, Nicolas quickly looked over at his other companions, with the expectation of seeing...anything, really. They all stayed the same. Shift caught him looking and realised what he was doing.

'It's arrangeable.' They grinned.

Not knowing how to respond to that, he shrugged and turned back to Jorish. 'So you're a centaur. That's established now. So what's this League of Light then?'

Jorish stared at him for a long moment, one that almost became uncomfortable. 'As a spy, giving secrets out does not come naturally to me.' The centaur allowed himself a small smile. 'But it has given me the chance to meet you. Your tales and deeds are well known. I must say, it is an honour.'

'Where did you hear these tales exactly?' Nicolas asked, keen to know how his legend was spreading across Etherius.

Now it was the centaur's turn to shrug. 'Word gets around.'

Doesn't it just.

'If we could get back to the point,' Silva cut in testily.

'Of course,' Jorish said with a slight bow. 'And I will tell you all. Especially as you are the reason for the league's existence.'

Nicolas blinked several times. 'I...I'm what now?'

'Because of your deeds, the non-human kingdoms of Etherius are no longer blind to the connection between the evils blighting your lands. Your efforts have shown us the threads connecting these tragedies, and the potential fallout from them if men like Tobias Helstrum have their way. The league was created to investigate and neutralise what is happening. To veer events away from the inevitability of war. Just like you, Nicolas Percival Carnegie, and your brave friends have been doing.'

'A noble endeavour,' Garaz said.

'Indeed,' Jorish acknowledged. 'I have been tasked to learn about this vile conspiracy and support you in your quest. I heard a rumour you would be returning to Ivilar soon, and men had been sent to kill you, so I positioned myself and waited. I had hoped we would have the chance to talk before now. But I can see the tales of the danger you constantly face are not exaggerated.' The centaur put his hands on his hips. 'After the border fort, I lost track of you, so I made my way here, to learn what I could.'

Nicolas was trying really hard to pay attention, but he was still more than a little boggled by the idea that he'd missed a centaur standing in front of him...twice.

But his hooves must've clopped on the floor, so how did I not hear it? What about when he needed to...well...move...evacuate his...oh for Deities' sake...how did he take a shit? Someone must've noticed that.

'So, the league was created because of me?' he asked, waving away all the other nonsense in his head.

'You have made many allies on your travels,' Jorish confirmed. 'Chief amongst us is Zal Numar, a great proponent of you and your companions.' Nicolas remembered the merman fondly. He'd been a great help when there'd been a pirate base to overrun. 'Governor Morrow is also a key member of our group. There are more, many more. We aim to shine a light on these conspirators for the good of all. Before it is too late.'

'It is good to know we are not in this alone,' Garaz said, getting up and approaching a nearby tree. Reaching behind it, he produced a large sack.

'What have you discovered so far?' he asked the centaur as Garaz placed the bag on the ground near them.

'That all roads lead to Tobias Helstrum,' Jorish replied, a hint of anger creeping into his noble voice. 'But we need proof before we can move.'

'Oh, don't worry about that,' Shift said. 'We're here to kill him.'

The centaur blinked several times at the shapeshifter's bluntness. 'I beg your pardon?'

'We are on a quest to assassinate Tobias Helstrum,' Silva said. 'I should have thought that sentence was quite clear.'

'It was.' The centaur took a second to compose himself. 'I just did not expect you to be taking such direct action.'

'He's the Maestro,' Nicolas said, the hint of anger now in *his* tone. 'A dying enemy told us. He's obviously using those fauns we met to stir up trouble so he can build his army.'

Jorish paused for a moment. 'That is the conclusion we are beginning to draw,' he admitted. 'Though for someone with such...extreme views of non-humans to be working *with* those fauns seems a stretch.'

'Kid,' Auron said, perking up. 'Repeat after me...'

Nicolas raised his hand to silence the spirit momentarily as he turned to explain what was about to happen to Jorish. 'You know we travel with the spirit of Auron of Tellmark, right?'

The centaur nodded.

'Well, he likes to tell stories about his time as a hero. Sometimes, they're pertinent to whatever adventure we are on, and sometimes, he just likes to brag about killing and shagging things.' Auron's aghast look made him realise what he'd said, and he quickly corrected himself. '*Killing things* and *shagging things*. Two separate ideas. He doesn't kill things then, you know...'

'Remind me to tell you the story of the Galus Vein, the Romantic Necromancer, sometime, kid.' Auron grinned.

'No. I won't do that.'

'Thank goodness,' Garaz said, as he opened the sack and began to remove their gear from it. Eagerly, Nicolas put on his armour and returned the *Dawn Blade* to his belt. The familiarity and protection they offered was comforting after the ordeal in the castle. 'I took the liberty of making sure I brought our things.' The orc smiled.

'Fine,' Auron said with faux offence. 'But repeat this...'

Nicolas began to speak, echoing the spirit's words. 'So, this one time there were these two warlords, Yjorig the Grim and Severn the Thrice Foul. They *hated* each other. They tried to kill each other on several occasions and even managed to take out a few of each other's relatives. When they weren't doing that, they were pillaging and raiding villages on the outskirts of Tannath. Old King Mackal finally decides to deal with them and sends an army after Yjorig.' Auron frowned for a second. 'Or was it Severn? Either way, the other knew the army would come after them as soon as their competitor was finished off, so they did something no one expected and teamed up. With their combined forces, and the home terrain advantage, they managed to drive the army back.'

'And they were best friends forever more?' Shift ventured.

'Deities no.' Auron laughed. 'As soon as the battle was over, they each saw the other in a weakened position and struck. Idiots wiped each other out.'

'I suppose the point of the story has merit,' Jorish said. 'The fauns have been everywhere recently, sowing seeds of chaos. Social crises, economic disarray, fostering conflict. These are all things that would play into the agenda of a man like Tobias Helstrum. Conspiracies do make strange bedfellows.'

'Did he just explain my story?' Auron asked indignantly.

'So either the fauns are in league with Helstrum or this is the biggest coincidence in the history of Etherius.' Shift shrugged.

Or Helstrum is right?

The implications of that question made him shudder, so he focused on a better one. It was a reach, and he knew it, but the slight hope that he might get the answer he wanted spurred him to ask, 'In your investigations, have you heard anything about the people of Hablock?' he asked tentatively. 'They were taken by Helstrum's men, and we've found no sign of them since.'

Jorish took a moment to answer, likely knowing how invested Nicolas was in the answer. 'I'm sorry, but no.'

Dammit. Worth a try.

'We need to move on,' Silva said as she stared towards the fortress. 'The orcs will be subdued soon enough, then they will likely be searching for us.'

Nicolas glanced back. Entire buildings were consumed by raging yellow flame. The smoke pouring into the sky blotted out some of the stars.

It'll take them a while to put those out. But still, best not to dally.

But the question was, where did they go next?

CHAPTER 45

With no actual destination in mind, the consensus was to head in the general direction Tobias Helstrum had gone and hope for the best. The next day yielded nothing, but sometimes a day passing without incident was a victory in itself. It had attempted to rain, but what fell barely earned the name. It was as if the clouds needed to burst but just couldn't be arsed.

The next morning, they had some luck. Auron picked up the trail of the carriages Tobias and his cronies had left in. The spirit stayed on the main road, relaying instructions to the others as they walked parallel to it. Walking on the main road with so many people hunting them would've been some epic-sized insanity.

Facing another potential day with nothing to show for it, the monotony of travel began to sink in.

It would be so nice if the bad guys came to us for a change. We just sit ourselves down in a field, and they do all the leg work. Then at least we'd be nice and rested for the fight.

Nicolas was getting used to the travelling, but that didn't mean his feet didn't still ache and his muscles didn't grow weary, especially directly after a battle and being roughed up by his *friend*. As they passed through the hunter's trail adjacent to the main track, Nicolas found his gaze continually wandering to Jorish.

'Do you ever let people ride you?' he blurted out before he even realised his mouth was open.

'*Nick!*' Shift cried, spinning around wide-eyed.

Garaz let out a few derisive snorts, and Silva looked at him as if he'd just vomited on her boots.

What?

Jorish visibly bristled but calmed himself before answering. 'It is considered the height of rudeness to ask to ride on a centaur. It is on the level of asking a kascat warrior if he *licks himself.*'

His hand shot to his mouth. 'Deities, I am so sorry. I didn't know. Please excuse me.'

The centaur was blatantly controlling his breathing, as one would do when fighting back anger. 'It is well. No offence given.'

Tell your face that.

'No, please,' he continued, starting to ramble. 'I am really sorry. I honestly meant no offence.'

Jorish looked away from him. 'I said it was okay.'

'I just—'

'What's going on?' Auron asked, appearing literally through the bushes.

'Nicolas just asked Jorish if he let people ride him.'

Thanks, Silva.

The spirit's eyes widened then narrowed as he shook his head. 'What's the matter with you, kid?'

'Naïve village boy?' he ventured.

'No, no, no,' Shift said. 'You don't get to be all *'whoopsie, I didn't know better'* anymore. Especially with all the places you've been and things you've done. You travelled with Dieter Von Ostric, for Deities' sake. Did you not think to try to learn a few things from him?'

'Oh, you know Dieter?' Jorish said, the ire dropping from his noble brow. 'He stayed with my cousin for a year, learning about our culture. Where is he now?'

'Living amongst the orcs,' Shift answered.

'Pfft,' the centaur snorted. 'Good luck with that. He'll get himself eat...' His voice trailed off as he looked at Garaz. 'I am so sorry about that.'

'No offence given,' Garaz said with a slight bow.

So he just gets let off?

'I don't think it's fair that—'

'Shhhh.'

The urgency in Silva's shushing made him stop instantly as he reached for his sword. The warrior had her head turned slightly to the side, as if straining to listen. Nicolas tried to copy her, but unless she was just listening to the soothing ruffling of leaves, he was out of luck. Shift was clearly dying to ask her what the problem was but was waiting for Silva to enlighten them.

'Do you hear that?' she asked Auron finally.

'Raised voices,' the spirit stated. 'That's what I came to tell you. I just saw a pair of very aggravated villagers running across the road ahead. I think it's fair to assume that the two things are related.'

Nicolas tried to listen again, but a bird chose that moment to start its mating calls.

'Guess we should go investigate,' Nicolas said with a shrug,

Carefully, the group stalked forwards, alert and attempting to move silently. Soon enough, he could hear what Silva had heard. Some people ahead certainly sounded irate. Straying from the hunter's path, they entered the foliage proper, the outraged shouting allowing them to relax a little with regards to moving silently. Finally, they reached the edge of a clearing, which contained a quaint little cottage by a pond that a group of people were shaking their fists at with gusto.

'It ain't right,' one yelled, hocking and spitting right after speaking.

'We don' wan' none tha' round 'ere,' another cried, holding a tomato menacingly.

In fact, a few of the crowd had vegetables that they were clearly ready to launch. Nicolas doubted having a lettuce lobbed at it would affect the house even slightly. The mob were all peasants, most likely from a nearby village. And Deities were they not the stereotype of *peasant*. The great unwashed masses, complete with shabby rags.

I thought Ivilar was a prosperous kingdom? Evidently, they aren't rich in clothing vendors.

A woman appeared through the door of the cottage, and the mob, for there was no better way to describe them, began to boo like they were at a cheap play and the villain had appeared on stage.

The woman took a few careful steps forward, well into veg-etable-throwing range, holding her hands up to try to shush the crowd, who were not compliant.

'Please,' she said, her voice filled with emotion that threatened to break it. '*Please*. We're your neighbours. You can't—'

'We ain't neighbours with deviants like you,' one woman yelled with a copious amount of fist shaking.

I wonder what she's done.

Nicolas found himself manoeuvring his neck to try to see around the crowd. What was this woman's crime? Was she a witch? A seer who'd given a bad prophecy? A prostitute who'd riddled the town with pox?

Whatever she is, she has certainly wound this lot up.

'I had no' a single fish bite t'day, and I know tis 'cause we're cursed with you abouts.' The man with the wide-brimmed hat carried a fishing rod, just to reinforce the point that he was a fisherman. Unless he planned on perching by their pond and trying his luck. 'You and yer damned husband—'

'Enough.' A figure appeared in the doorway. 'I will not have our family abused thus.'

The crowd seemed to have become possessed by snakes, hissing at the sight of the kascat male who emerged from the doorway. Judging by his thin limbs he was no warrior, but he carried a small wooden stool with intent, his reddish fur bristling in anger.

'We have lived here for years amongst you, and you would simply turn on us, mob our home, and insult us?' he cried.

'There's some difference between *livin' with* yer and *puttin' up* with yer,' a tubby fellow yelled, pointing an accusing finger. 'And we's done puttin' up with yer and yer lil' half-kitten monsters.'

Stepping forward with his stool, the kascat was stopped by his wife, but it did nothing for his ire. 'You dare insult my children.'

Nicolas caught the twitch of a curtain and saw a couple pairs of small eyes peering out.

'Them *children* of yers is an abomination to—'

That'll do.

Nicolas put his fingers to his lips and let out a single sharp whistle. There was a start as all eyes turned to him. There was a bigger start when they noticed Garaz. The peasants were so shocked some actually dropped their vegetables.

What a waste of food.

'What are you doing?' he shouted accusingly. One man opened his mouth, and Nicolas held up a silencing finger. 'It's rhetorical, so shut up.' The man closed his mouth. 'You're here in force, trying to intimidate some poor family. Have they hurt you?' The fisherman opened his mouth to speak. 'You can't blame them for your poor luck fishing,' he interrupted quickly, before he had to listen to some nonsense.

'Look, sir,' a man said, nervously aware of the fact that they were all armed. 'There's stuff goin' on and things like their *relations* ain't proper.'

'Neither's the way you speak, but you don't see me laying siege to your home with a leek,' he retorted dryly. 'How long have you lived here?' he asked the woman. Getting the kascat to talk was likely only to rile the crowd up more.

'I was born in this community,' she said, casting a filthy look at the rest of the *community.* 'Shar has been living here for gone eighteen years now.'

The tubby man huffed. 'That ain't the damn point. They—'

'It's exactly the point,' he interrupted curtly. 'These people are part of your village, part of your community, and you suddenly decide to shun them because their family are no longer fashionable? Or because you blame them for the rain not falling on your crops?'

'Mr Helstrum says that the *integrators* are the first step towards us being bred out and overthrown,' a red-faced woman cried. 'They only bring misery with them. And we're miserable.'

Every time I hear his name, I want to kill him just a little more.

'If you're miserable, it's your own fault,' he snapped. 'What happened to kindness and acceptance?' he asked, pleadingly. 'Humans are built to be kind or cruel. But we were given the gift of being able to choose between the two. You should listen to your own hearts, not the words of a man who—'

'What we ought not ta be listenin' ta is the words of a man travellin' wit' a green monstrosity.'

'I shall assume that was aimed at me.' Garaz sniffed in annoyance.

'You should listen to me because I'm speaking the truth,' he said, trying hard not to let the annoyance show on his face.

'Well, Mr Helstrum—'

'Is an ass,' he snapped, unable to control himself. 'He is a vile man who drips poison into the ear of anyone who will give him the time of day.'

Dammit, I've lost them.

A wave of outrage swept over the crowd in an instant. He might as well have called their children goblin droppings. There was a lot of disgusted muttering and head shaking.

'Of course you'd say that,' a man whose head was shaking so vehemently he was liable to get a crick in the neck, cried. '*Of course.*'

'*Appeasers,*' a woman shouted, a cry echoed by others until it became a chant. Discarded vegetables were picked up off the floor.

One single tomato hits me, and I'm letting Silva loose.

Nicolas sighed and pursed his lips. He'd been in enough frustrating conversations with Shift to know when to quit and cut his losses.

'When you retell this story in the tavern later,' he said, surprised by the growl in his voice, 'remember that I tried to use reason first.' The crowd gasped as he drew the *Dawn Blade*. 'Now, piss off and leave this family alone, *or else...*'

Silence.

A second sword was drawn, and suddenly everyone remembered that they had somewhere more important to be.

I'll never complain about Silva being more intimidating than me.

He watched the crowd through narrowed eyes as they indignantly shuffled away, until he was sure they were completely gone. Only then did he sheathe his blade.

'You know,' Shift said, patting him on the shoulder, 'every so often you do something noble like that, which reminds me why I let you share my bed...and makes me want to do it soon.'

'Well, if driving off a bunch of peasants by threatening them with a sword is what gets you... Hang on. What do mean '*reminds me*'? You need *reminding*?'

The grin told him he was wading directly into another frustrating conversation.

Sometimes, I wish I could be mad at you.

CHAPTER 46

B reathing heavily, most likely due to a combination of fear and frustration, the kascat, Shar, dropped his stool and held his wife. Nicolas
didn't need to hear her sobbing to know that tears fell from her cheeks
as her husband shushed her gently.

'Thank you,' Shar said, with a nod.

Nicolas waved the thanks away as the woman broke from her husband's grip, smoothing down her dress to compose herself. 'Yes,' she
said quietly. 'We are indebted to you. Please, come in and accept our
hospitality.'

'We would be delighted,' Garaz said with a bow.

As they proceeded towards the house, Nicolas caught Auron staring at
him strangely. 'What?'

'Sometimes, kid, you make me pretty damned proud of you,' the spirit
replied with a smile.

Nicolas coughed awkwardly, knowing his cheeks were flushing red.

The inside of the cottage was as quaint as the outside, which unfortunately made it difficult for them all to fit in. But he was soon squeezed
along the side of a table made for two on a bench beside Silva, Shift, and
Garaz, elbow to elbow.

Once Jorish entered the room, it was more obvious he was a centaur.
Items of furniture and quaint knick-knacks cluttered and banged as if
a ghost was moving them. The couple eyed Jorish suspiciously, as the
centaur's noble features creased with awkwardness.

'Just look at him and expect to see a centaur,' Shift told the family.

Elora, the lady of the house, furrowed her brow in confusion. 'Forgive
me, but I don't understand what manner of jest this... Oh my gosh.' Her
eyebrows rose quickly. Her husband, whose arm had never left her side,
held her a little tighter.

They've got it.

Jorish gazed around at the room and all the potential to cause damage.
'It may be better if I stand outside.' Seeing a centaur act sheepishly and

back out of a room was strange indeed. Though nothing would ever top the cow-dragon...or Silva smiling that time.

Disappearing back through the door, the centaur instead appeared at the window, leaning in on folded arms.

How big are centaur houses to accommodate their size? Are they called stables?

Better not to ask; he'd managed to offend their new companion once already.

A rustling in the corner got his attention.

'It's safe now. You can come out,' Elora said warmly, crouching and opening her arms wide.

Two children emerged from behind a cabinet. Both had feline faces and patches of fur but also patches of smooth skin.

'What lovely children.' Shift smiled as the young ones ran into their mother's arms, still warily watching the strangers in their house.

Elora brushed the two boys' heads protectively. 'That they are. Though not everyone feels that way.' Her face became hard as she seemed to play what had happened over in her mind.

'Would you like some tea?' Shar asked, pointing to a nearby pot. 'It's herbal and freshly brewed.'

And it smells lovely.

Nicolas nodded, as did his companions, and soon cups of a steaming hot purplish beverage were served. After blowing on it heavily so he didn't burn his tongue, Nicolas took a sip. The taste was strange, slightly sweet with a flavour he couldn't put his finger on. But the warmth and whatever was in it soothed him. Until that moment, he hadn't realised how tense he was. Now he could map every line of stress and every pinched muscle.

That's what betrayal will do to you.

How had it come to this?

He knew the answer: an arrow in the chest. But were there signs before that? He'd known Potter was a bit roguish, but attempting to kill Nicolas for a job was a stretch. Combing through his memories, he desperately tried to find some sign of what had come. Nothing. Just the odd pang of jealously at Nicolas's adventures.

Probably a good job I didn't give him the message from the Deities to deliver himself. He'd have ended up joining the necromancer.

'Thank you for what you did.' Shar looked at him with an awestruck gaze, making Nicolas thoroughly uncomfortable.

'I don't think it actually achieved anything.' It certainly hadn't soothed the mob's hatred. Personally, he was concerned the villagers were just leaving to go and arm up, rather than think about their intolerance and how they could be better people.

'But you tried.' The kascat smiled. 'And that is more than most people would. It means a lot to us.'

I just wish it had worked. 'Thank you.'

'Excuse me.' One of the two children had been brave enough to leave their mother's side and was tugging gently on Garaz's cape. The orc looked down with a warm smile and gestured for the little one to speak.

'Are you a goatherder?' he asked quietly.

'What makes you think that?' Garaz asked after taking a moment to comprehend what he was being asked.

'You have a goat-shepherd's crook,' the other boy explained from beside his mother's apron.

The smile faltered slightly. 'This is a wizard's staff,' Garaz explained. 'The shape is because the person who gave it to me thought they were funny.'

'I don't get it,' the boy said after a long pause.

Nicolas knew Garaz well enough to tell he was suppressing a sigh. 'When I first met the person who gave me the staff, he mistook me for a goat.'

The little boy by Elora wrinkled his nose, which was absolutely adorable. 'That's silly. You look nothing like a goat.'

'Thank you.' The slight firmness behind the tone suggested Garaz was still irked about that to this day.

'Yer shouldn' bleat like one then,' Shift muttered, putting on their best impression of senile old man T'goth's voice.

Garaz pursed his lips but said nothing.

'I can't believe your neighbours would treat you like that,' Nicolas said, more thinking aloud than expecting a response. 'You'd think at least one of them would say *'um, guys, I don't think this is a good idea.'*

'Mob mentality, kid.' Auron shrugged. 'I have a story about that, but I'll tell you later.'

Concern surged in Nicolas as he turned to Auron and looked him over. He seemed to be his usual ethereal self. But then why...

'Five people in the room can't see me,' he explained when noting Nicolas's concern. 'I'm not wasting my storytelling flair on half an audience.'

Plus, it may look rude if the four of us suddenly start staring into thin air.

'It's hardly a surprise.' Neither was the bitterness in Shar's voice. 'Tobias Helstrum has everyone round here riled up. The closer you get to his manor the worse it is.'

'Manor?' Silva asked, suddenly interested in the conversation now that it might yield some tactical information.

'Yes,' Elora explained. 'Just east of here is his manor, near a major town, Irelise. Apparently, he's holding a ball there soon. Many lords and ladies across the Nine Kingdoms will be attending...'

'No doubt to be seduced by his forked tongue,' Shar muttered, clenching his cup tightly.

No doubt at all.

On the one hand, they now knew where he was going to be. But being surrounded by the titled and powerful of Etherius would probably make it infinitely more difficult to walk in and kill him.

He could tell Shift's mind was working as their gaze didn't really focus on anything at all. Likely they were considering the possibilities of some grand heist where they disguised themselves as the well-to-do in order to sneak into the ball, where no doubt Nicolas would do something to give them away, like use the wrong spoon or release an ill-timed burp. Then they'd be due a free stay in whatever straw-covered cell Tobias had on site, complete with single pot to defecate in. It'd happened before, and he was sure they were going to use up their *'daring escapes'* soon enough.

I've been captured twice on this adventure already.

Shift's eyes flicked to him, and he shook his head slowly. Their face imparted well enough how much of a spoilsport they thought he was without the theatrical huff, yet they added it anyway.

'The manor will be heavily guarded.' Was Silva warning them or savouring the idea? She'd become a little obsessed with fighting that warrior woman, who was sure to be there.

'Don't worry about it,' Shift said, firing a little *'don't you dare disagree'* glance his way.

'Look, you seem like nice folk and all,' Shar began diplomatically, 'but I'm not sure we should be hearing this. Whatever you all are planning on doing, it makes us complicit. And we're in enough trouble as it is.'

'I would not concern yourself with that,' Jorish said, hanging in the window. 'I shall have you away to safety soon enough.'

The couple exchanged a wary glance as the kids giggled in delight, muttering something about *'adventure'* between themselves.

'As much as we appreciate the offer,' Elora said slowly, 'this is our home.'

'Not if the locals have their way,' Garaz said sympathetically.

'Is it a home anymore when you have mobs at your door?' Nicolas asked.

'Of course it is.'

It seems he'd taken the wrong track with Shar, who saw that as a challenge to his pride, and his ability to protect his family.

'This is only going to get worse,' Shift said, pulling funny faces at the children. 'At the moment, you are an island in a choppy sea. Soon it'll be an all-out storm, and you'll be isolated and alone.'

'Or I could get you to sympathetic people, who could spirit you away to somewhere safe,' Jorish added.

The couple still seemed uncertain. Nicolas could relate to that. He hadn't wanted to leave his home when he was told to.

Hopefully, their journey ends with less violence.

If they stayed, violence was almost certain.

An unspoken conversation occurred, the sort that can only be had by a husband and wife of many years, who know each other well enough to translate small looks into long and well-thought-out arguments. On the outside, they appeared to be having an intense staring-contest.

Finally, the pair looked towards their children.

'We will go.' Elora didn't want to, that much was clear, but when it comes to protecting your children, there is no such thing as too big a sacrifice.

CHAPTER 47

C ertain that the villagers would return sooner rather than later, Nicolas and his companions helped the family pack what they needed
for the road—which for the children included a large number of stuffed
animals—with all haste. Once they'd set their minds to leaving, Shar and
Elora went about their business efficiently, and soon enough they were
ready...as ready as you could be when being driven from your home by
an angry mob.

'Which direction are we going?' Nicolas asked Jorish.

'You and your companions will not be coming with us,' the centaur
replied casually as the family mounted the wagon which now contained
all their essential possessions.

'You don't want us to escort you?' Given the danger the family were in,
that shocked him considerably. He wasn't sure if he could even let them
leave without him.

'I believe we will travel faster with fewer, and certainly less conspic-
uously,' the centaur pointed out. 'I will have them at a safe place soon
enough, and from there, my people will smuggle them away from this
diseased place.'

'You will see them to safety, right?' Nicolas kept his voice low as the
family settled their children in the wagon.

'Of course. You have my word,' the centaur replied. 'And I hope I have
yours that you will complete your task. We have a golden opportunity to
see into Helstrum's operation and cut the head off the snake. We cannot
miss it.'

'And you trust us to do it?'

The centaur smiled at him. 'If the accounts are true, then you've been
beaten, whipped, had your home stolen away, been imprisoned multiple
times, and been the subject of various assassination attempts by this
organisation. I think your heart is in it.'

He couldn't deny the logic. When he offered his hand, Jorish shook it.

'Well met, Nicolas of Hablock.'

Where did my last name go? I'm not having it replaced by a village title, that's almost worse than the other *name.*

'Well met, Jorish. Hopefully, we meet again.'

The centaur smiled. 'I'm sure you will require rescuing in no time.'

'Maybe if some of us were more careful, we would not require your assistance.'

Thanks, Silva.

Nicolas turned to walk back to his companions, but stopped beside the wagon, looking up. 'For what it's worth, you're doing the right thing.'

'It's hard,' Shar replied with a strained smile. 'But I know you're right.'

Another handshake was exchanged, reins were snapped, and the wagon began to move, the children waving back at them with enthusiasm. People so young shouldn't have to see the evils of the world. In fact, there shouldn't be evils to see.

'Should we bed down here for the night?' Garaz asked, gesturing both to the cottage and the darkening sky.

'Yes,' Shift said gleefully. 'Then, when those idiots come back, they can kick the door in and find a full-grown basilisk coming at them?'

'You can grow that big?' Nicolas asked.

Shift screwed their nose up. 'Late teenage basilisk then.'

'What if they decide to just burn down the house instead of kicking the door in?' Auron asked.

'I, for one, have no wish to be trapped in a burning building so Shift can amuse themselves,' Silva said, already walking toward the forest. 'Now come on. We need to make camp soon.'

Making camp turned out to be a longer task than expected. They didn't want to stay anywhere near the village, but around it were open fields, so the group had to make a long trek to find somewhere suitable. With Auron scouting ahead, they relied on torches lit by Garaz's fire magic.

'Not at all spooky,' Nicolas muttered as he noted where the light suddenly stopped as the darkness finally overcame it.

'Don't worry,' Shift said behind him. 'Silva's the scariest thing in this forest.'

'I'm the scariest thing in most places,' the warrior called back from the front.

For a moment, Nicolas indulged a fun fantasy where he let Silva loose on Potter as he sat back and watched with a cool drink. His fingertips touched his armour where the arrow had struck him. Now that he was really thinking about it, he could see the signs. The slight faces Potter made when he let his mask slip. The ambition. Asking him to go against the will of the Deities—well, the choosing stick—and simply give him the message. It was all there. Nicolas now was beginning to see it clearly.

Nicolas then had been none the wiser. Briefly, he entertained another amusing fantasy. That he'd given Potter the message, and Grimmark had turned his stupid egghead to paste on that damnable bridge. The amusement lasted a second then he replayed the conversations with his friend over in his mind again, cursing himself for not seeing what was there.

I need to stop obsessing over this. I'll drive myself insane.

There was a light in the darkness. It got bigger and brighter until it resolved itself into Auron, who jogged up to them. 'I've found something.'

Within ten minutes, the group were peering at a large building on the edge of one of Etherius's enchanted forests. Though it was dark, Nicolas guessed the building was a brewery of some kind. Attached to the building was a large warehouse with a couple of wagons out front, hitched and ready. Figures milled about by a hitching post and—

That horse.

Torches near the door of the building illuminated a very particular horse with a white mane...that belonged to the man in the leather mask.

'One of Helstrum's bodyguards is here,' he whispered. 'The masked one. The one from the border fort.'

'Are you certain?' Garaz asked.

'Yes, I recognise his horse.'

'It is dark,' Silva said quietly.

'And mistakes get made,' Shift said warily.

'And you've been hit in the head a lot recently,' Auron added.

'I'm astounded by your faith in me,' he snapped. 'It's the right damn horse. I know it.'

The lack of instant agreement was infuriating, but at least no one argued further.

'There are guards patrolling the perimeter,' Auron said, pointing to two pairs of shadowed figures. 'I'll go and find this masked man, then you can grab him, and we can make him tell us the best way into Helstrum's manor and where his master is likely to be when we get in.'

'Did you ever have to sneak around this much on your adventures?' Nicolas asked suddenly.

Auron frowned at him. 'What do you mean?'

'Well,' he huffed. 'Hiding in bushes is getting a bit tiring.'

Hiding from the authorities. Hiding from the enemy. There's been a lot of bloody hiding on this adventure. Or getting captured. Who are the bloody good guys here?

'Yes,' Auron said after a moment. 'There was plenty. But we didn't call it *sneaking around*. We called it *stealth missions*. Has a bit more flair to it.'

'Doesn't feel like flair.' He grunted. 'Feels like cowardice.'

'Are you all right?' Shift asked.

No.

'Shhhh.'

At Silva's warning, they all got down. Two guards were approaching. Their steps were cautious, and they were clearly examining the bushes. But they didn't have their hands on their weapon nor had they raised the alarm. That made them easy pickings.

'I swear I heard something,' one said with a furrowed brow.

'Animals.' Judging by the other's tone, this happened quite often.

His muscles tensed as he readied himself. Silva would take out one guard—or probably both of them if he let her, but he wouldn't get better without practice. They just needed to draw them in further, and Nicolas needed to pick the right guard. If he and Silva both went for the same one, it could be disastrous, and embarrassing.

'Mrrrroooowwwwww.'

He actually turned, searching for the cat, when his brain kicked in. Shift winked at him and made the sound again.

'It's just a stupid cat,' one of the guards said.

The other picked up a rock and threw it into the bushes. 'Piss off, cat,' he shouted in a nasal voice, before he and his companion made their way back towards the building.

'Woof.'

Both men turned slowly. 'There's a dog in there too?' the first man said, frowning.

'What's a dog and a cat doing in a bush together?' the other asked. 'Sounds like the start of a bad joke.'

Bad joke or not, curiosity got the better of them, and they ventured in. Two seconds later, both men were unconscious. Trying to minimise the rustling of leaves, Nicolas dragged his man's feet from view.

'Nicely done, kid.'

'Now to—' As the doors of the building opened, the rest of the sentence died on his lips.

And so we hide again.

A troop of men came out, some carrying barrels slung over their shoulders. Amongst them was the leather-masked man. He held some parchment and appeared to be marking off the barrels as the men loaded them onto the wagons. Once the task was complete, the drivers took their seats, and the escort mounted their horses before the convoy got underway. Suddenly, there were a lot fewer men as those left returned to the house, thankfully not noticing two of their guards were missing.

'We can take them,' Silva said.

'We do not really know how many more are in there,' Garaz counselled.

Silva's eyes suddenly lit up. 'Maybe the warrior woman is in there.'

Mental note: Silva really *wants to fight that woman.*

'The building's not big enough to house an army,' Auron said as he scrutinised the structure. 'The old hero instincts say there won't be many more than the handful we saw.'

'Gotta trust those mighty hero instincts.'

The spirit looked at Shift as if he were a father who'd just caught their child sneaking cake, when they'd expressly forbidden cake. 'Yes, you do need to trust my instincts, finely honed from over twenty years of adventuring and hero work.'

Shift held their hands up in surrender. 'Calm down, ghost.' The ensuing smirk grew wider at Auron's string of expletives.

'So, get to the door, make our way inside, grab old leather mask, and get him to tell us the layout of Helstrum's manor and the best way for us to get in.' Nicolas repeated the basics aloud, just to make sure he had it right.

Auron nodded in response.

That's a sound plan.

'What about the other two guards.' Garaz gestured to the shadows that were getting gradually closer.

Shift held up a finger then their features changed into a perfect copy of one of the two unconscious men at their feet. 'Hey guys, give us a hand over here.' The voice was the perfect imitation of the nasally man.

Upon hearing the call, the other two guards obediently jogged over. They looked around in confusion when they couldn't immediately see their comrades.

'Eric, where are you?'

Getting no response, the men entered the foliage.

CHAPTER 48

S ilva took down the first guard with her usual violent efficiency. Naturally, Nicolas got the struggler of the pair. The man tried to cry out, only managing a wheeze as Nicolas's arm tightened around his throat. Flailing desperately, and making the bushes around them rustle enough to attract attention from the neighbouring kingdom, the guard tried to push Nicolas backwards. Going with the motion, Nicolas kicked the man's knee out from beneath him and essentially dragged him back by his neck until he was unconscious. Laying the body down, he pointedly avoiding Auron's reproachful glaze and shaking head. He could already hear the spirit's voice in his head. *That took way too long kid. And all the noise? I've taught you better than that.*

'Having a shapeshifter around is so useful,' he whispered to Shift as Silva checked to make sure there were no other patrols they'd missed.

Shift gave a half smile then their features shimmered into his. 'I completely regret all those times I ogled Silva's breasts before I realised I was crazy about Shift,' they said in a perfect replica of his voice.

Seeing his own face on the body of someone he'd been intimate with was a little unnerving. 'I don't think there's any—'

'Not now, children,' Garaz admonished. He was right too. This wasn't the situation for levity.

Without argument, Shift returned to their preferred form.

'It's clear, let's move,' Silva told the others, still keeping one eye out for trouble.

Keeping low, the quartet ran across the open ground towards the building, Auron strolling alongside them. Nicolas's gaze flicked from window to window, but he could see no shadows suggesting watchers. And there was no sign of alarm by the time they reached the building. Moving up the several steps to the porch carefully, lest an errant creak give them away, the group assembled by the door.

'Okay then,' Auron said with a smug grin. 'I'll go in, see what there is to see, then you guys can come in and kick ass.' Rubbing his hands, the spirit strode towards the wall.

'Well?' Nicolas whispered a moment later, as Auron stood before the old wood.

The spirit's head twitched this way and that. Reaching out, he began to feel the air around the wall. Several times, he tried pushing against it. Each time, he pushed harder, the exertion clear on his face.

'I...I can't get in,' Auron said, taking a step back. 'I can't walk through the wall.'

Holding his palm out, Garaz slowly waved it where Auron had been pushing, as if he were enacting a mime in front of an invisible fence. 'There is magic here,' the orc said thoughtfully. 'It seems they have found a way to keep Auron out. This site must be important.'

'The cheeky bastards,' Auron roared, levelling a kick and several more expletives at the barrier. 'This is what I do. I scout, I throw things, and I poke things. And they aren't going to let me scout?' The foul language grew worse.

'Calm down,' Nicolas whispered, just in case those inside could hear. 'What do we do?' His eyes flicked to the door. Who knew what was beyond it?

'We're coming up with a plan right on their doorstep?' Shift snorted. 'Why don't we just knock and pretend we're travelling preachers.' They changed their voice to a haughty, pious tone. *'Hast thou heard about the love of the Deities?'*

'Preachers with armour, swords, and an orc?' Garaz asked.

'If thou shalt not receive the love of the Deities, thou shalt receive mine blade, infidel.'

'Usually, they just try to give you parchments with scripture and move on,' Auron said with a raised eyebrow. 'I'm not sure what sort of preachers *you've* met.'

Silva rubbed the bridge of her nose. 'It is simple. We need to go around the building quietly, slip in the back, and take it room by room, subduing any opposition silently until the house is pacified.'

'What are the chances of us doing all that silently?' Shift asked. 'I'm sneaky. But the rest of you...'

'Why are you looking at me?' Garaz queried. 'Do you actually wish me to calculate the odds of me being the one to give us away instead of any of you?'

Sneaky. Quietly. Silently.

Nicolas wasn't really listening to any of it as he stared at the door. In his mind, he was replaying the confrontation with Potter. The arrow. The abduction of his people. The betrayal. All they had already been through since leaving Golthorak just to make it to this door.

'No.' His voice was a growl as his eyes narrowed at the door, not really caring anymore if anyone inside heard him.

'What's that?' Shift asked.

'I said no,' he repeated, maintaining his stare. 'I've had my fill of sneaking around. We're the bloody good guys, and we run, and we hide, and we sneak.' Now, he turned to the others. 'Twice. *Twice* on this bloody mission we've been captured. We've been hunted and chased all over.' He prodded his chest plate. '*We're* the good guys. *We* shouldn't be the ones sneaking around like assassins. *They* should be the sneaking ones. I'm tired of running around whilst the bad guys get fortresses, and nice houses, and get to stand around in the bloody open without a care in the world.' His body shook with rage. 'And I am not going to have it, not one second longer.'

'Nick—'

Everything, every slight, both to him and to innocent people, like the family they'd just helped, piled into his mind, adding fuel to his ire, until he was a raging dragon with a fire that needed to be set loose.

He stomped towards the door, sword in hand, then kicked it in with a feral roar. Stepping into the entrance room, he focused on the group of men who'd just turned towards him in surprise.

Clenching his fists, he cried out, '*I am Nicolas Percival Carnegie, the Dawnblade, and I have come to bring you to justice. Yield, or else.*'

Somewhere in the back of his mind, he heard the others talking.

'*Did the kid just charge in there and shout his name?*'

'*He even shouted his middle name.*'

'*Shouting Nick Carnage would've been so much better.*'

One short and slender fellow was standing just inside the doorway. Deciding to be proactive, he punched Nicolas in the face. The instant Nicolas slowly turned his eyes to the man, he could tell by the way he shrank back that his attacker knew he'd just made a terrible mistake. But he tried again anyway. The punch landed, but Nicolas barely reacted. With a gulp, the thug gazed in disbelief at his fist, as if wondering if he somehow hadn't used it right.

Nicolas stabbed the *Dawn Blade* into the wooden floor to free up both his hands. Grabbing the thug by the collar, he headbutted the shorter man three times, before running with him and launching him through the nearest window. Glass shattered as the limp body burst through it. Then he turned back to the other assembled villains, including the leather-masked man, all of whom were frozen in shock.

'Right then,' Nicolas growled, retrieving his sword. 'Who's next?'

The leather-masked man was the first to move. Reaching for his belt, he pulled out something that looked like a smaller version of the fire-sticks. Time slowed as he pointed it at Nicolas. In that moment, a stone flashed past his head. The stone struck the weapon, knocking the aim off just as it fired. Wood splintered somewhere behind him.

'Auron of Tellmark, ladies and gentlemen,' the spirit boomed from outside the building. 'I can't come in and scout around, but I still find a way to be damned useful.'

The leather-masked man's look of surprise became a snarl. His men stood around nervously, unsure what to do. Slowly, the masked man held up his closed fist then opened it abruptly, splaying his fingers wide. The group broke and ran, fleeing in all directions. Some of his men ran upstairs or ducked through doorways, but the masked man disappeared into a door to the left.

He's mine.

'They appear to have fled at the very utterance of your name, kid.' Auron sniggered.

'Are you pleased with yourself?' Silva rebuked. 'Now we have to play hide and seek with the bad guys.'

Actually, I'm pleased I got that door open with one kick. My leg's obviously healed nicely.

'For Deities' sake, Nick,' Shift said, shaking their head. 'There were better ways to do this.'

Probably...yes, actually.

The wind was going out of his sails now. Anger was fading and logic reasserting itself, telling him this might not have been the wisest thing he'd ever done. Mentally, he cursed himself. Sometimes, he just got carried away.

Never used to be the case, mind you.

With a huff, he looked at each door an enemy had fled through in turn. 'Then we split up and find them.' He was determined not to admit he'd done something stupid. That'd come later. 'If they're hiding, it's because they know they're outclassed. The masked man's mine.'

'Are you sure splitting up is the best strategy?' Garaz asked.

'They're scattered. We can't give them time to get away.'

Yup. Definitely made a mess of this one.

CHAPTER 49

The others looked less than impressed with Nicolas as they spread out to play Find the Villain. Slowly, ready for anything, he approached the door the masked man had disappeared through.

'Don't kick that door in,' Auron shouted from the open door to the house. 'He's lying in wait and expects you to do just that.'

I know. I know.

Calming his breathing, he gently touched the door handle. Keeping his eyes on the crease where it would open, he pulled the handle down and began to push. There was no instant attack. But he knew his enemy was near. His hero instincts were jumping up and down and screaming at him that danger was close by.

Opening the doorway more, he slipped into the room.

This...is the worst kitchen I've ever been in.

Maybe the second, if he took the Oracle's into account. Either way, for a moment, Nicolas let his attention wander to the fact that the place was filthy. Dirty plates and bowls covered a countertop near a basin that looked perfectly functional. Some ambitious soul had gone as far as filling it with water, but that was all they'd achieved to date. Pots and pans crusted with old food sat beside the crockery. Nicolas brought his hand to his nose as the sour smell hit him. Part of him wanted to drop his sword, roll up his sleeves, and clean the place. Another part of him didn't want to touch a Deities damned thing in here.

I imagine there's a room like this in the Underworld, where someone has to clean this for all eternity, only for it to reappear when they've finished.

There was a danger here other than the hidden enemy. Food poisoning.

Silently, he stalked through the kitchen, keeping his sword in line with where he was looking. Always on guard. Nicolas was very aware he'd barely survived his last fight in a kitchen. Hopefully, this one went better.

Where is he?

A foot flashed out of nowhere, aiming for his hand. Nicolas's reflexes took over and he dodged the blow, countering with a swing of his sword. His attacker met the swing with a spinning kick, knocking the *Dawn Blade* from his grasp. Before he could react, the same foot kicked him in the chest, sending him crashing into the counter by the basin. Even with his armour on, it was a darned fierce kick. He went to move, to regroup, but a knife pressed to his throat.

'Not everything they say you are, are you?' The masked man's voice oozed smugness.

His eyes flicked to his sword, just there, on the floor. Ready to be picked up.

The knife point dug into his skin as Leather Mask reached out with his foot and kicked the *Dawn Blade* away. 'Ah-ah,' he tutted. 'I hear you're the big hero, but being heroic now would be a fatal mistake.'

Nicolas winced as the tips of his fingers pressed down on the mushy food stuck to the rim of the bowl he'd just gripped.

'Now then,' Leather Mask said with a half-smile. 'You are going to walk me out of here, past your mates and—'

Nicolas swung the bowl, launching the grey water that had festered in it for who knew how long right into Leather Mask's face before smacking the bowl itself down on his knife hand. His grip on the blade broke, and it clattered to the floor a second before Nicolas kicked it away.

'You filthy little bastard,' Leather Mask snarled, wiping his face clean and spitting several times. 'I'll kill you for that.'

A blur of movement caused Nicolas to duck. The spinning kick meant for him destroyed some old crockery probably already well beyond saving anyway. The sounds of muffled fighting came from other rooms.

Leather Mask stood up straight, nodding appraisingly. 'You've got some skill.' Unbuttoning his jacket, he slipped it off and discarded it. 'This is gonna be fun.'

'Not for you, but for these,' Nicolas snapped, raising his fists.

He knew it was a terrible line the moment he said it. Inwardly, he cringed. This whole thing was going really badly for him.

Which I can live with. As long as I take him alive.

Ignoring the heat in his cheeks, Nicolas tried to continue being tough. 'I'm assuming you won't come quietly?'

Leather Mask let out a single harsh laugh. 'I just hope you don't die too quickly, boy. I want to savour this.' Dropping into a stance, the thug raised his guard. 'Your ass is mine.'

My ass? He's no better at this than I am.

Nicolas got himself into an opposing combat stance. It was clear his opponent knew his stuff.

Well, so do I.

Carefully, they circled each other. A couple of times, Nicolas probed his opponent with punches, and vice versa. Then Leather Mask came at him. Nicolas blocked a jab, only to discover it was a ruse. His blocking arm was gripped at the wrist, and he was pulled in as a hook sailed towards him. Managing to turn his hips, he brought his elbow up to block the blow, before sending over a punch of his own, which was sidestepped.

The pair parted, studying each other. Leather Mask got back into his stance, tapping his beak nose twice with his thumb as he readied himself. Nicolas was ready too. His opponent lashed out with a kick, which he parried, before launching one of his own. Nicolas's kick got the same result.

'You've been schooled,' Leather Mask said, appearing impressed.

'And now I'll be schooling you,' he shot back.

'Urrgghh,' Auron cried from outside the kitchen window. 'Please, kid, enough with the tough talk. You can't do it well.'

His gaze flicked to Auron for a second, and Leather Mask noticed the distraction. Nicolas barely stepped away from the swinging foot in time. His opponent came at him with everything. Nicolas blocked and parried kicks and punches. A couple got through his guard, and damn well hurt. Ducking, he let a punch sail over his head, but Leather Mask stopped the momentum suddenly and turned it into an elbow strike. Grabbing the elbow and his attacker's wrist, he used a pull and push motion to stretch the arm out. Leather Mask grunted but went for a low kick that could've broken Nicolas's knee had he not released the grip and dodged.

The air between him and Leather Mask became a blur of punches, kicks, knees, and elbows. Blows were traded and blocked at almost lightning speed. A few of his struck home, but the same could be said for his opponent, who could hit pretty damn hard.

Leather Mask went for a low sweep that somehow became a high spin kick. Stepping over the sweep, Nicolas caught the incoming kick, driving his knee into Leather Mask's ribs and punching him in the jaw. As his attacker's body spun around, Leather Mask attempted to counter with a backfist. Blocking it, Nicolas drove his fist into the small of his back, before another crack to the jaw and a follow-up elbow strike. His opponent was thrown into the counter with a loud crash.

A bowl hit Nicolas in the head, dazing him for a moment. Quickly, he brought his arms up to cover himself as several plates struck him. Stepping back from the crockery onslaught, unable to see, he was surprised by a kick to the gut. He caught a smack to the cheek and an uppercut that caused him to crash back into the counter, sending pots and pans clattering to the floor. Thinking quickly, he brought up a pot to use as a shield. Leather Mask hissed as his fist connected with it. Then Nicolas launched it. Unfortunately, his opponent had decent reflexes, catching it and throwing it back at him.

Even as his forearm redirected the incoming pan, Nicolas stepped to the side, guessing it to be a ruse. A heel slammed the counter where his head had been a second before. Nicolas drove his elbow down into the top of the leg, eliciting a satisfying grunt of pain from his opponent, before unleashing a flurry of chain punches on Leather Mask's unprotected torso, forcing him all the way back to the opposite counter. When he went for a hook punch across the jaw, Leather Mask blocked his arm.

His world blurred as a plate smashed over his head. An open-palm strike caught him in the nose, not quite breaking it, but hurting like an hour in one of Sha'then's torture rooms—he imagined. Leather Mask grabbed his collar, most likely readying to throw him to the floor. Remembering his training with Ban Dro, Nicolas used his hips to channel his weight into a single punch, an inch from Leather Mask's stomach. His opponent was launched back to the worktop, grunting with pain and doubling over. Nicolas brought his fist down across the masked face, and his opponent fell to his knees.

'Are we done?' Nicolas asked hopefully, breathing heavily but not dropping his guard. Blood trickled from his lip. Despite asking the question, he knew the answer already.

Apparently, Leather Mask was done, just not in the sense he'd hoped for. With a flick of his hand, Nicolas suddenly had a fork in his bicep. Grunting with pain—and disgust at the dirty implement—he pulled it out as his opponent made a run for the door on the far side of the kitchen.

With a snarl, he threw the bloody fork down then launched himself across the counter, rolling through the crap left on it to come to a standing position on the other side, right between Leather Mask and the door.

Leather Mask looked at him aghast, and Nicolas couldn't help but respond with a theatrical wink. What parts of the man's face he could see were covered in angry purple and black bruises. He imagined he looked the same, with the addition of a fork wound to his arm.

'Damn you,' Leather Mask hissed, drawing a pair of knives from behind his back. 'Just die.'

His opponent came for him, swinging wildly. Apparently, now that he'd remembered he had knives, Leather Mask was quite keen to continue the fight. Using his vambraces, Nicolas intercepted most of the fierce slashes, but his arm became warm and wet as one managed to get through. A stabbing blade came at him, and Nicolas blocked it with his armour. He kicked Leather Mask away then rolled back across the counter, buying himself a few precious seconds to think.

I need to defend myself, but I need to take him alive.

What could he use? Quickly, he scanned the kitchen.

Knife...no. Fork...no. Skewer...no. Why are there so many stabbing implements here?

His eyes settled on something, and he got a flash of—hopefully, genius—inspiration. He grabbed a nearby towel and dipped it into the murky sink water, soaking it, before winding it tight and holding it between his fists. He'd learnt a little chain fighting in his short time with Ban Dro, which hopefully crossed over to using a wet towel. Only one move had really stuck, but he was sure it'd be applicable here.

Leather Mask smirked at his choice of weapon and came forward, only for the towel to slap him in the face with a wet *thwack*. Pulling it taut, Nicolas launched it again, striking one of the knives from his opponent's hand with a snap, before kicking it under the counter, which was now becoming a mini armoury.

'No,' Leather Mask snarled.

And so they fought. Knife against towel. Leather Mask's onslaught was furious. Nicolas ducked and dodged the swinging blade, snapping in with the towel whenever a target presented itself. Pulling it taut proved an effective way of blocking incoming attacks, but even with his reflexes, Nicolas still earned a couple of shallow cuts to his upper arm. The more his attacker missed, the more frustrated he became. When he came in with a wide swing, Nicolas ducked under the arm, flicking the towel and catching Leather Mask in the temple with a satisfying *thwack*.

With an enraged cry, the thug stabbed at him with his dagger. Nicolas struck down on the stabbing arm with the towel, wrapping it around Leather Mask's wrist, turning and using his hips to throw his opponent over his shoulder to the floor. Leather Mask crashed to the ground, winded, dazed, and thankfully disarmed. Standing over the disoriented man, Nicolas stared at the killer, before circling his towel several times and pulling it as taut as he could. Straining his muscles, Nicolas launched it again, striking the killer heavily on the top lip.

Leather Mask's eyes went wide with surprise, and he clawed at his mouth for some reason. The hands moved to his throat as he began to make desperate choking sounds.

What in the Underworld?

Nicolas took a step back as Leather Mask convulsed, white foam appearing at the edges of his lips. He was at a loss for what to do as the thug's body bucked and thrashed across the kitchen floor.

Then with one final, epic spasm, Leather Mask was dead.

CHAPTER 50

M outh gaping, Nicolas looked between the dead body on the floor and the weapon he'd apparently used to kill him. A wet towel.

'What? How?' he asked shakily.

Bending down, he inspected the masked man's body for signs that someone had, maybe, shot him with an arrow. He was so engrossed, he didn't realise Leather Mask's ghost was stood beside him until he made a shocked groan. The apparition stared at the towel in disbelief, before fading and vanishing.

'What...what did I do?' Nicolas asked, turning towards the window.

Auron squinted and peered down at the body. 'Some in the Assassin's Guild have been known to use a false tooth containing a poison powder, for use should they ever get captured. You can't tell someone who hired you if you're dead. I reckon that's what beaky there had. You must've knocked it out with the towel.'

'But I didn't...'

'Oh, you did.' The spirit grinned. 'You just killed someone with a wet towel. The legend of *Nick Carnage* continues in epic fashion.'

Dropping his apparently deadly weapon, Nicolas put his head in his hands. 'Not again,' he cried. 'Why do we struggle so much to take villains alive?'

Cursing himself and his luck, he reached under the counter and re-trieved the *Dawn Blade*.

'Drop it,' a voice demanded.

But I only just picked it up.

By the kitchen door, a hulking thug had Shift by the back of the neck. Their cheek was bruised, but they looked inconvenienced more than hurt.

'Drop it,' the thug reiterated. 'Or the girl gets it.'

'I'm not a girl,' Shift corrected snottily.

The thug looked his hostage over leeringly. 'Tits and a pert ass. Oh, you're a girl, love. Maybe we'd 'ave a good ol' time if you weren't 'angin' around with this lot?'

Shift craned their head so they could look at the man retraining them. 'I beg your pardon?'

Oh. He's dead.

The thug yelped in surprise as his hands were prised apart by his captive suddenly expanding. Cloth tore as their skin greyed and turned to stone, the transformation into a rock monster complete. A boulder of a fist struck the man right in the nose. When it drew back, there was a bloody indent where his face had been. Nicolas averted his gaze quickly as the man fell to the floor dead.

'Clothes, please,' the rock monster boomed.

'Here,' Silva said, strolling into the room with the packs they'd left by the door.

The warrior rummaged in Shift's bag and produced some new attire before their companion's bulky rock body sidestepped through the door and vanished. As they did, Garaz entered the room, holding something.

'The building is secure and—' The orc looked down at Leather Mask with a deep frown. 'I thought you wanted him alive?'

'I did,' he muttered sourly.

Garaz rubbed his chin as he looked at the body. 'What is that foam around his mouth? Did you poison him?'

'The kid killed him with a towel,' Auron helpfully shouted from beyond the window.

Garaz looked back at Auron then shook himself. 'I believe this is the item keeping you out.' In his green hand was a small orange gem, which glowed softly. The orc closed his hand into a fist, and there was a whoosh of fire. Smoke slipped from between the orc's fingers, before he opened his hand and let the dust that had once been the gem fall to the floor. 'Try to enter now.'

Within a moment, Auron burst through the wall. 'Yes, that's better,' he cried. 'Anyway, the kid killed someone with a towel. I mean. A *towel*. A Deities' damned *towel*.'

No need to be so giddy about it.

'He did *what*?' Shift asked as they returned to the room, finishing pulling their top down.

'Smacked him with a towel and knocked out his suicide tooth,' the spirit cried. 'I mean, I've killed people with some random things...but a *towel*?'

'A *towel*?' Silva repeated, furrowing her brow.

I really wish people would stop saying towel *like that.*

'It was a wet towel,' Nicolas said, as if that made any difference.

'I'm sure plenty of people have described you as that in the past.' Shift earned themselves a filthy look for that one. 'For someone who hates killing, you are getting really good at it.'

'I didn't mean to,' he protested.

'And yet here lies a dead body,' Garaz remarked soberly.

'A towel.' Silva was clearly struggling to get her head around the notion as she crouched down and searched Nicolas's latest victim, to no avail. Removing the man's mask didn't yield any information either. Nor why he bothered wearing a mask. His face was fine, save the wide dead eyes, the foam around the mouth and the slight lolling out of his tongue.

'He kicked the *Dawn Blade* out of my hands, and he had knives. I needed a weapon.'

'You have knives,' Shift replied instantly. 'You've got throwing knives on your belt, and another blade in your boot.'

Ah. 'Well, I needed him al— Never mind. I guess it's too much to hope that you guys left anyone else alive?' The question was directed more at Shift and Garaz. He very much doubted Silva would've bothered.

'Capturing him was the point of this.' Garaz shrugged. 'So, no.'

'Ooh,' he said suddenly, clicking his fingers. 'What about the guy I threw through the window?'

'Shard of glass to the throat,' Auron said, miming blood pouring from his neck.

Great. All this for nothing.

'I did find something interesting, though,' Shift remarked. 'So you don't need to look so forlorn, o' mighty wielder of deadly towels.'

Before he could ask what it was, Shift made for the door. The others followed. Nicolas gave one last sad look at his latest victim then at the weapon he'd technically used to slay him, before leaving the room too.

At the back of the building was a storeroom that doubled up as a production centre. One side of the room was filled with large barrels whose contents, if Nicolas read what he was seeing right, were being split between numerous smaller ones, exactly like the ones he'd seen leaving on the wagon. What was most interesting were the piles of red powder on the tables and in, he guessed, every barrel.

'Boost?' he asked.

'And a lot of it,' Shift confirmed. 'From the parchments on the desk over there, it looks like this was a distribution hub. And they are sending that stuff *everywhere*.'

'Well, this building just earned itself a burning down,' Auron said, inspecting the parchments.

'Which I will gladly provide,' Garaz snarled.

'Do they make it here?' Silva asked.

'No,' Shift said. 'I had a quick look at the paperwork before the now-dead idiot grabbed me. They import it from somewhere called The Vault.'

That's next on the list to hit then.

'It looks like this is one of a number of distribution hubs. And they all seem to be near enchanted forests.'

What is it with the enemy being so bent on corrupting these places?

At the desk, Shift picked up one particular document and handed it to Nicolas. On it was a map marking the location of Helstrum's manor, as well as the number of barrels requiring shipping there.

'Must be some wizards attending his little shindig,' Nicolas muttered.

'And what better way of buttering them up than by getting them off their heads on the latest designer wizard drug,' Auron said solemnly. 'I wonder how many of them know it blows up?'

'I doubt any do,' Garaz said. 'If they did, they would not take it.'

Auron straightened, rolled his shoulders, and twisted his neck from side to side. Once he was finished, he looked seriously at the group. 'So, this one time, I heard about a guy who liked to run through gorgon lairs.'

'Why?' Nicolas asked.

'You know when a fight's done and you get this little rush because you survived?'

'Yes.' He was currently experiencing it.

'That. So, he finds a lair he likes and whenever the need for a rush takes him he goes running through it ,whooping and hollering and making a nuisance of himself, dodging the gorgon's gazes so he doesn't turn to stone. After a while the gorgons are pretty damn fed up with the guy, which I sympathise with. So they set a trap. Next time he comes in, he charges around making an ass of himself, anticipating the rush when he comes out the other end...only to find the exit blocked off.' Auron shook his head. 'So instead of a quick high, he gets turned into a statue, to live there forever more.'

'How do you know that?' Shift asked.

'What?'

'What happened when he didn't come back,' they clarified. 'It's not like anyone would've gone and checked or interviewed the gorgons. So how does anyone know it happened like that?'

'Oh, I'm sorry,' Auron said haughtily. 'So he goes in again and slips on a rock. Instead of turning him to stone, the gorgons put him on a slab and feed him to their snake hair. He dies in excruciating pain as hundreds of snakes nibble him to death. Is that better?'

Shift shrugged. 'It's an equally likely outcome. I was just asking how you can be sure.'

'The point is,' Auron said through gritted teeth, 'that sometimes we do things we know will be bad for us because it's fun.'

'Indeed. Well, let us be the ultimate spoilsports,' Garaz said as he looked around in distaste. 'If we could all vacate these premises with haste, please, I am quite keen to burn it to the ground.'

There was no argument as the others filed out.

CHAPTER 51

E ven from their camp deep in the forest, they could still see the faint glow of the flames from the burning building. Garaz had been quite thorough, to the point Nicolas thought he would set each individual piece of wood it was built from on fire.

The group had half-expected a mighty explosion as the red powder ignited, but there'd been nothing. Obviously, heat wasn't the trigger for this volatile substance.

'So, you went full Gornak then,' Shift said from nowhere.

He looked at his companion's head lying on his shoulder. 'I did not.'

Shift's face suggested they disagreed. 'You were one moment away from shouting *'whoresonsssss,'* when you charged into that place.'

'I...' It was hard to defend a position he knew was indefensible.

'I get it,' Shift said knowingly. 'This has been an especially tough one.'

'Is this about that Potter asshole, kid?' Auron asked. 'He was the one in the black armour on the battlements, right?' Nicolas nodded. 'I don't know how you didn't guess he was a rotten apple. A brief glance told me he was an utter and unrepentant wanker.'

Nicolas sighed sharply. 'You shouldn't eavesdrop.'

Raising his eyebrows, the spirit slowly viewed their camp. 'It's hard not to,' he said finally. 'We're all about six feet apart.'

'Look, I really don't want to—'

'No.'

He looked sharply at Silva. 'What do you mean, *no?*'

'How many times have we had problems because you have issues you refuse to discuss?' the warrior replied levelly.

Well, I can hardly sit here and argue that it's never happened.

'Sometimes,' he conceded.

'And that shall not happen here.'

Okay, no need to glare like you'll gut me if I don't share.

The words needed coaxing from his lips, but the others were patient...enough. 'We were friends, back in Hablock. He was my best friend.

223

He was, I suppose, everything I wasn't. Outgoing. Confident. Daring. Knew what he wanted. And then he shot me in the chest with an arrow to show Koth how amazing he was, and it landed him a job.'

'And he ended up a *black knight*,' Auron scoffed. 'I think I'd prefer being a collector of the dead during a plague than one of *those*.'

'Apparently, we even got him promoted when we killed Alric Tavish.'

'How nice of us,' Garaz mused.

Shift punched Nicolas lightly in the chest. 'I'm sorry you friend turned out to be scum.' They smiled sympathetically.

'Me too.' He laughed. 'I knew he wanted to do great things, but I didn't think he'd betray everyone he ever knew to get a job.'

'I will kill him for you,' Silva said calmly. 'You can choose whether it's slow or fast.'

In Silva's odd way, that was quite sweet. 'Just the two options?'

Silva allowed herself a half smile. 'There are varying degrees of slow. Fast is just fast.'

'Tempting. Thank you.' Nicolas chuckled. 'But when the time comes, he's mine. I owe him one puncture wound in the chest. Though if any of you feel like beating him and softening him up, I'm not going to complain.'

'None of you do that with the warrior woman,' Silva exclaimed suddenly, pointing at them with her skewer. 'Our battle must be a battle of equals.'

'She's all yours,' Shift said. 'Though I don't know why you're so obsessed with her.'

The way the warrior's eyes suddenly became dreamy was quite unnerving. 'Because she is my equal. I knew the minute I saw her that she and I were destined for a truly epic confrontation. She will know the same, when she sees me.'

'Maybe it's love,' Shift whispered, before yelping as Silva's skewer stuck in the floor between their legs.

'It is nothing so base,' the warrior chided. 'It is about challenge, honour, and glory.'

'I am all for honour and glory,' Auron said. 'But don't forget that what fighting is really about is *winning*.'

'And so I shall.' Silva bit her bottom lip in the manner of someone more interested in a lover's kiss than a fight.

Time to move on. This conversation was becoming creepier by the second.

'Let us figure out who is fighting whom once we actually make it inside,' Garaz said calmly. 'I have no doubt there will be plenty of violence to go around.'

'As long as the warrior woman is mine,' Silva said firmly, holding on to the point like a dragon did to its gold.

'And for that, I think we should pass it over to Shift,' Auron said, ignoring Silva's comment but giving her a slightly concerned look. 'If we're breaking into a manor, you're the one with the most experience in that area.'

Shift took a moment to answer, theatrically pretending they hadn't realised they were being spoken to. 'Well,' they said finally, 'if you're happy to defer to the master...'

Nicolas gestured for the shapeshifter to continue.

'I think it's best to strike when this gathering's happening,' the shapeshifter began. 'My initial idea was to disguise ourselves as guests and sneak inside.' They looked pointedly at him. 'However, I think we may have tried, and failed, that as a group once too often. Though I'd like it noted this was never a problem *before* I started travelling with you amateurs.'

'Noted. Get on with it.' Auron sighed.

'With said amateurs,' Shift grinned, 'I'm tempted to keep it simple. We survey the place on the night, find an unguarded door, slip inside. I break off and find Helstrum, draw him away to some discreet corner so Nick can kill him...with or without his towel. Provided Nick doesn't give us away by kicking the door in and howling his name like a werewolf at the moon.'

And lo, another embarrassment to haunt my every step.

'And it will be as easy as that?' Garaz asked.

Shift shrugged. 'It's only as difficult as we make it. Besides, with such an illustrious guest list, if the tales are to be believed, the guards will have their hands full with drunk and rowdy nobles. Once we're in, we're just part of the crowd. If we don't give them any trouble, they should ignore us.'

'Nobles get that bad?' Silva asked.

'Give these people a free bar, and suddenly, the burden of maintaining one's composure due to noble birth goes right out the window. As does a fair amount of clothing.' Shift's eyes briefly took on a haunted look. They'd seen some things, about which Nicolas wanted to know nothing.

'Can't Garaz just...blow the place up?' Nicolas mused.

'Ah, why defeat your enemies the honourable way when you can lazily magic them to death from a distance?' Auron nodded wisely.

'Ha bloody ha. All I'm saying is that there may be a way to do this without fighting our way through whatever security Helstrum has.'

'Three problems, kid,' Auron said, holding up three fingers, just to reinforce his point. 'One, we won't know for sure if Helstrum is there. Two, if we *blow the place up*, we'll be assassinating half the nobles in the Nine

Kingdoms, and you got squeamish about killing a faun in self-defence once, never mind blasting Lord and Lady Snootyass to oblivion. And three, and this is a big one, so listen carefully: *That's. Not. How. Heroes. Behave. Kid.*'

'Just an idea,' he muttered sourly.

Shift sat up and stretched. 'So, I think we're settled on following the lead of the master thief then. Deities, you lot are lucky to have me around.'

'If we are going to slip into the manor, we may need to have Garaz—'

'You certainly will not,' the orc protested, before Silva could finish. 'I am coming with you. I did not support you in the fortress, and young Nicolas was almost killed. I will not let you out of my sight again. And that is final.'

Silva took a second to close her eyes and gather her patience. 'Garaz, I—'

'That is final,' the orc repeated.

Touching. Especially as he nearly didn't want to come with us at all to start with.

CHAPTER 52

Tenderly, Nicolas probed his face. Certain areas were painful to the touch. And there was obvious swelling. Rising with a slight groan, Nicolas walked over to the stream where they'd made their camp. The trickling of water was soothing, as was the chance to rest. The group needed some time to recover before making their move on Helstrum, whose party was the next night. Standing at the edge of the water, Nicolas waited for a long time, unsure he'd like what he was about to see. Kneeling, he leant over and looked at his reflection.

Deities, this one's taking a toll on me.

His face was black and blue in several places and his cheek swollen. Part of it was from the fight with Leather Mask, but, really, he'd been hit a lot on this adventure, and he wasn't having the proper time to heal. His leg was doing okay, but it still bothered him on occasion, like after the numerous long walks they had between the moments of heart-pounding danger. Then there was the fresh scar on his temple...

At least they were taking the chance to rest now. Behind him, the others sat around the small grass area on which they'd made their camp. They all knew how hard what came next was going to be.

'You should've taken the towel with you.' Rolling his eyes, Nicolas turned to Auron, who stood behind him. 'I'm serious, kid. You've found your special move. I have *the finger poke of doom.* You have the *towel of death.*' The spirit mimed flicking a towel at opponents.

'I'm all right, thanks,' he replied dryly.

'You are, actually.' There was a certainty in Auron's tone that surprised him. 'All the beatings you're getting. That moron Potter. And you're still going.' Stepping forward, Auron flicked the rising sun on his armour. 'That's one of the reasons you get to wear that.'

Nicolas looked down at his armour, and the symbol of the *Dawnblade,* Auron's former mantle, which he'd bequeathed to him.

Will I live up to it? Deities, will I live to see next year?

'Are the other reasons my handsome features and wit?'

Auron laughed. 'Well, calling yourself handsome definitely shows your wit. But you have a long way to go before you catch me up in either of those stakes.'

'I'll never get more handsome doing what we do.' Nicolas sighed, pointing to his face. 'I only get more scarred and bruised.' His words summoned the itching in the whip marks on his back that troubled him occasionally. His leg joined in, just for fun.

'Scars make men more handsome,' Auron replied. 'It's science.'

Nicolas raised an eyebrow. 'Please explain.'

Auron rolled his pupilless white eyes. 'It's simple. Women love men of action. The more scars you have, the more of a man of action you are, therefore, the more attractive you are.'

'Surely more scars just mean you're more careless or accident prone?'

'Look, kid,' the spirit faux-reprimanded. 'Who knows more about the opposite sex between the two of us?'

'Hey,' he said indignantly. 'Just because I haven't shagged my way across Etherius, unlike some, doesn't mean I don't know anything. I'm in a relationship.'

'Not with a woman, though.' Auron smirked, waving his finger in the air. 'Therefore, I know more about the opposite sex.'

Technically Auron had him there. Shift didn't class themselves as either man or woman. Being a shapeshifter, that did make sense. Not that it mattered to Nicolas in the slightest. He just didn't like Auron being right all the time.

'You win,' he conceded grudgingly, once a counter-argument failed to materialise.

Sometimes it'd be nice if Auron failed to materialise.

'Of course.' Auron's grin was at its full level of smugness. 'It's what I do.'

'What I need to do is recover,' Nicolas said. 'I'll be in no state to face anyone if I don't. And the Maestro still has more bodyguards. And an army.'

'Imagine the tales when you fight your way through them,' Auron suggested, raising his eyebrows.

'I don't want any tales. I just want to get this done.' Nicolas thought for a moment. 'What do you reckon the odds are of Tobias coming out if I walk up to the gate and challenge him to honourable combat?'

The spirit let out a long whistle. 'I think we are looking at minus numbers there, kid.'

'Still, imagine it.' Nicolas smirked. 'Me walking up to the gate and bellowing a challenge. I might even get caught up in the moment and accidentally call myself *Nick Carnage*.'

'You do get caught up in the moment sometimes.' Auron nodded.

The pair laughed. It was nice, but it made his face hurt. Wincing, he massaged his jaw softly.

'Here.' Beside him, Garaz was holding a leaf with some kind of paste on it. The orc knelt beside him and inspected his face. 'This balm will help the bruising.'

Eyeing it warily, Nicolas took the leaf and applied the balm. It had an instant cooling effect on his skin. The orc removed a bottle from his cloak.

'Drink this,' Garaz said. 'It is a healing potion. But I have been watering them down, to ensure they do not have a negative effect on you.'

Somehow, because of his trip to the Underworld, healing potions now burnt him, though much less so than Garaz's healing magic. He accepted the bottle and took a swig. It still burnt a little, but like drinking something really spicy.

'Let me see to your leg.'

At Garaz's request, Nicolas stretched his leg out. The orc rolled up his trouser leg. Admittedly, the wound had healed nicely. But there would be a scar.

Another scar.

'Preparing him for the final battle?' Silva asked, leaning against a tree at their makeshift camp.

Nicolas scrunched his face up in distaste. 'Can you not use that term? *Final battle.*'

The warrior appeared confused. 'If we kill the Maestro, it may well be.'

'I know.' He shrugged. 'But it has other connotations. Like *I might not survive this one.*'

'Kid, where's your sense of the dramatic?' Auron tutted.

'I don't have one.'

Naturally, Shift chimed in. 'Oh really? Kicking down a door and bellowing your name seemed a little dramatic to me.'

'Auron must've possessed me or something.'

'Something possessed you,' Silva chided slightly. 'And it cannot when we get to the manor. I know what Helstrum took from you, but this mission will only succeed if we are careful.'

'I will be,' he said firmly.

This may be our only chance to kill him. I will not let it slip by me by again.

Once Helstrum knew he was a target, he could go into hiding. Then it could take years to find him, if ever. And too many people had died already. He wasn't going to let the Maestro hurt any more people.

My parents. Tallith. Avin. Countless others...I'll do it. For all of you, and all those that might be.

A thought occurred to him. 'What about getting out again? We've got an idea of how we're getting into the manor to do the deed. Then we kill him. What then? How do we get back out?'

Likely, there would be a lot of pissed-off guards around them. Maybe armed with fire-sticks.

'Already thinking about getting out.' Auron folded his arms with a proud smile. 'That's nice and optimistic. You're getting better.'

'An escape plan would be nice.'

Shift looked up thoughtfully for a moment. 'I think we will have to just improvise that one. Worst case scenario, Garaz sets a couple of fires, and we slip out in the confusion...'

'Leaving a trail of bodies of all those who dare try to stop us.' Silva's expression clearly stated that she meant the warrior woman.

Auron could see it too, and shook his head slightly, his pupilless eyes bouncing towards the sky.

'Start a fire and escape in the confusion has worked before.' Nicolas was thinking specifically of Avus Arex's fortress. 'I'm happy with that.'

Anywhere Tobias Helstrum lived should rightfully be burnt down. All the better to wipe every trace of the Maestro and his schemes from Etherius once and for all.

CHAPTER 53

Nicolas's eyes widened at his first glimpse of Tobias Helstrum's manor. Cast in the light of the torches surrounding it, the place was vast. It likely dwarfed some castles. There was certainly wealth in hatred. He didn't know how, but despite how plainly Helstrum dressed, he wasn't short of a coin or five hundred thousand.

'It's got more wings than a flock of chickens,' Auron said with an impressed whistle.

'I bet there's some treasures in there.' Shift was looking at the place the same way Silva had looked at the warrior woman.

The group lay in a patch of grass with a good vantage point that Auron had found just up the road from the manor. Even the spirit lay beside them. Tobias seemed to have at least one necromancer on staff, who was evidently taking precautions against intrusion by spirits. That was frustrating, to say the least. Auron was one of their biggest advantages. He could go in, scout the area, find Helstrum, then tell the group exactly where he was. Now, they'd have to do it the old-fashioned way.

Searching that place could take days.

But at least they'd arrived on time for the party. Gaudy carriages were passing them at a steady rate. So much so that there was now a queue to get in, as guards thoroughly checked invitations.

'They're even checking under the carriages,' Shift noted as they watched the guards conduct their searches. 'They're thorough. No going through the main gate for us.'

Even the guards were dressed for the occasion, wearing well-polished armour with a plumed helmet. There wasn't a mask in sight. Probably to make sure they didn't unnerve the guests.

'Deities,' Auron gasped, studying the side of the nearest carriage. 'That's Lord and Lady Shiyen from Secos. Old Helstrum doesn't mess around with his guest list.' Servants with trays appeared and walked the line of carriages, serving food and drink to those waiting to get in. 'Looks like he's covered every base.'

Auron continued to reel off a list of notables, the vast majority of whom Nicolas had never heard of. Shift broke the monotony of this by noting the one or two they'd robbed in the past.

And here we are, ready to sneak in like robbers ourselves. Except really, we're assassins.

'It is highly disturbing that so many well-to-dos would arrive for anything put on by this man,' Garaz rumbled soberly.

'There's Fliaphor the Cosmic.'

Nicolas turned his head to see who the spirit was talking about. After a moment of confusion, he followed Auron's gaze and looked up as a shadow passed overhead.

Oh, wow.

Garaz went from zero to utterly aghast in an instant. 'The Head of the Academy of Magic? But... How... What...' It was strange seeing someone usually so careful with their words unable to speak.

Auron scrunched his face up as he continued his watch. 'I don't care how magical it is, flying in on a rug just looks daft. Poor sod looks like he's half frozen from the altitude too. There's a limit to showmanship, you know.'

Never thought I'd hear Auron say that.

The carpet that flew over them seemed to be moving in a less-than-straight line. Ushered down by the guards at the gate, it descended until it hovered just above the ground. Even then it was very shaky. It looked like it might tip its rider, a proud-looking blond man in a deep blue robe—who did indeed seem freezing cold—off at any moment.

'At least we know who the Boost is for,' Silva said with distaste.

'Judging by the way he's flying that rug, I'd say he's out of his robe on it already.' The spirit sniffed. 'Oops, there he goes'

With one sharp motion, the carpet finally did tip to the side, sending its rider sprawling to the ground. Once he was no longer aboard, the carpet dropped to the grass like a stone, whilst some of the guards tried to help Fliaphor up.

'Looks like he's bumped his head,' Shift noted as the scene unfolded.

'Good,' a certain orc muttered.

As the guards attempted to help him rise, Fliaphor's leg got tangled in his own cape, and he fell to the ground again.

'The tit's attracting quite a crowd,' Auron chuckled as people leant out of their carriages to watch the show, their reactions ranging from bemusement to distaste.

'We did not come here to watch intoxicated wizards fall over,' Silva said. 'Let's move.'

It was a fair point, but the show was also quite entertaining. Having hauled him to his feet, a couple of the guards were escorting Fliaphor into the grounds, whilst trying to make it look like they were *not* actually carrying him. A servant dutifully rolled up his carpet, picked it up, and followed them.

The group made a wide arc around the manor, coming to the point where the side wall met the back one. It was slow going, as they kept low and in the shadows, stopping regularly to check for patrols. But it was necessary. Getting spotted now would give the game away. And give the Maestro a chance to flee.

Parallel to the wall, the group waited for a few moments, carefully scanning for traps. After stashing their packs in a hedge they ran to the wall, one by one, keeping low but moving with speed. As Nicolas made his run, he checked in all directions, senses sharp for signs of guards. Finally reaching the wall, he pressed himself to the cold stone beside the others.

'They haven't put a charm on the wall,' Auron said, putting his hand through it. 'So I can come a bit further with you.'

It obviously hurt the spirit that he might get left behind. Nicolas wanted to say something to make it better, but he didn't have any words that'd magically fix it. He wanted Auron in there with them as much as the spirit wanted to be there. They had more chance of success if they were all together.

'Can you check that the way is clear?' Silva asked.

Carefully, Auron put his head into the wall. Clearly concerned about getting spotted, he didn't just pop his head right through it. Nicolas could imagine his ethereal face sticking slightly out of the stone on the other side.

'No sign of any guards,' the spirit confirmed. 'But there's a lot of hedges. There could be patrols.' Then he vanished entirely through the wall.

'Avert your eyes.'

Confused, Nicolas looked at Shift. His eyes widened as he realised the command was because they were stripping off. He was about to turn back around, when the shapeshifter winked at him and blew him a kiss. His face reddened, and he wasn't sure why. He'd seen them naked plenty of times now.

Undressed, Shift quickly turned into a black cat. Bracing themselves, they leapt at the wall. There was a scrabbling of claws as they didn't quite make the jump and frantically climbed the rest of the way. But then they were over, vanishing into the grounds.

After a moment, the group heard a single *meow.*

'Does that mean the coast is still clear?' Garaz asked with a furrowed brow.

'We should have established the code before they went,' Silva huffed slightly. 'But let's assume it is.'

'Yes, it's still clear,' Auron huffed from the other side of the wall. 'I'm literally stood here watching for trouble. I don't need some furry...*hey*. Stupid cat.' Nicolas heard Shift hiss at the spirit. 'Just hurry up.'

The warrior picked up Shift's clothes, slung them over her shoulder then gestured to Garaz and Nicolas. The pair held their hands out low. As Silva stepped on them, both lifted her upwards, until she grabbed the edge of the wall and pulled herself up. After dropping the clothes on the other side, Silva shuffled around and reached for Nicolas. Jumping slightly, he grabbed the warrior's hand. Putting his feet to the wall, he climbed up and joined Silva atop it. Then, together, they did the same for Garaz.

Once the orc reached them, the group jumped down into the grounds, where Shift was already dressed and back in their preferred form.

'First step successful.' The shapeshifter smiled. 'We're in.'

In Nicolas's mind, a fanfare of trumpets played. He hoped it continued.

CHAPTER 54

There was a hint of music in the air, a teaser of the party within the formidable manor. Lights lit every window, bathing parts of the gardens and illuminating the numerous gargoyles that stared angrily down into the garden.

And it'd be really nice if you chaps stayed on the roof. Thank you.

The gardens were well-tended and filled with numerous large hedges that created corridors almost like a maze. It made it easier for Nicolas and his companions to approach the manor without being seen but also made it more dangerous, as each corner could conceal a patrol. Several times, the group had to stop and duck down to avoid one. The consensus was to let them pass unless absolutely necessary. Leaving unconscious or dead guards lying around would give away the fact that they were there, and hiding them would take precious time.

The several patrols they did see, around the sides and back of the manor, were all the masked men they associated with the Maestro.

As they wove through the ornamental bushes, Nicolas briefly glimpsed the carriage park, where all manner of fancy conveyances awaited their masters and mistresses dutifully. It reminded him of the Big Boss's arena. Inside was likely equally seedy.

With care and caution, the group were soon in sight of the back of the manor.

So close now.

Unfortunately, the rear of the building was quite the hive of activity too. A group of what looked to be performers in a myriad of tasselled and frilled outfits were preparing themselves for whatever they had to do inside. Judging by the leg stretching, it was a dance of some kind. Around them were numerous boxes and trunks, most likely their costumes and props.

'Brilliant.' Shift smiled excitedly. 'Just pretend we belong.'

That seemed very simplistic, given they had an orc with them, but Shift strode from the bushes before anyone could argue. All they could do was follow and hope the shapeshifter knew what they were doing.

'And who, pray tell, are you?' A haughty man positively caked in powdered makeup asked as they approached.

Shouldn't he be more shocked by Garaz?

'We're the Valiant Four, the company of Players from Horsestead,' Shift answered without hesitation.

The powdered man looked at his peers. 'The who?'

'Oh, I'm sorry,' Shift scoffed, adding a foppish tone to their voice. 'I mistook you for a cultured fellow.'

The man recoiled as if slapped before regaining his composure. 'Ah, of course. The Valiant *Four*. I thought you said The Valiant *Tour*. Lucinda over there has been going over her pitches, and it's left us all with our ears ringing a bit.'

Lucinda took the total amount of offense she could from that comment, to the point she stormed off into the building.

'So, you are putting on a show?' the man asked gleefully.

Shift clicked their fingers theatrically. 'That we are, my good sir. We are here to entertain the cultural elite with a little play of ours. My young friend here will be playing the notorious non-human lover *Nick Perverse Carnage*.'

It took every ounce of Nicolas's will not to react to the name. Obviously, Shift trusted him. Or just didn't care.

'Oh *him*,' the powdered man said, coming up close and examining him. He stank of sweet and sickly scents. 'Well, he certainly looks the part. He has the scrawny nervous look down to an art. And the beady eyes. Tell me, young man, are you a method actor? You're practically sweating.'

Shift took the man by the elbow and led him away. 'You know he can't answer that, he's in character. You can't have him...'

A guard appeared at the door. 'Dance troop to stage.'

He didn't react to Garaz either. That's bloody odd.

'Ooh.' The man became giddy. 'Here we go.'

Quickly, he rustled up his dancers and herded them through the door.

'Break a leg,' Shift called after him.

The man turned back and shrugged. 'Wouldn't be the first time, darling.'

Go ahead and break both, if you fancy it.

Nicolas was about to breathe a sigh of relief, but they weren't alone. An extraordinarily buff fellow in fur pants, who'd been painted green then sprayed with water so his abs and pecs glistened, strolled up to them. He wore clearly fake ears and tusks.

Oh.

'Hey,' he snapped at Garaz. 'I was told I was the only orky working tonight.'

Orky? What is he? Some kind of dancer?

'Clearly you are not,' Garaz replied without hesitation.

'That means splitting the tips.' The man shook his head in frustration, before he took a moment to calm himself and look Garaz over. 'Gotta say, man, I'm impressed with the costume,' he said an enthusiastic nod. 'You've nailed it. The tips you're going to get tonight. I mean, the feral eyes, the leathery skin, the odour. Proper ugly. I commend you...'

Garaz headbutted the man, and he crumpled to the floor. The orc snorted at the unconscious man before realising something. Taking two fingers, Garaz wiped the green paint from his forehead with disgust.

'The amulet working okay, big guy?' Shift asked.

'That was just regular angry,' Garaz admitted grumpily.

'Don't worry,' Nicolas reassured his companion. 'I wanted to do the same thing to the powdered guy.'

'That might've caused a dust cloud that would've had you sneezing for hours, kid.' Auron smirked.

'Apparently we are not worried about leaving bodies lying around any more,' Silva muttered in annoyance, already grabbing the painted man's legs and dragging him away. 'But that's okay, I'll move him.'

A gentle elbow in the ribs got Nicolas's attention.

'Looks like I get my wish to sneak in disguised, after all, Mr Carnegie,' they said with a wink.

Not much of a disguise, if we're just dressed as ourselves.

'Hey, look at this.'

Nicolas turned to Auron. Slowly, but with much excitement, the spirit put his arm through the manor doorway. 'No barrier. I'm in.' The spirit tutted. 'You'd think they'd have more sense. But I've won as many victories through others' ignorance as my own smarts.'

Drug dealers manage to have tighter security than a hatemonger in a manor having a fancy party for the Etherius human elite? I'll never make sense of anything.

That was a boon indeed. Auron could come with them. The group would be whole. Nicolas started to allow himself to get optimistic about this endeavour.

'When we're in, we need to stay together,' Nicolas said firmly. 'We split up in the fortress, and that was a disaster. And if we do get caught, we're going to need strength in numbers.'

'Agreed,' Garaz said.

A sickening snapping sound caught their attention. Everyone looked in the direction of Silva, who was closing one of the trunks.

'What was that?' Nicolas asked wearily.

'He wouldn't fit,' the warrior answered.

'He wouldn't...' It suddenly dawned on Nicolas what was probably in the trunk. 'What did you do to him?'

'I just broke his legs.' The casualness with which the warrior said that was staggering. 'No one should find him for a good while.' Silva held up the key to the trunk, which she'd removed after she locked it.

Focus, Nicolas. At least he's still alive. He just won't be dancing for a while.

Instead of arguing with Silva, he glanced towards the open door to the manor.

'In we go then.' It was hard to keep the nerves from his voice.

CHAPTER 55

D espite Nicolas's misgivings, just walking around as themselves was the best disguise. It made them a source of entertainment for the guests, who seemed to be excited at the outrage they suffered at their appearance. Apparently, Nicolas and his companions were quite infamous amongst the intolerant asshole community. Some of the guests feigned horror or comically begged for their lives. One lord even spat on Nicolas's armour. Nicolas only just caught himself before he punched the man, his fist raised and ready. This seemed to add to the *show*, the man theatrically crying about what a *brute* he was.

'Oh, look at his little face, Perry,' the lady accompanying him said to her husband. 'It looks like he may set his ghost on you.'

'One must stand up to these miscreants, darling,' Perry said, waving his handkerchief at Nicolas as if it were a battle axe. The foppish laugh that accompanied it made Nicolas want to vomit.

'Best not, dear.' His wife giggled. 'He may get his inhuman-loving stink on you.' Playfully, she dragged her husband away, allowing the group to progress.

Auron frowned, nodding with pursed lips. 'You guys go ahead,' the spirit said after a moment. 'I'll catch you up.'

Halfway down the corridor, they heard a voice cry out, *'Ow, my eye.'*

'Finger poke of doom?' Nicolas whispered as the spirit joined them.

'You're Deities-damned right,' the spirit scowled. '*Ghost* indeed.'

Once they'd left the back rooms and entered the main corridors of the manor, the place was bustling. Inebriated notables walked from room to room, gossiping, eating and doing whatever else they did at these sort of things. There were also plenty of people dressed up, wearing elaborate costumes that made them look like minotaurs, fairies, or other non-human species. Which was bloody odd, considering where they were. Sweet orchestra music carried down every corridor. Nicolas assumed there was a grand hall somewhere, which was most likely where Helstrum would be.

The building itself was as grand on the inside as it was on the outside. Fine red carpets ran through corridors of beautifully varnished wood-panelled walls. Nicolas could tell how fancy it was by all the little bits of crystal dangling off the lights. It was just a shame he'd chosen to decorate the walls with portraits of some of the sourest looking people he'd ever seen.

Maybe holding a smile for a portrait would be a test of endurance...but at least try.

Guards lined the corridors at regular intervals. But they appeared to be taking no notice of anyone who passed them. Nicolas assumed they were just being professional.

'I say, you there...'

The group turned as a lord with a large handlebar moustache jogged towards them, puffing and panting, waving them down as his wife...maybe daughter...held his arm and followed along.

The pair marched up to them and stood directly in front of Garaz, appraising him as one might do meat in a butcher's shop.

'Ah yes, a fine specimen indeed,' the lord huffed, still trying to catch his breath. 'Certainly looks the part, I do say.'

'Mmm, yes, darling,' his wife cooed on his arm. It had to be his wife, by the way she was stroking his arm. 'He looks delicious.'

Garaz was staring at the pair politely, but anyone who knew him could tell that inside he was screaming. 'Why, thank you.' A slight tremor in his voice nearly betrayed him.

'If you aren't already taken,' the lady smirked, as if telling a dirty secret, 'we have a playroom ready.'

'Oh yes, we shall have a lot of fun, I do say.' The man twiddled his moustache mischievously. 'And I have plenty of coin for the right sort of entertainment, yes I do.'

Playroom? Entertainment?

Nicolas barely contained his choke of horror as it dawned on him what was being asked and why there were so many people walking around dressed as fauns, kascats, serians, and more.

Thankfully, Garaz didn't headbutt the lord; instead, he smiled politely. 'Unfortunately, I'm already on my way to a...ahem...play date. But as soon as I am done, I shall come and find you.' The orc finished with a polite bow.

The lord and lady were visibly disappointed. The lord leaned in and whispered conspiratorially, 'Well, see that you do, man. We are keen to play *Bride of the Orc*, if you know what I mean. So don't overexert yourself with your next booking, my good fellow.'

Garaz gave another bow. 'I shall be along shortly.'

The lady tittered and clapped her hands. 'Whilst we wait, shall we go to the buffet? Those little gorgon eggs are to die for.'

'I believe we shall.' The lord beamed. 'Don't worry, young chap. We won't get too full. We'll make sure we have just enough to ensure our energy when you return.'

'Oh, and please practise your growl,' the lady called back as her husband led her away. 'I do love a feral growl.'

As they watched, the lady slipped her arm from her husband's. She ran back to Garaz, holding her skirt so she didn't trip. Coming to a halt, she reached out and placed her hand on Garaz's chest, patting it twice and exhaling breathlessly. Beginning to retract her arm, she suddenly reached in, gave the orc's nipple a playful tweak, and ran back to her husband with a girlish giggle.

'He will be perfect,' she said as she now began to lead *him* away.

Beside Nicolas, Shift's lips were pursed fiercely, their face red as they fought to hold back their laughter. Auron had no such restraint.

'Are you okay?' Nicolas asked, turning to a wide-eyed Garaz.

'Not at all,' the orc rumbled finally, seeming paler for the conversation.

'I do not understand,' Silva said, eyeing the retreating couple warily. 'They are at an event for those who hate non-humans. Why are they partaking in these...activities?'

I suppose that's the most diplomatic way to put it.

'That just makes it naughtier,' Shift replied with distaste. 'Butter folks up with booze, drugs, and kinky stuff, and they'll listen when you talk.'

'And in the morning, when they're disgusted with themselves, it's all the non-humans' fault for enticing them,' Auron remarked with a disgusted scowl.

'Indeed,' Garaz snarled, before wrapping his cloak tightly around him, and trying to ignore the coy glances of those they passed. 'Can we hurry this up before I have to wash my soul?'

'It's a big house.' Shift shrugged. 'And a party. He could be anywhere. We need to check every room.'

Nicolas opened the nearest door and slammed it shut seconds after, his eyes wide.

Shift looked at him in concern. 'You okay, Nick? You've gone pale.'

'...orgy.' His voice came out as a hoarse whisper as the image he'd just seen embedded itself in his mind for all eternity.

Auron promptly popped his head through the wall for an uncomfortably long time. When it came back out, the spirit was smiling broadly. Then he started nodding in a dreamy fashion.

'You should embrace stuff like that, kid,' the spirit said with passion. 'Enjoy the pleasures.'

'I'm not embracing anything that's going on in there,' he replied quickly, pointing at the door.

'Good answer,' Shift muttered sternly.

Auron rolled his eyes. 'None of you are any fun.' Again, the dreamy looked crossed his face. 'So many memories...'

If I hear, 'So this one time...' I'll find a way to exorcise him.

In another chamber, robed men were strewn about the place on pillows, giggling or murmuring to themselves. Around the room were trays laden with goblets filled with Boost.

'Old Helstrum doesn't mess around when he throws a party,' Auron said after a long whistle.

Nicolas eyed the goblets warily. 'He must be pretty confident that this stuff isn't going to just blow up.'

'Wouldn't do his attempts to gain supporters much good,' Shift said. 'Though I wouldn't complain about this place going up in flames. It'd be good for future generations.'

'I say, you two look amazing. Spot-on costumes, yes, indeed.' Fliaphor staggered up to them. It took Nicolas a second to realise what had been said, as the man's ability to speak had been reduced to a string of drunken murmurs. 'Is it true what they say about that Nick fellow and his shapeshifting consort?'

'Is what true?' he asked nervously.

Fliaphor put a hand on his shoulder, which he soon realised was only to keep the old wizard standing. 'That when they have carnal relations, he gets the shapeshifter to turn into a talking chicken?'

I do whaaaaaaat?

'Unfortunately, we will never know for sure,' Shift answered quickly. 'But I wouldn't put anything past those degenerates.'

'Exactly,' Fliaphor said, pointing a finger at Shift. Or possibly at a wall. 'Going around aiding the great enemy against their own kind. The boy is an example of everything wrong with humanity. Turning on his own. Despicable. But old Tobias has his number, yes, indeed. Says he'll be dead soon.'

So at some point I've become the figurehead of their enemy? Fantastic.

'Well, I'm sure they seduced him somehow.' Shift smiled. 'Say, speaking of Tobias, you haven't seen him around?'

'Why yes,' Fliaphor said with a dazed grin. 'He's in the west wing. He said we should enjoy ourselves whilst he attended to some sort of important matter. There's so much Boost here, how can one *not* enjoy himself?' The wizard's eyes opened wide as if a lantern had just lit above his head. 'And here's me talking to you when I should be planting my face in it. Good day.'

As the wizard turned, he attempted to fan his cloak out dramatically but instead looked more like a cold husband trying to wrestle the bedsheet away from his wife.

'What a wizened master the Academy has.' Silva snorted as the old wizard staggered away.

'Degenerate,' Garaz growled quietly.

'I really want to leave.' Nicolas sighed. 'This is just too much.'

'You need to work on your fortitude, kid,' Auron said with a raised eyebrow. 'You can't let a load of kinky, drug-loving nobles put you off finishing the battle for the soul of Etherius.'

Judging by this place, the battle was won. And not by us.

Nicolas was about to reply when a naked old lord ran down the hall with his arms in the air shouting, *'Eeeeeee,'* gleefully as a man dressed as a faun chased him with a whip. Nicolas gestured to the lord and raised his eyebrows.

'I know, kid.' Auron sighed. 'But we still have a job to do. Just think, this will make an amazing story one day.'

'Yes,' he replied dryly. 'I cannot wait to sit in a tavern and tell the tale of *Nicolas Percival Carnegie and the hundred wrinkly dongs.*'

'I would suggest not entitling your tale *that*, for starters,' Garaz said, suppressing a chuckle.

Closing his eyes, Nicolas rubbed the bridge of his nose. 'Let's just go kill Helstrum. West wing, wasn't it?'

The group progressed down the beautifully carpeted corridors whose doors were like small portals to worlds of excess and depravity.

'You'd think they'd have an issue with Helstrum allowing them to engage in such debauchery,' Silva commented, before giving the rotund lord ogling her a fierce scowl. It only seemed to spur him on.

'One does not take issue with the man who provides the sex and drugs.' Auron chuckled. 'Because then there wouldn't be any more of it.'

'There will not be any more once we are done,' Garaz said firmly. 'And the notion of burning this place down is becoming increasingly enticing.'

'We'd be doing Etherius a favour,' Nicolas replied, doing his best to keep his eyes straight ahead.

After killing Helstrum, I think this world will owe us a few favours.

CHAPTER 56

Following the maze of corridors in a vaguely westerly direction, the group soon—and thankfully—found themselves away from the main party. Finally, ahead of them was an ornate door with the symbol of the Custodians of Humanity carved into it. It had to be the door separating the west wing from the rest of the building. Two guards stood to attention on either side of it.

'Helstrum invites them in then buggers off whilst they play,' Auron scoffed.

Nicolas pictured Tobias. 'I can't see him as the playing type. Speaking of which, how do we play this?'

'I'll attempt to bluff our way in,' Shift replied. 'If that doesn't work, you and Silva can knock them out.'

At least all the security was focused on the party. They could take two guards.

Using the same breezy stride that had gotten them into the manor, Shift led them down the corridor towards the door. Before they could reach it, one of the guards stepped forward. 'Your business?' he asked in a gruff voice.

'We need to talk to Mr Helstrum about renumeration for our performance,' Shift answered with a slightly aggravated tone. 'The lords keep spitting on my companion who plays *Nicolas*. One even tried to defecate on his shoe, so we want to renegotiate our fee if we're to stay for the whole event.'

The pair of guards exchanged a brief look.

'Very well.' The guard who'd addressed them turned and opened the door for them.

Oh. Okay.

'Thank you,' Shift said as if that was exactly what they'd expected, before leading them all through.

Without a word, the guard shut the door behind them.

'You're good,' Nicolas said, staring at the closed door in wonder.

'Apparently so.' Shift shrugged, eyeing the door warily. 'I was expecting more of an argument.'

'Don't knock it,' Auron cautioned. 'We're in.'

This part of the house was a stark contrast to the rest of the manor. Here the corridors were simple stone. It appeared more like the corridor in a castle. Everything was plain and understated. And thankfully quiet. The door had even muted the music to nothing.

Maybe the rest of the place is for show? Perhaps this is what Helstrum is really like?

It was more in keeping with how Nicolas viewed the man. 'Now to find him,' he whispered.

That wasn't all, really—they had to kill him too—but the end was in sight. The end of the nightmare that had become his life. Grab Helstrum, make him talk, kill him, go and find his people, lead them home, and live happily ever after. All of that sounded really appealing and very achievable right now.

Passing through the corridors, the group entered a long room filled with pillars and what looked to be antiquities on raised pedestals. The range of items on show went from old pottery pieces to types of tools from the past.

Shift's gaze darted from pedestal to pedestal. 'Do you think these are worth anything?'

'I would imagine so,' Garaz replied. 'But you can control your thieving urges until after we have completed our mission.'

'But we may be fleeing then and not have time to—'

'You shall touch *nothing*.'

From the other end of the room, the ebony-skinned warrior emerged. Nicolas was sure she'd gotten bigger since he'd last seen her, though maybe it was because she was closer now.

'You dare plan to defile my lord's treasures,' the warrior snarled in outrage. 'I shall have your—' Suddenly, her face dropped and her eyes widened. 'You.'

Following her gaze, he realised the warrior was staring at Silva, who returned the intense look she was getting.

'Me,' Silva replied in a hushed voice, filled with anticipation.

The warrior woman shrugged her furs to the floor and unslung her weapon. 'Finally. A worthy opponent,' she whispered, looking Silva up and down. 'You are Silva Destrone?'

Silva stepped forwards, sword at the ready. 'I am,' she confirmed.

'I heard tell of you,' the warrior woman said as she and Silva met in the centre of the room and began to circle each other. 'Somehow, I knew that one day we would meet in combat. I hope it is everything I wish it to be.'

'I look forward to providing you with a glorious death,' Silva replied.

The ebony warrior let out a single laugh. 'We shall see.'

They're both as bad as each other.

Nicolas was torn. On the one hand, he knew how vehemently Silva wanted to fight her one-on-one, and the likely retribution if he got involved. But it didn't seem right letting Silva fight alone.

'Stay put, kid,' Auron said, reading his mind.

The pair stopped circling and stared at each other. The ebony warrior was a good head taller than Silva and a little broader. The air in the room became tense with the anticipation of combat. The ebony warrior made the first move.

With a grunt, she swung her mace. Silva raised her sword to block, but the mace batted it aside. With a quickness belying her size, the ebony warrior booted Silva right in the chest, throwing her backwards to the floor. Silva went with the fall, rolling and rising quickly as the mace took a chunk from the floor where her head had been.

Silva ducked another swing then leapt in for the attack. Three times, she swung her blade at her opponent, but the ebony warrior could move her weapon at great speed for something that looked so heavy.

'Ha,' the warrior woman exclaimed as they parted. 'I knew you would be a good match for me.'

The pair circled each other again, taking it in turns to launch probing attacks that were dodged or parried. The ebony warrior swung low, going for Silva's legs, a shot which would surely have snapped them in two if it hit. But Silva jumped at the last second, spinning as she did and kicking the warrior across the jaw. Staggering back, the warrior put her thumb to her lips, eyes wide with rage as she saw the blood upon it.

And then she came on like a berserker, screaming a battle cry as she swung the mace this way and that, taking chunks out of pillars and smashing the pedestals. She appeared to have lost interest in protecting her master's treasures now. Several were already in pieces on the floor.

Silva grunted in frustration as the sword was knocked from her hand and sent spinning across the room. Crying in victory, the ebony warrior brought her mace down towards Silva's head. Their companion caught its shaft in both hands, falling backwards and using her foot in her opponent's gut to throw the warrior woman overhead. As she crashed to the floor, Silva discarded her mace.

The pair rose, coming face to face and staring at each other with an intensity that made Nicolas uncomfortable.

'You are good,' the ebony warrior rumbled.

'Better than you,' Silva snarled.

Then, to Nicolas's surprise, the pair started trading punches. Each would take a turn smacking the other in the face as hard as they could then wait politely for the other to have their go. The sounds of the punches made him wince. How were either of them still standing?

Soon, the punches quickened in pace. Silva was the first to give, staggering back a step. The ebony warrior pressed her advantage, grabbing the back of Silva's head as she laid in punch after punch. Finally, Silva brought her forearms up to block, creating an opening and driving in with her own punches, which caused her opponent to retreat one meaty smack at a time. Nicolas was sure at some point he saw a tooth flying.

The warrior grabbed Silva and lifted her overhead as Nicolas might do a pillow and launched her into a pillar. His companion gasped in pain as her side struck the stone, before she fell to the floor with a thud. Gleefully, her opponent kicked her in the side, picked her up, and did it again. Something went crunch, and Nicolas didn't want to guess what.

The warrior woman went to kick again. This time, Silva blocked it with crossed arms, before lunging upwards and unleashing a flurry of blows at her opponent's stomach. Nicolas didn't know how effective it would be; the woman's stomach looked rock hard.

Going for a hook punch, Silva's arm was caught, and she was lifted into the air again. Wriggling, she managed to free herself from the grip, falling behind Helstrum's bodyguard. Grabbing the warrior woman around the waist, Silva heaved with a cry, strain on her bloodied face as her leg muscles tensed. The warrior woman cried out in surprise as she was lifted from the ground and thrown over Silva's head. Her shoulders crashed into the floor on the other side of the warrior.

For a moment, both fighters lay on the ground, panting and trying to recover. Slowly, they turned their bodies to face each other and rose. With a mutual cry of fury, they ran at each other. Nicolas watched out of one eye as blows were exchanged, until the ebony warrior wrapped her power arms around Silva's waist and lifted her into the air, squeezing tightly. Silva cried out in pain, her back spasming.

Nicolas went to step forwards.

'Let her do it, kid,' Auron said quickly.

Torn, Nicolas looked at the others. They all appeared to agree with Auron, so he stepped back.

Fine. I'll just stand here and watch her die then.

As the ebony warrior roared, hoping to snap Silva in two, their companion headbutted her in the nose then slapped her palms over both her ears simultaneously. Staggering back, the warrior dropped Silva, clasping her ears as blood poured from her nose.

Deftly, Silva swung her leg, catching the warrior with a spinning kick to the head. The force caused her to turn, and Silva kicked out her knee. The warrior woman cried out in pain as her body buckled to the side and she was forced to the floor. Snarling, Silva staggered over and took hold of her opponent's long hair in both hands after wrapping it around her forearms.

Straining with the effort, Silva turned her body, using all her strength to lift the warrior from the ground by her own thickly braided ponytail. The warrior turned in a large circle, face reddening with the exertion as she swung her screaming opponent through the air and slammed her torso first into the nearest pillar.

Helstrum's bodyguard slid to the floor, her breathing raspy, as if ribs had been broken, which was highly likely. Silva staggered drunkenly over to the warrior and slipped her arms around the woman's neck. Feebly, she tried to break the grip and fight back as Silva squeezed, clawing first at her arms then her head. Silva let out a cry, and there was a snap. The fighting stopped. Releasing her grip, Silva let her dead opponent drop, before looking up at her companions. She was barely able to stand up straight. Her face, a swollen and bloody mess, was drenched in sweat.

'Told...you...I...could...beat...her...'

She crumpled to the floor.

CHAPTER 57

They ran to Silva, Garaz already preparing his healing magic.

'Ishta?' a voice called from the room beyond.

Three other figures entered the room, the maned man and two wizards—Tobias's other bodyguards. There was a moment of mutual surprise then the gaunt man acted. As Nicolas watched, his body became intangible, until it was almost like Auron's. As a terrible avenging spectre, he surged forwards through the air, entering Garaz before the orc could act.

Garaz fell back to the wall, clawing at himself as if he could somehow pull the intruder out. Then he became still.

'Garaz?' Nicolas asked warily.

The orc rose, but his yellow eyes were now pupilless white orbs. Fire gathered in Garaz's clawed hands. The orc snarled at them.

Apparently, the healing charm doesn't cover that type of possession. Fantastic.

'Ah ha, a guy who possesses people.' Auron beamed, flexing his fingers. 'This looks like a job for Auron of Tellmark.'

Without another moment's hesitation, the spirit jumped into Garaz too. The orc suddenly went stiff before his body began to convulse. It took Nicolas a second to realise it was the fight going on inside their companion. Garaz suddenly threw himself to the floor. Rising, the orc then flung himself all over the room in haphazard, staggering steps, crashing into anything and everything. More vases were smashed. But he knew Auron would prevail. Auron of Tellmark versus some malnourished wizard wasn't even a contest.

That just leaves two.

The man with the thick mane stood before them, pumping his arms until the veins popped out on his muscles, his face set in a growl. The other wizard stayed near the door, but power glowed around his hands.

'Do you know who I am?' the maned man roared, every word finishing with a growling upward inflection. 'I am the annihilator, the widow maker. I'll break your bones and turn your organs to mush. I'll drop you like a—'

A throwing knife hit him in the throat.

'Nice shot.' Shift gave Nicolas a faux round of applause.

'Auron does go on about the virtues of a good throwing knife. And...' It suddenly dawned on him that the man was still standing.

The muscled warrior's furious eyes slowly lowered to the hilt of the knife sticking from his throat. And then back at them. More veins popped out on his temples.

'Nick, why isn't he dead?'

'I...I don't know.'

'You must've thrown it wrong.'

'How?' he cried. 'It's in his bloody throat.'

There was no more chance to conjecture as the maned man barrelled into him. It was like being hit by a boulder flung from a catapult. He was winded before he even hit the nearest pillar and collapsed to the floor. He didn't have the luxury of resting to shake it off, so he jumped to his feet then ducked aside at the last second. The man collided with the pillar, wrapping his outstretched arms around it and squeezing until it was crushed into rubble.

Deities...

Oh shit. I dropped my sword.

'Savage,' the wizard at the door cried. 'Get out of the way. I can't get a shot.'

Savage wasn't listening. Snarling, the maned man began to swing wildly at Nicolas, which he ducked and swerved. Where the man punched stone, it left an indent. Soon, the warrior's fists were covered in stone dust.

I can't match fists with this guy. Look at the size of him.

His attacker was, indeed, a beast. His torso a rippling mass of muscles down to...

His legs.

Nicolas wasn't sure how those stick-like things were supporting so much upper body weight, but the warrior had obviously neglected to work on them.

Be a real shame if someone snapped one of those twigs.

Slipping beneath a grab that would've surely broken him in two, Nicolas swept low, knocking the man's legs aside as if he were blowing a feather in the breeze. The crash to the floor echoed around the room. Nicolas didn't waste any time before jumping on him. Handily, there was a weapon ready to use. Clasping his hands together, he struck down on the blade of the knife in the man's throat, until it went in all the way to the hilt.

The warrior let out a choked cry of pain then grabbed Nicolas's neck with two huge hands. 'Just...die...already...'

Taking hold of the hilt of the knife before he blacked out or his neck was snapped, Nicolas twisted the blade. The grip around his throat vanished. Making sure to duck to the side, he pulled the knife out. A spray of blood blasted into the air where Nicolas had just been sat.

Falling to the ground, he massaged his neck. Beside him, the maned man's eyes were wide and empty, his tongue lolling out of his mouth.

That seems to have done it.

A shard of ice flew past his head, and Nicolas remembered that danger still abounded. Garaz was thrashing all over the place, whilst Shift was dodging more ice shards launched by the wizard. His companion ducked and dived, until their opponent changed tactics. Lowering his aim, the wizard turned the floor to ice. Shift slipped, their legs flailing as there was no solid ground. They landed heavily, smacking their head on the ice, and stopped moving.

'Nooooooo.' Grabbing an ornamental plate from the nearest pedestal, Nicolas launched it like a discus. It cut through the air and caught the wizard in the temple. The man staggered backwards as Nicolas charged him, sliding on the ice and snatching up the *Dawn Blade* as he passed it.

Seeing Nicolas coming at him, the wizard began to gather his power, holding his hands together as if in prayer. Slowly, they parted. As they did, ice gathered between them in the shape of a sword.

'Ah-ha,' the wizard exclaimed, brandishing his blade.

Nicolas swung the *Dawn Blade*, which cut right through the ice blade, shattering it. Spinning with his sword swing, Nicolas came full circle and ran the shocked wizard through.

'*Ah-ha* yourself,' he grumbled as he yanked his sword free.

Before the wizard had even hit the ground, he was cautiously running over to Shift. In his peripheral vision, he caught glimpses of the spirits of the dead bodyguards, which he ignored. Frantically, he took their head in his hands. There was a giant bulge on the back of it. His companion wasn't moving.

'Shift? *Shift*?' he cried. 'Say something?'

'Something...' came the murmured reply.

'Thank the Deities,' he gasped.

'My head.' Shift winced as their eyes opened. 'It feels like a giant stepped on my brain.'

'How many fingers am I holding up?' he asked desperately.

'Three,' came the thankfully correct response.

Nicolas didn't have time to enjoy the moment. There was a crash behind him. When he turned, Garaz was lying on the floor.

'What happened to Garaz?' Auron asked as he stepped out of the orc, dusting his hands off. His aura seemed diminished, like it had been when his companion possessed him that one time. But it seemed to have taken less out of him this time. Though he could tell by Auron's overconfident smile that the fight had drained him a bit more than he was letting on.

'Your fight was throwing him all over the place,' Nicolas said.

The spirit sucked his teeth. 'Shit. If I'd known that, I wouldn't have made such a meal of the fight. It was no challenge, but it's been a while, and I wanted to make the most of it.' The spirit bent down. 'Sorry, Garaz.'

There was a mumbled reply. At least he was alive. But as a group, they weren't in a good state right now. Nicolas cast an eye around the room. Yes, they'd beaten the bodyguards, but it'd taken a toll. Silva was still out cold. Garaz was only just starting to move slightly, and Shift was stubbornly slapping his hands away and trying to get up, looking like a newborn deer taking their first steps. The fact there was still ice on the floor made it trickier still.

'We have to get out of here and regroup.' The fact weighed heavily on him. They'd never get another chance like this. As soon as Helstrum found out his bodyguards were dead, he'd start travelling in the company of ten thousand armoured knights.

'No.' Shift's speech was slurred slightly. 'This is the best chance we'll get. You have to go on.'

'But you guys...'

'I'm up,' Shift snapped. 'I'll look after the other two. You go and finish this. It's too important.'

'Shift's right, kid,' Auron said quietly. 'It's now or never.'

I know that but...what if I fail?

'I'll be with you,' the spirit continued as if reading his thoughts, again. 'And I'm a lot handier than I was when I first died.'

'But you're—'

'Getting better already,' Auron interrupted, his aura already visibly stronger. 'Now let's go.'

Shift quickly began to tend to Garaz, who would then heal Silva. And Tobias Helstrum was an old, crippled man. All in all, Nicolas fancied his chances.

'See you soon,' he said with a thin smile for Shift, trying not to focus on the giant lump on their head.

'I shalt be ready to celebrate your victory, mighty hero,' they replied with a pained wink. 'Once this mighty hangover has buggered off.'

Steeling himself, Nicolas readied the *Dawn Blade*. Looking towards the doorway ahead, he got an unnerving sense of finality about what would happen next. One way or another.

CHAPTER 58

Two corridors down, they came to a pair of large wooden doors.

'This reminds me of the tower in Yarringsburg,' he whispered. Back then, it had been him and Auron facing the necromancer Avus Arex together. Now they were here to put the sword to the man behind him and who knew what else.

'This will go better than that, kid,' the spirit said firmly. 'You aren't the boy you were then. You can do this.'

He stared towards the doors. 'I know.'

Yet there was the anxiousness of not knowing what was beyond that door. Was it just Helstrum? Did he have more fancy bodyguards? A dragon maybe?

Nicolas would get one chance at this, do or die, and the fate of their entire world was at stake. On *his* shoulders.

Slowly, he put a hand on the wood of the door, hesitating slightly just before he touched the wood. This door would hopefully lead him to the man he had to kill. Not in anger, but out of necessity. Though after all of this, he couldn't deny he was a little angry. But he wasn't about to give into it. His enemies had taken enough from him, changed him enough.

'I'm not about to achieve the ability to see through doors, so I'd best go in.'

'Do you want me to scout it out for you first?' Auron asked.

'Oh Deities, yes,' he said with passion.

With a knowing nod, the spirit stuck a finger in the door. It seemed this room wasn't protected from nosey ghosts either. Then Auron unceremoniously stuck his head through the wood. Nicolas stared at the spirit's body nervously as he waited, imagining monsters, or an army beyond the door.

Or an army of monsters.

'He's in there,' Auron said as he popped his head back out of the door. 'And he's alone. No sign of any traps.'

Nicolas couldn't help but smile.

Auron gestured towards the door. 'Shall we then?'

'Let's.'

Nicolas pushed the door open and stepped into the room.

And there he was. Tobias Helstrum, the Maestro, the man behind all his suffering and the suffering of untold others across the world...sat eating soup.

The room itself was quite large. A grand dining hall, maybe. But now it only had a single six-chaired table in it, at the head of which sat Tobias. There was no one else with him. Scanning the room for surprises, just in case Auron had missed something, he found nothing. There was some kind of altar on one end of the room, a semi-circular carving of people reaching up longingly to something that looked like an angel.

Stepping forwards, Nicolas opened his mouth to issue a challenge, only to find himself silenced by a raised finger. Slowly, Helstrum brought the spoon to his lips and closed his eyes to savour the taste.

He even slurps his soup like an asshole.

Tobias lowered the spoon and dabbed the corner of his mouth with a napkin. Re-folding it, he didn't even look at Nicolas as he spoke.

'I take it my bodyguards are dead then?' The old man sighed, before continuing. 'A shame, but hardly surprising, truth be told.' Now the hard eyes deigned to look at him, sizing him up. 'For someone who gives us so much trouble, you really aren't much to look at, Mr Carnegie.'

Wrong footed, Nicolas attempted to steer the conversation where he wanted it to go. 'Where are my family? Where are the people of Hablock?'

Using his cane, Tobias rose to his feet, the chair scraping on the stone floor as he pushed it away to get up. 'I neither know nor care, young man. You're here. That's all that matters.'

'I... What?' Nicolas was starting to get nervous. He was the man with the drawn sword, so he should, therefore, be in control of this situation, and he was very much getting the impression that he wasn't.

But I've come here to kill him. Shouldn't he be at least a little nervous?

Tobias rolled his eyes. 'How could I expect intellect from a child who sides with the great enemy?' He sighed.

'You knew I was coming?' Nicolas asked warily.

'I was told, yes,' Helstrum confirmed. 'You are on some misguided mission to silence me for your non-human masters.'

'Of course we came for you,' Nicolas cried. 'You're the Maestro. You took my family.'

Tobias shook his head irritably. 'Foolish child. I am not the Maestro. I am merely a humble servant, doing good work in his name. You thought you came here to kill, when the reality is, you came here to die.'

A gallery ran the circumference of the room. Nicolas hadn't noticed it before. He noticed it now, because it was full with men armed with fire-sticks. All pointed at him.

No. Nonononono.

'Even now, my men are picking up your companions,' Helstrum continued. 'The orc monstrosity will be exterminated, and the shapeshifting thing shipped to where it needs to go. Silva will be re-educated. She was very useful before, and she can be again.'

Instantly, Nicolas turned towards the door, which slammed shut in his face. A heavy bolt clacked into place.

It's a trap. This whole thing is a trap.

'I take it the ghost is here with you too?' Helstrum asked casually.

'Of course he is,' Auron snarled, even though Tobias clearly couldn't hear him.

'Yes,' he answered, realising why there'd been no barrier around the manor to keep Auron out.

'Excellent, because his time is nigh too.'

How is a guy with a limp one step ahead of us all the time?

This was too much to handle. Nicolas couldn't get his head around it. 'So, you aren't him? You aren't the Maestro?'

'No, boy,' Helstrum replied. 'I am just a tool of the one true god. He who will remake this world as a haven for all right-minded folks.'

Nicolas's heart sank. Even if he made his run at Helstrum and killed him, Helstrum wasn't the Maestro. This wouldn't end.

'*One true god*,' Auron whispered thoughtfully. 'I swear I've heard that before?'

'How can you call anything you do *right-minded*?' Nicolas cried. 'All you do is spread hatred and evil.'

'I do what I must to save my people,' Tobias retorted firmly.

'So that includes using demons to murder people, does it? How about fauns? How do you justify consorting with them?'

'What are you blathering about?' Tobias snapped. 'Fauns?'

'You don't know...'

'Silence, child,' Helstrum snapped, cracking his cane on the floor. 'I am done bandying words with foul heretics. I would have you shot down like dogs here and now, but *he* wants to meet you.'

'The Maestro?' Nicolas ventured.

'I would not wish to sully his divine presence by having to look upon race-traitor filth, but he insisted. And his word is my command.'

Light caught Nicolas's eye. Turning, he saw the altar bathed in tendrils of green energy that spread out in all directions before congregating around the pool at its centre. Slowly, a semi-liquid substance rose from it, taking on a roughly humanoid form. Tobias Helstrum bowed as much as he was able whilst still being supported by his cane.

'My Lord.'

'There he is, at last,' came a sickly sweet voice. 'Right where you are supposed to be.'

'Where I'm supposed to be?' Nicolas frowned. This was all too much for him.

The humanoid form shook its head and let out a harsh laugh. 'You still do not understand? Allow me to spell it out for you. The Visitor didn't write the message for you. The Watcher did.'

'The what?'

'The tentacled creature on his neck.' He enunciated every word, as if talking to an infant.

Oh shit.

'It was a failsafe, both to make sure Avin continued to obey, and that if he failed, you would be sent to me,' the Maestro said matter-of-factly. 'When you went home to Hablock, we knew where you were. You were easy to find and therefore easy to kill. Well, that was not as easy as we'd hoped, it turns out. But once that attempt on your life failed, you began to move around a lot, always interfering in my affairs, fouling up my plans, and delaying everything.' There was a vicious anger in the Maestro's voice. 'It was harder to pin down your location, and that of your damnable companions, save the fact that you'd appear wherever was most inconvenient to me. Finding you takes time and effort. Making you come to us does not. So I gave you Helstrum's name, knowing you would walk right to him. And here you are. Herded to us like a good little sheep.' The Maestro chuckled dryly. 'In truth, I had hoped the army would flush you out and finish you off. But really I knew better. It's true purpose was to serve as a final prod to encourage you to make your run at Tobias.'

In the corner of his eye, Nicolas caught a perturbed frown from Tobias. He clearly hadn't known he'd been made into a target. But he recovered himself quickly.

'Is there anything else I can do to serve, my lord?' he asked, keeping his gaze low.

The featureless metallic liquid head turned to its servant. 'Thank you, Tobias, you may leave us now.' The voice was almost melodious.

'As you wish.' Tobias shuffled across the room, to a door in the back Nicolas had previously not noticed. As he did, the men in the gallery disappeared. Though he was in no less danger for their absence.

'Stay calm, kid. All is not lost yet.' He wished he had Auron's confidence.

'At last, we are alone.' He couldn't see the eyes, but they were definitely on him, burning into him. 'So, you are the Carnegie boy who has repeatedly stuck his nose into my affairs? Interesting. In truth, I should not really be here. It is a risk. But I could not resist seeing in person—after a fashion—the thorn in my side, and watching your brutal death, of course. I feel I deserve it for all the trouble you have caused me.' There was a ponderous pause. 'And now I do see you, I find you quite unremarkable, even for your kind. The stories about you tell of a mighty hero who brings peace and justice to the land, spreading hope where I intend to spread chaos. I confess, I expected...more.'

Part of Nicolas was paralysed by fear at the knowledge that he was slap bang in the middle of a nest of vipers, and they were all awake and hissing at him. But he reminded himself of everything that had happened to him and those around him thus far, and all because of this being. Slowly, he regained his composure.

'If you come closer, say, within range of my sword, I'd be happy to prove your notions about me wrong,' he said defiantly.

'The tough talk is improving,' Auron told him.

The Maestro gave an exaggerated sigh. 'Please spare me your chittering monkey noises. All I want to hear from you is your death screams.'

'We will see who's screaming by the time we're done,' he growled back, readying himself.

'Again, monkey child, I'm here to watch,' the Maestro explained. A metallic hand gestured behind Nicolas. 'Koth will be the one doing the actual killing.'

A shiver of fear ran up Nicolas's spine as an unnatural chill descended on the room.

CHAPTER 59

The temperature in the room had dropped markedly. Nicolas wished he had some furs on. And an army at his disposal. His next breath was visible as ice crept across the windows around him. The malevolent presence behind him was practically tapping him on the shoulder.

'What in the Underworld is that?'

When Auron was surprised, it was time to worry. Following his companion's shocked gaze, he slowly turned. In the corner, where every shadow in the room had seemed to gather, stood Koth. The monster was just as he remembered: disproportionate limbs on a huge frame, the random explosions of bone from the skin, the goat's skull with empty, dead eyes. Nicolas's bowels made a couple of spasming motions, but they didn't clench in terror as he'd expected. Instead, he began to summon his fortitude.

I stood him down once. And this time, he hasn't got an arrow-shooting backstabber to do his work for him.

'That's Koth,' he said, fighting to keep his voice level.

Auron turned to him in shock. 'Kid, you faced *that* down? *Alone*? You have got the biggest pair of testicles in Etherius...now that I'm dead.'

Koth lumbered forwards. Nicolas wanted to take a step back. But didn't.

'Nicolas Percival Carnegie, we meet again,' came the whispering, overlapping voices that made up the creature's speech.

'For the last time,' the Maestro interrupted from the altar. 'Because you are going to kill him, properly and finally. And Koth, I want it done slowly. I did *not* come all this way for a quick splash of gore. Do I make myself clear?'

Koth inclined his goat-skulled head slightly. 'As you command.'

'Where are my family? Where are the people of Hablock?' Nicolas shouted at the demon.

'Facing death, and *still* he goes on about the other monkey folk,' the Maestro scoffed. 'If it weren't so silly, it would be quaint.'

Facing death. *I suppose that's my only option now. To face it down.*

With a deep breath, Nicolas took a couple of steps forward. Keeping his eyes on Koth, he used the tip of the *Dawn Blade* to mark a line on the floor between them, before getting into a fighting stance.

Hopefully, this is where history stops repeating itself.

'At least you aren't alone this time.' Auron smiled as he stood at his side, drawing his sword. 'I can hit demons, remember? We do this together.'

'What about it, Koth?' Nicolas asked. 'Got a little tremble of fear now Auron's with me and you don't have your arrow shooting mate to bushwhack me?'

'He who commands me has commanded that you die,' Koth answered, approaching. 'If the ghost gets in my way, he shall be sent to oblivion.'

'Just so we're clear,' the Maestro interrupted, 'I want the ghost destroyed as well.'

'Hear that?' Auron smiled. 'Your master has put me on your list now. Kind of him.'

'*He who commands me.*' There was a slight tone of annoyance behind the correction.

'Whatever,' Auron scoffed. 'Right then, kid. We come at him from both sides at once.'

The spirit began to circle the monster, as did Nicolas. Defeating this creature was a tough ask, but then so was escaping the Underworld or literally anything else he'd done since being given a message to deliver. Nicolas's eyes widened as thick bone blades grew from Koth's hands.

You can do this. For your family.

Mentally, he said a prayer for his parents' souls.

The demonic creature appeared almost idle, at rest. But Nicolas knew better. He could sense its hollow eyes watching them both carefully. There was a terrible intelligence inside the creature.

This isn't getting any saner.

Nicolas charged in, swinging the *Dawn Blade.* Like a flash, Koth brought his arm up, and the sword deflected harmlessly off it. Auron's attempted attack was dissuaded by a lazy swing of the bone blades.

A pang of fear gripped Nicolas. The sword had done nothing. Swords were supposed to cut through arms.

You can't fight this thing.

Yes, I can.

Doubt tried to get his attention, but he couldn't let it. If he did, all was lost. Instead, Nicolas leapt forwards, thrusting with the *Dawn Blade.* All his sword stabbed was air, Koth had moved aside with surprising speed. A large swinging hand crashed into his chest plate, sending him flying six feet through the air. If the maned man hitting him was like a boulder, this was like a mountain. Descending in an arc, he hit the stone floor hard, before rolling several times. Groaning, he coughed a glob of blood onto the floor as the room finally stopped spinning. His chest was aflame, and it was only a taste of the creature's power.

Nearby, he heard the sounds of battle as Auron thrust and parried with his own sword before being sent to the floor beside him, his aura fading briefly.

The spirit exhaled pointlessly. 'This guy's tough.'

'And fast.'

Auron got to his feet, a determined look on his face. 'But we have the numbers.'

Nicolas rose and dusted himself off. Making eye contact with Auron, they exchanged a nod before charging forwards as one. At speed, he swung his blade: cut, thrust, chop, hack. Beside him, Auron did the same. Koth blocked every single attack with his own weapons and an upsetting casual ease.

He's putting on a show for his master.

Nicolas didn't even see the arm that hit him. The first thing he knew about it was when he was halfway across the room again. After landing painfully on the table, he rolled off the other side and ended up on the floor in a heap.

There was a cry, and he looked up just as Auron was knocked through a nearby wall.

Shaking his head, trying to fend off the dizziness, Nicolas grabbed his sword and got to his feet as Koth advanced. He planned to keep the table between him and the demon until he came to his senses, but the demonic creature threw the large dining table aside as if it were an empty sack.

As he watched in horror, Koth continued to approach. Nicolas jumped aside just in time as the demon stabbed down at him, taking a chunk out of the floor instead. He began to fence with the demon, barely managing to deflect attacks which appeared to be the product of minimal effort on Koth's part.

And then he slipped, his foot stepping on stone made slick by Helstrum's soup, which had spilt on the floor when Koth threw the table. Nicolas fell to the ground with a bump. The shadow of the demon passed over him.

'Barely entertaining.' The Maestro sighed from the altar. 'Finish it.'

Clasping his hands together, Koth readied himself to deliver a hammer blow that would likely turn him into a mushy stain on the floor, armour or not. Nicolas readied *himself* to not be there when it happened and hoped he was quick enough to do it.

'Surprise, demon scum.'

Auron appeared on the creature's back, stabbing at it as Koth reared and roared in rage. When he spun around, Nicolas could see the stabs were doing nothing to the creature's thick hide and bone armour...but at least they were pissing it off and had given him a reprieve.

Koth turned again, too close for Nicolas to use his sword, so he swung a fist at its head instead. The impact nearly broke his knuckles, and he howled in pain. The demon rewarded his initiative with a fast trip to the back wall of the room. Slamming against the stone, he slid down it to a seated position. Spat a little more blood. The armour was absorbing enough of the impacts to keep his bones intact, but the fight was taking a heavy toll on his body.

This is it...we're doomed. We can't fight this.

He looked at the door Helstrum had left through. It might as well have been on the other side of Etherius with Koth between him and it.

I need to get out of here, to save the others and—

Koth finally grabbed Auron from his back and flung the spirit right at him. Holding his hands up, for no practical reason he could fathom, he closed his eyes.

There was a sudden burning sensation in his insides, like he'd greedily swallowed scalding hot food. In his mind, he saw massed images flashing by too quickly to sort. Opening his eyes, he couldn't see Auron anywhere.

Hello?

Hello?

Kid, is that you?

Auron?

Yeah.

Where are you?

I'm...I think I'm inside you.

You've possessed me again?

I suppose, after a fashion, but it wasn't like this last time.

The burning faded but didn't disappear, continuing in the background, but at the same time, Nicolas somehow felt reinvigorated. The last and only time Auron had possessed him, it had been like he'd been pushed into the very darkest corner of his mind. Now, it was like...they were sharing his body. Carefully, he moved his arms. He was still in control.

How strange.

He rolled aside just as Koth's giant fist crashed into, and through, the wall where he'd been sat.

How did I dodge that?

Koth looked surprised too...as surprised as you can be when you have a featureless goat skull for a face and no eyes. The creature swung again, but it didn't appear as fast as it had before. It was like the monster was moving slower.

No. We're moving faster.

Is that my thought or yours?

Who knows, kid? Duck!

Nicolas ducked the sweeping blow, and the five that followed it. Without thinking, he swung his sword. It cracked the demon on the side of the face. It didn't remove Koth's head or anything useful like that, but it did make the head move slightly with the impact.

What did I...?

Stop thinking, kid. Just go for it.

Throwing himself forwards, he launched furious attacks with the *Dawn Blade* which Koth couldn't block. He struck the demon again and again. Each time, the beast was forced back a step. He could tell they weren't doing any damage, but it was a start. In between, Nicolas – and Auron – slipped and dodged around the demon's attempts to skewer him – them – on his large bone blades with a fluidity that made the demon growl with frustration.

'Koth,' the Maestro snapped from the back of the room. 'What are you doing? What's going on?'

With a snarl, Koth swung at him. Nicolas leapt over the blow, rolling to the floor, before turning and driving the tip of his sword right into the demon's chest. For a moment, Nicolas didn't move. Koth's goat skulled head slowly tilted down and regarded the blade pressing against its body. Then Nicolas jumped back and rolled the blade in his grip, just as Auron would. He cast a quick eye towards the secret door. He was on the right side of the demon now. The question was, could he make it to the door before Koth caught up to him?

'Koth, what is happening?' the Maestro demanded.

The demon stood silently, either at a loss for words or unwilling to speak.

'Annoying human,' the Maestro roared, clasping his metallic hands. 'I really shouldn't, but as you appear to need help to squash one human, Koth...'

Green energy lashed around one of the Maestro's arms as he stretched it out. It was only the distance between him and Nicolas that allowed the latter to get his sword up in time. He slid back across the floor as the energy struck the blade.

Then the most curious thing happened.

Instead of reflecting the energy as he'd expected the sword to do, the *Dawn Blade* absorbed it. It began to glow brightly as the last few tendrils of energy were sucked into it.

What's happening to the sword?

I don't know. I've not seen that before.

'No,' the Maestro gasped. 'That isn't... It's not possible...' The metallic head shook in disbelief. 'That sword...'

There was movement in his peripheral vision. Koth's clawed hand came at him, and he swung the blade. There was a roar of pain. When the monster stepped back, he had two less blades on his knuckles. There were pinpricks of red in its normally empty eyes.

Nicolas looked back at the altar. The Maestro had vanished.

What's going on?

Right now, who cares. Just give that damnable demon what for.

With a cry, Nicolas ran forwards. Now each time he caught the demon with his blade, a piece of it was sheared off, leaving a pulsating red wound in its place. He moved at speed, ducking and weaving and cutting, each time taking a small chunk of the monster. Slipping under an attempt to grab his head, Nicolas ran his blade across the demon's side. Koth roared in anger, his eyes flashing bright red for a moment.

But Koth was still fast. His neck jerked forwards as the demon's large foot kicked him in the centre of the chest plate, flinging him across the room. Managing to somehow spin in mid-air, Nicolas landed on his feet with a slight skid.

The demon moved laboriously, retreating into the corner of the room as its gaze twitched from between its various wounds to Nicolas.

He ran at Koth, pushing his legs hard, moving faster than he ever had before. But as the creature reached the corner, the shadows enveloped it...and it vanished completely.

Nooooooo.

CHAPTER 60

T here was no time to indulge his disappointment. Doubling over, Nicolas gritted his teeth as the burning sensation became slightly worse. As he did, Auron fell out of him, lying on the floor at his side. The spirit looked greatly diminished, barely there at all, as he gazed up at the ceiling.

'What *was* that?' Auron asked quietly.

'I don't know.' Each word was an effort. The fight with Koth had taken a heavy toll on him, and he'd only been hit a couple of times. But then, Helstrum's bodyguards had softened him up first. 'I'm glad it happened—'

'Yet I'd rather it didn't happen again,' Auron said, finishing his sentence for him. 'Agreed. But at least we saw off the demon.'

'But we didn't kill it, or the Maestro, or Helstrum, or save the people of Hablock.'

'We cut a swathe through his minions though,' the spirit said with a chuckle.

And yet they always find more.

Slowly, Auron turned to him. His aura was very weak, as was his voice. 'You can't rest. You have to get the others.'

The others. Get up Nicolas. Now!

Using some reserve of energy he'd been unaware of until now, he forced himself up, using the *Dawn Blade*, which had now stopped glowing, as a crutch. His legs wavered under the weight of his own body, but he stood. Every step hurt as he staggered towards the door at the back of the room, the tip of the *Dawn Blade* scratching across the floor as he was unable to lift it properly.

Beyond the door there was a set of stairs leading down.

Underground lair...of course.

Briefly, he glanced back at Auron. It felt wrong leaving his companion here, but the spirit waved at him to go. The wave was a laborious one, telling how much the possession had really taken out of him.

As fast as he was able, he made his way down the stairs, clinging to the wall for support. He was weak. Very weak. And injured. But the urgency of his mission drove him on. His companions had minutes to live...if they still did.

Shift.

Rounding a corner to a landing with doors on either side, he bumped straight into Potter.

'Nicky boy?' his former friend exclaimed in surprise. 'You survived Koth?'

'And you survived the orcs,' he panted. 'Shame that.'

'That's because I'm a survivor, Nicky boy.'

The smugness in Potter's face made him want to heave. It also made him want to finish what he'd started in that courtyard.

He raised the *Dawn Blade*. 'Not for long.'

'Oh, it's like that, is it?' His former friend chuckled.

'I don't want to sound childish, but you started it.'

Potter drew his own sword and looked him up and down. 'You're nearly spent, Nicky boy. Look at you.'

Nicolas let out a harsh chuckle. 'Then that'll make it easy for you, just the way you like it. Or do you want me to wait whilst you go and hide around the corner with your bow?'

'I did what I had to do,' Potter snarled.

'No, you didn't,' he spat. 'You did what you wanted to. For your own personal gain. Don't you dare act like a victim when you stood by and let them kill *my parents*.'

Potter shook his head. 'You're such a self-righteous little prick. I can't believe I ever deigned to be your friend. But you know what, killing you myself...that is going to be the real making of me. And yes, you pouty child, I'm doing this because I want to. Then I won't have to put up with your disgusted stare any longer.'

Shaking his head, Nicolas took a step back. 'How is this so easy for you? We were friends.'

There was a hint of regret on Potter's face. If Nicolas had blinked, he would've missed it. Then a dark resolve set in. 'I've had a long time to come to terms with killing you. This...this is just correcting a mistake.'

'Before I run you through, where are my friends?' he growled.

'That's not information a dead man needs,' Potter said, but his eyes betrayed him. They flicked to the door behind Nicolas. 'And they'll all be getting theirs soon enough. Especially that shapeshifting creature you're so bloody fond of.'

Pouring rage into his aching legs, Nicolas lunged forwards with a cry, swinging the *Dawn Blade*. To his weak arms, it was like trying to swing a sack of rocks. He was much slower than he ought to be. Potter intercepted the blow with his blade and pushed him away.

The black knight came at him, and the pair began their duel. Nicolas had never known Potter to be interested in the sword, and judging by his technique now he'd never bothered practising with the weapon he was now using to try and kill him. But he was an enthusiastic amateur fighting a severely weakened opponent. Probably just the way Potter liked it. If Nicolas were at one hundred percent, he could've finished this quickly—could've kicked his ass all over the manor, in fact. But he was in a bad state right now, having been thrown around by a demon only minutes ago, and the bodyguards before that. His muscles yearned for rest, screaming at him to stop, even though that wasn't an option.

If I stop, I die. They die.

Up and down the landing, the pair fought. The black knight would press his advantage, until Nicolas found an opening and forced him back, and vice versa.

Potter ducked under one of Nicolas's swings and drove his armoured shoulder into his chest. Nicolas was thrown back against the wall, his ailing body taking the blow as if a giant had kicked him. With a heave, he rolled aside as Potter's thrust came straight at him. The sword chinked off the stone wall. Nicolas smacked it down with the *Dawn Blade* and pressed his attack.

Blades clashed until finally their swords met, each man pouring his strength into his blade as they tried to push the other back.

'C'mon, Nicky boy.' Potter smirked. 'Join us. One last chance. You don't *have* to die here. Sometimes, even you must want to go on a killing spree after everything that's happened to you?'

'If that's an attempt to turn me evil, it's a piss poor one,' he snapped back.

Potter looked genuinely confused. 'I'm not evil. I'm pragmatic. This is the way of the world, Nicky boy.'

'Seriously?' In his surprise, he was forced back a step.

He's trying to get in my head. Distract me.

'Give it up, Nicky boy.' Potter grunted. 'I'm being taught by Rey Gelder.'

Huh, he is bothering to try and learn then.

The name had been said like it was someone Nicolas should've heard of. He hadn't. 'Who?'

'The man in the leather mask, I know you must've seen him at the fort before I had you beaten and chained.'

'Oh, him. I killed him with a towel.' *Two can play at mind games, asshole.*

Shock creased Potter's features, the force he was pouring into his sword wavering slightly. Which gave Nicolas the opportunity to headbutt

Potter right in the bridge of the nose. As the black knight stumbled backwards, Nicolas tried to grab him, to keep him close. There was a scream of pain.

Nicolas looked at his hand. In his palm was a clump of hair that had once belonged on Potter's face. Outraged, Potter touched the red and bloody skin on his cheek where the hair had been whilst pinching his nose, which wasn't bleeding. Nicolas hadn't had enough energy to break it with that headbutt.

I need to finish this quickly.

Potter roared and charged him. Nicolas ran back a few paces and jumped onto the higher step just as Potter swung. His former friend took another swipe at his legs, and Nicolas jumped again, the blade missing him. As he landed his embattled legs nearly gave out completely taking him down the stairs the quick way.

How does Ramirez make jumping around during a sword fight look so easy?

Potter looked up at him, aghast.

'High ground,' he exclaimed, raising his eyebrows twice, before kicking the black knight in the jaw.

Nicolas charged forwards as his opponent staggered away. But he was getting slower by the minute. Potter sidestepped his swing and punched him in the face. Any other day, it would've been a normal punch. Right now, it sent him staggering to the opposite wall. Pressing his hand against it, he willed his legs to stay in the fight, but he stumbled and fell to a single knee.

Shit.

Like a true hunter, Potter could sense weakness and came at him. Nicolas managed to push himself to his feet. Crying with the confidence of someone already victorious, his opponent swung his blade again and again. Each time, Nicolas just managed to block or dodge it. Just.

His inevitable defeat was coming. It was the same as on the bridge, when dodging Grimmark's bear-shaped war hammer. There was only so long this dance could go on for.

His arms as heavy as if they were made of stone, Nicolas raised his sword to block the downward attack. He was rewarded with a kick to the gut that sent him reeling backwards. Potter came in with several fierce swings, the clashes of metal echoing up and down the stairway. Nicolas grunted in frustration as the *Dawn Blade* was knocked from his grip, before the hilt of Potter's sword caught him under the jaw. He tumbled backwards, and his weakened legs finally gave out, dropping him to the floor.

Potter stood above him, smirking as he pointed his blade at Nicolas's throat. 'I guess we found out who's the best then, eh, Nicky boy?'

'You know this isn't me at my best,' he growled back. 'Try fighting me then and see how it goes.'

The black knight pursed his lips for a moment. 'Nah, I don't think I will. I'm quite content knowing that I'm the better warrior. I did give you a chance, but you wasted it, so...' Potter shrugged before raising his sword to make the final blow.

'Just...let the people of Hablock go,' he said, keeping Potter's attention. 'Please.'

Staring down at him, there was that element of conflict in his former friend's eyes. 'I can't,' he said finally. 'They're where they belong. Now it's your turn.'

'When he was teaching you, did your master ever tell you to be mindful of your environment?'

Potter frowned at the question. 'What?'

'Because my teachers did.'

The black knight followed Nicolas's pointing finger. He exclaimed in surprise as he realised Nicolas had hooked the back of one of his ankles with his foot. With a grunt, Nicolas kicked the knee with his free leg.

Potter cried out in pain as his knee buckled and his body turned. At the same time, Nicolas pulled his hooking foot back sharply. The black knight tripped, his leg taken out from beneath him. With an almost comical amount of arm flailing, Potter toppled over and began to roll down the stairs. The slowly receding sound of armour crashing on stone was so pleasing. There appeared to be a lot of stairs.

Bye bye, bastard.

CHAPTER 61

Nicolas rolled over laboriously. The fact that he was still in an enemy stronghold and his friends were captives wasn't lost on him. But neither was the fact that he'd been thrown into walls about ten times in the last hour. Pressing his hands to the floor, he tried to push himself up. His body lifted off the floor a little then his shaking arms gave out, and he ended up lying on the stone again.

'You okay, kid?'

Side-eyeing the stairway, he saw Auron stumbling down towards him. The spirit's aura was still dull and his face appeared gaunt.

'Fight with Potter.' His voice was a wheeze, his throat burning for some reason. 'Beat him. Knocked him down the stairs.'

Auron glanced past Nicolas down the stairway. 'All those stairs?'

'I bloody hope so.'

The spirit pursed his lips thoughtfully. 'If there's any justice, he's bashed his head in on the way down and won't bother you again.'

Nicolas had a bad feeling that wouldn't happen. But he could still hope.

'Right then, get up, and let's find the others.'

'I...I can't...'

Crouching beside him, Auron looked him in the eye. 'What do you mean *you can't*?'

A tear welled in his eye at the admission. 'I think I'm spent,' he said with a heavy breath. 'I've been beaten by bodyguards, by Koth, and by Potter. I haven't got anything left. I'm...done.'

Slowly, Auron reached out and flicked him hard in the temple.

'Ow.'

'Who are you?' the spirit asked, fixing him with a steely gaze.

'Nicol—'

'*No*,' Auron snapped. 'Who are you?'

'I'm...' He suddenly realised what Auron wanted. 'The *Dawnblade*.'

Auron flicked him again. 'Is that a word you say meekly?'

'No.' Taking a deep breath, he repeated himself, with a little fire this time. 'I'm the *Dawnblade*.'

The spirit nodded. 'And who has been taken by your enemies?'

'Shift. Garaz. Silva.'

Getting on all fours, Auron put his face directly in front of Nicolas's. 'And what are you going to do about it?'

He remembered his companions. The state they'd been in when he left them. They had no chance without him.

They need me. They need...me.

Forcing himself to move, he planted his hands on the ground, one at a time. Preparing himself, he pushed, pouring his fury and his love for his companions into his arms. Slowly, he began to rise. When he got to a kneeling position, he heavily put one foot on the floor and pushed himself to his feet. Instantly, he had to lean against the wall to steady himself. When he was sure he was staying standing, he carefully bent down and picked up his sword.

My sword.

'I'm going to get them back.' He didn't imagine he cut a very heroic figure in that moment, exhausted, bloodied, and sweating. But he meant every word.

'Glad to hear it,' Auron said, jumping to his feet. 'So...which door?'

Stretching his back slightly, Nicolas gestured to the one Potter had indicated. Thank the Deities he wouldn't need to search this manor forever. Sooner or later, there would be an army on his ass. They needed to get out of here as quickly as possible.

Staggering like a drunk, dragging his sword, Nicolas walked over to the door and entered. With Auron in tow, he made his way down the corridor. There was only one direction to go; he just hoped it was the right one. Keeping himself half leant against the wall, he followed the path he'd been given. As always.

Three corridors later, things were not looking good.

Do I keep going? Or go back and try another way?

Doubt racked him, as did guilt. Had Potter's eye flick just been a twitch? Or had he imagined it? If he'd gone the wrong way, he'd miss them completely, and his companions would be long gone.

'Listen,' Auron said in an urgent whisper.

Nicolas stopped and did as he was bid. There were voices. And they were getting closer. There was another sound amongst the chatter. The rattling of chains. The sort of chains you put on prisoners. Elation struck him as he exchanged a triumphant look with Auron. It lasted a moment, then the weariness reasserted itself. It couldn't be denied for long.

We've found them. Now I just need to save them.

Just. Like it was going to be that easy. He doubted there would only be a couple of guards to deal with. Helstrum wouldn't risk that. Not with his companions. Wondering how many there would be, another worry suddenly struck him.

What if they aren't all together? What if Helstrum sent Shift, Garaz and Silva off in different directions?

All he could really do was hope. The same way that he *hoped* that he could take care of the guards. Which he would need to do soon. They were very close now.

I may as well wait here and let them come to me.

Quickly, he extinguished the nearest torches, creating a shadow that he could stand in. Well...lean in.

Soon enough, several guards rounded the corner, with his companions in tow. Calming his mind, he readied himself.

You can do this. For them.

'They won't know what's hit them,' Auron told him firmly, as if sensing his uncertainty. Though is was most likely written all over his face.

Let's find out.

'All right, lads.' As he stepped into the light, he nodded with a confidence his body could no longer match.

Instantly, the group came to a halt. It was hard to see much past the guards, but he could tell his companions were alive and bound by shackles.

'Nicolas?' Garaz asked in surprise, looking very much worse for wear.

'What's left of me,' he shrugged.

'Quiet you,' one of the guards shouted at the orc, as he and his five comrades assembled between Nicolas and his friends, swords drawn.

Behind the men, he caught Shift's wink. 'Are you sure about this?' he asked the guards.

'Sure about what?' the leader snarled from behind his mask.

'About facing me,' he answered with false cheer. 'I've gotten through Koth and made it down here. And you *must* have heard of all the other stuff I've done before that?'

A little bit of uneasy shifting suggested they had. But he knew they wouldn't back down. He was just buying himself time.

'Look at you,' the leader hissed. 'You look half-dead. I don't think you're going to be a problem for all six of us.'

Nicolas smiled broadly. 'I'm not looking to be a problem for all six of you. I'm just keeping you busy whilst Shift sets the others free.'

The guards started at the sound of shackles hitting the ground. The clanging of metal echoed down the corridor in both directions.

Finally free, Garaz drew himself up to his full, imposing height, glaring at the guard who was carrying his staff. Beside him, Silva picked up one of the chains that had bound her. The warrior pulled it taught between her hands. Clearly it was about to be used to bludgeon whichever poor guard was closest. Shift had already begun to change into a long clawed kascat warrior.

Suddenly, the guards seemed less sure of themselves. They grouped together, back to back. There was no way they would surrender, no more than Nicolas would. A tense silence descended on the corridor as everyone waited to see who would make the first move.

'Get them,' the leader shouted, breaking into a charge straight towards Nicolas.

As it turned out, Nicolas only had to worry about two of guards. Even in his weakened state, he managed to kill them both by pushing the leader into one of his men, forcing them back against the wall and skewering them on the *Dawn Blade*.

By the time he did, the other guards were all dead.

'Deities,' he gasped, as he saw the state of Silva's face properly. He was surprised she could see, let alone kill anyone. Yet behind her swollen eyes, she still managed to glare at him.

'Getting out of here is going to be a lark,' Auron commented, looking over the group. 'How are we going to get past the guards?'

'By keeping them occupied,' Nicolas said firmly, before turning to Garaz. 'Would you set this place on fire, please?'

'Nicolas,' Garaz said with a slight bow and a weary smile, 'it would be my absolute pleasure.'

CHAPTER 62

The sounds of frantically fleeing nobility could be heard over the crackling of flames as the west wing of the manor was consumed. Nicolas had to admit to taking a perverse pleasure in the sounds of the deviant people in distress. It didn't take long for the other wings to catch fire, as the destructive element fed on whatever fuel the building offered it. Through the plumes of smoke, Nicolas caught sight of the guards trying to herd the stampeding nobles, so that they didn't accidentally run back into the fire due to their intoxicated state.

Part of Nicolas knew he should jump down. He was currently perched atop the wall surrounding Helstrum's manor. But he couldn't resist one last look at the burning building. It was just so damned satisfying.

Garaz had been good enough to make sure that the fire was obvious, so Helstrum's *guests* had plenty of time to evacuate. They were assholes, but innocent assholes, in the main.

Though it probably means he escaped too.

A shadow overhead caught Nicolas's attention. It was a certain magic carpet, and its rider was doing a worse job of steering it than before. It headed directly for some trees, crashing straight into the branches with a cry from its rider. Leaves scattered as Fliaphor fell from the tree, hitting several branches on the way down.

'Good,' Garaz grumbled from the other side of the wall.

Nicolas finally jumped down, hitting the grass with a soft thump. It was a small drop, but pain shot up his legs, causing him to wince and stumble slightly. Garaz went to hold him up, but he waved the orc away. His companion was in as bad a state as he was and didn't need the extra burden.

Recovering from this will take a while. For all of us.

Turning back to the wall, he reached up and helped Silva down. The fact that the warrior allowed this showed how badly hurt she was. Her speech was slurring slightly and some of the swelling seemed to be getting worse. But there was no chance to stop and heal in the midst of the enemy.

With a deft jump, Shift landed beside him. They too winced on impact, though he knew that was because of their head injury. The shapeshifter offered him a pained smile, which he returned.

'There's no one pursuing us,' Auron confirmed as he appeared through the wall. 'They're all too busy with the fire. So let's get the Underworld out of here.'

There's an invitation I'll happily accept.

There was nothing graceful about their flight to the tree line. The group moved haphazardly, as if they were all as high on Boost as Fliaphor. Nicolas had no idea what time it was, but there couldn't be that much night left, and they had to use its cover before hunting parties were gathered to come after them. The foliage seemed miles away as they sprinted towards it, but it was only his perception. He was exhausted, mentally and physically...probably spiritually too if he bothered to take the time to think about it.

Reaching the trees, everyone took a moment to stop and rest. Not a choice but a necessity.

'We failed,' Nicolas said as he caught his breath. 'We didn't kill Helstrum. He wasn't even the Maestro.'

'It isn't him?' Shift asked.

'No,' Nicolas scoffed. 'He's something else. I don't know what. All I know is that this was all a trap and we walked right into it.'

'Trap?' Silva slurred.

'They lured us here to kill us,' he explained. 'Instead of going to the trouble of finding us and killing us, they used Helstrum as bait so we'd come to them.'

'How efficient,' Garaz snarled.

'Nobody failed,' Auron said firmly. 'This wasn't our finest hour. But we're still alive. That is always a victory.'

'Is that the best we got out of this?' Nicolas chuckled. 'Still being alive?'

Which is actually amazing, considering the odds.

'No. We burned down two enemy buildings. Oh, three now.' The spirit gestured to the manor and the smoke billowing into the sky. 'And we killed all of Tobias Helstrum's fancy new bodyguards. Thinning out the minions is always handy.' The spirit looked away thoughtfully for a moment. 'I think we should call that a draw.'

'I'll take it.' Standing up straight and stretching, Nicolas couldn't help but smirk when he looked back at the burning manor. 'That'll be another one to lay at the door of the inhuman menace.'

'We are terrible like that,' Garaz said without a hint of regret. Nor should he have had any.

'Technically, they are right,' Shift replied. 'It was an inhuman who did it. And of course, their figurehead, the disgusting *Nick Carnage*.'

Two clicks signalled that they weren't alone.

'Turn around, slowly, and keep your hands in the air.'

Bollocks.

Doing as he was told, he turned. Waiting for him were two masked men with fire-sticks. One was aimed directly at Nicolas, the other slowly moved between the others and back again. Nicolas exchanged a glance with Silva. Well, he thought he did. It was hard to tell with her swollen eyes. There were four of them and two fire-sticks. Once they fired, they'd need time to reload. It was just a case of what they hit when they fired. He began to ready himself to jump aside. Though whether or not his legs would allow it was a different matter.

'We should take them prisoner,' one of the men said.

'Are you insane?' the other asked. 'Do you know who this is? I'm not taking any chances. He dies.'

We'll see. I didn't fight through bodyguards, Koth, and Potter just to be killed by some random guard.

The men visibly tensed as they readied to fire. Nicolas readied himself too. Hoping to improvise something genius to save their lives.

'*Wait.*'

Nicolas started. Mainly due to worry that the sudden shout would cause one or both of the men to fire. Fortunately, it didn't.

Another figure appeared. His mask had horns on it, so he was probably in charge. He was certainly tall enough to be. The big man stepped between the other two. 'The master will want them alive,' he explained. 'Do you want to risk his rage?'

Neither man did, so it seemed.

The officer took several steps closer to Nicolas, until he was in front of the armed men. 'What about it?' he asked. 'Are you coming with us?'

'No,' Nicolas snarled again, setting his stance, before raising an eyebrow.

Is that voice familiar?

'Okay then.'

Suddenly, the two other soldiers flew backwards as if struck. Dropping their fire-sticks, they were catapulted into the nearest trees, where they slumped, unconscious.

The officer removed his mask. 'How about with me then?'

'Jorish.' Nicolas beamed. Suddenly, the horse part of the centaur came into view, and he realised what'd happened to the two soldiers.

'No one expects a centaur,' Shift said, shaking their head and grinning. *The guy can kick.*

'I gather things did not go to plan?' the centaur observed as he looked them up and down.

'Not at all.' Garaz grimaced. 'We need to get out of here, and we need somewhere to lie low.'

'I can help with both of those,' Jorish confirmed. 'After getting the family to safety I came straight here. I was going to come in after you, but with the party...well, I would be bumping into people all over the place. Someone would see through my disguise sooner or later. So I waited to see what you would do.' The centaur nodded towards the burning building. 'And you did not disappoint. Is Helstrum...'

'No,' Nicolas answered quickly. 'We couldn't. It was a trap.'

There was a flash of disappointment on the centaur's proud face. 'Another time then,' he said finally. 'Let us get you out of here. A mutual friend leant me some horses and offered you safe haven.' Jorish raised an eyebrow. 'Which you sorely need, judging by the state of you.'

Mutual friend? Who?

CHAPTER 63

The location of their haven turned out to be one they were familiar with. Allegard's Gallery of Wonders. And the *mutual friend* that Jorish had mentioned was the owner of said store. Old Allegard had been a member of the League of Light for a while now. His basement was designed to house families fleeing persecution, including the family that Nicolas and his companions had saved from a potential mob.

Nicolas couldn't help but see a parallel between himself and Silva, and Allegard and Auron. Meeting the spirit—well, he was a living hero at the time—had clearly had a long-lasting effect on the former bandit-slash-mercenary. And he was now dedicated to leaving Etherius a better place than he'd found it. As were Nicolas and the others. Though the storekeeper seemed to be doing a better job than them.

Lying low in the basement for two weeks, the group took the time to recover from their visit to Helstrum Manor. They half expected the area to be swarming with masked men hunting them down, ready to enact the Maestro's fury at their escape. But there was nothing. The silence was almost more worrying. It was like everyone was taking a rest before the next round of insanity. At least it had allowed them to get to safety and recover, physically and mentally, from the ordeal.

Garaz had healed Shift and Silva quickly once they were safe. Beyond being drained, and unable to remember a time when he'd felt so tired, Nicolas had no injuries save the odd superficial cut and bruise. There was a recurring burning sensation in his stomach, but he put that down to the stress of it all.

Though Garaz had managed to heal their physical injuries, the orc could do nothing for the sullen mood that had descended on them during their time in hiding. Save for Silva, who was still riding high from defeating the warrior woman.

'You're doing it again,' Shift said as they watched Silva across the room.

The warrior's eyes opened. 'Doing what?'

'You know,' Shift muttered in disgust.

'I know nothing of the sort,' Silva protested. 'What am I doing?'

'Every so often you close your eyes and get this strange look of satisfaction on your face,' Auron explained. 'We know you're replaying the fight when you do it. It's getting a little creepy.'

Silva's jaw set in a scowl. 'I am reminiscing about a great victory. That's hardly something *you* can chastise anyone else over.'

Now it was Auron's turn to scowl. 'Ouch,' he replied dryly.

'At least one of us got what we were after.' Nicolas sourly stared at the wall. 'The rest of the mission turned into a giant turd of failure.'

'It certainly didn't go as planned.' Shift sighed.

'We learned something from it,' Auron counselled. 'Tobias Helstrum *isn't* the Maestro. At least we have that.'

'True,' Nicolas thought back to the metallic figure the Maestro had appeared to them as. 'What *is* he then?'

The spirit shook his head. 'I have no idea.' Admitting that he didn't know something obvious pained Auron, judging by the telltale wince as he said it. 'I've not seen that before. It was some kind of golem, or something. He's definitely keen on hiding his identity.'

'At least we are alive,' Garaz soothed. Apparently healing magic didn't work so well when self-applied, so the orc had to rely on potions supplied by Allegard and was still looking a little worse for wear, even now. Not surprising really when he'd had two ghosts fight inside him. Still, at least he was past the worst of it—which was when his constitution had been upset enough to return whatever he ate not long after the orc had consumed it. Garaz often glanced at Auron as though the spirit had violated him, which was technically true. But the necromancer, or whatever he was, had started it.

But I can sympathise. I know the feeling first-hand.

'There is that,' Nicolas said. 'But this was a loss for us. Nearly a big one...'

'We came close, kid,' Auron said firmly. 'Close to victory and close to total defeat. Yet we live. Ready to fight again. Take heart in the fact that you're still in the fight.'

He wanted to, but he just couldn't. With the added gut-punch of Potter's betrayal, he was starting to feel uncomfortable in his armour, as if it was the wrong size.

'At least I vanquished the warrior woman.'

There was a general groan.

I bet she'll commission a statue or painting to commemorate that one day.

'As much as I like to be the optimist,' Shift said, looking at their boots. 'I've got to agree with Nick on this one. They played us, and we barely made it out. We need to be smarter than that.'

'So what *is* our next step?' Garaz asked.

'Well, Helstrum can't exactly hide out at his manor anymore,' Auron remarked thoughtfully.

Jorish had informed the group that the entire place had burnt down. Which was a bloody good thing, in Nicolas's opinion.

'We now have the same problem the enemy had,' Silva added. 'We do not know where he is. Etherius is a big place.'

'We'll find him again.' Nicolas sighed. 'He's not exactly inconspicuous.'

'Neither are we now.' Shift laughed dryly.

Though the Maestro's men weren't openly hunting them, there was a consequence for their mission. Apparently, trying to assassinate a prominent citizen was frowned upon in Ivilar. According to Jorish and Allegard, wanted posters with their likenesses now adorned towns and villages for leagues in every direction, which certainly wouldn't help their claim that they weren't orc spies. Jorish had even been good enough to supply them with copies. The likenesses were exact. And the reward... Well, if anyone wanted to buy themselves a small castle, turning them in would be a huge step in the right direction.

Our lives get more complicated by the day.

And he was learning new things too. Reaching out, he grabbed the *Dawn Blade,* which was propped against the wall, and unsheathed it, studying the reflective blade and then himself in it. Since the battle with Koth, it had showed no sign of the mysterious glow.

'Has it ever done that before?' he asked Auron.

The spirit took a second to realise what he was talking about. 'No, never. In all fairness, I don't usually stay in the spot the magic bolts are being hurled at, but that was strange. It reacted to the magic then took chunks out of Koth. I just... I don't know.'

At least there was one heartening thing they could take away from this. As determined as Nicolas had been to find Koth, killing him had appeared insurmountable. Now they had a weapon they could use.

If we can figure out how to make it glow again.

'Do you still have a headache?' Auron asked suddenly. 'Because I do.'

'Yes,' he answered honestly. He knew it was from Auron possessing him, or them sharing his body, or whatever in the Underworld had occurred. 'I don't know what happened there either.'

'It was nothing like the last time,' the spirit said thoughtfully. 'You were in charge but together we were more powerful, faster.'

'It still wasn't enough to beat Koth, not without the sword and—'

'But you had the sword,' Garaz said with sympathy. 'And you fought him. You drove him off, and from what Auron tells me of the power of the creature, that was no small feat. Yes, we have not succeeded in our goal, but we have taken steps in the right direction, I think.'

I really want to believe that, but the word defeat *just hovers over my head.*

'At least Helstrum is down five bodyguards.' Shift shrugged.

'And one of them was defeated in a battle for the ages.'

Shift picked up their pillow and hurled it at Silva. 'You're turning into *him*, you know.'

Auron did not care for being pointed at.

'When you have bested a worthy opponent,' Silva began haughtily, 'you will—'

The door at the top of the stairs opened, and everyone went for their weapons.

'Calm down, calm down, you jumpy bastards.' Allegard chuckled as he entered the basement. The large shopkeeper shook his head with a smile as they all sheathed their weapons and Garaz dismissed the small flame in his palm. 'Since the wanted posters were brought round, no one's come asking about you.'

'What tidings?' Silva asked.

'You're still hunted high and low,' the shopkeeper confirmed. 'We've spread the rumour that you're headed back towards the orc wastelands. I think it's believable, so they will focus their search there.'

'But where *do* we go?' Nicolas asked. 'We can't stay here forever. Someone will find us—'

'Or we'll kill Silva for going on about that woman she fought,' Shift interrupted.

Allegard frowned and sighed. He'd heard enough of that too. 'I've spoken with Jorish, and we have an idea.'

'Being out of options, we are all ears,' Garaz said.

'We need to spirit you away to Babylon,' Allegard said, pursing his lips. 'We have friends there who will take you in. From there, you can plan your next move. You are honoured friends of the League, so we will find Helstrum for you and then you can finish what you started.'

'One problem,' Nicolas said. 'It's a long journey from here to Babylon, and it's through a kingdom hunting us.'

'True,' Allegard said, pointing at him. 'But I have a wagon with a false bottom you can use. I can't go with you. If I suddenly vanish, people will ask questions, and I need to be here to help other families.'

'Can Jorish take us then?' Silva asked.

'Unfortunately, no.' Allegard slumped a little, as if there was a burden on him. 'There has been a side effect of your attempt on Helstrum's life.'

Worried glances were exchanged. 'What?'

'The Custodians have decried the attempt, saying that non-human civilisations sent you to kill Helstrum. There is a wave of non-human hatred spreading across the area.' Allegard's mouth became a thin line.

'Jorish has gone with others to start evacuating certain families. That's another reason I need you gone but must stay myself. This hideaway is soon to become very crowded.'

The room shrank around him. For all the good they wanted to do, he'd ended up making things worse.

'What can we do to help?' Garaz said earnestly.

'Get to Babylon and prepare for what comes next,' the shopkeeper replied. 'You are good people, and we need you in this fight. You've done more to thwart the Maestro's plans than we could've achieved in years. Finish what you started, before it's too late.'

'Of course we will. You have our word,' Nicolas said firmly. *The least I can do is clean up my mess.* 'But even with the wagon, how do we make it to Babylon? We're still us and— *Ow.*' He rubbed the back of his head where Shift had smacked him.

'*Shapeshifter*, remember?' His companions chuckled. 'I'll just make myself look like Cuthbert and drive the wagon.'

'Who in the Underworld is *Cuthbert*?' he asked.

Shift frowned at him. 'The Oracle's wagon driver.'

'His name is *Cuthbert*? I didn't know that.'

'You allowed him to drive you around in a wagon and did not ask his name?' Garaz was aghast. 'That is a little rude.'

'Oh, come on,' Nicolas protested. 'He isn't exactly a personable fellow.'

'Probably because of people like you.' Auron smirked.

'I had a lot on my mind when I was in the wagon.'

'At least your manners are improving,' Silva noted. 'And thankfully you are far less whiny than you used to be.'

Now it was his turn to hurl a pillow at Silva, true though that was.

I really was an irksome guy, wasn't I? At least I've grown out of that. Mostly.

'When do we go?' Nicolas asked, wanting to change the subject.

'Now,' Allegard said. 'It's night, and the wagon is ready. I've put supplies in the wagon, enough for your journey. And I'm expecting a dwarven family within the next few hours.'

Thank the Deities we don't have much to pack then.

After grabbing their gear, the group progressed into the shop. It was kind of eerie when it was deserted. The open doors showed the wagon that awaited them.

'Thank you,' Nicolas said, offering the shopkeeper his hand.

Allegard shook it. 'Think nothing of it. Some of us need to be beacons of light in the darkness. And anything I can do to help you, you need but ask. I wish you and your friends a safe journey.'

'We wi—'

His words were cut off by the female voice that spoke when people crossed the threshold into and out of the store. '*Someone is attempting to steal.*'

Irritably, Allegard looked towards the door, drumming his fingers on the counter. Then he brought those fingers to his lips and whistled. Instantly, his demon hounds leapt onto the counter, growling.

Slowly, Shift took whatever it was they were trying to pinch out of their jacket and put it back on the shelf, smiling nervously.

'You said *anything you can do to help.*' Nicolas sighed. 'Can you start by not setting the dogs on Shift, please?'

****

The wagon bumped again.

'Garaz, move your elbow,' he hissed.

'Where would you like me to move it?' the orc replied tartly.

He wasn't wrong. Nicolas, Garaz, and Silva lay in the false bottom of the wagon. Just as they had done for the entire previous day...and the rest of the week they'd been travelling in it before that. They came out to camp at night – thankful of the chance to stretch their aching limbs – but now that it was morning again, so they'd returned to their hiding spot and set off.

I swear Shift is hitting these potholes on purpose.

'If you could just—'

'Will you two be quiet?' Silva hissed.

Nicolas turned to talk to the warrior. His gaze slowly dropped to what was practically in his face.

'Those are *not* my eyes,' Silva snarled.

'Then maybe you ought to stop rubbing them against me.'

It was hard to keep his temperament in this environment. It was cramped, and the air was close, filled with their combined body heat and odour. It was, in summation, not a pleasant way to travel.

Nicolas nearly headbutted Silva's breasts as the wagon lurched to a halt.

'Guys, get out here.'

Auron's voice sounded urgent, so Nicolas grabbed the latch that opened the false door, and they climbed out of the wagon. It was a delicate and uncomfortable process, but they managed it.

'What is it?'

The spirit, sat on his horse, and Shift in the guise of Cuthbert, were looking towards the horizon. In the next valley, beyond some trees, smoke rose into the sky.

'I'd say that's at least two or three houses on fire,' Auron said, craning his neck to study the scene. 'Most likely a village being raided.'

Narrowing his eyes, Nicolas looked towards the fires. He trusted Auron's judgement. Which meant there were people who needed saving.

'Let's go then,' Nicolas said firmly. 'I'm really in the mood to kick some ass.'

EPILOGUE

P o's gaze flicked from his cards to his brother's. Problem with Go—if you considered it a problem, which Po didn't—was that he was an awful bluffer. And right now, he looked like he was trying to hold in a crap that was as insistent as a battering ram on a castle gate.

'I raise.' Po smirked, putting three more coins onto the table.

Go snarled pleasingly, glaring at his cards in a way that told Po he'd been right to raise. Then his attention turned to his other brother. Yo was nervously playing with his horns, an obvious tell. But he was one of the youngest, too young to have learnt any better. Go was older, but bigger and a bit dumb with it, so that explained that.

I've got them. And their money.

'So, what about it?' Po probed smugly. 'In or out, fellas?'

With a dual cry, his brothers threw down their cards. Po reached across the table and pulled the coins towards his already impressive pile.

Maybe tonight I'll lay all my new coins on the bed and roll in them. Or I could spend the evening stacking them into piles.

'I swear you're cheating.'

His head snapped up, staring daggers at his brother. 'I *beg* your pardon?'

Go rose from the table, utilising his impressive bulk in a pathetic attempt to intimidate him. 'I said, I swear you're cheating.'

Pushing his chair back from the table, Po rose to meet the challenge. 'Family or no, nobody accuses me of cheating. Ever.'

'Give me back my coin, and we won't have a problem.' His brother's fist hardened to rock. Soon stone would engulf his whole body.

So that's the game you want to play then.

Holding up his thumb, Po let a single spark of lightning dance around the tip. 'Is this the road you want to go down?'

'Depends on whether or not I get my coin back,' his brother snarled.

'Guys,' Yo said, rising and raising his hands in an attempt to keep the peace. 'Don't do this. If Mother finds out we were gambling again, never mind...'

'Urgh,' Po scoffed. 'You sound like Bo.'

Yo's face contorted in rage. 'Don't you *dare* liken me to *The Anomaly.*'

'Don't act like him then.'

The temperature in the room dropped. Yo was summoning his ice powers.

Now we have a party.

Each brother eyed his siblings murderously. Fights between the family were annoyingly common, but all his brothers knew not to take it too far. Mother wouldn't like that, and when she didn't like something, she punished them. Po shivered at the thought of what she'd done to Zo when he'd brought news that he'd messed up the coup in Secos. The strips of skin she'd taken from his back still hadn't regrown. Zo's hasty and half-assed attempt to smooth things over by burning down a university hadn't eased her wrath any.

Still, she never killed any of us.

Though sometimes they'd wished they were dead. But no. Mother had a line. She wouldn't kill her own. Anyone else was fair game, but not her offspring. That Carnegie boy had no such line. The bastard had killed two of his brothers. *Two*. It was unheard of. So much so that Mother had forbade anyone from uttering his name aloud. Yet still his brothers would say it from time to time, using it in stories to try and scare each other. Until they found a new moniker for him.

If you aren't careful, the Faun Killer *will get you. That's what they say.*

Mind you, part of him was glad Fo was dead. The bastard had been a great one for using his power to instigate fights then acting all innocent in the aftermath.

But if that's what these morons want, that's what they'll get.

The fight was moments from breaking out when a noise distracted all three fauns. It was a familiar, liquid-like noise, as if something large had been thrown into a swamp.

'What was that?' Yo asked, looking towards the back of the room.

'Sounded like...the portal,' Go answered uncertainly.

'Can't be,' Po scoffed. 'No one's out.'

But it did *sound like the portal.*

The three brothers exchanged a look, a nervous one. If someone had messed with the portal when they were supposed to be on guard duty but were off gaming instead, Mother would tear them apart. Literally.

As one, the three fauns marched cautiously towards the back of the room. Po clicked his fingers to the four constructs that stood idly along the wall. The creatures' heads raised at the command, their eyes filling with red light as they awoke. Obediently, they skittered behind their masters, their scythe arms already deployed.

Hooves clopped on stone as the fauns entered the portal room. Everything seemed in its place, and the portal was closed. Glancing at each other, the brothers moved through the corridor to the adjoining room. The slave pens. Even here, everything was as it should be. All the slaves were curled up in the corner of their pen in their chains, just as they'd left them.

Briefly, he cast a disgusted glance over the pathetic figures. Filthy and emaciated, none of them dared look at their masters, knowing what would happen if they caught their gaze. He still remembered when they'd been brought here, herded in crying by the Maestro's men. Apparently, they had been a tribute, a repayment for the fate that had befallen Ro, killed by that stupid Nicolas creature. Po supposed it was quite fitting that they should have his village as slaves to appease Mother's rage. Though it had been stoked again when the little human bastard had killed Fo. He shivered, not wanting to think of the human or what he'd done. Instead, he focused on what he was supposed to be doing.

The slaves were in the right place, and the portal was shut, yet Po couldn't shake the feeling something was amiss.

We did hear something.

'Fan out,' he told the constructs.

Wordlessly, the quartet disappeared amongst the stacks of boxes in the portal room. The boxes the three were supposed to be cataloguing instead of playing cards. Even out of view, he could hear their clawed feet skittering across the stone.

'What do you reckon?' Go asked, searching the room.

'That we should've been here doing our jobs instead of slacking off?' Yo suggested.

Po cuffed him around the ear. Sometimes he was as wet as the ice he summoned.

'You lot see anything?' he shouted to the slaves.

None answered. Usually even if they answered a question, Po or his brothers would punish them for speaking. The people of Hab-whatever were learning.

Stupid humans don't know anything anyway.

The trio waited. They were just starting to relax when they heard a crash.

Running towards the sound, they found one of the constructs, dead. An arrow was sticking out of its forehead, its eyes dark.

'Oh dear, oh dear, oh dear,' Yo whimpered. 'We have an intruder. An intruder.'

'We do,' Po snarled. 'So shut up, and let's find him.'

The trio spun around at a flash of movement. Po unleashed his lightning, scorching the wall as it slammed against it, but hitting nothing else.

Yo suddenly howled in pain. There was an arrow through his hand.

'What's going on?' Po gasped.

A door opened.

'There,' Po yelled. 'After him. Go. Go.'

The three constructs emerged from the maze and charged through the door. Po followed them at a safe distance, leaving Go to tend to his crying brother.

Through the maze of corridors, they ran. He knew the intruder was ahead, he felt it, but couldn't see him. Whoever he was, he was bloody quick.

Bam.

Another of the constructs fell, an arrow in its right eye.

Bam.

The third one dropped.

Po jumped behind the last one, using it for cover. He cried out as an arrow tip emerged through its head, only an inch from his eye. The final construct crashed to the floor.

'Oh shit.'

Suddenly, Po realised that he was very alone. No brothers, no constructs. Just him and whoever this archer was.

His gaze slowly moved up from the felled constructs. At the end of the corridor, he could make out a shadowed figure.

Po licked his lips nervously.

I am not messing about with this guy.

Summoning his full power, Po blasted a beam of lightning down the corridor, filling it with light and sparking fury. Torches were consumed by the blast and the walls burnt and scorched as he cried out with the exertion.

The beam spent, he fell to the floor panting. There was no sign of the intruder.

Hopefully, he was burnt to ash.

Somehow, Po knew that wasn't the case. But either way, he'd vanished. Now he needed to try to think of a way to explain this to Mother.

It's definitely going to be Yo's fault, I just need to word it right.

As he manifested his excuses and explanations, he kept one eye nervously on the corridor. Just in case. Though his mind became increasingly occupied with Mother's reaction to all this.

Maybe...maybe we just clean this all up and she never needs to know?

Yes, that'd do it. Pretend it didn't happen, and he'd get to keep all his limbs attached.

ACKNOWLEDGEMENTS

Well, I have to say, this one was a lot of fun to write. And it was nice to revisit it myself, as I wrote the first draft back in 2023.

I felt that after the emotional rolle-rcoaster of The Pursuit, you deserved a nice all actioner based on a simple premise...what if *John Wick* was a bit inept and didn't really want to kill anybody. And so I wrote Helstrum.

Did you ever really think old Tobias was going to be the Maestro?

Actually, a better question...Potter's betrayal, did you see it coming? Have you picked up Wrath and Wraiths to see if I wrote in that Koth was holding a bow? I'll save you a job, he wasn't.

I really enjoyed writing the fight scenes for this book. I think my favourite is when Nicolas finds out about Potter's betrayal and absolutely batters his men (for a bit). I think angry Nick shows the skill he is capable of when he stops overthinking it, and dropping his sword.

Now, as much as this was an all actioner, it also nicely advanced the main story, I think. It showed what's going on in the world at large, how things are changing in Etherius. And it continues to plant the seeds I'm dotting throughout the series. Maybe you can see them, or maybe you'll have that 'oh, that's what he meant in...' in about four books time? I met with a fan the other day who told me that she chatted with others as they read the new releases. And wow. I know people read my books, but talking to other people about them too? That amazes me. Every so often I hear something like this and it just makes me realise why I love publishing. Not writing, that's its own thing. But publishing, putting my books out there and actually letting people read them.

Oooh. One quick piece of self aggrandisement. I challenged myself to get a famous quote from a sci-fi film in this book, just because it amused me to do it. Did you catch it? It's in there. I don't think Dani noticed, because she didn't comment on it.

Speaking of Dani, as per usual I need to thank her for her amazing work on the book. She helped me tidy up the rough edges and gave me some really great notes to improve the manuscript. This is exactly why every book goes to her first. There weren't many points this time. I think that means I'm getting better?

And naturally I need to shout out to my mum Christine, for hunting down the typos with more efficiency than Nicolas managed hunting down Helstrum. For example, I'm pretty sure she wasn't taken captive in forts twice as she searched for where I wrote their, when I meant there. Or put two full stops at the end of the sentence.

I also have someone very important to thank. You. Eight books in and you're still reading? I tip my cap to you. Don't worry, there's plenty more to come.

Which means a ninth book.

I don't think it's very spoilery to say that book 9 will pick up directly where Helstrum leaves off. I can't just write about a burning village and then ignore it, can I? Well, I could. But that'd be boring and silly. But that's just the beginning. The rest of book 9, The Vault, I can sum up in a single word. Fauns.

(It's plural because there's going to be a lot of the little buggers).

But until then,

Keep adventuring,

Andrew

ABOUT THE AUTHOR

Andrew Claydon has an imagination, one full of variety.
Sometimes it's funny, sometimes it's adventurous, sometimes it's shocking, and occasionally it's outright strange...but it's never boring!
Andrew is a UK author who grew up loving fantasy movies such as Conan, Krull, Beastmaster and Willow. The epic worlds and battles of swords and sorcery therein inspired him to create his own fantasy worlds, adding to them his own brand of irreverent humour; because sometimes it's good to chuckle in between sword fights!
He wants to inspire the imagination of others, just as he's been inspired; with dashing heroes, epic quests and vile villains.
So reader beware, you aren't just opening a book, but a doorway into Andrew's imagination. It'll be a strange journey, but an entertaining one!
When he isn't writing, he loves to read sci/fi and fantasy novels. It's one of the things that inspires him to write himself. He also enjoys playing Warhammer 40,000 and is a keen wrestling fan.
He has degrees in both history and psychology, as well as black belts in several martial arts.
When he isn't creating vast fantasy worlds and populating them with good guys and bad guys to run around fighting each other, he works as a supported employment coordinator, helping others to try and achieve their aspirations.
Subscribe to my newsletter for the latest publishing news (and a FREE prequel novella) at: www.andrewclaydonauthor.com
Or follow me on social media:
Facebook: Andrewclaydonauthor
Instagram: @authorandyc
Tiktok: @authorandyc
If you enjoyed the book, then please leave a review with your preferred retailer.
Reviews are really important to indie authors to help them get their work out there.
If you do take the time to leave a review, thank you.

ALSO BY

Chronicles of the Dawnblade Series
The Simple Delivery
Strange Companions
The Odd Sea
Wrath and Wraiths
Trail of Death
Demons and Disorder
The Pursuit
Helstrum

Novellas and short stories
A Grudge is Born
The Gathering
Don't you know who I am?
How I learned to hate adventuring
Refilling the Pot
The Shopkeeper

The adventure continues in *The Vault*
Coming June 2026